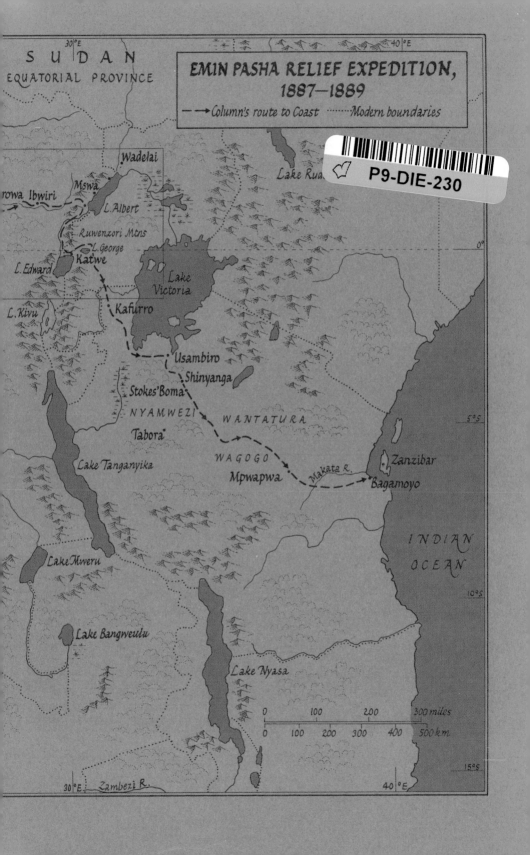

VALIANT
GENTLEMEN

VALIANT
GENTLEMEN

SABINA
MURRAY

Grove Press
New York

Murray

First published by Grove Atlantic, November 2016

Published simultaneously in Canada
Printed in the United States of America

FIRST EDITION

ISBN 978-0-8021-2545-3
eISBN 978-0-8021-8970-7

Grove Press
an imprint of Grove Atlantic
154 West 14th Street
New York, NY 10011

Distributed by Publishers Group West

groveatlantic.com

16 17 18 19   10 9 8 7 6 5 4 3 2 1

For Esmond

PART ONE

I

Matadi

September 1886

The first time Casement sees him, Ward is turned away, working on a sketch. He's in a white shirt and the sleeves are rolled to the elbows, showing strong forearms darkened with exposure to the sun. The stance is perfect contrapposto, the hips angled, the right foot casually set forward. As if sensing Casement's gaze, Ward turns and smiles. It is a romantic image that Casement has played over in his mind: first, the sight of the shoulders, the sun hitting the fair hair, the subtle movement of the arms, the hands, Ward's attention drawn to some compelling subject.

"That's ridiculous," says Ward. "The first time we met was in an office. I was waiting for you to show up so that we could share the transport to Vivi. We shook hands. In fact, I think I saw you before you saw me."

"How can you be so sure?"

"Well, for one thing, I wouldn't be standing in the sun without my hat."

"I remember the absence of the hat because it was exceptional."

"Also," adds Ward, "you can't see my forearms from behind, not if I'm sketching. My left hand is holding the book and I've got the pen in my right.

3

From where you were standing"—Ward presents his back to illustrate—"my arms are completely blocked by my torso. If you were an artist, you would know this." Ward turns again to Casement and shakes his head. He's wondering why Casement would find the need to create such a scenario. "That's the problem with you, Casement. You're a romantic, always making things up."

"One of many, I'm sure."

Casement grabs Ward's sketchbook and flips through to an illustration of a mad bull elephant with a flailing native raised high in the beast's trunk: Elephant and native lock eyes. Casement holds the illustration to Ward as evidence.

"Might happen. An elephant could get a native like this, and this is what it would look like," says Ward. "But bodies don't lie. You could never see my forearms from behind if I were sketching."

Casement and Ward are company men, once employees of the International Association of the Congo, now members of the Sanford Exploring Expedition. Both are relieved to no longer be employed by King Leopold of Belgium, but the complications of working for England in this Congo Free State—a plot marked out as one might a flower bed—now under Belgian rule, are many. Casement and Ward have both run stores, but transportation is where skilled people are really needed. On the lower Congo, there are no roads, no rails nor navigable waterways that can accommodate more than a dugout canoe. Therefore, the only method of bringing things in (brass rods, cloth) and things out (ivory, rubber) is to engage porters. And one needs a lot of porters.

For sure, there are some Zanzibaris, people who showed up with the explorer Henry Morton Stanley and couldn't find their way home, but the majority must be gathered from the local villages. And none of them are eager to leave their homes, wives, children, and fields. Also, the regulation load is an impressive sixty-five pounds. This the porters carry into the unfamiliar interior, where there are all manner of snakes and enemies, tribesmen who would rather eat you than call you brother.

"Looks like rain," says Ward. Casement looks up at the sky. It does look like rain. "Actually it looks like deluge. Can one say that?"

"Ward, you can say whatever you want. This is Africa."

Ward has engaged a young boy to carry some of his things and to gather firewood and cook. The boy is carrying sketchbooks and pens, also Ward's razor, shaving brush, needle and thread, and extra cartridges, though Ward carries his own rifle and it is loaded.

Casement travels with his dog that he has named Tom, after a dog back in Ballycastle, who was probably named after a person.

In Kikongo, Casement asks the boy, "What is your name?"

"You know me, Mayala Swami," says the boy, using Casement's nickname. "I am Mbatchi, son to Luemba."

"Yes," says Casement, "now I can see it."

Usually it is Casement traveling alone, or Ward traveling alone, the other white man needed to stay in camp, a civilizing presence in the village as on a map a pushpin signifies rule. But with the shipment of the *Florida*—a paddle steamer—has come a hoard of Belgians and Englishmen, so Casement and Ward can travel together and as twice the normal number of porters is going to be needed to bear the *Florida's* tons of metal to the edge of Stanley Pool, perhaps twice the normal number of porter procurers is justified. Casement wonders how many porters are left in the Bakongo villages in the immediate surroundings. How far will he and Ward have to go to meet the quota?

Down the gentle slope he sees his camp demarcated in thatched fencing, a square ensnaring the regular shapes of huts, a large barracks, white men in white clothing, black men in black skin. He thinks his heart is ensnared—fenced in like that, and dismisses the thought. There might be poetry in that, but none he'll write.

"Come on, Casement," says Ward. "I'd like to get ahead of that rain."

It is a narrow path, single file, and breaks into a wall of greenery. Down that path the birds call to each other in undecipherable phrasing. The air is heavy with moisture. Down that path exists an eternity of savages and

5

savage custom. Behind him the sun beats down on the present. Ward picks up the pace and soon will no doubt start whistling something, an absurd folk song that he learned in Australia or, more likely, some shearing ballad from his time in New Zealand. He'll break into song. Ward loves to sing, although Casement has the better voice.

"You're dawdling," says Ward.

"What's the hurry?"

"Oh, I don't know." Ward is hoping for some hunting.

The rain, miraculously, holds off. The dog sniffs with focus, halts, then plunges off the path and into the jungle. There is a fierce rustling, then silence. One hopes poor Tom won't be gutted by a boar. Little Mbatchi looks around for an explanation.

"Think he's coming back?" says Ward.

"Of course," says Casement.

"What's the word for 'dog' in Kikongo?" asks Ward.

"You are going to make a joke."

"Is it *mbwa*?"

"That's Swahili."

"I'll think of it," says Ward.

And he will. Ward is certainly proficient in the Kikongo of the lower Congo, and the Kibangi of the upper Congo. He is learning Swahili and has some knowledge of Kibabatu. Ward is proficient in turning one word into another. His vocabulary is enormous, but the words do not always add up. Ward manages to spin sentence after sentence without ever really speaking the language.

First the dog returns and then a dense rain moves over them. Mbatchi slips in the mud and is very nervous that something in his bag has broken, but on inspection, all is still intact and he smiles and his smile is radiant, and then there's lunch: yam, mandioca, dried fish. That's the eight hours done with and now they should be close to the village. Casement likes this walking—it reminds him of his early years in Ballycastle where there was little to do but walk. It was a childhood split between the lush green of the

Antrim countryside and the rattling commerce of his cousins in Liverpool. Then, he had thought Liverpool and Ballycastle opposites, but here, in the Congo, this feels like an opposite.

"Ward," says Casement. "Can there be three opposites?"

Ward responds with a dramatic sigh. He stands, shaking his head.

"Ward," says Casement, coming to stand beside him. He was going to ask what was wrong, but now he sees. The Bakongo village has been deserted. A goat reveals itself from the far side of a hut. Ward is down on one knee studying the ground. He picks something up.

"Casings," says Ward.

"Arab?"

"It would seem."

"Well," says Casement. "Let's hope our friends got away."

Just two weeks ago there had been a decent field of sorghum, but someone has harvested it all and the rich empty dirt looks like a fresh grave plot. Arab slavers normally stayed north of the river, but the Belgians too need labor and ultimately the difference between the Belgians and the Arabs is a matter of brass rods and the possibility of returning home. Better that Casement hires these natives for the English, who will at least pay them for their labor and treat them well, and with kindness, as these dark cousins ought to be treated. Mbatchi has found rope to tie up the goat and is leading it around.

"Mayala Swami, can I keep it?"

"It's yours," says Casement.

"That could have fed us," says Ward.

"Carrying meat through the jungle has never been a favorite activity of mine," says Casement. This is a reference to leopards.

"Even alive," Ward counters, "it's still meat."

Mbatchi is tying the goat to a tree and the goat seems relieved of the burden of freedom.

"I've never understood why they call you that," says Ward.

"What? Mayala Swami?"

"Doesn't that mean 'ladies' man'?"

"Yes. That's a reasonably close translation to the Kikongo."

"But you aren't a ladies' man, Casement. As far as I know, you're a perfect gentleman." There's the edge of disdain in Ward's voice.

Casement smiles, looking at the ground. "How would you, Mayala Mbemba, understand?" Mayala Mbemba is Ward's nickname. It means "wings of an eagle" and refers to the fact that Ward managed to walk forty miles in one day. Ward is very proud of this nickname and calls attention to it and explains it to anyone who will hear him.

"Do I detect envy, Casement?"

"Without doubt." Casement fixes his gaze to the left and then the right. "We should eat."

Mbatchi has collected a good pile of firewood. Because of the rain, it will not burn easily, but should get them through the night. Mbatchi is terrified of leopards and as one rather large print revealed itself at the edge of the stream when he was collecting water, his concern is justified.

"I'd love to bag a leopard," says Ward.

"It wouldn't be the first time," says Casement. "And we're not here to hunt. We're already a day behind and who knows where else the Arabs have been."

Ward is cleaning his gun. Casement brings out a bottle and takes a swig. He hands it to Ward.

"I don't suppose that's whiskey," says Ward.

"Better. Malafu." Palm wine goes down rough but does the work. A few mouthfuls of this and one sleeps through the night, no matter how many mosquitoes are biting.

Night falls with an almost audible thump. The frogs, tensed for action, begin their croaking and bellows, and giant moths—who also have been waiting for this moment—palm the air with their wings. Ward and Casement chose this shimbek to sleep in because of the rough Hessian curtains, made from sacks, covering the windows, and the old sheet draped across the door. Still, there is the constant rattle of insects worrying at the sheet to get in and—Casement suspects—to get out. But he is used to it. He remembers Taunt, the Chief Agent, saying just that morning—the wage ledger open in front of him, the inked numbers winking seductively—that this was not the life for an older man. Actually, what he'd said was, "It's all right for you young men, walking about from village to village, camping beneath the stars, but for a man my age . . ." He of course was giving a bucolic wash to the actual work ahead since the "young men" made a tenth of what the likes of him made for sitting in one office or another and making order after order that was executed at far distance from the place of issue, and often to ill effect.

Casement is twenty-two, but feels significantly older. And then as he settles into this older way of being, feels suddenly and impossibly young with no direction and no purpose.

"Ward, are you still awake?" he asks the dark. "Ward?"

"Now," Ward replies thickly, "awoken."

"We'll need a tent and not just any tent. I want a big officer's tent. And no more of this malafu. I want a case of Madeira and a porter to carry it."

"What are you talking about?"

"When they finally have the *Florida* in pieces and we're doing the portage."

"Why now?" asks Ward. "Why all of a sudden do you want to travel like a gentleman?"

"You can be a gentleman and no one treats you well. But I think if we demand a case of Madeira and a servant or two, then we might be able to negotiate a better rate."

"That's ridiculous," says Ward, rolling over, "and absolutely brilliant."

The *Florida* is a paddle steamer imported for the purpose of getting goods from Leopoldville on the southern edge of Stanley Pool across to the northern bank, and, more importantly, of bringing goods—ivory and rubber—back. Nothing larger than a dugout can make it up the Congo, and then, not even the whole distance. The mighty Congo in no way resembles any of the rivers of Casement's youth. There are waterfalls and cataracts and currents that would make the most scientific mind conceive of long-fingered sorcerers plucking unlucky souls from the surface and dragging them beneath. There is a bubbling quality to the cataracts; one named "Hell's Cauldron" is just downriver from Matadi. More than once Casement has seen a native, arms raised up, mouth shouting, voice obliterated by the crush of water, spin round and round and disappear as if there were an enormous drain at work. The upper part of the Congo, from Stanley Pool to the east, is navigable and there are two or three boats—missionaries—chugging industriously, perhaps transporting souls back and forth across the pool, in some sort of God-pleasing transaction.

The only way to get the *Florida* to the shore of Stanley Pool is by porter and the only way this can be accomplished is in pieces—many pieces. At present no better way exists, and—in fact—no other way. There is talk of a railway from Boma to Leopoldville, which would tear up the country but most likely have a civilizing influence. Maybe that would be fine, but the work involved (would he sign on for that?) gives one pause. And Casement's grown tired of dealing with caravans, and porters who are ambushed and injured and often run off with their loads into the jungle where it's impossible to find them, as if the jungle folds her own in her arms to protect them.

Two weeks have passed since Ward and Casement assembled the caravan and they are back in Matadi, making final arrangements. All in all, Casement's pleased with what they've managed—many Bakongo, who are an honest people and hard-working and with whom, since he's known to them and speaks the language well, he shares an easy relationship. The rest are mostly well-traveled Loango, who are therefore skilled at distinguishing friendly chiefs from hostile chiefs. But the territory from Matadi along the Congo to Leopoldville has all been opened up anyway and Casement has no reason to predict hostility from the many chiefs he will encounter.

Some villages have no more than twenty inhabitants, and some upward of 300, and all a chief and witch doctor to keep things lively.

Many of the pieces of the *Florida* cannot be broken down to the regulation sixty-five pounds and will have to be carried in hammocks strung between bamboo poles, the weight shared by two porters. The shaft of the *Florida* is nearly a ton and cannot be taken apart and so will have to be transported by cart. Some higher-up has remembered the cart, although neglected to provide anything with which to pull it. Ward left earlier in the morning to find bullocks and has already taken an hour longer than Casement thought he would. Casement exhales into the heat. A child, whom he knows by sight, comes up to him.

"Mayala Swami, do you have a gift for me?"

Matabicho is the word the child uses, which culturally is somewhere between a gift and a bribe.

"I might," he replies in Kikongo, "if you can tell me where Mayala Mbemba is."

"By the river looking at the Dutch trader's women."

Casement gives the child a piece of hardtack, which was in his pocket when he put on his trousers this morning. When did he put it there? The child seems happy and Casement is satisfied because he knows, from experience, that the child's information is correct.

There is Ward standing on the riverbank watching the spectacle of De Groot's harem—four women, their glossy skin set off by yards of embroidered snow-white muslin, arrange themselves into a canoe amid a musical chatter.

Casement sees his shadow standing next to Ward's, but is still.

"I know you're there, Casement," says Ward. "And I can feel your disapproval."

"Of the Dutch trader?"

"Of me."

"Four is a lot of women," says Casement.

"One would be enough."

"It's easily arranged."

"And a lot of money. It wouldn't be worth it with the work we're doing."

"Not unless she could walk forty miles in one day."

"Very funny," says Ward. He turns from the spectacle of the women with some effort.

"Did you get the bullocks?" Casement asks.

"It has been decided that we should have no bullocks," a little humor here, "as they are highly susceptible to the tse-tse. So instead it has been proposed that the enormity of the shaft," more humor, "be offset with a significant number of porters."

"Porters?"

Ward nods.

"I would recommend at least a hundred men," says Casement. "One hundred, no fewer."

"Which is what I recommended and that number is on their way up from Vivi."

"How?"

"The Arab Tippo Tib is supplying the porters."

"Tippo Tib is a slave trader," says Casement. "Are we now in business with him?"

"Someone is," replies Ward.

There's a moment where both Casement and Ward contemplate their insignificance. *We are pawns,* they think together. *We are powerless.* Then the moment passes, carried off by a doctoring wind.

"Did you get the Madeira?" asks Ward.

Casement nods. It would seem they are provisioned.

II

The *Florida*

March 1887

Today there might be rain. Ward looks upriver, at the sandbars rising like the vertebrae of some giant creature. Navigation on these stretches will always be dicey. A group of four birds flies speedily up the river and Ward follows them with his hands grasped around an imaginary rifle, as if he's setting up a shot. Mbatchi disturbs his reverie by pulling on his pants leg.

"What?" says Ward. "Does someone need me?"

Mbatchi nods.

The messenger speaks Kikongo, although he's Kibabatu, from upriver. He tells Ward about a village just over the ridge that has food to trade—sorghum for the porters, maybe some goat stew for him and Casement—which is good news because two years ago and not far from their present location a French missionary was taken out by a spear, although the flinger of the spear was never seen: as if the jungle herself had flung it unaided by human hands. According to this messenger, there is no need for concern: All here is peaceful. Perhaps there will be something of interest for Ward to sketch. He shows the messenger a few pages from his sketchbook and the messenger is very impressed and smiles warmly. The next village has beautiful women, says the messenger. Ward explains that his art is not confined to what is beautiful. The messenger says that that is good because the men of this village (a head shake here) are very ugly. Ward gets the joke and laughs very loud—too loud, because he is so pleased with himself for understanding humor in Kikongo. He and the messenger laugh together. Next, Ward asks about elephants.

After Ward has arranged a meal for the messenger, he goes to look for Casement, who is redistributing the contents of one of the baskets as the man who was carrying it has gone lame. Casement is looking at the man's foot where a thorn has become imbedded. The foot is inflamed.

"Shoes would solve some of this," says Casement.

"We would need a lot of porters to bring shoes to this many porters."

"And those porters would also need shoes." Casement smiles. He tells the man, one of the Loango, that he is welcome to go home now. He will be paid for his labor and should take care with his foot so that it heals now rather than becomes more infected.

"We're not supposed to give partial payments," says Ward. "The job is the whole portage, not just two weeks."

"It's only a few brass rods," says Casement.

"I'm not arguing with you," says Ward. "But we're about to have a rash of people stepping on thorns. And I think we're up to ten people who have run off. The porters are supposed to be chained."

"And then when one falls, we risk injuring the entire column."

"Which is why we're doing it your way. But I'm not sure if it's the right way."

Casement pretends to consider. He shrugs. He looks up at Ward. "I heard there was a messenger."

"From Stanley Pool."

"What did he say?"

"He said there was a lone bull elephant maybe four miles from here. He didn't get a good look at the tusks, but surely resting the men for a couple of hours would be good for all."

14

"And surely they didn't send a messenger from Stanley Pool to tell you that."

"No," says Ward. "Troup wanted to know if we have the brass wire for the boiler assembly."

"I'm not sure," says Casement.

"I already checked and the wire's missing. It was supposed to arrive at Stanley Pool with a bunch of Manyema porters supplied by Tippo Tib," says Ward. "Tippo Tib insists that it's either on its way, or has arrived and been misplaced, or that maybe the Manyema porters got mixed in with ours."

"I think we would have noticed that."

"That's what I said."

"Anything else?"

"There's a village less than a half day's march from here." Ward shifts his weight. "Can I go after that elephant?"

Casement thinks. "If you bag it, that's meat for the men, and they could use something better than manioc. What if you go with Mbatchi and eight men to carry the meat in case you're lucky, and I'll pitch camp in another five or so miles, which should bring us closer to the village, and you can meet us there."

"You could wait for me here."

"Mayala Mbemba," says Casement, "what's another five miles to you— you, who walked forty miles in one day?"

They finally find the elephant after trekking close to six miles. One of Ward's men, Mboko, an exceptionally tall fellow at six feet four, sights it at good range. Ward, who is on the short side, something that served him well when he was an acrobat in Sydney, can barely see over the top of the long grass. But he's good at balancing.

What he would really like to say is: *Mboko, would you mind terribly if I got up on your shoulders?* Instead, he says: "Mboko, I sit on back." And mimes shooting with his rifle.

Mboko nods in response. Ward clambers onto Mboko's back and then onto his shoulders and another man hands him back his rifle.

There's the elephant feeding, stripping the bark from a young tree. The elephant is flapping its ears, swinging its tail peacefully. Mboko, aware of the shifting breeze, moves to right and left, anxious to stay downwind. A lone bull elephant is very dangerous and even if all seems quiet—bucolic—Ward knows that if the elephant picks up their scent, it will attack. He nudges Mboko with his heel and Mboko edges forward through the grass.

Ward has a straight shot to the back of the beast's head. Not the most exciting way to kill an elephant, he thinks. If he gets this shot, he won't be charged, and the brute will most likely die instantly. If he gets this shot, he won't have to track the elephant through the jungle for a day and a night—he's done that before—and there won't be much of a story. If he gets this shot, he'll walk over to see what sort of tusks there are, rather than seeing the tusks come at him. And he's witnessed people who have been gored by elephants, although he's never actually seen someone in the process of being gored.

He feels Mboko tense up beneath him. They're close now and Mboko is wondering why he doesn't take the shot. And then the rifle is raised. Ward holds steady and sights, finger exerting an even pressure on the trigger, squeezing calmly. BLAM. A perfect hit to the back of the head. The elephant shudders. Reload. BLAM. And the elephant falls. After one more shot for certain death, they cut the thing up and cart what can be carted back to camp.

Casement is fiddling with some verse. Yes, fiddling. He looks at the lines:

The barren hills of Ulster held a race proscribed and banned
Who from their lofty refuge viewed their own so fertile land

It's a bit stiff, but the meter's right. He thinks of Ward's drawings, all Africans, and his poems, all Irish history. Is this what makes them different, that Ward constructs himself out of his own personal history, while Casement's personality demands a further reach? Why write about post-Plantation Ulster in the Congo? Well, the Bakongos are somewhat displaced as they shuttle around carrying things for the English. And he is somewhat displaced, first as one who is Irish when he's not being British, British when he's not being Irish, and sometimes both simultaneously. He checks his watch. It is closing in on eight, although time means little here—only daylight and darkness. He hears a swell of expectant chatter. Ward must be back.

Sure enough, there's Ward bearing his usual cheerful expression as if he's just walked into a parlor for a Saturday chitchat, or bumped into Casement on the way to a cricket match. The porters' baskets are full of meat.

"What's for dinner?" says Ward.

"Looks like elephant," Casement replies.

"I'm not eating elephant," says Ward.

"It tastes just like hippo, and I know you eat that."

"It does not taste like hippo, well, not much. And I only eat hippo if it's very young." Ward sits on a crate by Casement's chair. "What have you got there?"

"Poem."

"Any good?"

"Not yet."

Ward flips open his sketchbook and finds the picture. "What do you think?"

"It's an elephant."

"That all?"

"It's dead."

"The perspective was very difficult. Look at the legs."

"That is some accomplished foreshortening. Why'd you do it?"

"They were going to chop it up. It seemed a shame not to preserve it."

"Then why'd you kill it?"

The tent has been erected, prepped for eating rather than sleeping, with the walls rolled up and buckled in place. There are chairs and a table and a cloth on the table and the Madeira is there, half full, a reminder that sometimes these young men are rewarded. A moth enters from the right side of the tent, inspiring a bat the size of a cat to dispose of it midway.

"Stanley's book, *Through the Dark Continent*, have you read it?" Ward asks.

"Yes. Hasn't everyone?"

"It's full of bravado," says Ward.

"I think that's the typical writing style of short, ill-tempered men."

"So you were not taken in by Stanley?"

"I think I was," says Casement, and he tops up his glass, "which has contributed to my assessment of his writing style."

Ward fixes Casement with an appallingly earnest look. "Casement, all we do is walk. First we walk tens of miles finding porters, then we march them back to Matadi or Vivi or Boma or wherever. Let's say we do this in the pouring rain. Then we put things in baskets and the porters put the baskets on their heads, and then we walk some more. The rain clears up and it gets really hot. And then. Well. More walking."

"What does this have to do with Stanley?"

"What made his experience spectacular and adventurous when ours seems so boring?"

Casement considers. "He was the first. He got shot at. He ran out of food."

"We run out of food," says Ward.

"And isn't it exciting when that happens?"

"You're making fun of me." The insects crawling on the lamp are casting fantastic shadows on the inside of the tent.

"Yes."

In the porters' camp, some have started singing. More join in, the chorus of porters rising and falling as if carried back and forth by a fickle current.

"God," says Ward, "you would think they could sing something better."

"Are you homesick, Ward?" The porters' singing grows louder and now there's a drum in with it. Casement smiles. "Do you think we could teach them 'Greensleeves'?"

18

Ward slams his glass down, tops it up, and drinks. "I hate England," Ward responds, "and England hates me. But that doesn't mean that I like the Congo Free State."

"'Alas, my love,'" starts Casement, "'you do me wrong,'" his voice catching with the distant porters', "'to cast me off, discourteously.'" This is not a military drum. "'For I have loved you—'" This is a heart beating.

"'—well and long!'" sings Ward, who voices like a drunken publican even when sober.

And together, "'delighting in your company.'"

After "Greensleeves" they sing "Jerusalem." And after that, some interminably long Irish thing to which Casement knows all the words and now, after hearing the chorus once, Ward knows it, and he too wants the young lovers to "come to the bower," although he has no idea what exactly that means, or ever meant.

The day enters with its usual blanket of heat. Casement might welcome rain, but that would transform the path into a river, which would, in turn, give way to a mud track. And the brief relief from the insect population that happens in the wake of these torrential downpours would only offer up the intense humidity that mosquitoes love so well. One discomfort is merely exchanged for another, which makes the absence of choice about such things almost tolerable. Or at least promotes a philosophical stance regarding his lack of control.

Ward is dissatisfied and restless. Before he agreed to this latest venture, Ward had been about to leave Africa for England and return home—even if he denied having one. He was ready to find a career for himself, although he seemed more focused on finding a woman. Ward is only involved in the transport of the *Florida* because the pay is very good. Ward is now making twenty pounds per year more than he himself is, but he can't begrudge Ward anything. For his company alone, Casement would have paid the difference in their salaries. It is Ward who punctuates his days: Ward in the morning by the edge of the water in his breeches; Ward's signature high-noon squint; Ward's rangy walk as he patrols the length of the column, his constant interrogation of messengers and locals about the possibility of game; and late-afternoon Ward with his sketchbook, wandering in search of something to draw. Casement envies the basic appeal of drawing—one's vision is, if nothing else, oversubscribed—whereas he, with his poems, is often faced with the blankness of his own mind that he struggles to populate with long-dead Irish kings.

Casement sees Ward chatting with one of the cook's assistants. The corners of Ward's mouth are pulled back in displeasure, while the hands of the cook's assistant, fingers splayed and heels of palms supporting invisible riches, describe some gustatory delight.

Ward catches Casement staring and—for one long second—holds his gaze.

"Bush rat," he shouts.

"Bush rat?"

"On the menu," says Ward, coming over. "What did you think I meant?"

"I wasn't thinking," says Casement. "It isn't rewarded, so why bother?"

Ward is flipping through his sketchbook. "What?" he says. This particular "what" means that Ward has missed what's been said.

"Anything interesting today?" asks Casement.

"Just some Manyanga," says Ward. He flips through his book, brushing bugs off as he goes, bugs that become pressed and preserved like the flowers pressed and preserved by women at home. There are sketches of plants, a porter with radiating facial scarring, a still life of gourds and pipes.

"Stop," says Casement.

Together they look at a woman, full-lipped, erect carriage, hair shaved close to the head. "You like her?"

"Not the woman. The necklace." It's endearing, Ward's ability to chronicle everything without actually seeing it. "Her necklace, Ward. Look at it."

"It's quite unusual." The necklace is formed in a fine coil about the woman's neck, like a loose spring.

"It's wire."

"Probably."

"It's brass wire."

"Oh," says Ward. "That's right. The missing brass wire for the boiler assembly."

Certainly this is funny, but the effort required to gather up the brass wire—or what is still collectable—will be significant. He'll send out some men tonight, before the women and their wire disappear. Of course this was all predictable. Tippo Tib is corrupt as they come and if only the supervisors would acknowledge that there is a difference between a dissembling Arab slaver and, for example, an honest Bakongo chief, such mistakes would be rare. As it is, the Belgians, the English, the French would all rather do business with the Arabs because of their smattering of European language and their inclination to wear clothing.

"Here," says Ward, pushing the sketchbook into Casement's arms, "take a look. Maybe you'll find something else."

"Where are you going?" asks Casement.

"To go find something that's not a bush rat." Ward calls out to Mbatchi and then heads towards the greenery. And, waving, "See you at dinner." Mbatchi, loaded down with rifle and bag full of shot, follows after him, the pale soles of his feet raising up, lifting a low cloud of dust as he runs to catch Ward.

Ward does not appear that evening, nor Mbatchi, and although Casement knows he should not worry, his sleep is troubled by thoughts of poisonous snakes and the heavy crush of jungle that precedes the leopard's kill. And there are natives who can see the value of capturing a man like Ward, with his golden hair and straight shoulders. Casement opens his eyes expecting the darkness but it is now bright. He can hear the river rushing against rocks, tearing at the banks. He has managed to sleep. Tom is panting and smiling on the floor beside him. He sits up in his cot and hears a child's voice—it's Mbatchi—chattering away to someone, although the camp still holds the quiet of early morning. He hears, *Englishman*, and, *many Arabs*, and, *like a goat only bigger with very long ears*. Casement gets up from his cot and parts the canvas flap to leave his tent. He reminds himself that he is not Ward's keeper. He will be cheerful, not scolding.

"Mbatchi!" he says, too jovially. "You're back. What is this goat with long, long ears?"

"For the Arabs to sit on."

"It's a donkey," says Casement. "Don-key." It would be good for the boy to learn some English. He pats Mbatchi's head. He smiles, straining to be relaxed. "And where's Mayala Mbemba?"

"With the white man," says Mbatchi. "There were so many people," he gestures around him, "and the great English chief is there too, but I didn't see him."

"The great English chief," says Casement.

"His name is donk-key." Mbatchi shakes his head. "No, Stankey. His name is Stankey."

"Stankey? Do you mean Stanley?"

"Yes!" says Mbatchi.

"And what is Stanley doing in this region?"

"He is going to save another man, another great man."

What nonsense is this?

"Mayala Mbemba says to go on without him and that he will find us in the afternoon."

"Ah," says Casement. He is walking away when he changes his mind. "Mbatchi," he says, "this white man that you say Mayala Mbemba was speaking with, he wasn't Stanley?"

"No."

"What did he look like?"

"Like you, like Mayala Swami. He is a white man."

Which is, of course, the correct response. What is Casement looking for from Mbatchi, who sorts into either the familiar or the unfamiliar? To Mbatchi, this anonymous white man appears in same alien register as a donkey or a crowd of Arabs. And what did he expect Mbatchi to say? That this other white man is tall and strong? That this other white man makes Mayala

Mbemba laugh, or that they went hunting together? This is insanity and all diseases of the mind are easily succumbed to in Africa. One must be vigilant.

"Mayala Swami," comes a voice.

"What?" says Casement, startled from his thoughts. It's Kiskela, a Bakongo, and a supervisor.

Kiskela thinks before speaking. "We have gathered together the Manyanga women with the brass-wire jewelry, but they do not want to give it up. These are gifts, they say, from their husbands. We can take it from them, but they will be very angry, and the Manyanga are usually friends, but if we take jewelry from their women, they will not be so kind to us, and they have the fields just to the north. We will need to buy manioc from them—"

"I understand," says Casement. He feels rescued by duty. What to do? "Take a case of brass rods and some cloth from the stores and buy the jewelry back. Bargain hard and keep track of everything. We'll try to recoup some of our losses when we're purchasing food." Kiskela has a photographic memory for numbers and amounts. His retention of such knowledge is impressive, a gift that many of his people have—necessary when there is no system of writing.

"Is there something else?" asks Casement, as Kiskela has not moved.

"Mayala Swami, the women will want to see you."

"Fine," says Casement. "I will go there and wave my big white head at them."

Kiskela smiles.

"I haven't had any breakfast," says Casement.

"You will have some soon," says Kiskela.

Casement appreciates this about Kiskela, that he follows orders cleanly but always makes it seem as if getting things done is of personal satisfaction. There is respect here, and kindness, but not quite friendship.

This is a lonely, lonely place. Casement is twenty-two years old. In another life, he would be elbow-on-the-bar with other men his age, or reading history at Trinity.

"Kiskela!" he shouts. "No bush rat, please."

*　*　*

What does Casement know of Henry Morton Stanley, the great explorer of Africa? He knows him as a charlatan. He's heard the gossip—Stanley, a workhouse Welshman who escapes to America and reinvents himself as a Wild West journalist and now, suddenly, he's the best expression of an intrepid Englishman. His first publicity stunt was finding Livingstone and delivering the droll phrase, "Livingstone, I presume." Anyone who had actually met Stanley knew that he had no wit, even poor wit, and could not have come up with that. Stanley had carted this print-ready statement from London, along with his silly outfit and notoriously bad feet.

David Livingstone was a mediocre explorer, famous for confusing the source of the Nile with the Lualaba River, which flows into Upper Congo Lake. He also had a missionary bent, or a savior complex, depending on whom you spoke to. The fact of his ever being lost is up for debate. Ultimately, Livingstone became so confused with malarial visions that he ceased all communication with the civilized world—and was presumed dead—for six years. That is, until Stanley paid a visit to him, where he was living on the shores of Lake Tanganyika, the whole venture funded by the *New York Herald.* The jury is still out as to whether Livingstone wanted to be saved, or found, or conversed with, or whatever it was that Stanley had actually done. Still, it was a good news story. And how to follow it up?

Apparently with this stunt of saving Emin Pasha. The whole thing is absurd and no doubt the copy was already typeset before Stanley left for Africa—more of a script just waiting for Stanley to act it out.

Casement and Ward are facing off across the dinner table but Ward, his legs extended and ankles crossed, seems more occupied with his boots, which could use a polish.

"You're not making any sense," says Casement. He hears the edge in his voice, is worried that he sounds womanly.

"Well, you're not making much of an effort to figure out the facts, are you?" Ward responds.

Ward is determined to attach himself to Stanley, since he fancies himself an adventurer. "I'm not the one who has been taken in by this ridiculous enterprise. In your effort to make the facts clear to me, it's obvious that you have no idea what Stanley is up to."

Casement reminds himself to sound less spurned, more like a counselor. "You must admit, there's something odd about the venture."

"Casement, I don't understand why you're so against Stanley."

"I'm against all this puffery." Casement shakes his head. "Who is this man?"

"The name is Ingham and he's a representative of the Emin Pasha Relief Expedition."

The clarity of this statement hangs in the air. Casement smoothes his mustaches. "And you said he was very interested in the *Florida*."

"Yes. And in me. He seems to think I could be very useful to Stanley."

"When we have the *Florida* at the edge of the Pool, it will be the only steamboat available for purely trade purposes." Casement says the Pool instead of Stanley Pool because he refuses to be complicit in a testament to Stanley. "Every other boat is in the service of God and in the hands of the missionaries. He wants the *Florida*. He means to commandeer it."

"Really?" says Ward. "And what if he does?" Ward empties the last of the bottle into his glass.

And so what? Casement will get nowhere with bullying. If anything he'll prove himself to be bad company, and then it's all over. "All right, Ward. So who is this Emin Pasha? What sort of man is he, and what has put him in such a perilous position?"

"Well, he's a good sort of fellow."

"He is?"

"He's a consul, or a governor. And he's an ally."

Casement nods, affecting patience as Ward tries to put it all together. He feels like a schoolmaster watching as a student flubs the lesson. "And where is he?"

"He's in Equatoria, southern Sudan."

"Equatoria," Casement considers. It's beginning to make more sense. "He's one of Gordon's provincial governors, isn't he?"

General Gordon, Governor General of Sudan, had been slaughtered by Mahdist revolutionaries a year earlier. At first, the English hadn't wanted to get involved, and when they finally came around to seeing that perhaps Gordon did indeed deserve some help, it was too late. Troops arrived two days after the fall of Khartoum and Gordon's death. Many British subjects had lost their lives and images of hanky-clutching women being carried off by turbaned men on Arab steeds had sold a lot of newspapers.

"If Emin Pasha is in Sudan, why is Stanley here in the Belgian Congo?"

"I wondered the same thing." Ward seems proud of knowing to ask this obvious question. "It seems that old King Leopold also wants to give a hand in saving Emin Pasha, and so Stanley is starting here, you know, getting porters and supplies, the usual."

"*That's* ridiculous. To get to Equatoria with as many men as seems is happening, one should go from Dar el Salaam. Perhaps Equatoria looks close on a map, but that region is almost completely unknown and what's known about it is not good. The Ituri Forest is notoriously populated with cannibal tribes and much of it's a swamp."

"It sounds like an adventure."

"No, it sounds like money. Leopold. He wants to know if there's something in that territory worth claiming—rubber, ivory. He's thinks that sending Stanley through the jungle to rescue this Emin Pasha with the support of England, under the English flag—"

"It's not, actually," says Ward. "It's not the English flag. They're marching forward under the flag of the New York Yacht Club."

"So there's American money too."

"Casement," says Ward. "You can be so cynical. And, frankly, you sound like an old man. All we have, you and I, is the fact that we're young and strong. We don't have families to worry about, well, not yet, and we can do anything we want, without hurting anyone but ourselves."

This sounds like Ward, but a little more like some unseen person filtered through Ward's idiom. Casement is tempted to ask Ward if he's thinking of joining this absurd Emin Pasha Relief Expedition, but he's worried that by asking such a question, he'll be validating the possibility. In his bones, buried far from thought, he already knows that Ward is gone. Casement realizes that he's rolling the empty bottle in his hands.

"Is that it for the bottle?" Ward asks.

"Yes."

"Don't you think we should call for another?"

They have left the riverbank to cut a shorter distance between two of the Congo's coils. The terrain here is flatter with long grass, grass that hisses when the breeze stirs. Birds are occasionally flushed from its pile and take to the air, their wings singing. A herd of deer the size of dogs had been sighted, but by the time the rifle was raised, Ward running up the column of men, eager to get a shot, they were gone. Casement had watched the deer escape. Leaping from the grass made them seem like fish breaking the surface of the water.

The cart carrying the shaft for the *Florida*, pulled by a hundred men, has presented more problems than even Casement, who has a gift for seeing potential disaster, could have predicted. The bed is low-slung, the wheels thick and wooden, a most primitive machine that it is hard to imagine any civilized people using unless one goes far, far back. And this track through the jungle—packed dirt when dry and when it rains a river of mud—is made for porters. This awkward, deformed vehicle requires something of a road. When a curve is encountered, a new path must be struck and the men must strike it. Casement knows something of surveying and with each passing day knows something more. How many times has he heard, "Mayala Swami, the wheel is off. What do we do?" And how many times has he responded, "When that happens, we put the wheel back." Which is accomplished as the insects swarm and the heat bakes down and the pause in progress reminds all the porters who have considered deserting that this might be their only chance, who set down their bundles carefully and take off at a good clip. But what to do now?

He hears the men calling out first and then Tom's barking. The hillock is low and although now Casement sees he should have been supervising, he was reviewing food purchases to be made that evening with Kiskela. He would like to blame this on Ward, but Casement had asked Ward to check the rear of the column since they were approaching the village and the temptation to run off was strong.

Ward comes up beside Casement as they view the disaster. Apparently, as the cart had begun to roll down the hill, the men behind had not been able to slow it. There were so many men pulling the thing that those in front were under the impression that the cart was once again on level ground, which is why they'd resumed their efforts. The cart had sped along briefly—a slow but unstoppable runaway—until it had managed to become beached upon a low boulder, breaking its axle in the process.

"Is anyone hurt?" asks Ward.

"One of the porters tripped on a root while trying to get out of the way and split his lip." Sure enough, there is the porter gingerly touching his swollen mouth, testing his teeth carefully against the wound as if to confirm that his own teeth are indeed responsible for the injury.

"Well, we should be grateful," says Ward cautiously, sensing Casement's mood.

"Oh, I am," says Casement. "I am as grateful as they come. Do you hear this?" He shouts at a deaf god, "This is gratitude!"

"Can we make—"

"No. Even if we find ironwood out here, we don't have the tools to fell it. And anything else will just snap immediately." Casement has lost. The cart has given Ward the excuse to leave him and Casement savors his defeat. "We'll need to purchase another axle."

"Well then," says Ward, "one of us needs to go to Matadi."

Casement nods. "True."

"Did you want to go?" Ward asks, forcedly casual.

If Casement goes, the entire operation will fall apart. Someone will see a fresh leopard print and Ward will go after it, the men will desert, and those who don't will be faced with meager rations as Ward will have forgotten to purchase supplies. "Me? Rather than you, Wings of an Eagle, and your forty miles in one day?"

"All right," says Ward. He looks around, twitchingly, for some reason to stay to present itself.

Casement presents a wan smile.

"Oh well. I should probably get going, you know, while there's light."

"That would seem to be what's called for." So that's that then. "I'll push on and leave a rear patrol with the cart." Casement is suddenly exhausted.

Mbatchi shows himself. The clever boy has been picking up some English. "Mayala Mbemba, are we going to Matadi?"

"You stay, Mbatchi," says Ward. "Too far for you, for little legs." He rubs Mbatchi's head affectionately and Mbatchi looks up at Casement. Casement, swallowing, looks back and his look says, *Yes, clever boy, we've both been abandoned.*

Sleep does not come for Casement. He pictures Ward making the trip back to Matadi, his long strides, his sweeping the track for prints, the hearty calling-out to the natives he encounters with his fumbling Bakongo and Swahili. Stanley is in Matadi putting together what he insists is the greatest rescue ever mounted. Stanley will push through the jungle, through hostile tribes, through unforgiving terrain, where Emin Pasha, surrounded by blood-thirsty Moslems, is sure to perish until Stanley—cue the bugle—sweeps down vanquishing the heathen: a cliché that would only appeal to Ward, who seems more of an adolescent than a man, although this is perhaps the source of his appeal. Casement's love for his friend, well, maybe it's better that Ward should leave before Casement has to acknowledge that it's something else. He stifles a low sob and instantly loathes himself. He thinks of writing a few lines, but, knowing that they will be awful, does not pick up the pen. A moment of painful consciousness, where he senses every corner of self flung out across the universe—exposed, without skin—ticks by. He wonders if the shot in his pouch has stayed dry. Sensing distress, Tom pants by the edge of the cot. Casement pats the dog, momentarily comforted. They stay like this a moment, but then Tom's head pivots quickly and he emits a low growl.

"Is there someone there?" Casement asks of the dark.

"Mayala Swami, it's only me."

"It's all right, Tom," Casement tells the dog. "Come in, Mbatchi."

Mbatchi steps inside. He's holding his bedroll.

"It's very late, Mbatchi. Why aren't you asleep?"

"Did I wake you up?"

"No, no."

"You couldn't sleep," says Mbatchi, "because Mayala Mbemba is going to Matadi. You think he isn't coming back because he wants to go with Stanley to save the other great man."

"How do you know this?"

Mbatchi thinks but doesn't answer. He too has had a feeling that has become a certainty.

"You should sleep, Mbatchi."

Casement watches him, but the boy does not move. He stands with his bedroll looking down at the ground.

"Did you sleep in Mayala Mbemba's tent?"

Mbatchi nods.

"I thought you slept in the cook's tent."

"I didn't like the smoke."

"Did you want to sleep here?"

Mbatchi clearly does, but he casts a nervous look over at Tom.

"Tom's all right. Come here, pat his head. He likes it when you scratch behind his ears."

Mbatchi comes over nervously but scratches the dog's head. The dog smiles.

"You can set up your bed in the corner," says Casement. "And Tom will make sure that no snakes come in." Casement raises his eyebrows. "You'll be very safe with Tom around."

Mbatchi takes his bedroll over to the corner and lays it out.

"Go to sleep now, good night."

Mbatchi is lying down but still not ready for sleep. "Mayala Swami, what will I do now?"

"Well, I can send you back to your parents with the next messenger. I'm sure you miss them."

Silence stands briefly as the boy thinks. "Can I work for you?" There's a nervous sadness in the voice, as if he fears that he's not wanted.

More silence. What is best? "All right," says Casement, "you can carry my surveying tools, but most important of all, you must make sure that Tom has water. He needs to drink several times a day, and I do forget. You will be very useful."

"Good," says Mbatchi. Casement hears the boy roll over and almost instantly a whistling snore can be heard from the corner of the tent.

Well, that's settled, thinks Casement. He'll take care of Mbatchi, make sure he is well fed and in good health, that he is always happy and feels safe, that he rests when he needs to and is protected from those that might harm him. And he'll work and perform all the tasks required of him, one after the other, until his life is wasted or there's nothing left to do.

III

Yambuya

June 1887

The camp hovers on the side of a river and is enclosed by a fence of sticks that—when observed all at once—resemble nothing more than the teeth of a comb. There are several huts made of tree limbs, planks, scrap metal, whatever was available during construction, and these are thatched with grass. Three months have passed since Ward signed on for the venture, and he has yet to do anything beyond presenting himself in various locations to little purpose. And now he is presenting himself here. Stanley and half the officers and the available porters have already left, their drums but a distant memory. Stanley is in a hurry to rescue Emin Pasha while he still needs rescuing, before the situation resolves itself.

Ward has been made a fool and he knows it. He and four other officers—Stanley's less desirables—are to wait in Yambuya until they have sufficient porters to join the expedition. They are to guard the supplies deemed unnecessary at this juncture. A Major Barttelot is the top-ranking officer. Ward explains that he has experience with porters, that he speaks local languages and is a good shot. Barttelot finds none of this interesting.

Barttelot doesn't want to look Ward in the eye but rather keeps swiveling—as Ward moves to face him—so that Ward remains sighted over his left shoulder. Ward asks, "Where ought I put my things?"

"Why should I care?" says Barttelot.

Which actually makes sense, but someone should care, shouldn't they? Ward ducks his head into a large hut and sees various bundles and crates of ammunition piled into a pyramid in the corner. On the cot Ward sees fragile nets, pens, and a series of leather-bound notebooks, folded clothes—someone else's traps, as they call personal belongings here, as if everything possesses a potential danger.

The next hut has a bare cot and no ammunition. It's very small, which seems about right for how Ward feels and is, at least, unoccupied. There are several empty sacks folded on the floor and these he'll fashion into crude curtains. Ward sets his bag down and sits, the cot responding with a creak. He takes his sketchbook from his bag.

There's a series of slaps on the doorjamb and Ward looks up.

"Herbert Ward, I presume," says the man, leaning in the entrance, "unless you are Selim ben Mohammed, who is also expected."

Ward stands and shakes hands. "I'm Herbert Ward."

"James Jameson," he says. "Perhaps I can scare up some sort of meal for you. Would you be interested in that?"

"I could eat," says Ward, following him out.

They sit on crates in the shadow cast by Jameson's hut, which is the large one with the ammunition. Ward starts on his bowl of goat stew. Jameson looks frail for this climate. He wears his mustaches long and has a dreamy, faraway look that seems better suited to less-obscuring landscapes. "I'm really not sure what the purpose is of my being here," says Ward.

"I'm thinking you're here to keep me company."

"How are the others?"

"Well, you've met them. Troup is all right, if you don't mind hearing—again—that this isn't Egypt. He's a soldier and is really only happy when he's killing for King and Country. And Bonny, well, was a sentimental addition for Stanley. He came along for romance and adventure. Obviously, the man's an idiot, but you still feel bad for him."

Bonny had punned on Ward's name, "to-Ward, and for-Ward," and Ward had chuckled to be generous but didn't really understand the joke. "Good for a laugh?"

"If you feel like making the effort." Jameson raises an eyebrow. "We've been here six weeks now. Barttelot is already mad, the first of us to lose his mind. He is, after all, our fearless leader."

Jameson might be the sort who quickly calls people mad, not realizing what it means in Africa.

"We could be here for months," says Ward. "Why would Stanley put Barttelot in charge?"

"Because Barttelot's ill-tempered, which can masquerade as having a sense of purpose. And he served in China."

"This isn't China," says Ward. He's tired of serving under people less knowledgeable than himself, but that's written into the running of Africa. People from home slide right into the highest positions, while those with actual experience have to fight for what's left over. "Why'd they leave you behind?" asks Ward.

"You're very direct," says Jameson. There's a Scottish purr to his accent, one that is carefully controlled. "The doctor thought I looked less sturdy than the others, although they brought Stairs along in a stretcher."

"Clearly, you think it's something else."

Jameson shrugs. "They're a bad lot anyway. Jephson bought a dog in Cape Town and one night, deciding he didn't like the look of it, tied a bar around its neck and threw it overboard into a black sea. I had its brother, until it ran off a week ago." From Jameson's expression, one would conclude that "running off" had been a wise decision. "Jephson and I tossed coins and I got the better-looking animal. If I'd known that Jephson would be so cruel, I would have taken the other."

"You're Scottish?" asks Ward.

"Actually, Irish, but raised in Scotland."

"Jameson, like the whiskey?"

"Oh, yes." Jameson looks at Ward from the corner of his eye. "Deceptively charming, but capable of knocking you off your feet when you least expect it."

"I meant—"

"Yes, that's my family." Jameson, holding very still, looks over Ward. His eyes stop on the sketchbook. "May I see?"

Ward hands the sketchbook over.

"These are very nice. You have talent." Jameson, someone who is accustomed to having his opinion matter, raises his eyes and nods at Ward. "I too am someone who draws, but I lack your vigorous line."

"I say, it will be good to have another artist—"

"Artist?" Jameson shakes his head. "Drawing is a gentleman's pursuit."

"Really?" asks Ward and regrets it.

Jameson's eyes twinkle. "Unless you're planning on taking up drawing as a profession?"

"No," says Ward. "That's not really my thing." He glances about him—at Africa, he supposes—which is currently what interests him.

"What has brought you here?" asks Jameson.

"Now you're being direct!" says Ward, on his toes. "I'm a bit of an adventurer, you know. I've traveled a lot. I've been to Australia and New Zealand. I lived in Borneo—"

"I've been to Borneo," says Jameson. "Do you hunt?"

"There's nothing I like better."

"This might work out," says Jameson. "Any interest in insects?"

"Well, not really. Insects, you mean scientifically?"

"Of course." Jameson laughs and notices Ward's ears, which are turning red with embarrassment. "Also butterflies. I collect them."

Ward doesn't know how to respond to this at all.

"And birds. I've been skinning them to stuff later—"

"There I can help you!" says Ward.

"Really?"

"Yes. My father was a taxidermist at the Museum of Natural History." Of course, his father is now living in America, but he'll not mention this just yet.

"Oh?" Jameson is pleased.

"And my grandfather traveled with Audubon in America." This last fact is true, but always sounds as though Ward is making it up. And Ward isn't sure if this pedigree really recommends him: He comes from a long line of bird-skinners.

"Jolly good," says Jameson, whiskey heir, as if he's produced the phrase as a gift to the "jolly" Ward. "We should make out all right on this muddy strip, even if it does edge onto the abyss of hell and is very, very slippery."

Ward has been at Yambuya three long, empty months. He has given up shaving and, possibly as a result of this, avoids looking in the mirror. Jameson occupies himself collecting butterflies and beetles, finding the wriggling, scuttling, fluttering things and quickly—with pins, chemicals, whatever—introducing stillness. Even with the sun shining, there is something gloomy about this reach of the Aruwimi River. Kingfishers hunt over the black surface of the river, their jeweled feathers catching the sun; they hover and hover, then drop, dividing their reflections with a narrow splash. The manioc plants, when stirred by the wind, flutter their hand-like leaves.

Casement had warned Ward that he risked being treated as second class because surely Stanley was recruiting in London from a pool of hundreds, mostly gentlemen. And that, because the finances on this venture were not clear, wealthy people who had interests beyond the rescue of Emin Pasha and other vaguely heroic undertakings would fill out the roster, and here was Jameson with his whiskey fortune and butterflies. Down to the last detail, Casement had seen it. He had pointed out the press clause in Ward's contract: *I undertake not to publish anything connected with the Expedition, or to send any account to the newspapers for six months after the issue of the official Expedition by the leader or his representative.* "If something goes wrong," Casement had said, "you'll have no way to defend yourself." Ward has begun to wait for that thing to go wrong.

A shadow falls across the doorway of his hut. It is Jameson, back from tending his snares. Jameson presents a pair of dead warblers: limp creatures with closed eyes and gentle beaks, their claws curled tenderly. Jameson and Ward will flay the birds and pack the skins carefully, so that their being can be reconstituted in England—stuffed with wood shavings and fiber.

"Ward," says Jameson, "you look tired."

"I'm all right," says Ward, "but I feel the ghost of a fever in my joints."

Ward flips the bird onto its back and slices vertically from the base of its head down the length of its abdomen. Ward left home at fifteen years, a boy, but already committed to being an artist. His father had laughed at him, although there were artists in the family. Uncle Rowland was very successful; King Edward VII had commissioned his bronze animals, which led to recognition. Ward is not a gentleman, never wanted to be. When he threatened to become a sailor, to journey to New Zealand, his father had told him, *Go. Go kill yourself*, sealing the deal. And, what Ward recalled most clearly, *Don't you know what happens to little golden boys like you on long voyages?* He remembers his father's growling laughter, his own fear. There is a little blood along the incision and carefully he peels back the warbler's skin. Ward was suffocating in London, amid the reek of chemicals from his father's work, his mother's wide-eyed, stupid beauty, his own furtive sketching, the cold corridors of the Mill School, where he excelled at boxing. And gymnastics. His pride at taking first prize for the horizontal bars and his father saying, *Go join a circus then*. The low, growling laugh. His father's glee as all the elements of failure fell in place for his golden, pretty son. Ward gently snaps the wings from the warbler's sockets. Somehow, it was all about the mother, who loved her son blindly and this blind love for Ward, after all love had died for her husband, infuriated the father. If she had really wanted to protect him, his mother should have loved him less. And now his father has taken all the family money, some of which should have been Ward's, and bought huge tracts of land in California. This is where his parents and sister now live, so far as to almost be beyond the reach of memory.

"Now if the rain will hold off," says Jameson, "maybe these skins will dry."

Ward skillfully scrapes all traces of fat from the skin. The work is soothing, an escape. "Why do you really think Stanley left you here, James?"

"To the point," says Jameson.

"You always say that," says Ward, "as if there's some other way of speaking."

"There is."

"Not if you want to be understood," says Ward.

"All right," Jameson demurs. "I think Stanley left me to Yambuya because he found me intimidating. He's a brute, old Stanley, has the worst manners, and is threatened by just about everyone, which is why he loves his Manyema savages so much. On a continuum, he's actually closer to them than he is to me."

"And where would you put me," says Ward, "on this continuum?"

"An artist?"

"It's a hobby," Ward protests.

"It shouldn't be."

Ward scrapes at his bird skin, looking over at Jameson, who isn't often serious.

"Artists are more angels than men," Jameson declares.

"What if I told you I used to be a circus performer?"

"No!" Feigned horror.

"I was. Even worse, it was in an Australian circus, in Sydney. I used to walk along this beam over everyone's heads. I'd get up there and stand on my hands." Ward regards his hands, dirty with bird blood. "Was I with the angels up there?"

"Closer to God? I think not," says Jameson. "You're demoted, back among the Manyema, with Stanley." Jameson smiles indulgently.

Ward is something of a pet, and he knows this, but that is all right. Better Jameson than Casement, who is clearheaded and fair to a fault. Judgmental. Noble. Arrogant. Blind.

Bonny sticks his head into the hut and lets Ward and Jameson know that Barttelot would like to speak to them. They make their way to Barttelot's tent. They stand awkwardly before Barttelot, who—spread across a makeshift couch, his legs splayed—reports that Tippo Tib sent 400 porters, but nearly all are lost. An Arab half-caste, Abddallah, is happy to escort the representatives of Stanley back to Tib's camp at Stanley Falls, suggesting they bring partial payment, so they can sort it out.

"I think Tippo Tib is lying," says Ward. "There were never any porters. He says this so that we will send rifles as payment."

"We haven't talked to him yet, have we? Have we?" Barttelot props himself higher on his elbow. "If we don't talk to him, he cannot lie. It is the Manyema that lie. The black man lies."

Ward holds steady. He sees Barttelot's fingers grasping the handle of his steel-tipped staff. Ward is careful not to look at Jameson, as careful as Jameson is not to catch Ward's eye.

"You must go to Tippo Tib and tell him where we are and tell him to send the porters again."

"It will take us at least three days to get to Stanley Falls," says Ward.

Barttelot waves him off with the back of his hand.

"We will need supplies and arms and men to accompany us. It's straight through Opongo territory and they are known cannibals."

"Of course they are!" Barttelot twitches and forces himself into a seated position, which he seems to resent having to do. "Take some of these savages—arm them, and good luck to you."

Ward, as a safety measure, has the escort made up half of Arabs and half of natives from around the Stanley Falls area. The Arab interpreter, Assad Farran, is accompanying them, no doubt lured by the promise of good food at the court of Tippo Tib. The path is narrow and leads through abandoned villages where formerly cultivated manioc blocks one's path. For dinner, one moldy biscuit each, since they had counted on purchasing food from the villagers, but there are no more villagers—nor villages, as all have moved to avoid Arab slavers and conscription as porters.

Jameson has folded in upon himself like a clenching fist. Ward attempts some cheer, pointing out birds through the scrim of drizzle, although they present themselves robbed of color and slightly out of focus.

"Tell me a story," says Jameson.

"What about?" says Ward.

"About your Congo cannibals," says Jameson.

"I've spent most of my time among the Bakongo," says Ward. "They would no sooner eat a man than I would. They are a gentle people."

"Then it is a boring story." Jameson is depressed at this. They are walking the length of a creek, ankle-deep in water.

"Unfortunately for the Bakongo, their gentleness puts them further down the food chain."

"Really?"

"The Bangala—mostly north side of the Congo—are quite fierce and unrepentant cannibals."

"Do they feast upon each other?" Jameson asks.

"No. No one does that. Mostly, the Bangala eat slaves, Bakongo wandering through the jungle who accidentally cross paths with them, or Arabs who aren't paying attention. Or they'll be at war with a neighboring tribe and win. That gives them some captives. That sort of thing."

"Were you ever in danger?"

"I suppose I must have been, but not anymore. I'm blood brother to the chief of the Bangala, Mata Mwiki."

"You should write a book about all of this," says Jameson. "You know so much. You could call it *Five Years Among the Congo Cannibals*."

Ward is flattered, yet he also knows he's been flattered—flattered purposefully, but he doesn't know why.

"You say the Opongo are cannibals. Are you sure?"

"Not having been among them, I can't be sure, but that is the prevailing wisdom."

"And you say we are passing into their territory?"

"Either that, or we're already here."

They march on in silence. There is another swamp to be crossed, another nest of vines that knocks your hat off and then follows up by tangling your boots.

"They're saying there's a village close by," says Jameson, "although they don't know much about it."

"Right," says Ward. "There's reason for cheer." He cheers himself by saying this.

Ward washes his face. The village they have reached is deserted, although now—as Ward sights across the manioc fields—he can make out a native zig-zagging in cautious approach. The native is carrying something—at first Ward thinks it to be a baby—dangled by its leg. Whatever it is, it wriggles. And when the man draws close, disappearing for a moment behind the wall of a thatched hut, reappearing just six feet from where Ward stands, he sees that the man is holding a dog.

Ward calls for one of the Stanley Falls natives to translate because he is sure he does not speak this man's dialect. Molangi presents himself with his usual droll reserve.

"Give the standard greetings," says Ward, "and find out who he is."

Ward smiles as Molangi delivers as instructed: salutations, friendship, an explanation for their presence.

The man listens, nodding, and responds pleasantly—or so it sounds—and as he speaks he gestures with the dog, which yelps and snaps.

"Well?" says Ward.

"He is the chief," says Molangi. "And this dog is for you, because he would not like it if you left his village hungry."

"This can't be his village. It's completely deserted."

Molangi thinks this over and says something to the chief, who, lifting the miserable dog, indicates some location to the west.

Molangi looks at Ward.

"How far?"

"Not far. One hour."

"Do they have food?"

"First take the dog," says Molangi, "then give thanks, and then we ask about other food."

"You take the dog," instructs Ward.

"Can I have it?"

"Yes, you can." Ward smiles at the chief with perfectly pantomimed gratitude.

Jameson has shown up for the interview. He looks poorly rested, pale and red-eyed. "So where's the village?"

"An hour from here. Are you up to it?"

"Is he Opongo?"

Molangi, hearing "Opongo," looks over the chief and nods to Jameson.

"Is he a cannibal?"

Ward supplies the Kikongo "cannibal" to Molangi. Jameson wants this communicated with the chief, but Molangi shrugs, unwilling to communicate things that aren't worth knowing, as unwilling as Ward to continue in this vein of conversation.

"Look at the necklace," Ward instructs.

The chief wears a number of bone fragments—teeth—strung out on a leather thong looped loosely about his neck.

"Human teeth?" asks Jameson.

"That's what it looks like," says Ward. "They must have food, at least fish and plantains. We should go with him. He seems friendly enough." Even if he is a cannibal, he won't injure a white man as the presence of Stanley's allies is so strong in the region. And the dog is a diplomatic overture.

"I'll get my sketchbook," says Jameson.

Ward's eyes follow Jameson to his tent. Molangi too looks in that direction and presents Ward with a quizzical look.

"What concerns you, Molangi?"

"I wish for the good health of the captain, that is all."

Ward too senses something about Jameson, and what could that be? Because when Ward sees Jameson he almost senses himself slipping, a sort of shared corruption. But this is the fever that has been lurking in his joints. Maybe his malaria is returning.

The following day, they reach Stanley Falls and the current location of Tippo Tib's camp. Ward and Jameson are presented at the entrance of his movable palace, constructed of paper and cheap paint—a stage set for this little drama. Ward runs his eyes over Tib's hundred wives, arrayed about him in flowing, spotless white, their faces veiled. Tippo Tib himself scans into vacant space as if he is a wolf testing the air for the scent of prey.

"I see it's true he's blind," says Jameson.

"But his hearing," says Ward, his voice dropping to the caliber of breath, "is very, very good."

Assad Farran makes the preliminary introductions, with appropriately flowery language and Ward and Jameson follow along.

"Friends of Bulwa Matadi are my friends," says Tib.

Bulwa Matadi is Stanley's native name and means "breaker of rocks," since once, recognizing a fracture and being in possession of a hammer, Stanley did manage to crack a rock in two. This impressive feat surprised all the natives and—no doubt—Stanley himself. They sit on the floor with the food and circulating all around, coffee replenished before it can cool. More rifles, says Tib. More porters, says Ward, and off to the side Assad Farran feigns attention, but his eyes—large black irises on the surface of brilliant whites—flit right and left, observing the veiled women.

Jameson whispers to Ward, "Is there nothing to drink, not even malafu?"

How does Jameson not know that with Tib, a devout Muslim, one does not consume alcohol?

The meeting over, Ward returns to his tent and falls into an exhausted sleep. His fast-approaching illness produces a great, clouded darkness as he drops off, as if a heavy blanket has been thrown over him, head to foot.

"Ward, wake up."

Ward awakes to find it bright already and Jameson standing, dressed, beside his pallet. "What time is it?" asks Ward.

"Almost nine. Are you all right?"

"Don't know yet," says Ward as he pulls himself to a seated position.

"Two of the Stanley Falls natives have stolen rifles. I'm going after them."

"I'll go with you."

"Not sure you're up for it," says Jameson. "Do you think you can make it back to Yambuya?"

"I will. Besides, one of us will have to report back to Barttelot. We're running a day late as it is."

"I'm not sure I should leave you," says Jameson.

"Go. Get back the rifles, and quickly, before they're pointed at us."

Ward asks Jameson to send in a boy with water and, after drinking, he feels refreshed, but his light-headedness informs him that the next three days are going to be a hellish slog back to Yambuya.

The first leg of the trip is by canoe, and after, on foot. When his porters, who are hungry, refuse to move on, Ward isn't sure how to persuade them. Then—with the fever growing—he no longer cares. He sees them terrorizing villagers, throwing women to the ground, decimating carefully tended stores, as he limps forward with one hand resting on the shoulder of his rifle-bearer who now must bear so much more. He wonders how Jameson is faring. After four days, he reaches Yambuya and collapses in his hut. Before sleep takes over, he manages to scrawl *very seedy* in his journal.

The next five weeks pass with Ward moving through different chambers of consciousness, his limbs vibrating with pain. Jameson is his near constant companion.

"Look," says Jameson. And Ward sees the first drawing: a young girl, her hands tied together, her face fixed in terror as an exchange is made. "She was purchased for six handkerchiefs. I provided them."

Ward's eyes, swimming, look at the watercolor—the girl, no more than twelve, seems to tremble on the page.

"So the sale was made—Assad Farran translating—and here we see how they dispatch with the slaves that are to be eaten." The girl's hands are tied with a chord, and this chord is tied to a tree. A wash of red spills out from her abdomen. At her side, her ferocious assailant still holds the knife. "They bled her out like that. She didn't make a sound. She was resigned, you see. She understood her fate."

Jameson has captured himself in the corner of the picture, drawing the scene. One looks over his shoulder at the event. Ward's fever makes it so that he feels himself stirred by that breeze, hearing the snap of wet twigs on the fire.

"And here," continues Jameson, "we see how they cut the body up. I'm sure you know how that's done. You must, given all your exposure to the savages."

Jameson flips to the next page.

"And here—well, if you don't know what they're eating, it just looks like any other stew. It's problematic, you know. When you think of all those Spanish etchings from the New World, they're always depicting feet and hands, because that's what makes us human. But these cannibals don't eat the feet and hands, and I did want to be accurate."

Then Jameson shows him a picture of a Manyema woman, her back patterned over with decorative scarring.

Next Jameson shows him a new butterfly fixed with a pin to a wooden board.

He says, "I'm getting bored with you so ill. I was down myself, for a couple of days, but with you as sick as you are, there was no one to notice."

Jameson returns to Ward's side with a cup of broth, caring for him with tenderness. Ward, choking on the broth, falls back against his cushion. "I had a curious dream," he says. "You purchased a girl for six handkerchiefs and presented her as a gift to cannibals so that you could watch her be eaten."

"That was no dream," says Jameson.

Ward sits up weakly.

Jameson says, "They would have eaten her anyway. There was nothing remarkable about the situation other than the fact that some old chief has six handkerchiefs and I have five watercolors."

Ward lies back down. Jameson does not understand the simple truth about the black man, that he—like every man—thinks himself the best expression of humanness, that the black man finds the white man less human.

October comes with smallpox and no Stanley.

In November, Ward catches one of the Sudanese stealing meat from his tent. Barttelot orders 150 lashes, which is extreme and should kill the man, but all the officers are frightened of what these hungry men will do. The Sudanese takes each lash, holding Ward's gaze, his teeth pulled back at the corners. It isn't even hatred in his eyes, rather incomprehension. Ward responds in his mind, saying, *You shouldn't have stolen the meat.* But of course he stole it. The men are starving. This man's eyes ask, *Why are you killing me?* and Ward replies, *Because you stole the meat.* And this man's eyes say, *I stole the meat because it cured my hunger. And you kill me because it cures yours.* Foggy thoughts. Shuddering images. Fever. All this is Yambuya.

Surprised that the man survives, it is decided that he be chained in the camp for all to see, as a warning: Do not enter our tents, do not steal our food.

"It's Christmas," says Jameson. "How shall we celebrate?"

"Sketching in the morning," suggests Ward, "followed by a malafu stupor."

"You are an African Scrooge, Ward."

"Scrooge would have been dead within two weeks of arriving here."

"You know that's wrong. People like that tend to have iron constitutions."

Jameson looks around Ward's hut. He picks up Ward's sketchbook and flips through, but Ward hasn't added anything since the day before, when Jameson last looked at it. "What should we do for presents?"

"Presents?" Ward sits up. "There's nothing here but brass rods."

"Then that's what we're getting. Now for wrapping paper."

Petty differences have been put aside and Bonny, Troup, and Barttelot agree to join the party. Ward rallies a little cheer. He shaves and trims his mustaches. He sits cross-legged on the floor sorting brass rods into piles, searching for the most entertaining scraps of newspaper with which to wrap them: plant-fiber makes a stringy, yet somehow appealing, bow.

And in the evening, a superb dinner of goat: first chops on the griddle, and then a leg roasted like lamb, which is extremely tough, but reminds of the Christmas spread that is happening back home. There is something that resembles a pudding. Barttelot produces a bottle of brandy, left by Stanley, which has enough for two good glasses, or four lesser portions.

"Presents!" says Jameson, handing each in turn. "You first, Major."

"Very well," says Barttelot, "I have an advert for a woman seeking employment—"

"I have an opening!" says Troup.

"And if you're lucky," says Bonny, "she does too!"

Oh, funny.

"Ward, read yours."

Ward smoothes the paper and says, "I got the agony column."

"I think we've all had that," says Bonny.

More laughter.

"It says," says Ward, "that Reggie has been going daily to Saint James Park Station and waiting for Lil and that Lil has not shown up."

"What does she look like?" asks Bonny.

"It does not say," says Ward, "but I imagine her to be very pretty."

"Oh, you bachelors," says Jameson. "I've no time for idle speculation as my lovely wife is waiting for me back at home."

There's a moment of quiet as people try to be respectful.

"Well, I wonder who's coming down her chimney," says Bonny, and they're off again. And Jameson laughs too, a good sport.

Then Bonny sings and his voice is a tremendous baritone so rich with emotion that he seems altogether a different sort of man. Then they sing together, different songs, and Ward would like it if they sang that long Irish ballad that Casement was so fond of, but Ward never learned all the words, just the chorus, and this is what's playing in his head when he falls asleep that night.

On New Year's Day, Ward goes hunting with Jameson before the heat sets in. Jameson sees a small bird dart into a tree. He's sure it's something new, but he loses it. Standing stiffly in silence, Ward waits for the bird to show itself. And then there is the sound of wings singing against the air and in two expert shots, two birds drop. Jameson has claimed the pair—a cock and hen—sunbirds, with jeweled feathers. Ward goes to retrieve them from where they have fallen on packed dirt, startled and almost saddened by their brilliance and beauty, those glinting feathers dirtied with blood.

Weeks pass, as if carried off in the sickly breeze. Late morning heat brings Ward to consciousness. There is a woman in the corner of his hut. A woman. She crouches, watching him guardedly. He inhales hard, trying to clear the fog from his mind. What will he say to her? Nothing.

He makes his way, still clumsy with drink, to Jameson's tent. How much malafu had they consumed the previous evening?

"Jameson," he says outside the entrance. "Jameson," he says again.

Jameson appears in his breeches, no shirt. He seems fresh, rested.

"I need to send her back," says Ward.

"Send her back where?" asks Jameson.

"To her village."

"Burnt to the ground by Selim's men," Jameson informs.

"She should rejoin her people."

"Who are at this point twenty miles from here and expanding that distance by the minute."

"Well, I can't keep her."

"That's not what you said last night."

"This isn't funny," says Ward. "I can't be keeping a slave."

"Apparently, you can," says Jameson, "although I don't know how you're going to get on without your boots. I suppose Troup might be able to dig up another pair for you."

Ward remembers—in a panicking flash—his trading of his boots for the Bolongo woman who had been captured by Selim's men. He had thought it valiant at the time, that he was saving her.

"You rescued that woman. She could have ended up in a brothel. Or a cooking pot. And if you give her up now, that's her likely fate."

"You don't know that," says Ward. Jameson's brow is smooth and untroubled. He could have that same look back in Scotland, standing on a wide verandah in the Highlands, ready to hunt elk.

"I can't prove I'm right, but you can't prove I'm wrong." Jameson looks over his shoulder at his tent flap, which has not yet been secured open to allow for a breeze.

"What about your wife?" Ward asks.

Jameson smiles. "You know nothing of women," he says. "I'll give her children and that will make her happy, but she doesn't want me snapping at her heels. A husband needs to keep his appetite in check."

All the officers have purchased women, even Barttelot, who is so volatile that one wouldn't think he had the patience. And it's more than mere memory that recalls the screams coming from Bonny's tent. The impression of them loops like birdcall, repeating in Ward's mind.

Ward, unlike Troup and Bonny, does not keep his woman locked up, as she is aware of her limited options. She spends most of her time with the other women, close by the huts, not showing up until the evening when she's wanted. She sits on the floor, her legs swung to the side, her full breasts exposed, traced over with decorative scars. Her hair is cropped close to her head, and her lips and cheeks are full. Ward sees her make that face—a cringe that shows the fine edge of her straight teeth—and then she meets his eyes. Those eyes are neither docile nor combative. They say, *I will give you nothing but what I have to,* and when Ward draws her, she is quiet, unlike Jameson's woman who talks and talks, asks if all white men come from the same mother, tells Jameson to lower his eyes more frequently because his intent look as he sketches might steal her soul, says that he must get her an extra helping of rice when the Arabs prepare it.

Ward asks his concubine (it's an odd word, but what else is she?) what her name is and she supplies it. Although he does not forget that she has a name, he doesn't use it—just directs her in small ways—as if calling her by name would be a violation. He will just say, *please come here,* and, *turn this way.* He will feel her flanks tense when he places his warm hands on this cool flesh; he will feel her force herself to relax. This is her role. Ward will let her play this role. Could it be that by not forcing her into the fullness of personality that she will be able to return to herself as she was before meeting him—as if her identity is something she could slip out of, like a coat? And maybe Ward too can do this, can slip out of himself at Yambuya, can put his golden self on a mental hook in the corner of his mind, his wide-eyed, adventurer self—Mayala Mbemba!—the linguister, hunter, and hero. This other Ward, a slippery creature, a man who assembles his moral code around his desires, he will leave in Yambuya with whatever pitiless appetites he wishes to sate.

And who's to know?

IV
Along the Congo

February 1888

The *Florida* has been wrestled back from Stanley and provided with an engine. Casement sits on her deck, waiting for his friend Edward Glave to be finished with the daily figures. Glave is the best sort of man. He speaks the local languages well and has assembled his servants from slaves that he himself has emancipated from Arabs and local chiefs. Glave is an unrivaled hunter and stalking prey with him is almost comically predictable; he can find the heart of an animal from any distance, from any angle. There's the animal. There's Glave. Pull the trigger. Animal collapses. Done.

He is also good at keeping order and inspires trust in everyone: delusional supervisors, pious missionaries, committed savages. And Casement. Glave appears from his office vigorously rubbing where his forehead meets his hair with the heel of his hand. He cracks his knuckles and looks out to the water where, in the distance, a hippo sinks from view. He gives a look of a surprise to see Casement sitting there.

"Casement, I thought you would have abandoned me. Sorry I took so long."

"Where would I have gone?"

"World's a big place." Glave flings his arm out, embracing the Congo and, apparently, everything else. "I have whiskey."

"I wouldn't want to take—"

"Nonsense," says Glave. He waves at one of his servants calling for some glasses, fried plantains, the location of the whiskey. Glave rubs his hands together and stands at the railing. He looks out again, perhaps making sure he isn't under attack from Arab raiders, then turns facing Casement in a fit of earnest inquiry. "What have you done now?" Casement's run afoul of the Sanford Expedition and will soon be unemployed.

"What have I done?" Casement smiles.

"That's what the whiskey is for, I suppose, to rob you of your characteristic reserve."

"I didn't like the conditions of the job at Luebo."

"What will you do?"

"What have I done? What will I do?"

"These are good questions," says Glave. The man arrives with the whiskey and Glave thanks him, asks after the plantains, learns that he hadn't stated how many he wanted, and Glave says to fry them all, keep half for the crew and bring the rest. He sees Casement and seems again surprised that he is there. "Well?"

"Don't suppose there's any work here?"

"Work, yes," says Glave. "Money, no."

"Well then, I'm going elephant hunting."

"And what about money?"

"Really, Glave, you sound like my mother." Although Casement really means his sister, or his cousin, since his mother has been dead a long time.

"Would you listen to her?"

"No, actually," says Casement, "I wouldn't. And I'm fine. I have savings from these last several months. If you haven't noticed, there's not much to purchase around here."

Glave pushes his chair around, finding a decent angle—although according to what criteria, who can say?—and sinks lightly into it. He gives Casement another searching glance, and then sets about putting good portions of whiskey in the tumblers. "I don't understand. You're the best man the Sanford Expedition has working the river."

"People don't like me," says Casement.

"That's not true."

"You like me. The locals like me." His sister likes him. And his cousin Gertrude. Ward likes him, or did. "I've run afoul of Taunt and Weber. I am reportedly too lenient with the natives. The only reason I am still here is because I'm necessary. Regional languages. Good at keeping the porters healthy. Things get from one place to the other."

"And you're honest."

"I don't know if that's one of the good things, Glave. Not around here. People think you're watching them."

"I'm honest," says Glave. "I wonder if people don't like me."

"Regardless, they wouldn't do anything about it. You're too good a shot."

Casement was tired of working for the Sanford Expedition. He was tired of the chain of command. He couldn't sit through another tedious meeting with a company officer, still in his costume of European fat, rivulets of sweat pooling at his neckline, blinking in haste as if it warded off ignorance, or illness, or loneliness, while Casement stood performing his role against this creature on the other side of the desk as the two raced towards the inevitable last line, which was never his, "You'll do it that way because that is what you have been ordered to do."

Glave says, "You have acquired a reputation for lacking respect for authority."

"That might be true," says Casement, "although it all depends on your definition of 'authority.'"

The plantains arrive carried by Mabruki, a child who is usually carrying Glave's rifle and shot bag.

SABINA MURRAY

"Ask him how old he is," says Glave, "in English."

"Mabruki, how old are you?" says Casement.

"Ten years old," Mabruki barks back.

"That's right," says Casement. Mabruki, pleased, walks off.

"If we actually knew how old he was. Ten seems about right," says Glave. "He's an orphan. A little English might put him in good stead with the missionaries for when I leave."

"Are you thinking of going home?"

"England? No. I've become curious about the Yukon."

"America?"

"Why not?"

After plantains, it's goat stew, and there's chili in it, which is not always available and is always appreciated. The whiskey holds. Both Glave and Casement drink slowly, valuing conversation. Glave asks after Casement's poetry and Casement laughs him off.

"Everyone else is drawing or writing books," he says. "And I don't have time for a book, and I can't draw."

Conversation takes a moment's rest. The thrum of insects sounds in high and then higher pitches. Water makes an even wash against the side of the boat. In the black river, some large creature dips from the surface with a full, low splash.

"You know people on the Relief Expedition," says Glave.

"Of course I know Ward. And there's Jephson, who bought a position and is traveling with Stanley. I don't know Jephson well. He's a cousin on my mother's side."

"Ward's in the Rear Guard, isn't he?"

"Last I heard," says Casement. He feels an anxious heat spreading. "Is there any news?"

"News? Not really. Stanley is out there trying to relieve Emin Pasha of his ivory. Tippo Tib is trying to relieve Stanley of his weapons. What porters Tib has provided are slaves. Anything new there?"

"No. And what of the Rear Guard?"

"Well, I hope Ward's all right. But there are rumors flying around. I pick them up from the Arabs passing through. The porters are dying off—everything from smallpox to starvation. Floggings of one hundred and fifty lashes or more are commonplace. Barttelot, who's still in charge, has lost his mind. One of the officers has a fascination with cannibalism and purchased a girl to see her eaten."

"I wonder who that is."

"So do I, but the Arabs think all the English look the same, so who's to know?" Glave packs a pipe with tobacco. "And, apparently, all the men have harems. Rumor has it that one girl was purchased with a pair of top boots."

Casement considers. He'll go over this later. He'll go over this alone. "Having a harem," he says—as a way of sending a representation of a thought, although it is not a representation of his thought—"is hardly remarkable."

The water is always coursing by, but on a river this size, the current seems more of time than of rain and run-off. The Congo wants to head to eternity rather than the seashore. And sometimes, here in Africa, Casement feels more on the underside of things rather than just in a different country on the same crust of earth. It's as if he's the altered version of his other self—his British self back in County Antrim—enacting different rituals and, somewhere, beneath a different sun, the different him is reading different lines, involved in different actions. One Casement hunts elephants through jungle. One Casement watches osprey circle salt air.

He has spent much time wandering the Antrim countryside. The sun felt good. You turned your face to it and the gentle heat was a benediction. That water song, like the rattle of oak leaves, the sighing string-note of doves on the wing, the splash of sunlight through summer foliage—all of it was in a gentle register. These were notes played with the right hand—a tinkling of ivory. This was, of course, back when ivory was just that: piano keys, combs in women's hair, chess pieces moved one at a time and with exacting precision. Here, the river moves with great power, as if the engine of God starts in the heart of Africa—as if the surging power of all that man cannot conquer, cannot understand, is here. The Congo is swift and deadly. Submerged stones tear entire sheets of steel from hulls, sinking boats. Rocks reveal themselves to be crocodiles. Like a massive engine belt, the river spins her circuit, revolving, churning, splitting green from green. Off the river, the sky obscures her face behind a veil of jungle growth.

The tree-filtered light creates a constant gloaming. Casement can hear the wash of pulse in his ears. He travels with two natives, Bongo Nsanda, who is Glave's friend and carries a spear, and Bongo Nsanda's friend, Mbwiki, who carries a rifle. Some ivory will supplement Casement's income, which, as Glave knew, needs attention. Now that they have left the proximity of the villages, the elephant pits will be spiked. People fall into them constantly and time, which allows hunters to forget a pit's location, also aids in its disguise. One must watch for cords of native twine strung low along the paths. This native device, the likongo, uses the cord to precariously hold in place a spiked beam, normally thirty feet above the ground. The wire, if tripped, releases the beam and this can fell an elephant and, therefore, anything else it manages to strike. Casement imagines his Irish self announce to a crowd of curious lyceum attendees. He hears his voice: "The likongo is a curious native device . . ." He hears the hush of surprise from the audience, the rustle of skirts and gossip, men coughing into curled fists, shamed by their ignorance of such things.

Bongo Nsanda raises his hand, fingers splayed. Casement stops, barely daring to breathe. Both Bongo Nsanda and Mbwiki listen, their eyebrows knitted in concentration, but Bongo's face soon opens wide—unconcerned.

"I thought I heard something," Bongo Nsanda says.

"I heard you hearing something," Mbwiki says.

They laugh.

"Is there any game here, except for us?" says Casement.

All laugh. Earlier, they had seen the imprint of a leopard's paw in the damp earth. And what is "game" after all, but the acknowledgement of an inferiority, as if we had lined up all creatures and decided, "You, gazelle, prey," and "You, lion, predator"? Bongo Nsanda shoulders his spear and walks lightly, the shaft end and spear tip bouncing. Would this same dividing intellect look upon Casement's rifle, Bongo Nsanda's spear, and say, "You, white man, predator," and "You, black man, prey"?

Bongo Nsanda stops again. His head shoots forward and then he raises his eyebrows in an affirmative. Casement lifts his rifle, although he's not sure where he'll aim. And then he hears a distant crash of greenery—an elephant and moving fast. Trees are crushed, vines ripped stringing masses of undergrowth, pulling the tops of trees downward. One never knows what one will see with an elephant. Why is it running? If it is scared, it runs. If it is angry, it runs. The snap and boom of breaking trees is coming near and Casement tenses. He has seen a man gored through a leg and tossed into the air. Or was that one of Ward's pictures? Representation and reality, the artifice and the basis, his colluding, corroding memories. And then the sun floods as the elephant tears the curtain of jungle from the brilliant sky and Casement is momentarily blinded as if he is seeing not a beast but the face of God itself.

Reverend Slade is sitting across the desk and Casement sits wondering what else creates a divide between the two. Casement needs employment and perhaps fanning the flames of his faith is not a bad thing. It's not as if he's made a conscious decision against God.

"I did not know you were a religious man," says Slade.

"I think that's because I was working for the Sanford Expedition. Which is the other church in the Congo."

"That and the Belgian Society. Still. Working for a mission, Mister Casement, seems to be quite a shift for you."

"Reverend Slade, you have the same needs as everyone else here. You need things transported. You need buildings. You need someone who can communicate with the locals. It's not that big of a change."

"But you are not religious."

"I am."

"You are."

"Recently."

"A convert?"

"Not so much a conversion as a . . . reviving." Why not try religion? It's not as if he is in favor of slavery, and he has worked with slavers. As for the Sanford Expedition, does he really believe that elephants need to be slaughtered for ivory? Is that something to believe in? "This is a country that forces convictions on a man," says Casement. He's being honest. "Your outfit—"

"The Baptist Church."

"The Baptist Church," he'll accept the correction, "cares for the well-being of the natives. I have seen men tied to the ground and flogged within an inch of their lives. I have seen the men who do such things, when their arm grows tired, hand the whip to some Zanzibari to finish the job. These same men go back home, kiss their wives, and tell of the frightening sorcerer and the horror of cannibals. This place will send you to hell or bring you to God." Casement sits calmly. He crosses his legs. He smiles at Slade.

"So it has brought you to God?"

Casement nods carefully. "I don't claim to be a favorite of our Lord," since God has a peculiar means of trying him, "but in the end he is a solace to me and I do think our native friends might benefit from some hope that there is a better place to which we all are headed. And just the fact that you seem to think the Bolongos and Bakongos and Manyema—and the rest—are eligible for salvation makes me like you."

"And my outfit?"

Casement gives a gentle nod.

"I'd have to pay you what we pay our missionaries," says Slade, "and they only accept the wage because it's some sort of performance of great sacrifice."

"We're poor, therefore God loves us?"

"That would not be inaccurate."

"Well, I'll be poor because it's all you're willing to pay me."

"It's all I have," says Slade.

And just like that, Casement is working for the mission.

Now he's bringing natives to God. In a way, so is King Leopold.

Just last month he was surveying for the railroad. Imagine. A railroad from Banana on the coast up along the river to Stanley Pool, where the Congo becomes navigable. How many men will die in the construction of this railroad? To this point, there still has been no path created that will accommodate a donkey, so how will they create this? Casement wishes they would stick to porters because the need for porters might inspire the Belgians and the English and the French to do something about the Arab slavers. The Europeans prefer not to use slaves, but instead of abandoning all these villagers to the brutality of the Arabs under pretense of righteousness, why not protect their freedom and give them work? Casement has been successful with porters. He has. These people execute their tasks and if one is just about the payment and the distribution of the goods, relations with the natives remain friendly. Why build a railroad? And how will they do it without enslaving villagers, scaring them senseless, whipping them? And now the practice of kidnapping wives and children has been introduced. If you want your wives and children back, you will have to work for us—that's the Belgians, right there. How is that not slavery? And this is King Leopold's work, who managed to have all the European powers hand the Congo to him, tied in a bow, because he had formed the Aborigines Protection Society.

So the missionaries don't always make sense to him. Casement's not sure why the sight of a black man wearing a suit—the buttons, the wool, the high-collared white shirt—in the searing heat brings such joy to the hearts of people like Slade. If it were up to Casement, he'd be happy to wander around without a shirt in his bare feet. The missionaries want to create God's kingdom on earth and seem to have decided that God's kingdom is in Suffolk—or some such place—and so the Congo will be Suffolked, one skirt-wearing woman at a time.

Casement looks over the inventory for a shipment for upriver. As usual, there are more loads than porters, although Casement has put together a good group of mostly Bakongo.

"We're going to have to winnow it down to forty loads," says Casement.

Slade goes about the baskets with great energy and little purpose. He does not know where to start. John Michael, the best of the mission boys, who speaks impressive English and has learned to read, looks on with a studied, affected seriousness.

"First," says Casement, "I'm not sure about the five baskets of bibles."

"But those have been sent by a congregation in Edinburgh that is one of our best donors."

"No one in that region speaks English. And even if they did, no one can read."

"But—"

"Next time," says Casement.

"What will I tell Reverend McIntyre?"

Casement looks sympathetically at Slade. He picks a bible out of a basket and tosses it onto a load of tinned biscuits. "You'll tell him thanks very much and we've sent your gift on. All the medicine needs to go, and all the seed and tubers, and the farming tools. There are four loads of assorted machinery and parts and those, of course, are necessary. When all's said and done, we have four loads to play with." Casement grabs at some rolled fabric and unfurls an odd garment, shapeless, white, and only identifiable by the presence of a neck-hole and arms. "And what is this for?"

"It's to dress the natives."

"The men or the women?"

"Both."

"And where did it come from?"

"A lady's group sent us two sewing machines and now we have some women making the garments," says Slade.

"My sister is making these dresses," says John Michael. He wants to laugh.

"Oh," says Casement, "the tyranny of generosity." He slips the dress over his head and pulls it on. The dress is so large and shapeless that it easily fits over his clothes.

"What do you think?" he asks John Michael.

"I think it is better for a woman," John Michael says.

"And you, what do you think?" Casement asks Slade.

"What are my choices?"

"Bibles or dresses," says Casement.

"It all depends."

"On what?"

"The will of God."

"Better consult quickly," says Casement. "We've got half an hour before we need to leave, otherwise we won't get far before the heat sets in."

Casement sets out with Patrick, formerly known as Makola, for Stanley Pool. It is not a difficult march, although the paths are now more crowded. One must step aside for caravans heading in the opposite direction, loaded with ivory. And these porters are a deeply miserable lot, malnourished and overloaded, living with the chicotte snapping at their heels. These men are strung along with iron collars and heave clanking chains. They are slaves hunted and captured by Arabs, leased to the Belgians. When Casement's little column passes them, he can feel the fear rise among his people. He'll chat to them, to try to keep them calm. In the past, he would have said, "Your load is not so heavy and you are not chained." Now he says, "Your load is still heavy and I'm sure you'd rather be at home." He's not sure what created this change in him. Patrick has planned a route different from the one that Casement used the last time, because Arabs have burned one of the villages to the ground and the land is now occupied by a hostile group of Bolongo. Or that's what Patrick thinks is happening. Regardless, what had once been a good place to purchase food is no longer, so they must hug the coast more closely, even though the terrain is rockier and more uneven.

"Do you understand?" Patrick had asked. He finds it hard to believe that Casement really speaks his language beyond barking orders or delivering salutations or bartering.

"Of course," Casement had said. "And I don't need to call you Patrick."

"I don't need to call you Mayala Swami," Patrick had responded.

But Casement is still calling Patrick Patrick.

Patrick is still calling Mayala Swami Mayala Swami.

Patrick abandoned his trousers at the limits of the mission and is now in his usual wrap, exposed to the elements, but looking less vulnerable as a result. He lopes along, circles back. He helps a porter redistribute the contents of a basket, which have shifted in the course of portage, making the load imbalanced. The porter explains animatedly about how worried he was that the basket would fall when they were passing close by the river. The porter says, "It would have been bad. Very bad." And Casement peeks into the basket that reveals the rolled-up dresses. How bad would it have been? He imagines crocodiles coming across the robes, their toothy snouts nudging the fabric into lazy circles.

"Are you well?" asks Patrick.

"Just a bit light-headed," says Casement.

Casement sits on a log and Patrick sits next to him. He can feel Patrick studying the side of his face and hears him calling to one of the others to fetch some water. The water arrives and Casement drinks. He focuses on his shoes, then on Patrick's feet. He sees a series of scars rising around Patrick's calf like bracelets, not elegant enough to be ornamental scarring, yet even in their progress. There must be close to ten of these encircling scars.

"What happened to your leg?" asks Casement. He's dizzy and Patrick steadies Casement by leaning him against his side.

"I had too much malafu and fell asleep in the path." Patrick could be telling a funny story, but his expression is droll as always. "I awoke to my friends shouting and shouting all around me. There was a snake that had started to eat my leg. He was moving as snakes eat like this," Patrick shows Casement a two-inch increment with his thumb and forefinger, "and like this," he shows him the same distance a little farther up in the air. "So my friends killed the snake."

"And then what happened?"

"I became a Christian. It is not good to drink too much."

This is a good story and once Patrick starts preaching will make sense to other villagers. "Did the snake really think it was going to be able to eat you?"

"I did not ask it." Patrick places his long hand along the side of Casement's face, feeling for fever.

"Is that why your name is Patrick?" As *Patrick* is unusual for the Baptists.

"My name?"

"Because of the snake. Saint Patrick cast out all the snakes from Ireland."

Patrick looks indulgently at this nonsense. "Are you better now?"

Casement nods. He must have just been dehydrated.

Once at Stanley Pool, Casement arranges for the baskets to be put on board the *Peace*, and moved to the mission upriver. He collapses, exhausted. His tent is an island in a river of ivory—traders moving back and forth—Flemish curses, English barking, a shuffle and shuffle of barefoot workers, a clank of chains, and the screech of the steam whistle announcing that a new shipment from farther up the Congo has arrived. He lies on his side with his arms in front and his legs stretched forward, as if he is a dog. This is the most comfortable position. As a child, he had found that lying like this helped him drop off. He remembers his mother singing him to sleep and decides the memory to be false—a fantasy of maternal attention. He has had such fantasies since his mother's death when he was nine. This mother baptized him Catholic, sneaked him off to some roadside church and willing padre. What would this mother think of his masquerading as a Baptist?

Then Patrick is gently rousing him.

"Is it late?"

"No. There is a man who is taking our people to carry his ivory."

Casement gets up, finding consciousness. He is quickly in a vicious argument in emphatic French with a lean, bearded Belgian whose faraway stare makes him seem mad. This man has a chicotte casually coiled in his hand. Casement buys some time. He tells Patrick in Bakongo that they have to leave immediately, for him to collect the men. They escape while the Belgian is arranging his ivory into loads, having—in his mind—already appropriated the mission's porters.

* * *

At the mission, Casement grows restless. There is not much for him to do. Right now he has been tasked with building a structure that will function as both school and church. Although he knows that permanent buildings in this climate should be of stone, such a building is beyond his knowledge and the available materials. So it will be of palm and thatch, and Patrick is happy to show him how.

"How much in the way of palm and thatch do you think this will take? And how many men to do the work?" Casement and Patrick stand side by side looking at the chosen plot of land as Patrick makes the calculations in his head.

And then he sees him, as he's just stepped out from the wall of jungle— he sees Ward. There's a tall, slim native beside him, and also Glave's boy. Casement cannot move and he wants time to also stop. He wants to look at Ward standing there, his haggard frame, his relief at seeing Casement. He might feel happy but instead is overwhelmed with an almost crippling ache that knocks the breath from him, that feels—although it is so tied to this present instant—like an awful nostalgia.

Casement watches Ward from across the table, his gaze open, as the long absence excuses this. Ward is thin and he's pacing himself with his food, taking polite portions of the chicken, which he eats slowly. His eating still seems actions of intermittent devouring rather than a civilized enjoyment of food. If it were up to him, Ward would just set the bowl of chicken at his place and shovel the sauce into his mouth, tear the meat from the bones, wash it down with this one civilized glass of Madeira: stuff Slade won't touch, but that he has offered to the guest.

"Casement, how have you been?" asks Ward.

"Well enough," says Casement. "And you?" This is said with humor.

Rumors must have started spreading. Ward considers. "I just missed you, you know, in Equatoria. I stayed up all night chatting with Glave. He said you'd gone elephant hunting. I was jealous."

"What were you doing in Equatoria?" asks Casement.

"On my way to Boma. Glave's headed to America. That's why I have Mabruki." Ward turns to Slade. "He's learning English."

"He seems like a nice boy," says Slade, understanding that Mabruki is now his boy.

"But what have you been up to? You've been sighted all the way from Stanley Falls to Leo, but in such a short amount of time, I thought there had to be a mistake."

"No mistake," says Ward. "It's a long story. I haven't been in Yambuya since March."

"Well, it'll be a long evening then," says Slade. "And I'll break my rule and get you another glass of wine."

Where to begin? Seeing Casement across the table makes it seem as if Yambuya never happened, or as if it happened to someone else. Jameson had been sent to Tippo Tib's winter residence at Kassongo to plead for more porters. Barttelot had gone off to Stanley Falls to look for news of Stanley. It was just Ward, Troup, and Bonny in the camp and there was nothing to do but supervise burials, send out work details, and retreat to one's tent where Ward's girl waited with her passionless eyes for him to make some demand of her. And then Barttelot returned madder than ever, with a new instruction that Ward return to the coast in order to send a cable to Mackinnon in London. Barttelot was of the opinion that Stanley was dead, swallowed by the middle of Africa, and he was damned if he was going to spend the rest of his life waiting for him.

Ward looked over Barttelot's orders. Ward would proceed to Bangala with a cohort of Zanzibari and Sudanese and proceed in canoes from Bangala. No white man had made it down the Congo in anything smaller than a steamboat that was armed with a frightening steam whistle and, should that not suffice, a Martini rifle. There was a gauntlet of hostile tribes all along the banks from Bangala to Stanley Pool. Traveling at night would increase the odds of their survival to about fifty percent.

Ward spent that last night in Bangala on the deck of the *Stanley*, chatting with Werner, the engineer, who was the only Englishman left in these parts. So many had died in the last couple of years. Ward had them listed in his diary. *First, Captain Bore committed suicide at Verona. Second, Benny shot himself; third, a Belgian officer died on his way up; fourth, Webster, who went home very ill; fifth, Deane who underwent awful perils; sixth, Dubois, who was drowned; seventh, Van der Welde, who died the other day at Leopoldville, en route to the Falls; eighth, his companion, Stillmann, who got sick and had to clear off home to save his life; and ninth, Amelot who died on his way to Zanzibar.* This sounds like a nursery rhyme, something that little girls rattle off while they're jumping rope or playing patty-cake.

"But you're still here," says Casement. "You survived."

"Barely," says Ward. "I hit all the missions on the way down to Boma and finally got on a steamer to Banana. From there, I made it to Loanda." At which point, Ward was not in good shape. His foot was inflamed, and his leg was covered in ulcers that had started as mosquito bites, but that Ward had gouged at and made into something much worse. He engaged Msa, who was about sixteen years old and very capable, who nursed him through.

A cable finally came from London and Ward started back upriver. Five weeks later, he was in Leopoldville. There were letters waiting for him—moldy missives in his mother's girlish hand with news from the year before. Then he found passage on a small paddle steamer and was heading as hastily as the conveyance allowed when he met up with the *Stanley*, chugging along in the opposite direction.

As was practice, the two boats had pulled up together in order to exchange news and letters. Ward was shocked to learn that Troup was on board, being invalided home. He was very weak, although he brightened when he saw Ward. Troup had not saluted, nor spoken of Egypt, as had once been his habit. Barttelot, according to Troup, had gotten into an argument with Tippo Tib that almost resulted in a small-scale war—one that would have wiped out all the officers at Yambuya. And now there was an awkward truce between Tib and Barttelot, but nothing was ever going to be accomplished by the two men. Jameson had been sent to Kassongo to work out minor things, to create some semblance of normalcy.

Troup was quite yellow and Ward wondered if he would ever make it home.

And of course Troup had a new set of orders from Barttelot.

Ward was to proceed to Bangala and thereafter wait.

And wait. And wait.

There would be no glory for Ward, no triumphant rescue for him, no picture in the paper, nothing. Stanley was skirting a major catastrophe. All sources seemed to indicate that not only did Emin Pasha not want to be rescued but that the whole thing had been an opportunistic ploy to subdue the Pasha's enemies—a cry for help to enable him to stay in Africa, not sweep him back to the bosom of mother Europe. Stanley was looking for scapegoats and Ward was once again watching boxes and stacks and things and garbage, the detritus of the Dark Continent, performing the tasks that gentlemen paid their way out of. There was no news from Yambuya, nothing, and then finally, a letter from Jameson.

Barttelot was dead. Jameson wrote, somewhat cryptically, that Barttelot had been shot, but there was no explanation. Jameson was now in charge.

Several weeks passed. Ward realized that he was sleeping much more than he needed to and was indeed laying himself out for a nap when a small boy rushed in to his cabin and, speaking in rapid-fire Swahili, announced that a white man had just come down from the Falls in a canoe.

It was Jameson.

Jameson was lying in the floor of the canoe, insensible, surrounded by his men—six Zanzibaris, who had been paddling day and night. They carried Jameson to Van Kerkhoven's house, since it was the best accommodation in Bangala and Van Kerkhoven—the local chief officer—was used to it being appropriated for such purposes. Some medicine was tracked down and administered, but Jameson was unresponsive. He was delirious, deep in the grip of hematuric fever. The next evening, Jameson was gone, having died in Ward's arms.

"He did recognize me," Ward says. "He kept saying he was getting better."

"So Jameson and Barttelot are both dead," says Slade, a candle splashing somber shadow on his face.

"Yes. And I learned of how Barttelot died in Jameson's diary. One of the natives, Sanga, shot him after Barttelot beat his wife for drumming at dawn. She'd woken Barttelot up. Sanga was worried that Barttelot was going to kill his wife. There was some sort of a trial for this man in Kassongo, but I'm sure he too is dead by now. I had to return to the coast to send cables to the families of Jameson and Barttelot." Which had been another journey of a thousand miles. "Miserable work."

"What are you up to now?" asks Casement.

"I'm going to Bangala, organizing the last of Yambuya—which should have arrived there by now. I think there are some crates that belonged to Jameson, and Barttelot—and upwards of ten boxes of Stanley's stuff that Barttelot shipped downriver, although I doubt that's what Stanley wanted. I sent a letter to him weeks ago and haven't heard a thing. I guess I'll bring it to the coast, although there's photographic equipment in there that Stanley probably needs."

"And then what will you do?" asks Casement.

"I've been engaged by Mackinnon to sell off whatever is left of our sorry expedition."

"To whom?" asks Slade.

"Probably the Belgians. If there's anything in there that you can use, I'll put it aside, if you like."

"Please do," says Slade.

"And after that?" asks Casement.

"Well, personal effects are to be transported back home. Mackinnon has me doing that, but in the last letter," Ward produces a piece of paper and hands it over to Casement, "I've been instructed to engage you to help."

Casement reads the note, the wavering writing flickering on the page, *Sell remainder goods to State. See Governor about this. Bring Bonny, all men Expedition, all Barttelot's and Jameson's effects and collections Banana; ship*

them England, care Dawes & Co. If help wanted engage and take back Case-
ment. Wire if these instructions understood.

Casement had not intended to go home, but he had not intended to be a
missionary either, and this haphazard landing of different professions and
roles was turning into something of a proclivity. And now he was a nurse.
As he and Ward waited in Banana for the next ship back to London, Ward
fell apart. First, the fever, which Casement is accustomed to dealing with,
and then the carbuncles, which in Casement's reckoning, Ward has never
suffered from before. Msa informed him otherwise. Ward was treated a
year earlier in Thome. Some sort of ointment had been effective, although
such a thing is not available in Banana. Good diet. Rest. Loose clothing,
and now for poor Ward, no clothing, as he has a carbuncle the size of a
saucer on his right buttock, something eased with cool water and a gentle
washcloth. Msa tends to Ward in this way, although Casement wouldn't
mind—anything to make Ward feel better—but that oozing, yellow crater
hardly puts him in his most attractive light. And makes Ward, who is already
down, profoundly depressed. Ward is like a child in a way. His being sad is
much harder to bear than the sorrow of other people.

"Good news, Ward," says Casement. "The *Afrikaans* is leaving for London in a few days."

"How do you know that?" asks Ward.

"Because she just docked and, after minor maintenance, is eager to get
the hell out of here."

"Is that a newspaper?" asks Ward.

"Yes it is."

"What's it say?"

"I haven't had a chance to read it yet."

Ward's eyes narrow. "You're lying. Why are you lying?"

"I'm not lying." But Casement is, and he wonders how Ward knows this.
Or maybe Ward is just clever enough to predict that he is to be slandered by

Stanley and that Stanley is rushing to his work, rushing to clear his name, happily tossing Ward onto the bonfire. "It's not that bad, Ward."

"Does he mention me by name?"

Casement nods and rifles through the paper. "He has things to say about all the officers of the Rear Guard."

"And what of me?"

Casement shakes out the paper, folds it open, and finds the place. "'Mister Ward, at an officer's meeting, suggested my instructions should be canceled et cetera, and consequently my kit and baggage were sent down the Congo.'"

"I was at Stanley Pool when Barttelot decided to ship Stanley's traps," says Ward, sitting up. "I was the only officer not present, a thousand miles away." Ward wraps the sheet around him and sinks his face into his hands. He looks like a classical tragic figure, toga-ed, wronged.

"Write a response," says Casement.

"Of course I'll write a response. But you know what this means."

And Casement does know. This is the first of many slanders to come as Stanley struggles to clear his name.

Ward adjusts his position and raises his golden head. "What did you hear of the Rear Guard?"

"Not much."

"I know you're not one to traffic in rumors, but Casement, I need to know. I need to know what people have been saying."

"Who's to say you're implicated?"

"You can't protect me, so you might as well help me."

Casement pulls the chair to the side of the bed and sits opposite. "One of the officers, apparently, purchased a girl and had her slaughtered in order to make pictures of it. Surely, that's not true."

"What else?"

"The natives were not well cared for. The diet was poor and disciplinary action was brutal in the extreme. The overall impression of the leadership of the Rear Guard," Casement is focusing on Barttelot's role, "was that of madness."

"And that's it?"

"All the officers were rumored to have harems. One of the officers supposedly purchased a woman with a pair of boots." Not that remarkable a detail for one who has been living in the Congo, but achieves a level of scandal when read in the parlors, drawing rooms, and dressing rooms of London.

"It's over," says Ward.

Casement keeps his expression gentle, sympathetic, as he expands his knowledge to include Ward as the officer in question. "What's over?"

"My future."

And what was in Ward's future? Probably he had some idea of making his fortune in Africa, mellowing in age, finding a nice wife, and having pretty children.

Ward contemplates the calm that he feels now that he's lost. It's that moment when all the cards are pushed to the center of the table and dealt again, the moment when unlimited possibility exists.

"You'll need to write your own account," says Casement.

"You know I can't."

"You can't write directly about the Emin Pasha Relief, that's what Stanley had you sign, but you can write. You can write a book about the five years you've spent in Africa. You can include your drawings."

"*Five Years With the Congo Cannibals.*" That's what Jameson had called it.

"If you like. Clear your name by letting people know who you are."

"Won't help if Stanley's lecturing all over England and America."

"You can lecture. I'm sure someone will sign you up."

"Stanley is famous."

"Anyone," says Casement, "can be famous."

V

The Saale

October 1889

Sarita sights across the rail: a straight view of uninterrupted North Atlantic, the same one she's been staring at for the last four days, since the boat left Plymouth. Sarita had been looking forward to the journey as she had much to think over, but now she's thought and rethought. She's looking forward to New York and its distractions. She knows nothing of men.

When Sarita was still a schoolgirl in Argentina, a trip was arranged to visit the countryside. One of the wealthier girls owned a hacienda, and she and the others were to spend the weekend picnicking, hiking, swimming, and eating good wholesome food. The girls were crammed into the back of the carriage and Madame Villa Juan forced to sit beside the driver, allowing the girls to descend into their tame gossip and gossamer fantasies. Madame was wearing an enormous hat that she kept in place with her left hand, while with her right she clung to the rail of the bench—small, desperate acts of control. The carriage dipped and swayed along the rutted road and the girls chatted and sang, waved off flies, and tolerated the heat and profound humidity that resulted from three days of heavy rain. At a bend in the road, the carriage drew close to several vaqueros at work with cows. Here, the road narrowed, and as the driver attempted to steer the carriage to the verge, clear of the deep mud, the wheels began to slip and the carriage became stuck.

At this moment Sarita noticed that one cow—in truth a bull—was mounted on top of the other, wiggling, and the activity in question was the breeding of the two animals. This realization was made by all the girls concurrently and met in turn with confusion, horror, glee, and meditative calm. Sarita, who had the unfortunate luck to be seated closest to the spectacle, now saw that the young vaquero who held the rope about the bull's neck was smiling at her, holding her pale eyes directly in his dark gaze, and although she knew she ought to do otherwise, she could not look away. This is how it was—the vaqueros at their husbandry, the bull at his—until Sarita woke to Madame Villa Juan, ankle deep in mud, yelling at the girls to please avert their eyes.

For weeks after, every time her mind becalmed or she was falling off to sleep, Sarita would recall that bull—its shifting as it met its mark—and the cow, that might have been distressed but wasn't. And the vaquero's smile that had spanned mere seconds in real time but was spinning into hours in its recollection.

She cannot marry Charles Brock-Innes.

Her mother is already on her case. If Sarita didn't like Charles Brock-Innes, then what was he doing at dinner? He has been a regular at Carleton Terrace and Sarita's mother, as she struggles to keep on top of what is socially acceptable, has made these invitations, expanded menus, ordered outfits, and vacated drawing rooms in order to let the match take. And Sarita has been happily occupying benches, taking elbows, sitting knee to knee with Mr. Brock-Innes, alert, complicit, and hopeful as the whole family struggles to clean up the American (and even South American!) money with this marriage. Her father is relying on her to steer them into the English peerage. Sarita understands what's needed but has no help. Her mother, this Sallie-from-New-Jersey, still wears the trauma of poverty, recalls too clearly her husband's first dollars made peddling boxes of unguents and pills in Buenos Aires, remembers burying a child in New Orleans in a plain pine box.

Sarita has no illusions about a life of poverty. She remembers going to the markets in Buenos Aires with her mother to bargain for chickens and vegetables and bread. Mother could do anything in those years, but her Spanish was rough, and Sarita—despite the flat, gray eyes and pale skin—made a convincing Argentinian once given a chance to speak. She wasn't bargaining for fun or pride or whatever makes the wealthy squeeze money from working people, she was bargaining because she was poor. Whatever cash could be had was being held by Father, who seemed to think if his family could just put off buying that new pair of boots, moving to better rooms, hiring a woman to help with the washing—eating—that he could take those simple coins and turn them into something real. Sarita remembers being cold. She remembers being unbearably hot. She remembers being hungry and the particular humiliation of being white—in a country where that meant wealth—and having no money. If this life of Carleton Terrace and Fifth Avenue is a gilded cage, try the prison of poverty. Sarita's mother retreats behind curtains, into shadows, up the stairs, with her false headaches and real pills, and Sarita would like to say that it is done. Over. Successful.

That it is marriage.

She liked Charles Brock-Innes. He made her laugh. Brock-Innes did impersonations, including one of her father—his probing eyes, his habit of stretching his fingers like a cat extending claws, the way he sank into a chair, silently observing until those attempting to speak to him dissolved into nervous chatter. But now everything Brock-Innes said is in a new light. She remembers his words, "Sarita, a woman should pursue her own goals, even in marriage." He must have thought her desperate, but it didn't seem that way.

The grinding of the ship's engine draws her closer to New York, farther from London (although they sailed from Plymouth) as if she is a dog on a leash, allowed to wander to a better location, only to be pulled back at another's will. Sarita shuts her eyes against the sun and the exchange plays through her head. There's the linen closet. There's Brock-Innes, exiting, and rushing down the hall. There's Valentine, her father's valet, close behind, tucking in his shirt. And there's Sarita, standing farther up the hallway, with Valentine processing her presence, having lost none of his composure. His usual reserved look read as challenging. And she'd said, utterly ridiculous, "Who is dressing Mister Sanford?"

Valentine had mumbled something about her father needing to compose a telegram before dinner and therefore having been done with his wardrobe early. And after that, she had again taken Brock-Innes's elbow into the dining room, had managed through the salmon and jellies and roasts and asparagus and puddings and cheeses, the different wines, the winking cutlery spreading out across the cloth like surgical tools. She had carved at all of it: fish, pheasant, fool. Never wittier, she had found humor in everything and there was Brock-Innes laughing at all her jokes. He enjoyed her company. He liked her spark. He wanted her to be the mother of his children.

The bull wiggles.

This is not the time to stir things up. She doesn't know what deals her father has going down with Barings Bank, but she knows it's risky. Father is on edge and his usually prickly demeanor has shifted to a disturbing calm—the calm indicative of a looming eruption. But there's no point in saying what happened. She has no interest in exposing Brock-Innes. She wonders if he thought she too had strange inclinations. She could be more fragile—which men seem to like—but she's always thought that her handsomeness and warm intelligence made up for that.

No.

She's not going to blame herself. She'll leave that to the others.

And then, a shadow.

"Señorita," says Paz. Paz is Sarita's maid.

"¿Qué necesitas?"

Paz holds the parasol, which she opens and extends in her direction.

Of course, Paz is right. At her age, twenty-nine, Sarita shouldn't be presenting her face to the sun. She also knows that pretty Paz enjoys making these reminders, easing waistlines, yanking the occasional gray hair from Sarita's head. The day is cold and the passengers are arranged about the deck, taking in the air, stirring about the exits, gliding as if on tracks. Sarita moves to the railing, her skirt trailing, and she trails a yet longer shadow. Her heels click as she steps, as she shudders to each new second, marking her progress.

Ward and Glave have another five days before they reach New York. Casement, visiting relatives in England, will join them in a few weeks. They share a small cabin, stacked one on top of the other in bunks, as if they're corpses. One crate of Ward's is jammed behind the door, making it difficult to enter. There is a small porthole window that spills light into the room, something that Ward argued against, but Glave prevailed—even offering to pay for it—and thank God, because without it, there would be no air. To be shared with the other passengers, there is a privy down the hall. Ward has heard the passengers say, "Better than nothing," but Ward, who has made do with nothing for many years, knows the statement to be false.

This is Second Class.

At dinnertime, Ward and Glave sit on long benches eating rich food ladled out of bottomless, frothing pots. There is salt and fat and gravy. There is pudding. There is silverware. There is as much wine as one can drink, included in the five-guinea fare, and Ward grows fatter, which is good, considering the countenance he presented in London—more of a specter. Major Pond has signed him on for a nationwide tour across the United States in anticipation of his upcoming book, *Five Years With the Congo Cannibals*. And Ward has packed up the masks, and spears, and gourds, the feathered rattles, the shields—this miniature Congo—and crated them carefully. There are four crates in all. One is inconveniencing Glave in the cabin. The other three are in first-class storage as Ward has bribed the First Purser to stow them there. Glave has joked that for Ward to present a genuine experience of the Congo, he ought to have gathered up a couple of whip-cracking Belgians, some Arab slavers, mosquitoes, fever, and an infinite coil of red tape. Glave is headed to the Yukon to do some exploring, which always sounds like it's something concrete and never is, more a condition of motion propelled by a particular state of mind.

Ward had started writing his book while still on the *Transvaal*, making the journey from Africa to Europe. Casement advised him to do this. The book had to be in good shape, in the hands of a publisher, off the presses, and ready to be shelved at the bookstores no later than six months after the publication of Stanley's account, the six months stipulated by Stanley in the contract.

"This will offset the damage," Casement said. "Just do a good job of it."

So Ward, sequestered in his cabin, had begun to generate page after page, while Casement fiddled with his lines. Casement was enjoying the journey, eager to get to Liverpool and see his fun-loving cousin Gertrude, his clever sister Nina. Casement had people to miss. He missed his friends in England, and people—as judged from the volume of letters Casement received—missed him. Ward's immediate family now lived in California. He would arrive back in London an Englishman with no one to welcome him, no one to care. Maudlin. Pathetic. And anyone who might have been intrigued by this young, golden adventurer would now know him as the man who had either purchased a girl to watch her be eaten or acquired a sex slave with a pair of top boots. Scandalous. Untouchable.

Distant Africa was looking better all the time.

In order to manage the last of the Emin Pasha Relief Expedition shipment, Ward had enlisted the Zanzibaris from Bangala—twelve of them—and they had strolled about the *Transvaal* decks in their flowing white robes, presenting ever-more-startling countenances as the *Transvaal* drew closer to Europe. Casement spent much time with them, working on his Swahili. And Ward, who was not feeling particularly sociable, drew deeper into his writing, trying to bring the life of the Congo—the heat, the women, the laughter, the terror—alive on the page. He thought of where his drawings ought to be placed and as he sorted through the sheaves of paper, his mind often wandered back to Jameson and how he would be remembered. What had happened to his drawings? Were those of the slaughtered girl in these crates?

Ward will have to meet with Jameson's family. He doesn't like this role, but he knows he's good at it—sympathetic and patient. He's done it before. After Hatton's son Frank was killed hunting elephant in Borneo, Ward had brought the body back to England. Hatton was grateful for the effort, of course, but Ward had been ready for a change. Hatton, missing the son, seeing the young man who had returned in his place, had been moved to help Ward. It was Hatton's letter of introduction to Stanley that secured for Ward his first employment in the Congo.

Now, he has another letter of introduction written by Hatton, this time for the American businessman Charles Sanford, who is running all sorts of deals in South America for Barings Bank.

"My boy," said Hatton, "you need two things to escape this Emin Pasha scandal. You need distance and you need money."

So, for a little distance and a little money, the United States and this tour of the lyceums with Major Pond will do. But for big distance there's South America, and for big money there is, apparently, Argentina. Ward wonders about the mortality rate as he turns this second letter of introduction over in his hands.

The wind rifles through his hair and his monstrous wing-coat, absurd, flaps about him, bringing an unwanted element of drama to everything he does. He feels like an old-time villain. The letter goes back into the pocket and he leans against the railing. Glave, head down, has somehow miraculously managed to light his pipe and he is drawing in quick pants, letting the cherry-smelling smoke fly into the salty air.

"Just give her the letter," Glave says.

"Well, it's not really for her, is it?"

"Then give it to Sanford."

"I don't think he's left his rooms since we got on board." Ward will try his luck with the daughter. At times like this, Ward misses Casement, who knows how to talk to women, earns "Mayala Swami" in drawing rooms and garden parties, makes everything seem so natural.

"Is she really so terrifying?" Glave is amused. "I could drop her with one shot right between the eyes."

"It would help if she didn't look so miserable."

"Is it misery?"

Sarita is wrapped in a blanket, as are all the women seated in the deck chairs. The chairs are arranged in a long row, angled for the warmth of the sun, but somehow the arrangement makes the ladies seem like vegetables— ripe for picking.

"Maybe she's just cold." Glave considers. "She's probably bored."

Although, just then, a look of woe rises in her features, as if some horror has been remembered. Ward brings out the letter. "All right," he says. "I'm going in."

Sarita has been eyeing the two young men. At times, it seems that they are looking at her but looking away. And there is something in their sunburned faces and restlessness that holds her attention. Why would they be looking at her? One is a bit older with a broad forehead, clean-shaven, and smoking a pipe. His friend is blond with mustaches, wearing a too-big coat. She wonders if these men have been playing the game where you pick a person and try to figure out their story. That's what women do because women have nothing better to occupy them. Maybe the men are Australians, which would explain the restlessness. Or maybe they've been working in South America, only they're going the wrong way.

Charles Brock-Innes exiting the linen closet. The scene plays through her mind—a theatrical retread.

Then the blond man is standing right in her line of vision. He's holding a letter.

"Miss Sanford," he says.

"Yes." He's blocking the sun, and the beams disperse around his head as if he is an icon or an Olympian.

"I have a letter of introduction to your father." He extends the letter, which she takes. She looks at it.

"Who shall I say it's from?"

"Herbert Ward." He extends his hand hastily, and she shakes it.

"Wonderful. I'll give it to him."

Ward nods. He thinks maybe he should just walk away, but that seems rude. Although hovering over Miss Sanford doesn't feel much better.

"Where are you from, Mister Ward?"

"Ah, the Congo."

"You don't seem sure."

"I'm also from London. And some other places." Ward looks hastily over his shoulder at Glave, who has been watching the exchange unfold as if he is at the theatre.

Glave rouses himself.

"And what is it you do, Mister Ward?"

Which throws Ward into more confusion, confusion that he tries to sort through as Glave introduces himself, exchanges—in his polite yet unadorned way—the details of their journey thus far, what they intend to do in America, what manner of business kept them in Congo.

"So you've written a book?" says Miss Sanford.

"I have a first draft. And a contract for publication."

"What is your book called?"

"*Five Years With the Congo Cannibals*. It's not out yet, won't be for a few months."

"You're a writer?"

"I feel more confident with my drawing."

"Ward is a great artist," says Glave. "Very talented."

"Do you have your drawings with you, Mister Ward?"

"I do."

"Would you be willing to share them?"

"I wouldn't want to take up your time."

"Please, take up my time," Sarita says, aware that the boldness of that statement is not correct, aware that she is ceasing to care. "We have five days before we land in New York and I have studied the line of horizon for long enough. I'm sick of my own thoughts." She waves her hand dramatically and follows this with a smile that's clearest in her eyes. "Show me something new."

Just like that, Ward had been reinvented: He had shown something new. He tries to think if he'd ever mentioned to Glave just how important his art was to him, how his artistic inclinations had fed the animosity between his father and himself. Had he ever told Glave the real reason he left for New Zealand at the age of fifteen? The truth of it—when he thinks back to that time—is that his father's complete dismissal of his admittedly ridiculous plan had made a reality of a fantasy, had packed his bags for him, had helped to scrape together the money and give a little steel to Ward's young backbone until—as Ward rounded the Cape of Good Hope—he realized that posturing had morphed into execution. If it were all a joke, the punch line had been delivered without Ward's noticing. He had both won and lost, now an adventurer who had to have an adventure whether or not he still felt so inclined. Until now, he hears his father's laughter rattling around his brain, that laughter that stirs itself whenever he is unsure, like the ghost-scent of perfume in a disturbed scarf.

He is unsure now. His old friend, Alfred Harmsworth, had laid it out for him over lunch in London. Ward needed a long-range plan. Ward wasn't getting any younger. Ward needed the real money that real men need as opposed to the coins and cups of soup that satisfied the appetites of youth. And Harmsworth pointed out that, although Ward was an adventurer, his time cavorting with monkeys and digging for Australian gold had left him naïve rather than worldly. Ward knew nothing of the manners and means of civilized society.

In those months between returning from Borneo and leaving for the Congo, Ward and Harmsworth had shared a ramshackle house in West Hampstead. Then, ambition had formed the bulk of their sustenance. Harmsworth had been writing for pennies but with complete conviction that all the scribbling would amount to something. Now he was editing, making deals, making real money. And Ward was starting over.

Harmsworth had flipped through Ward's manuscript as it stood, given him a couple of pointers, bought him a steak at a good London establishment, shaken his hand warmly, and predicted—with a fierce twinkle in his eyes—that they would be in business together soon. That would be good but was hardly something to rely on. And what exactly would Ward do?

Ward sits on the lower bunk, his head at an uncomfortable angle. The porthole is barely cracked because of the cold and the cabin smells of mildew and sweat, of damp wool, and, luckily, of pine as well, a result of the crate. Glave is sitting up on top of the crate, holding his pipe but not lighting it, as if that final odor in the room might cause some manner of explosion. Ward has his drawings spread across the thin wool blanket—all these pictures that seemed works of great accomplishment now appear to be the result of prolonged, committed dabbling. Ward hears Jameson's voice echo in his head, *Drawing is a gentleman's pursuit*. It's just pictures, he tells himself.

"You can't show her that," says Glave.

"Why not?"

"He's completely naked. And she's completely naked. It's not exactly polite. But this one's good, just a head with some nice ornamental scarring. And here's an Arab."

"Everyone's seen Arabs. The Congo natives are what's interesting and all these illustrations are going into the book anyway."

"All right then, Ward," says Glave. "Your call. Go sit with your Miss Sanford and show her pictures of naked Africans."

"I will," says Ward. "And she's not 'my Miss Sanford.'"

He tells himself, Miss Sanford needs distraction and he needs distraction and that's it. "My Miss Sanford." With her American money, her power, her Barings Bank, England in her pocket, the quickness in her eye.

He has not a chance with her and is not looking for a wife.

A marriage for men like him happens late in one's thirties, when one's health cannot handle the ravages of harsh climates and the adventure has been burned to the butt so that a cheerful face, a pleasant household, and maybe a couple of children to teach to shoot and to send off to school are actually welcomed. But family is barbed for him. He is more traumatized by his childhood than by anything that Borneo or New Zealand or the Congo could throw his way.

No. She is not his Miss Sanford. He's safe, fine with that. Still, he trims his mustaches, moves that stray hair into the rich bank of blond above his right brow, knocks his shoulders back: he's not tall but cuts a good figure.

Glave, chewing on his unlit pipe, smiles at him.

"What?" says Ward.

"Nothing at all," says Glave.

Miss Sanford is standing at the railing looking out at the waves. He feels odd approaching her with his satchel, as if this is a scene from another's life, purloined from a novel. There, she turns and smiles. There, the light spills from her eyes. There, she approaches. Ward clears his throat. He has no time for this, no interest in the sheltered girl trussed into her dress that makes a vase of her torso, the poof of her hair no doubt harboring a battery of pins, that armful of gathered silk suspended at her rear, her legs cocooned in silk, her arms constricted by the stiff mutton sleeves of her dress. She has sharp eyebrows and her pale gray eyes scan over him, searching for something, weaving like the head of a cobra.

"Good morning, Mister Ward," she says. "Are those your drawings?"

"Good morning," he says. He looks to the satchel and nods.

"It's so nice to be out on deck," she says, "but not that conducive to looking at pictures. I'd be worried one would blow away."

"We could duck into the saloon," says Ward.

There's a moment of silence.

"Well," she says, recovering, "I could definitely use some tea. Would you mind coming to our rooms? I'm sure my mother would appreciate seeing your work."

"Of course," says Ward. He's out of his mind. Miss Sanford can't go to the saloon, not with him, not with anyone. He feels the heat rising in his face. What should he say? "I'm sorry. I shouldn't have suggested the saloon. It's just that I'm out of touch. I've been in—"

"I know," she says, as she widens her eyes for comic effect, "Africa." She takes a step forward and Ward notices another woman, in a plain dress, stir from farther along the railing. This must be her maid.

Miss Sanford crosses the deck to the brass-handled, glass doors. Should he open the door for her? Should he wait for her to make a gesture, permitting entrance? The maid steps in front and swings the door out, permitting Ward to hold it open for Miss Sanford without presuming. The maid, chin raised, looks at Ward in the reflection of the door's glass pane: She's appraising him. Ward holds the door, allowing the women to enter first. His face is burning. Was he supposed to give the door back to the maid, to enter before her?

The room is a riot of red velvet and glinting crystal, thick rugs, damask ceilings—everything made into a soft cushion or a sharp, reflecting edge. Women are sunk into brocade conversationals, arranged across upholstered benches, and men inserted into the deep casings of wingchairs. A smattering of light conversation rises like the burble of pigeons. Newspapers shake open. Porcelain chimes. "The first-class lounge is a bit overdone," she says. "Maybe you already—"

"Glave and I are in second class." Ward announces this as if it's a matter of some pride.

"Of course," she says. "Roughing it."

Her manner is relaxed, yet oddly tragic. And cheerful.

"Here we are."

Another door and Ward steps into a world of painted landscapes and miniature Stubbs cattle, lacquered furniture, and weak light spattered about by a myriad of crystal. Crystal dangles from the lamps, loops through chandeliers, is arranged about reflecting salvers ready to be filled with bloodred wine or sparkling Champagne. But all the light is artificial, as if perfumed. Somewhere, is there music? No, but his imagination has supplied it. And there are several sinuous sculptures of naked Greeks—inflected with classicism, drained of blood, unsexed. But naked none-the-less. In one corner, a recent putica is draped in nothing but her modesty. Ward is pondering how this is accomplished when he realizes that his bald contemplation of the naked female has been noticed.

"Do you like sculpture, Mister Ward?"

"It is something I want to know more about," he says. It could be worse. She could be shy, short of words, exhausting, but as it is, he feels that he is being made fun of. She knows she's playing with the better hand and, although this might bother Ward, it is somehow a relief. "Do you always travel with this much art?" This is a good shot, he thinks, as if he's playing tennis.

"No, actually," she says. "My father just went on a bit of a binge in Paris—most of it is still in London. I think the shops of Les Invalides are now emptied of artwork."

"Were you with him?"

"For part of it, yes." Her face calms and then brightens. "Did you see the Paris Exposition?"

"No, I didn't."

"Well, that's a shame. It was quite the spectacle. They had African villages set up, so that you could see how the people live."

Ward doesn't know where to go with this. "I suppose I could have been a part of that, hung around the fire, asked if they had any malafu to spare."

Miss Sanford laughs, waves him off to dispel embarrassment. "That would have lent an element of realism, I suppose. What's malafu?"

"It's a drink. Very alcoholic. You wouldn't like it."

"How can you be sure?"

Is she charming him? Ward thinks she is. Why would she charm him? He pauses before a small oil of an Italian countryside and reads Corot in the corner. He hasn't spent much time in the museums since his Hampstead days when he would go to the Tate and the National and spend hours, slack-jawed, trying to determine how undeniable greatness existed on flat planes bordered in heavy gilt. "Are these your permanent rooms?"

"On this ship? No. I think we've had these rooms before, but we just book what we need and they stick us wherever. Normally, it isn't quite so crowded. For some reason, there wasn't sufficient room in the first-class storage—the secure area, anyway—and we had to keep a few crates in here. I had the maids unpack everything because I couldn't think of what else to do. And it stops them from getting grouchy. Long voyages, nothing to keep one occupied, you know . . . it's the not the way to run a household."

Ward thinks of his three crates that have displaced the Sanford collection and almost feels like telling her about it. He thinks of Msa, who was always busy without Ward needing to come up with activities for him.

"Mister Ward," she says. "Would you like tea? We do have coffee and I'm partial to it. It's part of my South American upbringing."

"I like coffee," says Ward. "Some coffee would be very nice."

Miss Sanford rings a crystal bell and her maid appears so suddenly that Ward thinks she was sneakily hiding behind the door. Or is it polite for a maid to keep out of sight?

"Paz," says Miss Sanford. "Unos cafecitos, por favor. Y donde esta mi madre?"

"Esta en la cama, señorita. Tiene un dolor de cabeza."

There's some other politeness that ensues, and then the maid retires.

"You speak Spanish," says Ward.

Miss Sanford nods. "It's not that difficult, and has been useful, but every time I encounter someone not speaking English, I find myself blabbering away in Spanish regardless of where I am. In Paris, I was speaking Spanish all the time and no one knew what I was saying."

"I do the same thing," says Ward. "Only it's Kikongo." There's a moment of silence. "Your mother has a headache?"

"So you speak Spanish too?"

"Just a tiny bit. You run into more Portuguese in my neck of Africa. Knowing French helps, and if you spend as much time with Belgians as I do, one's French needs to be at least conversational."

Miss Sanford nods introspectively. She clasps her hands, her eyes searching the room. "All right, Mister Ward, as an artist, what is your favorite piece in this room?"

"Which one did you pick out?"

She laughs. "Clearly you've never met my father, or you wouldn't bother asking that."

Together, they look around at the paintings, the statuettes, the little medieval triptych, the Chinese landscape carved from a tusk, and then—as if by design—they are looking into an oval mirror and see themselves, in naked intimacy, reflected side by side, as if they are the only two people in existence.

She can't decide if he's a new problem or the answer to an old one. Sarita taps the envelope on the palm of her hand. That first night she had brought the letter to the dinner table with the simple plan of handing it to her father, but he hadn't joined Sarita and her mother. He was eating in his study— which really ought to have been her mother's dressing room—as there were sheaves of documents to go through before the morning. So she'd left the envelope propped on the dining-room table. "Mr. Sanford" was neatly inked in an assertive, masculine hand across the ivory stock; her father should have picked it up. The next night, as she dined alone (Father had work, Mother had a headache), she had sat in silent conversation with the letter as if it were Mr. Ward himself: She supplied his dialogue. *What made you leave home?* she asked. *A life of adventure,* the envelope replied. *Really?* she asked. *No, not really. I was lonely and wanted to be in lonely places so as not to seem ridiculous,* the envelope responded. Sarita recognized that she was doing what women did—seeking out a rugged man and then looking for the weak spot, the vulnerability. She taps the envelope on her hand. Women couldn't possibly be that pathetic, looking to infect compromised men as disease infects compromised bodies. At breakfast this morning, the letter was still on the table, propped against a bud vase. And now she holds it as she contemplates knocking on her father's door. Sarita has her hand raised into a loose fist, knuckles ready to tap, when her father's footsteps start across the floor. She steps out of the way just in time to avoid being hit as the door swings open.

"Hello," he says, "what are you doing there? I almost walked into you."

"I have a letter of introduction." She extends the envelope.

"Why? I already know who you are."

"Ha, ha," says Sarita. "It's from a Mister Ward. Joseph Hatton wrote it for him."

"Hatton? Where's this Ward from?"

"He's from the Congo. He's been working with Stanley."

"The explorer?"

"No. Stanley the cheese monger."

"Ha, ha," says Sanford. He takes the letter and holds it up to the light, as if looking for a watermark. "What do you think?"

Sarita shrugs. "He's pleasant, has a gift for languages. I brought him for coffee yesterday so you could look him over, but there was no one around. Mother had a headache."

"Is he looking for work?"

"He must be." She keeps Ward's artistic ambition to herself.

"Does he know anything about railways?"

"They're building one in the Congo. He's done some surveying." Actually, it's Ward's friend who's done that. Why is she lying for him?

"Well, you like him. That's clear. What job do you think he's suited for?"

"You don't want to know." Sarita delivers a charming smile.

"Sarita, don't play with me. And what happened with Brock-Innes?"

"The truth is nothing happened with Charles Brock-Innes, at least not with Charles Brock-Innes and me."

"Doesn't mean it won't. We'll send you back in a month or so. That should give Brock-Innes time to miss you."

And to mull over the benefits of Sarita's fortune. Sanford waits for Sarita to excuse herself. He looks at the envelope and tucks it into the pocket of his bathrobe, which he is wearing for warmth, over a pair of wool suiting trousers. "You should meet this Mister Ward," says Sarita.

"Why?"

"I think he'll remind you of someone you like very much."

"And who is that?"

"You."

Glave is also working on a manuscript. Glave was one of the early Congo pioneers, appointed by Stanley back in 1883. And he is still held in high esteem by Stanley. Glave was given the task of setting up the station in Lukolela, when there was no post between Stanley Pool and the coast. The way he tells it, it would make one think that he'd been assigned to be a small-town postmaster in a place like Devon. But Ward knows that Glave was just abandoned in the jungle with some weapons, a linguister who had the local dialects and few words of English, some tinned meat and hardtack, and the charge to make the spot—chosen for its hospitality to boats rather than people—civilized. Most of the others assigned to opening new stations were dead, carried off by disease or the natives, but Lukolela and the Congo in general seemed to have agreed with Glave, until he made it safe and acceptable for the others—his job—and the place became overrun with Belgians, who had the authority and money but no good men. The occasional capable Belgian is usually French.

Glave's writing style is fluid and his vocabulary is broad. His work is nuanced. "You sound like a writer," Ward says.

"Generally a good idea when putting a book together."

"Your book's better than mine," says Ward.

"No, it's just different. Yours is colloquial and faster-paced. Mine is a little more contemplative."

"Better."

"People will like yours more. And you can draw." As evidence of this, Glave sorts through and pulls out his drawing of some Kroo boys: flattened figures with limbs akimbo, roughly sketched to illustrate their colorful mish-mash of European clothing and native flair. Glave's drawing is the equivalent of Ward's writing, capable of communication but not justified by some larger aesthetic truth. "I've a long way to go," Glave says. "The whole book seems to be about hunting. Currently, the book should be called *Some Things I Shot in Africa*."

"You have pages on the natives."

"I shot some of them too."

From the cabin, Ward and Glave make their way to the saloon, which is crowded. Ward likes the saloon to be crowded because the noise of others is shared by all. He and Glave have spent so much time together as of late that often silences spring between them, silences that they don't find uncomfortable but must appear less congenial. He was never silent with Casement. Glave has taken to bringing a short piece of rope with him, with which he practices increasingly quicker and more elegant knots.

"What are we drinking?" asks Glave. "Beer, wine, or whiskey?"

"I think whiskey," says Ward.

The bottle soon arrives with glasses and Glave knocks out some good portions, giving Ward a little more to start. The whiskey now poured, the rope comes out.

"One would think you were going to sea rather than the Yukon," says Ward.

"What, this?" says Glave, raising the half-executed knot.

"Knots and sailors," says Ward.

"Actually, stops me from wanting my pipe, and I don't want to be dependent on anything in the Yukon, so I'm cutting back."

So even the mystery of the knots has been dispensed with. Ward takes a mouthful of whiskey. The first belt tastes awful but feels sublime. The rest will taste good enough, and feel all right, as the effect on the senses evens out. Glave completes his knot, holds it up for inspection, and unties it. Lately, Ward has been thinking about Miss Sanford, which is a reprieve from thinking about Stanley and his slander. Although even Miss Sanford leads back to Stanley, as all lines of thought do, as all roads lead to Rome. A certain chunk of time passes with Ward going over the particulars of his conversation with Miss Sanford, their consumption of coffee, the maid's smirking around the corners as if she knew something, which she did: She knew that Ward didn't measure up for the family and, in the gleeful schadenfreude that makes the life of a servant almost tolerable, felt entitled to remind him—and Miss

Sanford—of it whenever possible. Every cup of coffee poured, every cake offered, every polite inquiry was an opportunity for Ward to improvise manners and with a woman unaccustomed to improvisation. Of course, Miss Sanford had been careful to keep things easy, but the maid—she read his mind. Cake on plate, coffee in hand . . . How did one eat the cake? Bite it directly off the plate? Of course, the coffee would be set down, but in this moment of hesitation—coffee or cake?—a gulf had sprung up between him and Miss Sanford, between his world and hers. And all this witnessed by the nostril-flaring, soft-hipped Paz. Another glass of whiskey and Glave is teaching Ward knots. Another glass and Ward, fumbling with the rope, seems to have unlearned everything he just mastered. Another glass and the saloon is shutting down. Glave is going to allow himself a pipe and then head for bed. And Ward is going to take in some fresh air, but he has a vague notion of passing by the first-class lounge—at least by the doors—not in pursuit of Miss Sanford but rather Paz, the pretty maid, who, in her subtle smirking and heavy-lidded, full-lipped condescension, has successfully convinced him that he is not only unworthy of Miss Sanford but uninterested. He sees Miss Sanford's trim figure, her repartee, her lively hands, her perfectly executed loaf of hair. But Paz is all direct gazes, heavy bosom, escaping tendrils. Should her hands be rough, even better.

The deck is quiet and Ward wonders how late it is. He allows himself to think of Bidi, his woman back in Yambuya—her glowing skin, her bottomless eyes, her rich scent. He allows himself to conjure that name—Bidi, Bidi—that he had never used in her presence, as if that small action allowed her to somehow not be present in his tent. She was soulful beauty. In his current state of mind, it's difficult to manage the regret and remorse that he normally performs with himself as his only audience. Still, remorse enacted leaves Ward some residue of genuine regret. Where is Bidi now? Where is he? The ship's engine sounds like the engine of time, as if he is waiting for this episode of his life to run out, this action that will take all of his Congo life—Bidi, Msa, Mbatchi, Jameson, Barttelot—the living and the dead, and bring them to history. The prow of the ship is cold metal and the surface of the water appears like beaten tin, like the hull of the ocean rather than a liquid surface. He feels this life to be a false life with no consequences even though reason tells him that the opposite is true—that Africa is that which is not real. He cannot fully articulate what he feels—a fathomless absence, a sorrow, an embarrassment at this current role of acting an Englishman. To bed, Herbert, he tells himself.

And then he sees her, down the railing. He'd thought it impossible that Paz would be there. The odds of fifty/fifty that he'd determined in the saloon, and with conviction, have evaporated in the sobering night air, although he still feels emboldened with whiskey. But there she is, so he's glad the liquor hasn't deserted him all together. Paz, he thinks, approaching. What will he say? *I hoped you'd be about, but thought the odds slim.* Does she speak English? It won't matter. Paz will want him because it will give her something over her mistress. Paz will know that all the lacquers and corsetry imposed on these society women—the sugary coating—rob them of their warmth. Paz will know how to hold his gaze, will know where to place her hands, when to push him away, when to laugh. Ward can almost feel the warmth of her skin beneath his fingers, the smell of sweat and powder along the nape of her neck. He imagines the tickle of her hair against his jaw as he unpins the braids. Ward draws closer and the woman, startled by his steps, turns. It is not Paz. Of course it isn't.

"Mister Ward," she says. He can tell she's been crying, but her voice is bright and composed, as always. "I see you also needed some fresh air."

"More than fresh air," he says. "I'd hoped you'd be about but thought the odds slim." That was his line, now delivered.

"It is very late."

"I thought all the young ladies were in bed."

He sees her reach for a comeback, but she doesn't find one. He takes a step closer and reaches for her wrist. The tiny wrist fits in his palm neatly. He closes his fingers around it and can feel the gentle thrum of her pulse, as if he is strangling a bird. He can pretend desire for this chilly dish, but he finds himself warming to her. She holds his gaze as if uncomprehending.

He waits for the rebuff. She also seems to be waiting for the rebuff, as if unaware that she is supposed to produce it. He pulls her gently to him and she goes with little steps, as if she's learning a dance—willing, but unsure.

"You look as if you're worried that you'll make a mistake," says Ward.

"That's a good observation," she says.

"You shouldn't be concerned. You don't have to do anything at all."

And, she thinks, how many mistakes are presented to her? Is going to Ward a mistake? Would retiring to her room be correct or the wasting of an opportunity? Each little step she makes into Ward's arms produces its own forking paths, a different fistful of fates. She was crying bitter tears up on the deck, angry that her choices were so limited, angry that she had been calculating and recalculating her options that she hoped had expanded with Ward's *deus ex machina* appearance the day before and had decided that all was lost. But now he's kissing her arm. Do men do that? Her experience is so limited. Once, in Argentina—she must have been about eighteen—she was visiting in the provinces, when she found herself abandoned in a church. What actually had happened was that her father had gone off with the surveyor to see about laying track, and she had been left with the maid, who was from that town and had a few quick errands to run. This maid had deposited her in the church, which was pretty, but Sarita wasn't Catholic, and as such wasn't sure if praying there helped to aid or compromise the future of her soul. After about an hour of tentative prayer, candle lighting, and perusal of statues—the feet of which had all been rubbed free of paint—she had wandered outside. There, beside the church, under the shade of an enormous tree, she had seen a young man in a cassock retrieving water from the well. When he saw her, his face brightened, and he began to make quick steps towards her. Sarita had stood there, holding the handle of her parasol, and wondering whether or not she should open it, or walk back inside, or say something and what something—should she say it—would be. She knew that action was called for, but this young man was suddenly before her—handsome, and with eyes the color of honey—and he had taken her in his arms and begun to kiss her, there, at the side of the church, where there seemed to be no one around. And then he had released her, smiled, and wandered off. Maybe the Catholic god had called him back. And then all the waiting for Brock-Innes to stop laughing at her jokes and admiring her clothes and to at least sustain the holding of her hand. And now Mr. Ward, who seems to think her innocence—more ignorance—is what might cause her to make a mistake. He has no manners at all, she thinks, although he is kind and gentle and she's never put much stock in manners. He's moved from kissing her arm to kissing her neck. Now she smells the whiskey on his breath. She wants to tell him that she's been drinking too. Sherry. Five glasses, with no one to notice except for Paz. She feels his hands moving up and down her sides, which, she thinks, probably feel like upholstered furniture through all that stiff canvas and whalebone, as if, should he get the whole contraption off, he'd find her dress stuffed with horsehair. She feels his fingers at the back of her dress and—steeling herself with a deep breath—manages,

"Please don't do that."

Ward steps back, suddenly full of reserve, worried.

"It's not that, Mister Ward," she says. "Unless you can fix it yourself, you better leave it as is."

"All right," he says. He steps closer and puts his hands on her shoulders. "Am I offending you?"

"Not at all," she says.

"Then call me Herbert."

"I really can't do that," she says. "And don't call me Sarita, but think it. Think it all the time."

"She's invited you for dinner," says Glave. "I'm impressed." Glave is digging through his trunk looking for his jacket because Ward's has a split seam. "How did you manage that?"

"How I managed that is unimportant. How I will manage the dinner, however, is."

"Well," says Glave, "I can't help you there. I'm just relieved they didn't invite me."

"They did. I said you couldn't come."

"Really."

"I needed your jacket and I didn't think you'd mind."

"You know," says Glave, "you might end up marrying her."

"That's ridiculous," says Ward. "It's just dinner. And we are friends."

"Heiresses don't have friends. Ward, if you don't want to marry her, you have to leave while you still can."

Ward shakes his head. "She couldn't marry a man like me anyway."

"So it would seem, but if she sets her eyes in your direction, what will you do? People like the Sanfords are used to getting what they want, Ward. And you, you've been compromised in the wake of the Emin Pasha scandal, so you are not seeing clearly. I am just reminding you, as your good friend, that you have a lot to give up."

Ward knots his tie, the kind of knot that never fails him. "Ridiculous, Glave. My mind is as clear as crystal."

"That's a meaningless phrase," says Glave. "And I don't believe it. You've had nothing but freedom and adventure for the last ten years. I'm not sure the transition into drawing rooms and continental holidays is going to make you happy."

Of course Glave is overreacting, but Ward remembers that Glave is always right, that even Casement—who is often right—thinks to himself "What would Glave do?" in times of difficulty. There has to be an element of truth in this little drama. "But what if I like drawing rooms?" He shrugs. "I like women. I like beds and horses and things like that—shaving with hot water. Maybe I'm not like you and Casement and Parminter and all the Congo crew."

"You're a country squire at heart, are you?"

"Who knows?" says Ward. "How do you find these things out?"

If she were ten years younger, Sarita would know that she wanted to marry Mr. Ward. She would know it. She would picture their lives, the kicked bed sheets, the pretty children, the laughter—ha, ha, ha—over the morning paper, the hand holding, the attentive listening for every minor concern one's spouse might have. But she's not nineteen and she knows she would like to spend time with Mr. Ward. She is sure of time, but not of life. All right. She cannot get him out of her mind. She thinks of his heat. She is pleased that being on deck alone (which she'd always heard invited scandal, but never quite believed) has caused her to indulge in some scandalous activity. Her advanced age of twenty-nine years has made her privy to all sorts of conversations from her friends—well-trained girls who occasionally manage to find themselves behind a hedge with an interesting young man and were kissed, or, if his looks or standing were deemed unsatisfactory, "violated." Clearheaded, still unmarried (and maybe never married), Sarita would sit and listen as these young ladies—Emily, Hazel, Garnet—would wonder out loud if it was love, as if love and these passing infatuations were mutually exclusive. Passing infatuations, one would think, masqueraded as love—love being the real thing—tricking girls away from their true destiny: the gallant young man who would give them passion and respectability. Sarita isn't buying it. She never did. Her father—for all his steamrolling over her desires and maneuvering her like a Hapsburg—has always been up-front with her. Father has no sons and because of his parental desire to impart wisdom somewhere, has taught Sarita a lot. She does have one living sister, Ettie, who married early—before she could marry well—and is now producing grandchildren in the Midwest, but other than that, she's it for Father. And he has told her so much that she knows that infatuation is love, that this greater patient, solid love doesn't exist, although—and this is important—patience and solidity do. Marry a rock. Don't expect love. Above all, do not be stupid.

So indoctrinated, Sarita had moved in the orbit of Brock-Innes and his ilk. Money. Prestige. Children. Respectability. She was all for it. And even if he was an invert, so what? All women were cheated on, and maybe this, added insult to her uxorial majesty, would work as a bargaining chip— better vacations, more say in the children's upbringing, more freedom. It all sounds very convincing but, despite weeks of considering this, she still finds herself unpersuaded.

And now Mr. Ward.

What does he have to offer? He is handsome. He is young. He is impulsive. Is that a good thing? He does not make her feel companionable and steady, but rather still deep in youthful compulsion. She remembers asking him to show her something new, and there she is, a new Sarita, who might have been there all along but that she is seeing for the first time. She is also aware that she doesn't believe in money the way that she used to and that the development of these sacrilegious thoughts exactly mimics her loss of faith in God. What if God/money didn't exist? What would I do without God/money? Am I brave enough to live in a world of self-determination without God/money?

This seems to be what Ward offers: a loss of innocence. How romantic.

Oh, but there are things against him. She knows about the Emin Pasha Relief Expedition, although not his role in it. The news stories make good reading, lit with an African light, buoyed by the heat and the drum beat of sorcery, savagery, insanity—the notion that these were civilized men lashing others to blood, succumbing to the glamour of cannibalism, losing themselves in embraces with black bodies: all of it such a welcome read, the perfect antidote to one's life where an entire waking hour each day is spent assembling the architecture of one's clothes—the garters, the bustles, the stays and laces, the buttons and overskirts, gloves and pins, hats and collars, jewels and perfumes.

After their encounter on deck, her hair lopsided, her face flushed, she returned to the cabin. Sleepy Paz had been waiting for her, had loosened her stays and let down her hair, first smacking the side of Sarita's head (although gently) to determine why half of it seemed to have collapsed. Of course, that's where Mr. Ward's hand had been digging around, as if trying to find where Sarita's head actually existed in all the fluff. Paz had yanked and unlooped, pulling the pins from the coif and dropping them on the salver where they pinged like angry hail.

Once the maid retired from her room, Sarita had immediately gone to her father's study. Miracle of miracles, he was not in there and, as she determined from the snores across the passage, actually seemed to have gone to bed. The letter was not in the stack on the small correspondence table that was serving as his desk, nor in the clutch of papers in his leather case. It had to be somewhere. And then she saw his bathrobe hanging from a hook on the door and sure enough, there in the pocket was the letter, the envelope torn open in haste, probably with her father's thumb rather than a letter opener, and the pages themselves thrust, slightly crumpled, back into it. She would learn what her father knew, what Hatton knew, what recommendations and reservations existed against this man. In truth, she felt, the letter of introduction was intended for her.

The letter is standard, recommending Ward's character, diligence, work ethic. Hatton goes on to say a word about Ward's iron constitution, his ability with languages, his honesty. And then something in strong admiration of Ward's moral character, which strikes Sarita as protesting too much. Hatton calls Ward a "pocket Hercules," referring to both his height and strength. Pocket Hercules? This makes it seem as if Ward is a circus performer. But Hatton ends on a somber note, saying that he has taken a particular interest in Ward since the death of his son. As far as letters of introduction go, it is solid.

What are the odds now?

If the newspapers are against Ward, Father will favor him, because Father prides himself as being a freethinker and seldom has an opportunity to exercise his skill as judge of character. What else? Brock-Innes must need money, or why would he be courting her? Father likes his money. Is the purchase of a title really worth the loss of capital? What else? Grandchildren. Good genes. Look at Ward, a shockingly handsome man with a hale temperament, devoted friends, strong physique—a fine example of masculinity. And Ward's not stupid, but regardless, Sarita has brains enough for both. This is her hand and she knows how to play it—the only question is whether or not she wants to. Sarita chooses her battles and doesn't see the point in parlaying with her father unless she sees her future raveled in with Ward. This won't be easy. She taps the envelope against her palm. She

98

could consult Ward and see what he thinks, but there's no protocol for that. She'll just move forward and fix the details as they arise.

Sarita's surprised at the surge of feeling she has for Ward when he enters the cabin. Is it nerves? She feels slightly breathless and wonders if her stays are too tight—although the dress is one that fits well. Paz, who is taking coats, is staring at her, although she lowers her eyes when Sarita catches her.

"Good evening, Mister Ward," she says. And he says whatever he needs to say, shakes her hand, and sizes up the scene. He gives Sarita an honest, nervous look. She smiles apologetically. He raises his eyebrows back to her. This is shorthand, which means they're in it together. And how the next half hour passes, who can say? There's some refreshment, some chatter, and Sarita is grateful when her father, who is an undeniable blowhard, starts on about the railroad in Argentina—grateful until she remembers that she said that Ward had done survey work in the Congo. She realizes her eyes are bulging—which is what happens when she's nervous—and then, thank whatever god you choose, Cook is at the door and they're ready to eat.

Mother's had too much of her headache medicine and seems to have forgotten that she is supposed to lead the way, with Ward, and this crazy dowager from Pittsburgh that Father dug up in the first-class lounge—intended to even things out—has proven herself to be of appropriate pedigree and fabulously wealthy, but also a bit deaf. The other man should have been Ward's friend Glave; however, Glave had already made plans—but what, and with whom? Regardless, he's not here and instead she has Mr. Smith, a nervous-looking man who keeps looking from end to end of the room as if he's a rabbit in a hawk-ridden meadow. Father knows him from import/export something or other, and Smith has been telling Sarita about his apiary, of which he's very proud, and although she knows it's bees, she keeps imagining him tending to monkeys. Suddenly, they've all stood up, although no one has made a move towards the table. Perhaps they're confused because escorting people from one side of a room to the other doesn't make much sense. Although, escorting people from one room of a house into another is also a bit extreme. But of course everyone's confused. Sarita's the host and she's confused.

"Mother," Sarita says.

"Hmm?" goes Mother, seemingly surprised to see Sarita standing there.

"You have to take Mister Ward in," she whispers. She gently pushes her mother's elbow in Ward's direction, who—if he were someone else—would have a better idea of what was going on, but is naïve and, although he seems to be ready for Mother, is not suave enough to take the lead. Mother toddles over to Ward, and together they make the ten-foot crossing to the dining table. After, it's Sarita with Mr. Smith. And, bringing up the rear, here come Father and the Widow Plumly of Pittsburgh.

Father finally seats himself and the servants spring into action. Sarita's glass is soon poured with sparkling wine and she looks at it for a moment before allowing herself to pick the thing up. Ward sits across from her in an ill-fitting, large jacket. His overcoat is also too big: He's lost weight, or maybe he just likes big clothes. She looks over at him and they lock eyes before quickly turning to their neighbors. The chatter starts up and Sarita finds herself yelling to Mrs. Plumly that she enjoyed her last trip to Pittsburgh and would like to see Mr. Carnegie's art collection. She finds herself repeating "Mister Carnegie's art collection" several times, and then, when "Mister Carnegie" has been successfully communicated, she soldiers on with the rest of the statement, increasingly loud, until the table grows quiet.

"Art collection," she says. "Art collection. Art. Art. Art."

Mrs. Plumly, smiling to one side and then the other, suddenly turns to the table and says, "I've always been a lover of art." Mrs. Plumly pats Sarita's hand with a warm concern for this slightly unhinged young woman.

"How wonderful," says Sarita, although she's taken aback by Mrs. Plumly's sudden ability to hear. "Mister Ward is an accomp—" Did Ward shake his head? He did, although almost imperceptibly. "Mister Ward is about to go on a lecture to promote his book"—she looks at him; he hadn't wanted her to mention the art, which is wise—"about his time in the Congo." And she was about to say he was an artist, after keeping this information from her father—must be the wine. He's not so inept, this Mr. Ward. He knew that talk of art would lead nowhere, particularly not with him, and now the conversation has been steered in a better direction. So Mr. Ward can now rehearse his lecture on the Congo cannibals for the Sanford dinner table and thank God. Apiaries and art. Is this the best that Father could do?

The food service wears on and Sarita is actually amused, as opposed to poor Mr. Smith, who delivers a series of feeble nods as Father batters him with an unrelenting squall of emphatic and not particularly interesting money-speak. At least Mrs. Plumly has a good sense of humor, and that, coupled with several glasses of wine and an eccentric family, passes the time. All Sarita has to do is to let Mrs. Plumly do all the talking. She can listen and laugh. That's good. Although she tries to catch some of Mr. Ward's entertaining stories—elephants, natives, bad weather, lack of food, and an awful lot of walking. Mrs. Plumly, now finishing up her tart, is momentarily quiet. Mr. Ward is relating his time among the Maori of New Zealand, which is a bit of surprise, but has Father interested.

"So what is there in New Zealand?" Father asks.

"It's sheep, Mister Sanford."

"Any money in that?"

"Quite a bit, although none for me, I'm afraid. I was sixteen years old and an amateur shearer, although I learned quickly. I'd say for you, Mister Sanford, Australia would be more of interest. More places to lay track. And there's mining there, of course gold for now, but who knows what else exists in that red dirt? It's an enormous country."

"Mining."

"I prospected for a time."

"Find anything worthwhile?"

"If I had, I wouldn't have left for Borneo."

"Mister Ward," says Mother, who suddenly seems to have achieved actual consciousness with the added benefit of speech, "what is the strangest job you've ever had?"

"Strangest?" says Ward. He smiles at Mother, who is charmed by his handsomeness, because he is really a handsome man. "I don't know if I should say in the present company."

"You really must," says Mrs. Plumly, who seems to hear everything she wants to.

"Right then," says Ward. "For a time, in Australia, I was in a circus."

Good lord, thinks Sarita. *Ladies and gentleman, I present to you the Pocket Hercules.* "You're playing with us, Mister Ward," says Sarita, hopefully.

"I assure you, I am not. I entertained with my ability to walk on a wire, high above the heads of the audience." She thinks this must be some manner of confession—know what you're getting into, young lady. "And believe me, they wanted me to be good, because if I fell, I would have landed right on them."

"I don't believe a word of it," says Sarita.

"Then you must show us something," says Mrs. Plumly, which was not exactly what Sarita had been hoping for.

"Oh, please do," chimes in Mr. Smith. Father, too, seems eager for this new entertainment.

"There's not very much room in here," says Ward, and he stands up. He takes off his large jacket and drapes it on the back of his chair. "But I can certainly manage a handstand."

"Please don't feel the need to put yourself to any trouble."

But then Mrs. Plumly gasps and Sarita sees that Mr. Ward is indeed standing on his hands. He takes a couple of steps like this, and manages to move to the side of the table, where Sarita can get a good look at him.

His blond hair is hanging down in a lump of pomade and his shirt-front is becoming untucked. Sarita can see his socks, a slight mismatch. His face is getting very red and yes, he looks silly, but she is astounded at how every muscle obeys and how steady—even in that stance—Ward manages to be. "What does the world look like from down there?" says Sarita.

"Much the same, only completely different." He's smiling at her. "I have a very nice view."

* * *

The guests were all gone. She'd only managed a quick exchange with Mr. Ward as they all stirred towards the door and were occupied with finding wraps and coats, although no one had much of a commute. Ward had said, "Perhaps we could do something together." A simple enough statement, Sarita had been completely flummoxed by it, and isn't sure what exactly her response was, although it was something positive. She knocks on her father's door and takes his grunt on the other side as an invitation to enter.

"You," he says to her.

"Who else?" She shifts some papers that have been deposited on the hassock and deposits herself there. They look at each other for a second, and then she reaches for the laces on her boots and loosens them, because her ankles are throbbing. "Well?" she says.

"I'm not sure," he says.

She waits.

"It is so much harder to maneuver with daughters."

She shrugs. "I wish you had a son."

"But I don't."

"You'll have to hold out for grandsons."

"Are *you* sure?" Father asks.

She's sure of how she feels, but that is not what he's asking. "I am nearly thirty and you need grandchildren."

"Brock-Innes would give me grandchildren."

Sarita doesn't know what flashes across her face, but her father sees it. "Brock-Innes would be a mistake," she says. "Another season without a marriage will seal my fate as a spinster."

"Sarita," says Father, "wasting the opportunity of your marriage will not be good for anyone in the long run."

So Father knew about Brock-Innes. Of course he did.

"What is the state of Brock-Innes's financial affairs?" she counters.

Father smiles as he neatly knits his fingers together. "So you are sure."

"I am sure," says Sarita, "that you will do anything you want. And I am sure that I will do anything you want."

"You should have married earlier."

"I would be living in the Midwest, producing grandchildren, like Ettie."

Father nods to himself. "You're pretty enough to go another season."

"Thank you, Father, but a part of me believes that you do not want me to marry at all."

No response.

"You can always count on me to be there for you, as I always have been."

In response Father pours out some whiskey. There's only one glass. He takes a sip and extends it to Sarita. She takes a sip. "Acrobats," her father says.

"If we go belly up," Sarita replies, "we can start our own circus."

Ward lies silent on the lower bunk, knowing that Glave is awake too, as his silence gives him away.

"I think I asked her to marry me," he says.

"You're not certain?" says Glave.

"I said I'd like it if we did something together."

"Are congratulations in order?"

But Ward doesn't know. He is thinking about Borneo—a place he hadn't known existed—but that had popped up, sprung from the ocean. Australia, with its harsh light and open sky, had stopped intriguing him, and Borneo, singing a siren song, cloaked in vines, scented with flowering greenery that shook with the passage of monkeys and jewel-feathered birds, had drawn him into her folds and held him close. Altered his life. In the end, Borneo—with its deluding fevers—had nearly killed him.

VI

The United States

November 1889

Ward and Glave are on an evening train headed for Boston. The deadline for the *Scribner's* article isn't for another couple of days, so Ward could put it down and start a letter to Sarita. He'd rather write in privacy—along with all the other things he'd rather do in privacy—but that's a luxury unknown to him.

"Ward," says Glave, "you know you ask her father for her hand. What she says isn't worth much."

Ward nods. "I'm not sure that's what I'm doing."

"It is what you're doing," says Glave. "If you can't see it, I can. We're back in New York before we head to Pittsburgh. That's in four days. I just want you—"

"To what, Glave?"

"Don't take this the wrong way."

Ward prepares to take it the wrong way.

"Things in your life can look accidental. If you're entering a marriage, you must do so with a complete sense of purpose. In our line, we do things because they have not yet been done. Others might ask 'Why?' and we ask 'Why not?' "

"And?" says Ward.

" 'Why not?' is a bad reason to get married," says Glave. "It doesn't work when you're involving someone else, in this case a complicated, intelligent woman of good reputation whom you obviously care deeply about."

"Well," says Ward, recovering some good cheer, "you're full of advice for a committed bachelor."

"Which is why you should believe me."

"Very funny," says Ward. He reaches for the flask of whiskey that Glave has extended to him. The train lurches, the lights dim, then brighten. Ward wonders what Sarita is doing now. He imagines her gliding around in her long skirts, pausing at the third-floor windows of her Fifth Avenue residence. He sees her retrieving his letter from the little silver plate extended by the maid or butler or whomever performs that particular task. He sees her as one of those stuffed parrots or hummingbirds—gorgeously dressed, carefully posed, stuck behind glass, and doing a good job of mimicking life.

Ward wonders what's happened to Jameson's skins, all those birds so carefully prepared, and the notes and measurements that had accompanied those fragile feathered hides, so necessary for bringing them back from the dead. He could easily write pages about Jameson, but Stanley has put that off-limits—nothing about the Emin Pasha Relief Expedition for another four months. Instead, he stuffs and stuffs the *Scribner's Magazine* piece with naked natives and cannibalism, more naked natives and more cannibalism. The train carriage shudders on the tracks, each little bolt and window casing rattling with impatience. An even darkness beyond the steamed-up windowpane—it's cold outside—makes the fact that they are moving seem more of a fancy.

It is midnight when they finally arrive in Boston. Stepping off the train, Ward sees his breath hold in the cold air. He doesn't feel much about Boston, so instead he finds himself recalling what other people might feel about Boston.

The Boston Tea Party. The American Revolution. He pauses, looking to the end of the platform for a porter. He thinks *Boston Tea Party* again. Finally, a tall man in a rough jacket approaches. He's wearing an official porter hat, but the sideways glance that he gives Ward is sizing him up in an unofficial way.

"Good," says Ward, "I have three crates that I'm going to need help with."

"Are you English?" says the man, checking the accent. He's Irish.

"Yes," says Ward.

"Let me find someone who will help you." The man begins to amble away.

"What?" says Ward. He's doesn't trust this man to help him with anything.

"I apologize," says the Irishman. He bows. "Let me find someone who will help you, Governor."

Glave, now exiting the train, is ready with his pipe.

"What was that all about?" asks Ward.

"He must be Clan Na Gael." Glave seems unperturbed.

"What? A Fenian?" Ward knows the bold strokes of this but none of the finer points.

Glave nods. "Boston is full of them, or so I've heard."

"Doesn't help us with our crates."

But sure enough, the Fenian has sent someone else along, and although this man could be the other's cousin and would not look out of place in Ireland—Ward has never been there, but certainly knows what an Irishman looks like—he speaks the rough twang of the American, with a harshness that must be the local accent. The crates are organized and Ward, now standing on the Boston street, is glad for Glave's company, is fearful of this Western place with the ice crusting over the puddles and the trams roaring out of the dark streets, the thin women in ratty cloaks darting aside as ladies with ferocious hats of stiff silk lay claim to the footpath. This place makes him nervous. Nerves caused by buildings, streets, industry, civilization. By men who find his accent an assault and who announce their hostility with sarcasm. He never had this feeling in Africa. Perhaps the difficulty of survival was enough that he didn't have the luxury to want to avoid working out transportation, or the novelty of speaking new languages so great that he wasn't hesitant to express himself, but here—in these large American cities—he feels both alien and not.

"Look, Ward," says Glave, and he points to a poster.

The Boston Explorers Club
November 18, 1889,
At 8:00 P.M.
Boston Lyceum, 64 Commonwealth Ave.
Lecture by Mr. Herbert Ward,
(the renowned African traveller),
SUBJECT:
"The Congo Cannibals of Central Africa"

Illustrated by stereopticon views from drawings and photographs taken by Mr. Ward. Membership tickets will admit member and two ladies. Admission to non-members 50 cents each person. Reserved seats 25 cents extra. Boxes $2.00 extra.

"They've placarded the whole town," says Glave. "You should have a good crowd."

And Ward smiles, but he's aware that he's stepped into this new life— lecturer, Boston—by accident.

Casement has been in New York for two days, booked into a decent little hotel on Broadway—recommended by Ward and Glave—which is noisy, but convenient. He has another five days on his own before his friends get back from Toronto and although he has many things he could do—and a list of people who will supply him with drinks and cakes and conversation— walking has been entertainment enough.

The day before he had wandered to the west, by the docks, and, confused, found himself at the end of an alley, the sky obscured by a web of clotheslines. His sense of direction had failed him. He turned a couple of times and headed back from where he came. At every door the chilly air would be cut with the smell of something decidedly organic and unpleasant. Casement tried to look like he knew where he was going, which involved a quick step, and that, in turn, made orienting himself impossible. Upon taking his third corner and reaching the end of yet another alley, he could not decide whether he should exit to the right or left and in this moment of hesitation attracted the attention of some rough types who were sizing him up as he stood there in his good traveling clothes. A clang of metal to his left startled him. It was a man at work emptying ash cans and Casement saw, with relief, that he was black—an American African—and decided that he was a good person to ask.

"Excuse me," said Casement, "I need to get back to Broadway and have somehow gotten completely turned around."

The look the man gave him was something between weary and incredulous, and then amused. This man also noticed the toughs across the street. There was a moment where he said nothing, as if hoping that Casement would go away. Casement was sympathetic. He too wanted himself to go away and was just waiting for assistance. Finally, the man responded, "Just follow me, sir. I'll bring you to where you can get back to Broadway."

Later, as he was checking for his mail, he mentioned the incident to Mrs. Sawyer, who ran the hotel.

"Where were you?" she said.

"I'm not completely sure, but it was probably directly west, not too far from the water."

"Mister Casement," she said, her face drawn dramatically to its opposing corners, "don't go there. It's dangerous."

"I'm quite capable of taking care of myself."

She shook her head dismissively. "This isn't Africa," she said.

"I spent six years living shoulder to shoulder with cannibals—"

"These people don't want to eat you," said Mrs. Sawyer. "They want your money and they don't mind killing you to get it. Stay away from the black people. And whatever you do, don't talk to any Italians. And the Irish, best avoided."

"But I'm Irish."

"And so am I, on my mother's side. But you've got to be careful." She considered. "Don't talk to any Irish south of Fourteenth Street and west of Seventh Avenue. You can go north as far as you like as long as you stay near Broadway. Why don't you go look at the Park?"

And then she waved him off. She had cooking to do and—judging from the size of her—food to eat.

Of course Casement is aware that he has romantic notions of the United States. These rough settlers had managed to throw off the yoke of British Rule and even as a boy, as he'd pasted the articles on Parnell and Davitt from *Freeman's* on his wall, his thoughts had wandered back to the American War of Independence—a war that was won—where the British suffered a humiliating defeat at the hands of these farmers. And cabinetmakers and eccentrics and silversmiths. He knows little of eighteenth-century America and his knowledge of American history quickly succumbs to a synedochic devolution. The accounts of the American War of Independence that he read as a boy had all been decidedly unsympathetic to revolutionaries and he suspected that English schoolchildren—without the benefit of an Irish gimlet eye—were all happily ill-informed, as were the majority of the British population, a situation that probably led to the revolution in the first place.

Casement had wanted a concise history of the American War of Independence. He'd also thought to try Whitman again, *Leaves of Grass,* which he'd looked at years ago and found interesting in some ways, but metrically unhinged. He did like his poems to have some music. Unsurprisingly, Mrs. Sawyer had no idea where a bookstore might be, but had fixed him with that look—oddball—and then sent him away with a reminder not to stray too far from the path.

That was this afternoon and now, after wandering off the path and discovering various parks, he has finally found the bookstore and it's closed. And he's hungry. Having walked a randomly chosen couple of blocks, he has discovered a lunch cart with a list of options and a few recommendations:

"Ham and Egg Can't Be Beat," "Have a Hamburger, There [*sic*] Fine," "Eat a Pork Chop and Be Happy." Something about this lunch cart is so richly American and un-English that Casement's astonished by it. He wishes he had someone to share it with. He is committing to his choice of meal when he notices that he has caught the attention of another man, finely dressed, who has him fixed with such a curious look that Casement is momentarily embarrassed by it. He is surprised that the man smiles—eyebrows slightly raised—when he sees that Casement has seen him, as if he thinks Casement has recognized him. Of course Casement has no idea who he is. Maybe this man has confused him with someone else. And then the man is walking over and then is beside him, looking at Casement, then back to the lunch cart. The man has a walking stick and he leans on it lightly.

"You look confused. I thought you might need help," he says.

"No," says Casement. "I was just wondering whether a pork chop would really make me happy."

The man shakes his head subtly. "Not this one, old chum. If you really want a pork chop on a Wednesday—one that will make you happy—you should go to Green's, on Twenty-Second Street."

"Thank you for the recommendation," says Casement. And he waits for the man to leave.

"Where are you from?" says the man. "I'm trying to figure it out. I'm going to say English. It's the way you carry yourself. But your accent—also English, but with a kick to it. Maybe from the north? Liverpool?"

"I'm Irish, but I've spent time in Liverpool." This man's directness is a wonder to Casement. He wonders if he's a swindler.

"Are you going to get that pork chop?" The man's eyes flit back and forth. "Or there's always the hamburger, but 'there fine.' Did you know they fined you for eating hamburgers in New York?"

Casement knows he should laugh, but he doesn't. He feels mesmerized. "I'm still deciphering New York." The man is not black and he is not Italian and he is not Irish from below Fourteenth Street, but somehow Casement doubts that Mrs. Sawyer would approve.

"New York is an open book, unlike you." The man extends his hand suddenly. "Sam Butler. I'm in sales, textiles. Let's go to Green's."

"Roger Casement. I've been working for the British Consul in the Congo." Which is easier—and probably more truthful—than confessing to his recent stint as missionary.

"Green's, then?"

If this were Africa, he wouldn't hesitate. Even if he didn't like the man—if he was a rheumy Belgian with a greasy mustache, pocked jowls, and pink-rimmed eyes—he would be there at the table, no problem. And here is a civilized man on a street lit with lamps, a police officer strolling there in the offing, and other men of good appearance occupying themselves in the getting to and from seemingly respectable pursuits, and he hesitates. "If you have other plans, Mister Casement, it's a shame, but it was a pleasure to meet you. And I do hope you have a pleasant time in New York." Butler tips his hat and is about to make his exit when something in Casement shifts.

"Mister Butler, I have no plans. I will take you up on your generous offer of company."

"Good," says Butler. "I hate eating alone and I'm not meeting my friends until nine o'clock."

Green's is a fifteen-minute walk and in that time some pleasantries are exchanged. Butler has seen the posters for Ward's upcoming lecture and thinks it might be fun to attend. He's never been to Europe, and never been farther west than Chicago. Butler finds the lure of travel alluring, but not enough to leave New York. He's surprised to find that Casement doesn't know the borders of the various neighborhoods. And standing here as Mr. Butler rattles off the different restaurants, theatres, shops, it does seem as if the world is brought to some sort of metonymic manifestation here in New York. Five thousand people are arriving daily at Castle Garden and, although it seems an impossible figure, Butler assures Casement that as they head farther south, it will seem about right. "I'll take you down to the Bowery after dinner, if you like," says Butler. "It's not the best neighborhood, but I kind of like it."

"I would find that interesting," says Casement, catching an image of Mrs. Sawyer's disapproval in his mind's eye.

And then they're at Green's.

"Do you drink, Mister Casement?"

"Not to the exclusion of other things in life."

"As an enhancement, to brighten things up?"

"At my leisure." Casement is aware that he has not had a real conversation in days. He runs through his minor exchanges—the black ash-can worker, Mrs. Sawyer, the man at the newsstand who directed him to the closed bookshop. He hasn't spoken much at all and now, facing Butler, is reminded of coming in from the jungle after weeks spent searching for porters, and suddenly being faced with the news from Europe. One world is reality, one world is dream, and the exchanging of one for the other seems almost arbitrary. Every sentence he says seems awkward and tentative.

"How long were you in the Congo?" asks Butler.

"Six years." Easy question.

"I have to confess, I know absolutely nothing about the Congo. I don't even know what to ask you." Butler is momentarily saved as the waiter arrives with bottles of beer. "What is it like?"

"What is the Congo like?" Casement repeats stupidly.

"Tell me about the Congo."

This Butler is full of exaggerated expressions and, to underscore his last statement, he pushes back from the table, swings one leg over the other, and fixes Casement with a look that anticipates horror. Should Casement tell him about rampaging elephants? Naked cannibals? Surveying for the railway? Fevers and deaths? Cowardice and bravery?

"It must be hot," says Butler with conviction.

"Yes, it is," says Casement. "With lots of insects and these insects bite."

And they're off and the conversation starts up as if cranked by an enthusiastic organ grinder and the chops arrive.

"How's the pork chop?" asks Butler.

"This pork chop," says Casement, "has made me very happy."

And he's telling Butler about his latest trip home, how good it was to see his sister Nina and cousin Gee, and about the *Transvaal* with Ward and all the Manyemas and how the Manyemas had to have suits made for them in Rotterdam—twelve suits of a uniform, inexpensive cloth—and the look on the German tailor's face as he saw the Manyema march in, filling his shop, and their patient waiting for the tailor to do whatever was done with measuring tape. And he tells Butler all about the portage of the *Florida* and—is it the third beer or the fourth?—what a wonderful artist Ward is, how he should devote more time to it, and how he's looking forward to returning to the Congo with Ward and Glave, looking forward to seeing the missionary friends and his boys and all of that, looking forward to hunting. Hunting with Ward. Working with Ward, just the two of them, and a thousand Africans, in the jungle.

"I'm so glad you have friends," says Butler. "I find it strange when people don't, or they don't talk about them."

Casement doesn't know what to make of that statement other than that Butler is extremely friendly and often finds himself talking to people he doesn't know. Perhaps this explains his facility with identifying accents, Casement's included.

"Ah," says Butler, with mild astonishment, "look at the time. I have to meet my friends, and I hope you will join me."

The two men exchange a look.

"Of course, if you have other plans . . ."

"Would your friends mind my intruding?"

"My friends? No. But I must tell you," and here Butler leans in, "it's a bit of a rough place. Your fiancée might not approve."

"My fiancée? What fiancée?"

"Your future fiancée. Or your friend the missionary."

"What kind of place is this?"

"Don't worry. It's not what you're thinking."

Casement doesn't know what he's thinking.

"If you can tolerate cannibals, you'll tolerate this," says Butler.

"Now I'm intrigued."

"Good," says Butler. He throws down some bills. "My treat, and we're off!"

A short carriage ride later Casement finds himself on a street that is primarily warehouses. Butler jumps out and, after a brief exchange of pleasant argument, allows Casement to pay the driver. The door announces nothing, but Casement sees other carriages pulling up—women and men, but mostly men—and then a nice-looking brougham disgorges several wealthy-looking patrons onto the sidewalk. They look around and one woman lets forth a high-pitched giggle. She looks at Casement and Butler and finds them disappointing.

An unexceptional door leads to a narrow corridor, and this throat in turn leads to a cavernous hall that is a shock of noise and smoke and greasy light. Butler looks around and Casement does too, his eyes slowly adjusting to the dimness and cacophony.

"They're at the bar," Butler shouts out across music, because somewhere a band is playing, but Casement can't see it from where he's standing. Casement and Butler push around the patrons, dodge through tables—seated at one are two women dressed in dinner jackets like men. Some men are wearing rouge. But it is very dark and therefore easy to assign such spectacle—at least temporarily—to poor light. They reach the counter and Butler is greeted by his friends, four of them, and extra bar stools are found, and they sit and are introduced. A Mr. George, with red hair. A Mr. Rourke, who looks instantly suspicious of Casement. A Mr. Smith, who has a firm handshake and strong gaze that seem almost rehearsed. A Mr. Abruzzi, who looks younger than the others, who are all about Casement's age, twenty-five, or older.

"Where did you meet this Mister Casement?" asks Rourke.

"I saw him at the lunch cart on Thirty-Fourth Street. He looked confused."

"And is he?" asks Rourke.

"To look at him," says George, "he's less confused by the minute."

"One day you'll find you've made one mistake too many," says Rourke.

"Your concern is much appreciated, Rourke," says Butler.

"One day I'll end up burying you," says Rourke. He studies Casement.

At the distant end of the bar there is a woman in a long, pink dress standing on the counter itself. There she is, stepping around the drinks. She turns and flips up her skirt and whoever is treated to the view laughs out loud. As no one notices, Casement affects not noticing. Her hair is shorn like a boy's.

"You need a drink, Mister Casement," says George. "I suggest you buy yourself one, and one for everyone else, me included. And I'll have whiskey."

Butler shakes his head. "Casement is our guest."

"I don't mind, really," says Casement. "You did get dinner."

"Do you know, Mister Casement, what is the only thing worse than a friend who is poor?"

"No. What is it?" Maybe this is a joke.

"A friend that is rich."

It is a joke.

"He never thinks about money, so he never has it," explains Smith. "Never," he repeats, looking at George.

"That's not true. I'm just a little short on cash tonight," says Mr. George. And laughter ensues. But Casement is buying the first round, and he's happy to do it. And there's nothing untoward happening, not yet, and if it does he can always leave.

Abruzzi leans in to Casement. He has olive skin, heavy lashes, a narrow face with thin, elegant nose. "Mister Casement," he says in an accent that he is burying under layers of studied etiquette and genuine grace, "don't mind Rourke. He's right to caution our Sammie."

"Where are you from, Mister Casement?" says Rourke. His accent announces he's a Dubliner.

"Magherintemple," says Casement.

Rourke shakes his head, but he takes the drink that Casement has bought for him. And at the end of the evening, when more drinks have been consumed than can be reasonably counted, it is Rourke who leads the way past the urinals and into the back alley.

Casement wakes early into the quiet of his room. At first, in the stillness, he hears his breathing and his breathing seems an alien sound, as if his inhabiting of his body is something new—as if he should be of the air. That's the sensitive thinking that comes after drink. And now the show in pictures of the evening, unbidden, begins. There is Rourke, "I'll show you the way," and Casement following him through the tables, Rourke checking over his shoulder to make sure that Casement is still with him. And then the marble urinals in a long row opposite the wooden stalls. And Casement is using the urinal, and Rourke too, although Rourke finishes first. And then Rourke ducks his head down, checking beneath the stall doors, which are all closed. Perhaps a stall is free? But no. And then Casement is buttoned up, thinking they'll head back to the bar, but Rourke grabs his wrist and jerks his head towards another door. Casement hesitates because he doesn't know what Rourke is on about and Rourke says, "Fresh air," and Casement says nothing, just wanders after him and then they're in the alley. And then Rourke presses his mouth on Casement's and Casement can feel the man's stubble. Then Rourke is unbuttoning Casement's trousers as expertly as he must handle his own and after that. Well.

At what moment did this happen to him? At what moment?

Was it when he followed Rourke into the alley? Or the men's room? Was it when he allowed his affection for Ward to grow? Was it when he chose Africa, a moral vacuum, which is why all the missionaries are drawn—sucked even—to that place?

Or his time spent in the company of Nina and Gee?

He doesn't feel womanly at all. Mayala Swami. No. If anything, he feels completely masculine. This is a life for a man among men. After this moment's delirious affirmation, it hits. And this miasmic self-loathing, because of the ecstasy of the previous evening, has a depth to it. A coldness. He is alone. He is alone.

He remembers the woman tripping her way down the bar, lightly, and when this pink-frocked creature drew near, his surprise that it was a boy—maybe sixteen years old. The dress was sliding down the front, showing smooth skin and sparse hair. He was sashaying along. He slipped the neckline off his shoulder and winked at Casement, spun around. He was wearing men's shoes, brutally beaten up, worn at such an angle on the heels that the shoe leather itself was wearing away on the outer corners. His legs were disarmingly hairy. And the boy's hands, obviously callused as they clutched the pink fabric, had red knuckles and dirty, rough-cut nails. His hair stood in a blond shock. Butler smiled at the boy.

"Here you go, Jimmy," he said, giving him a coin. "And be careful with your skirt. I almost got you with my cigar."

"Oh Mister Butler," said the boy, his voice an incongruous growl. "I am already on fire!"

Dry toast will do for breakfast. Sarita's agitated and with good reason. These weeks in New York have been a trial. The previous evening she ambushed her father by the water closet. She'd accused her father of being quiet, because that's all she could politely do.

"You've been quiet, Father," Sarita had said.

"No, I haven't." He'd looked her up and down. "Life is a job," he said.

She'd managed some sort of protest, although what she'd said was lost to her, lost in the eruption of incredulity following her father's last statement.

Father had raised his hand calmly, silencing her. "Has he talked to you? Because he hasn't talked to me."

And no, Ward hadn't really talked to her, just chatted, although she knew for a fact that his chat-and-chat-and-chat sprang from different reasons than Brock-Innes's. Men who didn't have money were supposed to talk about prospects. Even Ward knew that. But he'd talked about lecture sites, made jokes, played with her cat—done anything to be there in the drawing room without having a real conversation. Ward had no prospects, she thought, although—her stomach sinks—he had talked about his article for *Scribner's*. Surely that wasn't his prospect? Writing for the newspapers? But what on earth can she expect? She met an adventurer who has revealed himself to be a circus performer. And sheep shearer. And prospector. She pushes her plate—toast untouched—away from her.

"Aren't you hungry, dear?" asks her mother.

She looks at her mother's plate that is heaped with bacon and jam and eggs and bread—all untouched.

"No, I'm not," she replies.

And then, announcing himself as always with a flap of the paper and that dark chuckle with which he takes his first look at the financial page, here is Father. Sarita looks over at the maid who, bored out of her brains, is staring at the ceiling. "Coffee, please," she says. The maid stirs into motion with a bland look on her face, pouring the coffee well. Mother likes this one because her hands are nice and small, unlike her predecessor, who has been "promoted" to some role in a dark corner of the house so that Mother isn't assaulted with her manly paws. Sarita can still remember the early days in Buenos Aires, her mother sewing their drawers out of rough cloth on a borrowed machine.

Father tosses the paper down on the table and takes his seat. "Any New Year's invitations?" he asks Sarita.

Sarita gives her father an inscrutable expression.

Mother answers, "Three so far."

"Well, that's three more than last year," says Sarita.

"That's a good thing," says Mother.

"When is your sister getting here?" asks Father. "She's such a pleasant girl."

"Is that why you're in such a good mood, Father?"

"One reason. And then," low chuckles, "there's always the state of the Argentinean stock exchange."

Something in his chuckle bothers her. He must have a deal going down that's not quite aboveboard. Father gets particular joy from bilking the establishment.

"Anything from Mister Brock-Innes?" asks Mother.

Mother had sent Paz to the drugstore earlier that day, meaning that she was short of some medication, which might account for her sudden interest in life. "Mister Brock-Innes has gone hunting with some friends in Scotland."

"I hope there won't be any young ladies there," says Mother.

"Somehow, I doubt it," says Sarita. Father is hidden behind the *Wall Street Journal*. "I did get an interesting letter from Mister Ward. Apparently, his lecture in Boston was sold out. Based on that, they've booked a larger venue here in New York. And there will be tickets for all of us held at the door." Ward is still lecturing in Canada, or some such place.

"Mister Ward is becoming quite the celebrity," says Mother. She's unsure whether or not that's a good thing.

"I suppose he is," says Sarita.

"A little celebrity is all right if you don't mind work," says Father.

What is Father on about? "He lived with man-eating savages for five years," she counters, which was meant to prove something but, as Sarita thinks about it, only proves exactly what it states. "Are you using the carriage, Father? I'm supposed to meet Garnet for lunch."

"Where is she?"

"On the Park, at Sixty-Second."

"Take the carriage. I'll walk. Looks like a nice day."

"Who's getting Ettie?" says Mother.

"I am, Mother. The train gets in at seven."

"And who's going to get the trunks?"

"They have porters there."

"What if they steal everything?"

"Mother, this isn't Buenos Aires. You don't need to bring your own porters." Sarita hears herself. She sounds like an eighteen-year-old, even though she'll be thirty this August. Mother is right. Father is right. She is right. She needs to get married, if only to stop being a daughter. Of course she's getting Ettie. *And* she goes over the weekly accounts with Baxter. *And* she supervises the hiring of new maids, the shutting down of the house after the winter season, the booking of steamer tickets. She's incredibly useful. "More coffee, please." Maybe Father won't let her get married. Maybe she should elope. But that doesn't usually end well. She thinks of poor Isabella Linton in *Wuthering Heights*, manipulated, unloved, ankle deep in mud, the driving wind blowing greasy hanks of hair around her shivering shoulders.

120

But if Sarita stays here, she'll lose her mind. And if she marries Brock-Innes, she'll lose her mind. And Mr. Ward has such a short attention span—even if he loves her now (does he?)—who knows what he'll be thinking in another six months, when he's done lecturing? When he's a journalist, or a painter, or . . . What is left? A fireman? A magician? Her hands fly up to her temples and she knocks the coffee pot out of the maid's well-shaped hands.

"Sarita!" says Father.

"Well, I've probably had enough coffee," she says, getting up from the table. The maid is scrambling to wipe the up the rug and several assistants have been conjured from the paneling to assist in this. "I am sorry," she says to the maid.

"Quite all right, Miss," says the maid.

"Sarita," her mother calls to her as she's leaving. "If it's nerves . . ."

"I'm fine, Mother. I just need some air."

Sarita takes the carriage to Garnet's house, which is a grander residence with a marble vestibule, curving staircase, and an odd little Juliet balcony that Sarita doesn't quite understand. Maybe for puppet shows? Or perhaps it's one of those architectural pieces that Garnet's father brings back from Italy, although this one would do better stuck somewhere in the house in Newport, which—on account of its size—absorbs such eccentricities. Sarita hands her hat and gloves to the maid, slips out of her cloak, nods in a polite way, and soon—appearing on the crazy balcony, red hair flowing—is Garnet.

"Sarita!"

"Garnet, what are you wearing?"

"It's Japanese, of course," says Garnet.

Of course. It looks like a bathrobe—made out of high-quality furniture brocade—and on Garnet, as with everything, is stunning.

"Come up," says Garnet. "And hurry. I am simply dying to find out what's happening in England."

In the parlor, Garnet kicks off her slippers and collapses into a couch. To sit close, Sarita takes the piano bench.

"Tell me everything," says Garnet.

"There's nothing to tell," says Sarita, not intentionally lying, but just because that's what she usually says. "And where's Wallace?"

"Of course, he's at the bank. But you would forget that, because you've been in London, where no one works. How's the new house?"

"A bit bare. The location is very good. You'll have to visit."

"I wish!" Garnet closes her eyes. When she opens them, it is with profound, dramatic gravity. "I can't travel for a while."

"Really?" says Sarita.

"That's the bad news."

"And the good news?"

"I have a progressive doctor who says I should wear whatever I want and avoid headaches."

Garnet is pregnant. "Congratulations. That explains everything."

"It explains the state of my hair. But if you're ever getting rid of Paz, let me know."

Paz is known for her skill at executing the latest styles. "You'd have to learn Spanish," says Sarita. "Does this mean you're not going to any of New Year's balls? Because if you're not going, I'm not. I'm calling in sick."

And that's what she feels about her whole life right now. Could she call in sick? Garnet prattles on and on, divulging intimacies that would no doubt make Wallace very uncomfortable, but everything as communicated by Garnet becomes funny. "Did you know that could happen to men?" says Garnet, raising her eyebrows suggestively.

"No," says Sarita, and they laugh like schoolgirls and only later does Garnet say, "I'm terrified of the baby coming. I'm terrified of blood and pain and you know I never knew my mother. And everyone says I look—and am built—just like her."

"You could get lucky," says Sarita. "The baby could have Wallace's head," which comes to a point like a pencil and has been the subject of fun ever since Garnet met him. And Garnet laughs, but her terror is real. The sun cuts through the clear December air and floods the room, catching gold in Garnet's hair. "Don't worry, Gar. It will all be fine."

"Easy for you to say. Or say now."

"What are you implying?"

"You had a shipboard romance."

"You can't believe everything you hear."

"Unless it's from Mabel."

Mabel is Garnet's maid, who is good friends with the cook, who—having lived in Cuba—speaks Spanish and is friends with Paz. "I met an interesting man."

"He's African."

"Not that interesting," says Sarita.

"You must be scared," says Garnet.

"Of what?" says Sarita.

"I bet he's an animal."

"Why?" says Sarita. "Because he was in Africa?"

"Yes, absolutely."

But this is Garnet's fantasy. Wallace is nice but boring. She whispers in Sarita's ear. "It will be much larger than you think."

"What are you talking about?"

"You know exactly what I'm talking about." Garnet's voice drops lower. "But it will fit. He'll make it fit, that's what men do. That's what it's all about." And Garnet's rueful nodding starts them both laughing.

Ward is back in New York, having arrived the night before. He had originally told Sarita that he would visit in the afternoon since he'd hoped to see Casement right off, but Casement isn't at the hotel and, according to Mrs. Sawyer, has been keeping to himself and is out very late some nights—or so her nephew, who acts as the night watchman, has told her. So Ward decides to walk over to Sarita's house to see if she's about. He has had very little exercise of late and his trousers, purchased in Rotterdam when he had to get suits for the Manyema, are getting snug. And it's a nice day—cold and dry—although he still has the wing-coat that's on the large size and, here in New York where all the stylish people are wearing fitted topcoats, is even more ridiculous than on the boat. There are a lot of people about. Ward is drawing close to Sarita's house when he sees her, although he does not recognize her at first. She appears galloping along the footpath—not a real gallop, but a sort of skip that in its lopsided repetition recalls a horse and it's only when she stops and turns to the child (who he now sees is beside her) that he makes the connection. She's dusting her hands off dramatically and then she rests them on her hips.

He hears, as he draws closer, "But what if I don't want to be a monkey?"

And the child, a boy of maybe six years, says, "Then you can't be my friend."

"Why not?"

"Because monkeys and horses can't be friends."

She is about to respond when Ward interrupts her. "Miss Sanford," he says.

And Sarita, startled, looks to him. "Mister Ward, fancy running into you."

"I think you were galloping."

Sarita nods, matter-of-fact. "This is Henry, my nephew. Henry, this is Mister Ward."

"Tell her," says the boy.

"Tell her what?" says Ward. He hasn't been around children that weren't carrying his rifle and isn't sure what tone of voice one is supposed to use.

"Tell her that monkeys and horses can't be friends," says the boy.

"Monkeys and horses can't be friends."

"So we're all monkeys?" asks Sarita. "All right, fellow monkey, off you go, and wait at the corner." She smiles at Ward. "So what brings you over here?"

"You."

"I was expecting you later."

"I can come back."

"I think it's all right, provided you don't mind being friends with a monkey."

"Not friends," says Ward.

Sarita stops to look at him. He is so suddenly grave that she anticipates the punch line of a particularly well-delivered joke.

He says, "I think you should marry me."

Ward hadn't been in love with her. He had appreciated her, like a well-sighted rifle or some excellent wine. Maybe it was seeing her galloping down the street, unconcerned. Or her frank manner with the child. That too, surely, but more than that was the instant he recognized her face and felt a flood of relief. Relief. Seeing her on the sidewalk, he got the same feeling as when he finished a long, terrifying march and found a clearing, a fire, the promise of food and shelter. Sarita is the promise of something like shelter, and even though he does not know her well, he knows that she is home to him. She pats the back of his elbow, steering him back up the street, and lightly takes his arm. They're walking. Henry scuttles ahead, weaving through the legs of passersby. She turns to him.

"Mister Ward, I don't know you."

Ward thinks. "You might not marry me if you did."

Sarita gives him a curious smile as people on the sidewalk move in a hurried, jerky river of human activity, as the sound in the clear air ricochets, making every conversed word about him sound like laughter, as the birds sing in support of this marriage and the sun presents a particularly benign face. She looks at him, biting her lower lip, as if he's a piece of cake that she wants but does not really need, and he knows he's won her.

On the next block they reach the Sanford house. Through the windows one can see activity as the downstairs curtains are being changed and the lack of modesty—the house's exposure—is palpable. Maids are working as quickly as they can with ladders and stepladders. Manservants keep the drapes off the floor, extended between them to prevent wrinkling. "It's going to be a bit nutty in there," she says, "but we can probably get coffee."

Henry disappears down the corridor with a savage whooping. The housemaid takes Sarita's coat and—after a curious look—Ward's.

"Doris, what is Paz doing?"

"The curtains, miss."

"And my sister?"

"She's with the baby. She asked not to be disturbed."

"Well, the house is upside down. Let's go sit in the dining room."

Ward chooses a chair at the long table while Sarita heads to the kitchen, but he's restless. He pauses at a cabinet filled with silver—he's seen these before, but usually the urns and soup tureens are old family stuff, handed down, but of sentimental and historical value. All this silver finery is beyond doubt new. It sparkles, and then, as his eyes readjust, he sees his reflection in the glass panel. Ward gets a feeling of what it might be to have money. He then sees Sarita reflected behind him as she enters the room.

"Coffee's on its way," she says. "Seriously, how long does it take to put the curtains up with something like eight people involved?"

Is she dodging real conversation, or is this what's occupying her mind? "Are you thinking about what I asked you?"

She flips her chin up, and her eyes, now thinking. "It was more of a suggestion."

"Really?"

"You said, 'I think you should marry me.'"

"It was a proposal."

She nods but stays on the other side of the table.

"I'd like to talk to your father, but I won't if you don't want me to."

"Herbert," she says, trying out his name, "have you thought it through? I wouldn't want you to make a mistake."

"I'm thinking now," he says. "I think the marriage is a very good idea."

"Why?" she asks.

"Because," he considers, "I can't imagine life without you." He realizes that's a cliché. Strip the language. "Because," answer her question truthfully, "everything leads to you."

"The Congo leads to me?" She is skeptical, although curious.

"And the Mississippi."

"The Amazon?"

"The Nile. The Seine."

She sinks into a chair and for a moment he's worried he's upset her. She brings her hand to cover her mouth and every second or so shakes her head in a little shudder, as if in disbelief. She rests her hand on his arm. "Go and talk to my father now. Lunch will be served in twenty minutes and he'll be in a hurry to get out of the conversation."

"And that's good for us?"

"Unless he's hungry and in a bad mood."

Sarita waits with her sister, who never has much to say, which is most often dull but currently a relief. Ettie shifts on her chair, adjusting the sleeping baby that's limp as a rag doll, snoring, mouth open. "They're so precious at this age. I think she's going to look like Elizabeth. Don't you?"

Elizabeth is the sister who died in New Orleans. "I don't remember Elizabeth," says Sarita.

"I do. She had your gray eyes and my dark hair. And she was a tiny little thing, very slender."

That's because she was dying, thinks Sarita.

"Are you going to marry him?"

"Do you think I should?"

Ettie adjusts the baby and shifts on her hips. "It's all about the children, Sarita. What's the worst that can happen? If you two grow apart, you'll have the children. You'll see. You'll care about your husband for a while and I never wish James any harm. He gave me Henry and Annabel and this little angel, but I don't really care about him."

Sarita laughs. "That's not true. You do care about James."

"No, I don't. It's better this way. I do look out for him, you know . . . make him change his tie because it has soup on it, or something."

"You're being ridiculous."

"Do you think he wants me to care more? Of course not. We're the happiest couple I know."

Which is hilarious, but, on the face of it, seems true.

VII
Lecture Circuit

January 1890

Casement, Glave, and Ward, now reunited, are heading westward to San Francisco as Ward continues his lecture tour, bringing the spectacle that is the Congo into the still-spectacular United States. The train is rumbling, as trains do. Casement likes the meter of the word "thunderstorm" to describe the sound of it and the fact that the word itself beats in time with their progression across the country. He writes "thunderstorm" and looks at its presence on the page, a tiny tempest of ink upon a sea of cream-colored nothing. He should write an "American" poem but is not sure what that would entail. He knows that Whitman is all the rage but is not sure what is accomplished by the removal of rhyme and meter. What's left? And the stuff itself is oddly naked—exposed. He prefers Longfellow, but for him to pursue poetry in this vein seems uninspired. America itself is difficult to pinpoint, can seem like a nation of disparate historical facts that resist coming together into a recognizable whole.

The American Civil War has been over for a quarter century and, with it, slavery. The Transcontinental Railroad was completed twenty years earlier with Irishmen laboring from the east and Chinamen working from the west, this meridian seam sealed with a golden spike. Indian Wars are still being fought and the great Indian nations—the Apache, Sioux, Cheyenne—are losing and as they expire make all feel complicit in the extinction of a gorgeous, wild thing. As the natives are cleared, the space must be filled, and Europe has the stuff. In New York alone, 5,000 new immigrants are disgorged at Castle Garden every day, many of them Irish. In America, the Negro is black, but not African, although Liberia—the inverse of a Promised Land—has existed since the 1850s. The movements of people, the extermination of people, the enslavement of people, the creation of nations, the destruction of nations—it is all happening in the context of America. The sky in these United States stretches uninterrupted. The plain stretches uninterrupted. Ward stretches, belches in his sleep, with his hands folded neatly in his lap. Ward sleeps everywhere, an untroubled soul—uninterrupted. Casement looks at the blank page, which stretches: uninterrupted.

If he could only cobble a few lines together.

He would like to write about disappearing Comanche and the pride of Negroes, but his thoughts are degraded by the knowledge of Ward's impending marriage. He tells himself that it means nothing. This is where Ward was heading—his only destiny. Ward is not an eternal bachelor, like Glave. Nor an eternal bachelor, like him. And he does not know what it means that Ward has chosen this clear-minded, older, wealthy woman to be his bride. Perhaps this is why it feels like betrayal. This Miss Sanford is not what he had imagined for Ward. She is not a modern-day country maid with pink cheeks and a light laugh. The train lurches, waking Ward, who seems momentarily alarmed, but quickly settles—dog-like—back to sleep. The occasional farmhouses and barns register like sound across the empty landscape. And there it is, the plaintive wail of the train barreling along and this time—as every time now—Casement feels that he has made that howl, that it has come from him.

"Anything good?" asks Glave.

"No, not really."

"Every time I ask, you give me that or a similar response."

Casement smiles. "I hate to think of the reason for that."

"Do you really think you're a bad poet?" Glave is teasing. "Why do it all these years, then? Why not write articles? At least you get paid."

"Why do we do these things we do? I'm lazy," says Casement. "No one needs to see the poems and so they don't need to meet anyone's standards but my own."

"Why write at all?"

"I could tie knots. And then untie them." Casement likes creating, controlling, and his poet voice has an unmarred nobility to it. And he doesn't think he's bad, not really. It's more that the subject of his poems—his Ireland, her history—demands a certain sort of listener, and Glave, much as Casement likes him, is not that man. "I like writing," says Casement.

"Although when you're doing the composing, you look completely miserable."

"Poetry is difficult."

"Why not keep a diary?"

"I do." Besides, he finds much of what Glave and Ward produce to be utterly false—somehow stringing together bits of reality but in a way that creates a cheap, tin version of the Congo. Casement knows the transaction. The American and British public desire a particular cut of Africa and the scribblers work to produce it to the exact specifications as requested, using snippets of the truth but cobbling them in a way that is not representative. The Congo is hacked into pieces for shipment, as might happen in an abattoir, and these choice cuts no more represent Africa than roasts and cutlets and minced meat can represent a cow.

Ward has sent a telegram to his family in Sacramento, inviting them to his talk. Casement had watched Ward struggle to compose it, and then—unasked—helped with the wording. *In San Francisco Feb 17. Stop. Lecture at Platts Hall 7PM. Stop. Tickets saved at door. Stop. Your Herbert. Stop.*

Ward had not been sure about the "your Herbert" part, and he was not sure if the telegram would reach his parents. Ward had saved his mother's letter and of course this was the source of his information, but the letter—at this point—was over a year old and something in his mother's tone had made Ward think that all was not well. She had said something about "the good Lord" providing and exceptional lives requiring exceptional people. Ward was of the opinion that no one would show up and was frank about the dread and disappointment this would cause him. And Casement, initially tempted to tell Ward that his family would be there, of course, beyond a doubt, had instead just clapped him on the shoulder and said, "Have you told them about Sarita? That you're getting married?" Ward hadn't. They didn't. None of that had made it into the cable. Ward nodded, happy to be redirected to the future, which was comfort to him. Although no comfort to Casement.

The train is shuddering to a stop. Again. These trains. As they cross. This. Remarkable. Continent.

"Where are we?" asks Ward, now awake.

Glave says, "Somewhere between somewhere and somewhere."

Which is nowhere. Or perhaps Nebraska. "I'm getting out," says Casement.

There's a need for water, and cargo has to be moved to another carriage—things that Casement is glad are not his responsibility. The engineer tells him that they will be stopped for an hour. A ten-minute walk up a dirt path will bring Casement to a farm, if he's interested, where he can purchase a glass of fresh milk. Casement is not much of a milk drinker but as Glave is deep in his notes and isn't leaving the train, and Ward has nodded off again, he decides he'll take this stroll and buy this milk. It's cold and he wraps his coat tight, pushes his fists deep into his pockets.

As he makes his way into this broad landscape of no shelter that feels nothing like the Congo, but perhaps a bit like a frozen South African savannah, he is struck by the grandeur of absence. The farmhouse, although at a distance, is completely visible. For a moment Casement has the sensation that the only two points in existence are the train and this farmhouse and that he shuttles back and forth between them as if a walker on a tightrope. His leather soles slip on the frozen ground. At the front of the house, no one is visible, so he makes his way around it where he sees the edge of a barn and the planking of a hastily constructed corral. On the railing of the corral are several pelts—wolves or coyotes. Casement is momentarily intrigued and then he sees what is contained in the pen. There are five bison, a small herd, and they have been waiting for him because they all meet his gaze with theirs, judging and silent except for the sound of their rough exhalations. Great curls of steam escape their nostrils. These are enormous animals with sentient eyes. Casement is struck by their noble appearance and feels the tragic reality about their captivity. He thinks of Indians and wonders if there's a poem in that— *their fulminating breath, a sad few left*. He wonders how many poets have equated bison and Indians.

From the farmer, Casement takes a glass of milk and purchases a pie. And then Casement is retracing his footsteps back to the train.

"What have you got there?" says Ward, already with his pocketknife in hand, blade unsheathed.

"It's a pumpkin pie," Casement says.

"I already know that this pie," Glave adds, "will be the best thing I've ever eaten."

As Casement takes his seat, takes the slice of pie offered by Ward on his cloth napkin, he has a vision of the train reeled back to Albany, a vision of the plains being repopulated with buffalo and Indians, of triumphant natives and prehistory, all this pillaging and destruction erased by the reverse movement of the train as it industriously tugs the New World— like a great curtain—back and back, returning it to pre-history. He wonders what can be restored. He wonders what can be saved.

"How do you find it?" asks Glave.

"How do I find what?" responds Casement.

"The pie," says Ward. "How do you find the pie?"

He thinks. "I find it very nice, preferable to crumbling cheese and stale bread and beef jerky." Which was actually deer jerky, but why split hairs? And soon enough there will be a constant supply of good food, for in another five days they will be in San Francisco, although he needs to be cautious with his money.

Glave and Casement go to have a pipe at the back of the train.

Casement eyes the bowl of his pipe, which is slow to light. He wonders if his tobacco is damp. "Glave, do you have your funding for the Yukon straightened out?"

"Close. There's real interest from *Frank Leslie's Illustrated Newspaper* and a couple of other places." Glave spent the last week in New York dodging in and out of newspaper and journal offices. He was pursuing any and all options for financing his Yukon adventure. "You won't believe what kept popping up."

"Herbert Ward's impending marriage to the very wealthy, somewhat older Sarita Sanford?"

"Merely a sidebar, Roddie," says Glave. "It's Sanford père who has everyone's attention. You know Sanford's got Lord Revelstoke wrapped around his little finger and Barings Bank has underwritten millions of pounds of stock for Sanford."

"We know this," says Casement.

"Ah, but do you know what the stocks pertain to?"

"Something in South America."

"Right. Railroads." Glave had paused for emphasis. "Railroads in Argentina. If this Argentine stock doesn't show a profit very soon, Barings Bank is going to be on the hook for all of it."

"Sounds vaguely familiar," said Casement.

"Yes it does. This is the same cocktail that caused the Panic of 1873."

"I was thinking more of Trollope's *The Way We Live Now.*" Casement laughs. "Does that make our Herbert Sir Felix Carbury?"

Glave considers. "Felix Carbury was a penniless aristocrat, whereas 'Our Herbert' is just penniless."

Casement is attending Ward's talk. The hall is packed to capacity. Despite the December chill, the air in the lecture hall is still and hot. Casement sits in the balcony with the family of Ward's fiancée, these Sanfords: the neurasthenic mother, the avaricious father, the benumbed sister, and her husband—pleasant and dull. The odors of cigar smoke and sweat emanate from the men. The women—when they shift in their seats—lift floral scented clouds into the air. If he were the kind of person who said things were unbearable when they were, in truth, bearable, he would say it of this heat. His discomfort gives his disposition an edge, exaggerated because he is nervous on Ward's behalf.

A smatter of applause introduces Ward to the stage. *You were in a circus,* thinks Casement. How hard can this be? Ward begins to speak. Gesticulating in a manic way, he stalks the stage's perimeters. He will describe all of Africa, as that is what he's promised to do, and pull it off in the course of a single hour.

Casement is, as he well knows, indulgent towards Ward, but the presentation seems a combination of balderdash, the ravings of an egomaniac, and—awkwardly—the truth. Casement holds his breath through the first few minutes, waiting for Ward to be laughed off the stage. But he isn't. Although his talk has had an admittedly slow start, Ward quickly finds his pace. Now, he could be talking about anything—or nothing—and the audience would still be mesmerized. Ward struts and harrumphs and enacts—blam, blam of invisible rifle, awed face at felled elephant—and everyone follows along, as if children at a Christmas pantomime. Casement steals a sly look at the Sanfords, gauging their reaction, Mother Sanford, Father Sanford, Sister and Brother-in-Law Sanford, are rapt. But Sarita (surprise, surprise) seems equally bemused as Casement—on the point of laughing. He wonders what she's thinking and then she catches him—his looking at her—and her face breaks into a broad smile: They share a secret.

On the hall steps as the venue empties, she approaches him. Her vivid eyebrows dart around. "Mister Casement, does our Mister Ward do the Congo justice?"

Which is an odd choice of words, given the rampant injustice that is being unleashed upon its natives. Casement responds, "That's just what it's like. Inexplicably hot with Ward leaping around, keeping us entertained."

She laughs in an unguarded way, as if they're old friends.

And then her eyes had spark, her voice dropping an octave. "Do you know that man?" she asks. "He seems to be looking at you."

Casement hazards a look in the direction suggested by Miss Sanford's gaze. There is the red hair, rosy cheeks, and overly snug jacket of his friend Mr. George. George is accompanied by a thin, insect-like woman—his wife, or so Casement assumes by the way she has her tapering fingers sunk into George's elbow. He delivers a warm smile and as this smile slides into pity, quickly nods. "I have met him," says Casement, "over drinks once. He was a bit short on cash."

Miss Sanford has not worked to charm him. She has tried to win him over with her wit and fun and intelligence. And all this strikes Casement as very strange since wit and fun and intelligence in women certainly appeal to him, but the occasional European ladies who have previously drawn Ward's attention—the type Ward might marry—are all coy, retiring things, girls who duck behind fans and beneath parasols, daughters of missionaries or consuls who think of marriage as a process of adoption whereby one escaped the clutches of one's parents by escaping to a husband.

Miss Sanford is attractive—slim, elegant, with expressive gray eyes—but she isn't charming in the traditional sense. According to Glave, she is nearly thirty. Why, wonders Casement, has she decided to marry now? And why would this woman whose father controls—according to reliable sources—Lord Revelstoke, and therefore Barings Bank, and therefore England and all that that implies, choose Ward?

VIII
Sark

May 1890

He should be writing his story, generously commissioned by Harmsworth, but it is hard to focus knowing that Sarita is in the other room. Ward is going to have to get used to it, because marriage is all about the other person in the other room, or the other person in the same room—the other who, like a volcano, even when not currently commanding attention, can threaten to explode across one's landscape. Sarita will like this comparison. No. He won't share it, because, chances are, she feels more this way than he does.

Sarita had wanted to visit the Channel Islands ever since she'd read Hugo's *Toilers of the Sea*. She found Sark, with its plunging cliffs and surging ocean, preferable to hectic Rome, which she'd envisioned as swinging between gypsy mob madness and museum galleries filled with Londoners and Bostonians. Ward had gone along persuaded by Sark's remoteness and its promise of poor mail service.

Stanley has taken to lecturing on the horrors of the Rear Guard and Ward is so often implicated that he feels himself to be the Saint Sebastian of insult, martyred to the cause of Stanley's knighthood. He's promised Sarita he won't think about any of this on their honeymoon. So exile it is—exile from his thoughts, escape from reality, a little uncomplicated practice run of what married life is like.

Sark seems to fire up the imagination. And there's a lot to look at—rustic people, wild landscape. He's missed his drawing. London does not bear recording in this manner. Ward likes to draw things he might never see again—to save them—and London is proud of repeatedly presenting the same things at the same times: up at half seven, hot water for shaving at eight, dressed and at breakfast by nine, lunch at one . . . as if life were a wheel that hit its marks with numbing accuracy.

Toplis, the local artist, likes to paint the cliffs, which Ward finds strange, because he prefers, when at the shore, to stare out to sea. Doesn't everyone? He can't imagine sitting with his back to the waves, sketching more obstruction and less view, although the Sark coastline is dramatic and varied—mysterious. The island coyly gathers its cliffs around it. Ward jogs his foot back and forth, as if it might pedal his imagination off the curb. In *Toilers* one of the characters is, extravagantly, attacked by an octopus. Shall Ward borrow? He's leaning hard on his pencil and snaps the lead.

He is two weeks in to a two-month honeymoon, the purpose of which seemed obvious when he embarked on it—to learn about one's wife away from the predatory curiosity of one's in-laws—but now he is less sure. Sarita approaches the bedroom with a sort of cheerful wide-eyed fortitude, but he still isn't sure that he has the upper hand, even there. If his sexual experience might seem to privilege him in this regard, it somehow doesn't. He feels that he's stepped into a role, like a proven stud, although—to his knowledge—he has yet no children. The possibility that he might have fathered one in the Congo is enough to truly make him sweat, but he does not think this to be the case, and if he had done—unless the child were blond—no one would know about it. He imagines Bidi vanishing into the jungle and all traces of his presence in the Congo evaporating like the mists off the surface the river.

"Knock knock!" says Sarita, at the door. "Are you done with that piece for *Boys Own Paper*?"

Ward rallies his thoughts. "Do you think an octopus would attack a dog?"

"No."

"Well, then, I have nothing."

"Whether I think an octopus would attack a dog is beside the point. You're not writing for me. The readership of *Boys Own Paper* believe that the ghosts of Spanish pirates kidnap children and that hoards of Arabian treasure can be dug up in Harefield. So, how is it?"

"Why do you ask, Mrs. Ward?"

"I ask because it's a beautiful day and I want to go fishing."

"And where do you propose we go?"

"We could go to Creux Harbor. I've had luck there with the bream, but it's such nice weather that it might be fun to walk over to Gouliot Headlands."

"Let's do that," says Ward. "I could use some inspiration."

Sarita is good at fishing—another surprise—something she says she learned as a child. She's told him that she wasn't always wealthy but never supplied the details. Sarita doesn't like to show weakness. She knows her resilience puts her in a strong light, but that which necessitated this strength might temper it with vulnerability. He's watched her expertly dig the worms up, set the hooks, and cast. There's a nimbleness to all this activity—activity that awakens something in her, a memory of action tensing like a muscle—and he knows that once this fishing was more than a hobby.

"You carry the rods, Herbert," she says. "And don't poke me in the eye."

Sarita is lacing her own boots as she (the honeymooning radical) has forsaken her corset for a summer frock that doesn't require one.

"Let me carry the tackle," he says.

"What will I carry?"

"You carry the basket."

"That's what will be heavy coming home."

She walks quickly. He imagines if she could whistle, she would, but she doesn't know how: He's heard her try. "What are you thinking?" he asks.

"Me? I'm wondering if Garnet's had the baby yet."

"I wonder what kind of mother she'll make."

"I've asked her that," says Sarita, "and she points out how very attentive she is to her cat."

They laugh. The sun is high. The wind is stiff. Clouds scudding past cast exact shadows across the sheep pastures and nodding fields of wheat. A shepherd whistles to his dog and the dog comes. Another whistle sends the dog in another direction. The sheep are not around and this must be a lesson. Two horses, side by side, watch, heads at the gate, puffing and whinnying commentary as if they're two patrons at a bar.

"We are the only two people on earth," says Ward.

"What about that man with his dog?"

"We and that man with his dog are the only two people on earth."

Sarita likes this kind of joke.

At the Headlands, Sarita picks her way around the slope. If she slips, she'll fall a hundred feet down the cliff and into the water. She is confident, however, in her leather boots and heavy skirts, encumbered by the basket. She finds her preferred rock and settles on it. "Come on, Herbert," she says. He steps along the narrow path, placing one sure foot before another. She takes his rod and baits the hook, weaving the worm onto it.

"You didn't need to do that," he says.

"I just wanted to make sure it didn't slip off."

He shakes his head at her and then casts, a sure shot flying far across the waves, blown a few feet off course by a sudden gust, and then piercing the surface of the water. And then she casts farther off to the left. They sit and sit.

"You don't find this a touch uninspiring?" Herbert says after a half hour.

"I'm just waiting for the mackerel. I'm sure they're out there. Look how clear the water is."

They sit. And finally, Ward feels the knocking on his line that means that something has, at last, found his bait attractive. "Some luck," he says.

Sarita touches the line delicately, thinking. "It's a bream. Let it go a bit, and then strike it."

Herbert loses the bream—when he pulls up his line, there's nothing there, not even bait. Later, the mackerel do come in and Sarita hooks about four to Herbert's one. "You look busy, darling," he says. "Mind if I wander to the caves?"

"The tide's still high."

"I just want a peek. Thinking about my story."

"Be careful. Those heavy rains last week seem to have worn the edge off of that path."

"What are you, my wife?" Ward had used that phrase to admonish Casement on an almost daily basis, and Casement always had a response, but Sarita is completely taken with some development at the end of her line and she does not hear.

He moves around the grassy slope, the side of a rounded mound that has resulted from some long-ago geological event. Much of the gorse in the vicinity has been cut away for kitchen fires, but lucky for him, this gorse is in too precarious a position for easy harvest and is clinging along the cliff's border, holding some of the dirt in place. Agile as ever, Ward walks along the path, although he is aware of the gusting winds that, on more than one occasion, have knocked men into the sea. Here, there's a slippery bit, and then a few rough rocks, and after the opening to a chasm. If the tide were out, he would scale it downward until he was at sea level, but he spies a ledge. He'll lower himself in and find his way to it. There's a benefit to having been an acrobat. His body still responds in the old ways—balance, counterbalance—all of it instinctual and sure. Here on this rocky shelf, he feels safe. The sun struggles in from the mouth of the rock. The waves surge below, softly, softly, and then rise with a smack and spume of water.

He cannot see it, but he knows that all manner of treasure is hidden beneath the surface of the water. There are beadlet anemones—bright as jewels—and languid squid and rocks armored with mollusks. Eels inscribe their progress through the dark, vertical recesses. There are octopi. The shadowed walls of the cave drip with cold and a sense of comfort makes him both wish to stay there forever and to leave. He feels pushed to the edge of life, yet completely stilled. He puts his hand on his heart and feels it beating. Below, the water sings angrily against the rocks and the clash of pebbles raked by waves—an even, harsh hissing—echoes from the shore.

What has brought him here, from the Congo? What has brought him here, from Borneo? He remembers that youth walking on the tightrope in Melbourne, the drunken men jeering below, their stained teeth. He remembers that woman from the pie stand showing herself to him when he returned to his tent to dress. He was seventeen. He remembers shearing sheep in a long shed with Australian black fellows chatting amongst themselves and flies rising in clouds, sinking in waves. He remembers a red pelt flashing behind the trunks and vines of the Asian jungle. He remembers the sound of Jameson's pen scratching his horrors on the paper, and the thud of a snake falling from the hut's roof beam. In this cave he is meeting everything—all manner of everything. How does one continue?

In the harsh light and dry wind he approaches his wife. She turns to face him and now she looks quite small.

"Herbert," she says, "I wish the rest of my life could be just like this."

"Fishing."

"Fishing with you."

He's not sure that she was fishing with him. "Do you know what I'd like to be doing for the rest of my life?"

"What?"

He takes the rod from her and plants it in the ground.

"And then what happens?"

"Well," says Ward, "one of those waves hits them in the cave and goes and shoots the water up. You've seen that happen. There's a lot of force in that."

"But what does that have to do with the dog and the octopus?"

"Hendricks is very glad that he saved the dog from the octopus because, when the wave hits, he chucks the dog into the water and the dog gets shot all the way up through the entrance, back on dry land. And then the dog runs and gets help from someone."

"Maybe a shepherd."

"Or a farmer. What else is there around here? Anyway, the dog brings the shepherd or farmer back to the caves and Hendricks and Flanders grab on to a lowered rope and are brought to safety, all thanks to Rebel."

"Rebel is the dog?"

"Who else?"

"How many words is that?"

"About two thousand."

"Perfect," she says, "and perfectly preposterous."

They are walking down the avenue to get their mail, a part of their routine that has epically begun to take the entire morning. There are more visitors to the island and now when they stop at the Victoria Hotel, the tearoom is full of honeymooning couples and fancy families. One sees all manner of people crawling down the long ladders to reach the beach at Grande Greve. There are scrambling parties at Port du Moulin. The Coupee, that long narrow spine that connects to the encephalitic head of Little Sark, is now busy with Londoners—children running too close to the precipice, women obscuring the view with parasols, men rolling up sleeves to reveal unmanly forearms. Oh, she's been judging everyone. She can do that. Sarita doesn't need some local to carry her picnic basket and she's fine to scramble down the rocks free of ladders and ropes. With no Paz to remind her, she has been exposing her face to the sun and does not care should she return to London looking like a walnut.

Sarita waits as Herbert gets the mail. There's a damp edge to the wind and she wonders if the afternoon will bring rain.

"Two letters," says Herbert, exiting the post office. "One from Hatton for me, and this one, for you, from a Spencer Nyman."

Sarita reaches casually for her letter and Ward whips it out of reach. They exchange a look.

"Spencer Nyman. Garnet's brother."

"Does he look anything like his sister?"

"He is quite good-looking, but I prefer blonds."

Herbert lets her have the letter, and she taps it in her palm thoughtfully.

"Aren't you going to open it?"

"Not right now."

"Why not?"

Sarita smiles, raises her eyebrows. "What do you think that's about?" she says, referencing the Hatton letter with her chin.

Ward shakes the letter. "I have half a mind to burn it without opening it."

"You think it's about Stanley."

"No, because you've forbidden me to think about that, but if I were allowed to think about that, that's the first place my mind would go."

Of course it is about Stanley and Sarita gives Herbert a dispensation to mull it over, to wander down the well-worn ruts of his concern, to go over every little thing in this static past and quickly setting present, to turn and churn and torture each completed and possible development as he sits on the floor in the corner of the cottage, knees pulled up, imploring some uncaring God to fix it all. Through all of this, Sarita isn't even sure if he's entirely innocent. Herbert probably did have a woman in Africa, must have. At least one. To be honest, right now she doesn't even care, so long as he keeps stuck in this self-absorbed and all-absorbing monologue.

After a simple meal of pork cutlets and roast potatoes, after Greta has washed up and made her way across the moonlit field to her house, Herbert presents Sarita with Spencer Nyman's letter.

"I'm not sure why you don't want to read this," he says. "It's probably about Garnet."

"It's definitely about Garnet," says Sarita.

Herbert's eyes cross her face, looking for clues.

"Why is Spencer Nyman writing to me about his sister?"

Herbert looks at the letter, treating it with more respect.

"You open it, Herbert."

"Me?"

"I want you to."

Herbert settles into his seat across the table and tears open the flap. It's a short letter and she watches his bright eyes flicker across its information. She sees his mouth tighten and hears his sigh, although it is controlled and very quiet. "So," Sarita braces, "she's gone, then."

"I am so sorry."

"And the baby?"

"I'm afraid the baby did not make it. It was a girl."

Sarita does not move. Her eyes fill up, but she controls herself. She knows that Herbert is watching her and is so outside herself that she manages her sensations through what he must be seeing, sees herself slump into the chair, sees herself shake her head as if to find a preferable reality, sees herself draw deeper inwards.

"Sarita . . ."

"Garnet was my best friend," she says, although that was obvious to everyone. "I loved her more than anyone except my father." This much honesty cannot be good, but Herbert is not easily frightened and sits in place. "I'm to have a baby," she says. She gauges Herbert's surprise, his suppression of happiness. "Maybe it will be a girl too."

"I will welcome a girl," he says, small joy creeping past the caution.

"Maybe it will be a boy." Sarita shrugs. "Maybe it will kill me."

He feels he should comfort her but knows that is not what Sarita wants. She demands a constant, exhausting honesty. "I really liked Garnet." He feels his own eyes filling. "She made you happy and that made me happy. Her death does no one any good."

Sarita nods. "I'm going for a walk."

"I'll go with you."

"I'd rather be alone." Sarita stands from the table and pushes her chair back, grinding the legs across the floor. He watches her walk out the front door without her shawl. She is barely gone when he realizes that he has to follow her whether she wants it or not. This is what he needs to do.

The clouds have come in but somewhere behind this screen the moon is nearly full and the path—packed dirt—glows between the fields and cottages. He checks to the left, towards the Headlands, and then up the road and sees her—or some vague woman figure moving quickly—by the mill. As she rounds the curve in the path, he loses her in the shadows, but there she is again. He hurries to reach the corner of the Avenue and sees her by the gate of the old monastery. Ward clings to the shadows, not sure why he is hiding or why he does not call out for her to wait. He sees Sarita disappear at the corner. She is heading west. On his right, the blank fields fill with moonlight, but she has headed to the tunnel of trees and is no doubt weaving her way on the narrow paths that skirt the stream. Ahead, he can hear the leaves rustle beneath her feet, the occasional snap of a twig, and then there is silence. She must have reached the packed dirt of the cliff path.

Before him is blackness now, the moonlight obscured behind a wall of rock, and then he sees a perfect square of brightness. He has reached the Window, a lookout hole blasted through the cliff with man-made exactness. The drop from this ledge could kill, but now with the moon softened by the fabric of cloud and the crash of waves swallowed into the darkness, it seems almost as likely that one could float upward—that gravity would have relaxed her hold. Even the stars have been erased in the gray wash, hidden behind the clouds as sunken ships hide beneath waves. Sarita is in shadow—must be—sitting with her back against the wall, listening to the waves assault the cliffs.

"Sarita."

"I said I wanted to be alone."

"I'll be quiet." And he is, for a while, but there is so much he wants to say to her. Ward also knows that she's aware of his presence and is being silent as a way of disciplining him to her need for boundaries. "You don't want to be alone," he says. "You want Garnet to be alive." He hears her adjust her position. "Let's go home and have a glass of brandy." He gets up, extends a hand to Sarita, and helps her to her feet.

They walk together in silence until they reach the gate of the monastery. Ward stops and turns Sarita to him.

"When did you know?" he asks her.

"I didn't."

"I meant about your condition."

"I am still not sure or I would have told you."

But he knows that she is sure, even if her body has not confirmed it: She knows and she didn't tell him because she wanted to keep it from herself.

PART TWO

I

The Congo

June 1890

Casement is back in the Congo, despite his having vowed to have no more
to do with this Belgian enterprise. His old friend Parminter had begged
him, had said that he was the only person who could open up the new trade
route to Luvituku. When Casement had disagreed, Parminter asked him to
name his alternate. And the only name Casement could come up with was
Ward, who was both embroiled in a scandal and recently married. Casement needs the work, the money. Perhaps having a kinder presence here in
Matadi is better for the natives than a protest accomplished with absence.
Still, Casement's refused the usual three-year contract, determined to be
out of the Congo and free of Belgians in the next twelve months.

There is nothing to recommend Matadi. There is only a track coming
in, a track going out, and a mess of hastily constructed shacks that nod
towards settlement. A convoy of porters has just left for the interior, creating
a stillness in their wake, making the sloping piazza of packed mud rimmed
with shaky huts seem all the more arbitrary.

De Schepper, the station officer, emerges from his rooms. This shamble of planks and bent nails he refers to, improbably, as "the office." It is where official things happen. He waves at Casement, squinting into the sun, but then De Schepper always squints.

"That new Société man is here," he informs Casement. "I told him to put his traps in with you."

"Is he there now?"

"Taking a stroll." Which, given the size of Matadi, won't take long.

"What sort of man is he?" asks Casement, although, as Leopold's latest emissary, he doesn't inspire much optimism.

"Full of himself, if you ask me. Not friendly," De Schepper responds, a mediocre officer, who is also full of himself and not friendly.

"Belgian?"

"I don't think so, and not English. Something else."

"I'll do my best to make him feel at home," says Casement, an impossibility, unless this man's home—wherever it is—happens to be a tract of rickety tin shimbeks where the waft of sewage waits on the warm wind.

Casement looks up the dirt track towards the river. He sees only the usual: children and pariah dogs, shadows and heat. Two women start an argument and a chicken breaks into a run, stops, and flaps its wings, suddenly self-conscious. Casement wonders how long he'll be sharing his one-room hut with this man. At any rate, Casement will be away in Boma for some of this. He's committed to supervising a caravan of ivory back to the coast, and in the days leading up to this departure and after his return, Casement will be busy rounding up more porters for the Luvituku trail.

Casement turns to Mbatchi. "Did you get a look at him?"

Mbatchi nods.

"And what does he look like?"

"He looks like you." Mbatchi giggles because he says that about all Europeans. "He also has a beard like you, but his eyes are small and black and he looks angry."

"Wonderful," says Casement. He's about to whistle for his dogs but sees them both, Bindy and Paddy, panting behind him. "The dogs need water," he says, "and later maybe this angry man will want to eat and I'll need your help with that."

Casement is buried in some lines—surely there's a better word than *heart* to rhyme with *part?*—when the man shows up, darkening the doorway. Casement swings his feet off his cot. For a moment—as if roused from a dream—Casement can't remember who this man is. The two regard each other.

"You must be Mister Casement," the man finally says.

"You must be the new man from the Société," says Casement, who has momentarily forgotten his name. They're speaking English, rather than French, and the man does have an accent but Casement can't place it. He stands and extends his hand. "Roger Casement," he says.

"Joseph Conrad," the man replies. This is not the name that Casement was expecting. "Or Korseniewski. As you like," he shrugs, banishing importance. "I disturbed you."

"Oh, that," Casement looks at the papers spread across the cotton blanket, "should be disturbed."

Conrad approves of this, it seems, and smiles, looking less angry. He has the facial ticks of a Russian.

"Please take a seat," says Casement, gesturing towards the one chair in the room—a rickety wooden thing set by the desk—and makes an apologetic face for his forgetful manners.

Conrad sits down.

"How do you find Matadi?" asks Casement, sits through a second's silence, adds, "Or are you too polite to say?"

Another pause. "I was going to say that people talk ill of each other, but realized that in saying that I would be doing the same."

Casement laughs and this Conrad laughs too, as if in relief. Casement has been identified, correctly, as one of the few reasonable men of the area and, he thinks, this man sitting across from him is probably one of his tribe. "So what brings you here, Captain Conrad?"

There's a long pause, as if Casement's polite patter has opened an onto-logical chasm.

"The Société. We all must work. And I have my captain's license, but am now signed on as mate, until they find me my own boat. But I understand there aren't many boats here."

"Not now, but there will be."

"And what brings you here, Mister Casement? Are you a trader?"

"No. Not much good at that." He sees a look flicker across Conrad's face and he knows that the captain has already heard about his poor business skills, his useless, kind nature. "I'm establishing a new track that is necessary for the railroad. I work with the local tribes and find porters."

"How does one accomplish that?"

"Well, you go and talk to people. You say, 'I will pay you this much to carry that much,' and so on. And then you show them what to carry and where to go."

"You make it sound very simple, but I have heard," he smiles at the admission, "that no one is as good at this as you are."

"I speak the local languages," says Casement, "and I've been here since '85. So, enough time to develop a relationship with the local chiefs."

"And what are they like, these local chiefs?"

"Depends on what chief. I find the Bakongo, and Loanda—my boy is Loanda—pleasant and peaceful, although not exactly civilized. But of course there are the other tribes."

"Cannibals?"

"I know it's a horror," says Casement, "but if you're already dead, does it really matter if someone eats you? I've always thought the loss of life to be the greater problem than the provision of a meal, but around here, that makes me somewhat remarkable."

On cue, Mbatchi sticks his head into the hut. "Food now," he says in English. And then, recalling his lessons, and with a flourish, "Dinner is served."

*   *   *

For the next few days Conrad accompanies Casement to the local villages. He is a good listener, this Conrad, and he has a few stories to tell. He left home at sixteen, left like Ward, for a life of the sea. But this man is shuttered and the reasons for his escape to the Far East aren't explained. He is one of those people who creates an impression of having answered a question, although later Casement can't remember the answer. Just the opposite of Ward, who seems to be waiting for people to ask him why he left home at such a tender age in order to tell them about the monster that was his father.

Conrad does not remember Ward, although they might have met, and he leaves them in the possibility of their having crossed paths, which is far more provocative and romantic than had they in fact known each other. Conrad's home is actually Poland, although he has lived abroad for many years. But he seems not quite a Pole. Korseniewski is the name he was born to, but he has taken on the Joseph Conrad along with English citizenship several years ago when he got his Third Mate's license. Casement thinks to make a joke of this, to tell him jovially, "You're sailing under a new name," but something prevents him. Conrad will at one moment bend his head and reveal the intimacies of his life—his family's exile to remote Russia, his youthful gambling debts—but at another quickly retreat into a distant self. No matter what is going on, he has a capacity for isolation. And this is a good trait for a sailor to have. The boat is just a prison of sticks stitched together.

When Conrad signed his contract in Brussels, Stanley was also there, apparently celebrating the triumphant rescue of Emin Pasha. Conrad cannot help but thrill at Stanley's exploits but says that his desire to visit Africa predates by long years his knowledge of Stanley and even Stanley's knowledge of Africa. He, like Casement, has been drawn to the empty spaces on maps and he, like Casement, knows that he is performing their extinction.

In a small notebook, Conrad keeps track of certain words in Bakongo, in Loanda, in Bangala.

"If you just point at something, the natives know to give the word for it," says Casement. "They're happy to. They don't want us stumbling about as deaf mutes." But although Conrad sees the value in learning these words and has enjoyed following Casement, watching him palaver with the local chiefs, scratching the dogs' heads, observing with a pleased intensity, he does not feel the need to actively engage and if his appearance was not remarkable—his compact frame, black hair, eyes set to the offing even in the suffocating jungle—it would be easy to forget that he was there.

In the evenings, if not too tired, they have both turned to their writing, although here again—even though the manuscript is in plain sight—Casement has not felt at liberty to ask. And then there is the Conrad of late night, asking for Casement to pass the bottle, and divulging slowly, as one uncoils a rope, the complicated matter of his life. His Polish nationalist parents exiled to Vologda, his paternal uncles executed for opposing the Russians, his mother succumbing to tuberculosis, his father—a translator of Shakespeare—following her three short years later. And young Konrad Korseniewski, his face pressed against the glass, watching the agitated Russian landscape slip into memory as he barreled towards his homeland, his own exile completed.

"And yet you were destined for this." Casement gestures at the tin walls upon which dozens of suicidal insects tattoo a dissonant percussion.

"As opposed to what?"

"Oh, I don't know. That fate of rebel heroes, like your uncles."

"They were not rebel heroes so much as martyrs, Casement. Do you find that romantic?"

"Honestly, I do. Who wouldn't?"

Conrad gestures for him to pass the bottle. "I wouldn't. I would find it a tragic waste of life. I would find it suicide, a suicide at the hands of butchers."

Conrad says that England is the most civilizing place on earth. He finds the presence of red across the earth's maps symbolic of an improving influence, and Casement has to agree that the English in the Congo would be infinitely preferable to the Belgians, people like Rohm with the skulls circling his flower bed, and Van Kerkhoven, who thinks abandoning the corpses of fallen porters to the elements to be a force for good, a way of keeping order, although how this functions—or why other officers believe this too—is a mystery to Casement. He has tried with the Belgians, and the French. A few years ago, he had actually attempted to lodge a complaint against one of the State men, Francqui, who had beaten some poor servant within an inch of his life. Casement had put the man in his own hammock and in a state of outrage—one that he maintained for the entire fifty-mile trek to Boma—had fully expected to exact retribution for the groaning man, whose back, stripped to pieces, called to mind convict ballads and the Irish rebels whose backs were reduced to gore on the triangles of Morton Bay. And here, as then, no justice had been served. Casement was laughed at. He'd recalled his father—who was not consistently gentle—splinting the wing of a blackbird and the derision this tenderness had earned him, although when his back was turned, from the man delivering the coal. But that was a bird and this was a man.

Casement does not believe that England is always right and, in a later, quiet moment when he has stepped outside the hut into the dark where the night's stillness bows beneath a blanket of deafening frogs, he thinks that perhaps Conrad does not himself believe it, but rather in the conviction itself.

Casement rolls out his most recent map, one provided by the Société, one onto which he has added various things, places he knows about, sources of water, wild banana groves. He sets a bottle on one corner of the map, a book on another, and he and Conrad look down at Africa, which is in a struggle to return to its rolled, uncommunicative, obscured state. Casement indicates, his finger jabbing godlike.

"Here's the section of river," he says, "I'm not sure of the distance—it's somewhere just shy of two hundred miles. But you'll have to walk it. It's slow going. We'll have some porters to serve as hammock bearers."

"I think I'd rather walk," says Conrad.

"Wouldn't we all, but if you get hit with a fever, you'll be down for days, and as you just arrived here—"

"I have been hit by fevers."

"Far Eastern fevers. Different set of bugs." Casement squints along the map, his finger moving up the Congo. "No doubt, you've looked at this. There were villages all along here, but between the Arabs and Belgians, people have found good reason to relocate. And here's Stanley Pool. God willing, your boat is waiting, in good shape, and ready to go."

"You make it sound unlikely."

"Honestly, it is. But once that's figured out, you're on the river all the way to the Falls. Unless you rip out the hull, which can happen, and does. If you think it's a hippo and it's taking its time getting out of the way, it might not be a hippo."

"I'll keep that in mind."

"Equatoria here was a good a place to stop, but there have been all kinds of skirmishes with the Arabs. We lose it, and then we get it back, but the news is slow and so you don't really know what you're steaming into." Casement skids his callused finger up and down the Congo. "Bangala is probably all right, a good place to stop in. And then you're just playing it by ear, all the way to Stanley Falls."

"Upriver," says Conrad. He returns his attention to the map. "What's this?" he asks.

"Ah, Yambuya, right at the mouth of the Aruwimi. Have you heard of the Rear Guard of the Emin Pasha Relief?"

"A little," says Conrad.

"It's blowing into a major scandal," says Casement, rolling his map and returning the two men to the limits of Matadi.

"So it would seem."

"What have you heard?" says Casement. He stows the map and goes about packing his pipe. He lowers himself into the desk chair.

"Starving natives, poor management, people's sanity slipping away." Conrad's face settles into a hard smile. "To retell it from this vantage point seems to have robbed the situation of all its remarkability."

"But it is remarkable, because Stanley's involved and it makes him look bad. And certainly, sanity is a rare commodity around here, but Barttelot stands out because he was so immoderate that he was killed by one of the natives. Shot. That is not so common. The natives fear retaliation more than anything."

"Was it in self-defense?"

"Of a sort." Casement takes the bottle of gin and pours a glass for Conrad. "There was a woman engaged in some sort of ceremonial drumming, which happened to be performed at dawn. This woke Barttelot up and he, in a foul mood, was going to deliver some variety of excessive punishment when her husband shot him."

"Why did the native have a gun?"

"I'm not sure. The natives do trade for rifles, but usually they only have predictable sorts of weapons—knives and spears and clubs." Casement takes a thoughtful slug of gin. "Barttelot was mad. There's a saying around here that the definition of insane is whoever is crazier than you are. But Barttelot was unhinged from the start."

"The climate—"

"This place attracts the worst of Europe. It doesn't create monsters," but as he says that, Casement becomes unsure.

Conrad is quiet. Casement leaves him to that silence and, after a search, finds his pencil beneath a sheaf of loose papers. He moves on to the list he's been compiling. Conrad has four crates, so that's probably four porters just for him. And there are provisions that need to be purchased—tinned meat, coffee, sugar. Conrad says he's brought ample tobacco and his own medicines, foul-weather gear, and ammunition, but he might not have all the right pills. And he'll need cartridges for the Martini rifle. He wonders what they have stockpiled at Stanley Pool. The man who is traveling with Conrad to Kinshasa—Casement forgets the name—is also new to the area, so everything needs to be double-checked. Casement predicts that Conrad will end up in charge of the column by default, by his proven constitution if not his rank. No doubt, this new company man has lost some of his bulk due to the regular upsets and exotic diet, but still he is somewhere north of fourteen stone, which means, should some misfortune befall him, he will require—amusingly—three-and-a-half porters. Not his problem, Casement decides. But he should attend to Conrad's goods for bartering. "Conrad, do you have your cloth and rum yet?"

"No." All of this second-nature calculation is being reflected—by Conrad's bemused responses—as a curiosity. "How much rum do I need?"

"That depends on you," says Casement. "This is local currency. A bottle of rum is . . . I don't know if exchange rates are worth exploring, but it's as solid for trading here as the pound sterling is back home. And better than rods. Bring a combination of rum and cloth. Most transactions involve both. And if the station chief tries to push the yellow Manchester on you, don't take it. The natives don't like it. A fine check in blue or black is probably safest, although my last time out, I had a bolt of red damask and it was very popular. The villagers do check that the dye does not run, so you should too."

Casement teaches Conrad that most often, it is better to trade with the men than the women because the women tend to bargain harder and are difficult to read. Many transactions take several days. Ivory is sold by weight and one must probe into the larger tusks with a sharp object because the natives have figured out how to load the tusks with lead. One good-sized tusk—a forty-five pounder—brings to the native trader a hundred gallons of rum, ten cases of gin, 400 yards of Manchester cloth, twenty kegs of gunpowder, four guns, and a bushel of other nonsense: buttons, beads, and baubles. Of course, the amount of these rubbishy goods required to purchase just one tusk of ivory surprises Conrad. He wants to know if every trader has to track such exchanges in specific detail, but Casement assures him that once he is up in the interior, the quantities of ivory will require a different manner of transaction.

"Here in Matadi, there is business like that—natives wandering in with a couple of tusks. And I've gone hunting on occasion, supplemented my income, picked up my own supply of rum and whatnot to use to trade for other goods. But where you're headed, well. As you know, I'm not a trader and when you get deep enough into the country, it's hard to get a sense of the business. The climate doesn't agree with people. Equipment rusts out. Everything's in a state of corruption." Casement manages a smile for Conrad, reminds himself that all of the preparations and caveats are useless when presented with the reality that is the Congo Free State. "All good stuff to add to your already full trunk of experience."

Casement has his own trip to worry about. He's running a caravan of ivory to Boma—he'll be gone just a few days—and Conrad will be on his own. Casement's arranged for one of the local agents to include him in meals, but beyond that he is pretty sure that Captain Conrad, or Konrad Korseniewski, will be fine alone. It occurs to Casement, as he rolls an extra shirt and puts it in his rucksack, that instead of having many names, this Conrad has only one—that when Casement addresses him "Conrad" the name falls upon the captain's ears as that same name used by his long-deceased and still-mourned parents—that everything about this Conrad can be read two ways. And also, that Conrad has wondered about Casement, is curious about his reticence, and seems to think that, like his own, it springs from an inability to communicate what he does not know about himself. Conrad is made of one element in a constant state of flux—as if Conrad is the ocean itself—whereas he, Casement, like most men, is built of a tough exterior and a tender middle, his constitution only remarkable by the extent to which his inner self is kept secret. He ponders these differences as he checks the baskets, as he makes the final arrangements with the barges for crossing the Congo.

"Mayala Swami," says Mbatchi.

"What now, little friend?"

"You will buy me ice in Boma."

"Where did you hear about ice?"

Mbatchi, for obvious reasons, used the English word and at first Casement had thought the boy had wanted *eyes*.

"From Msa," says Mbatchi.

"Msa?"

"He was with Mayala Mbemba."

Of course. Msa had nursed Ward through the ulcers. "I'm not sure if there is ice in Boma. Maybe your friend meant down on the coast. They have it in Banana."

Mbatchi's face falls.

"If there is ice in Boma, I will get you some. And if there's not, I'll find some other small magic, and buy you that." Casement whistles for the dogs, but as he's about to step onto the track—the first of many stages for such a short journey—he feels the weight of eyes on his back and turns under this certainty. And there is Conrad, watchful, his gaze fixed, focused both on Casement and Mbatchi and the dogs, and on something else—something not visible—at the same time.

There has been traffic on this path. What was once wilderness has succumbed to some influence, although it is hard to call the snapped branches and muddy ruts, the denuded leaves and occasional corpses evidence of progress. The monkey population has all but disappeared. Casement remembers a ridiculous discussion he'd had with Glave and Ward back in San Francisco, when they were they staying in that decrepit hotel near the piers, where the wind blew in through the cracks and the traffic up and down the stairs just outside the door—back and forth, light-footed women leading stumbling men—had underscored the Wild West exoticism of their present location. Exotic, and just that morning, at a barbershop, Casement and Glave had been shaved by a Chinaman, his sloping forehead plucked bare, a long braid falling down his back. And Glave's comment, *If he goes for my hairline, I'm screaming*, and the man's laughing response, *You no think I'm handsome?* Such jovial fun. After a good-natured blunder around the city and a phenomenal steak-and-potato meal, the three young men had returned for bed but decided that they were not quite ready for sleep.

After a couple of drinks—the creaking stairs in call-and-response with a creaking iron bedframe in the next room—Ward had found the courage to say something that had apparently bothered him for quite some time.

"Once," he said, "I saw two monkeys and they were, well, face to face." He looked at Glave and then at Casement, waiting for some variety of shock to set in.

"I imagine," started Glave, "that monkeys are often face to face."

Which was, of course, highly amusing.

Glave leaned back into his chair. "Maybe they were chatting about the weather, or making introductions—"

"That's not what I mean," said Ward. "They were, you know," he nodded, "you know," and he gestured to the wall where the previously creaking bed was now slamming hard against it, threatening to break through, "face to face."

"Are you sure they weren't villagers?" Glave had asked. "Maybe it was dark?"

"Broad daylight," said Ward.

And the conversation had continued like that, Ward swearing vigorously that he had seen the two large monkeys copulating like people and that it had so disturbed him that he had been unable to comfortably—but here Ward stopped himself, not obliging with details. And of course this had raised questions about what opportunities for intimacy presented themselves in the jungle. Glave had peppered him with possibilities, progressively outrageous—cannibals, elephants, gourds—until Ward had lost patience, saying loudly, *Hold on! Hold on! Hold on!* And then an occupant of the slamming bed had yelled, *Can you not shut up?*

After they'd recovered from their laughter, Glave admitted—in a considerately soft voice—that he'd heard of these monkeys, and their face-to-face. They were a kind of chimpanzee. But why had Glave withheld his knowledge of this, Ward wanted to know, and pummeled him so mercilessly, played him for a fool? Of course, it was because of Ward's reaction, hilarious, and Ward is a good sport, and Glave always teases him as if they are brothers.

Ward had connected with his mother and younger sister there in San Francisco, but it was less than what Ward had hoped for. His mother—in letters—had not changed because her script and affection and youthfulness all remained intact in writing, but to see her, although Ward would not go into much detail, was to witness her decline. Ward's sister was a pretty thing, poorly educated and rough-mannered, wearing a too-big dress that was threadbare in places. His father had been unable to attend the lecture. Ward had thought his father unwilling to witness his success. Ward had wondered what had become of his family, and now he knew.

One evening, fortified by whiskey and the comfort of feeling foreign, Casement had excused himself to take a stroll down on the docks. Along the piers, dark figures mobilized the shadows, ducked into view and retreated. He was at first nervous, but realized that this was a place where courage wasn't required. A voice called, "Hallo, hallo," and he smiled back. Casement wondered if he should shake hands, but a quick grip on his shoulder let him know that it was not necessary. He followed to a tangle of nets thrown against a wall, offering his name, although the man was not interested. Casement felt curiously alive.

He knows to practice regret and remorse, but he doesn't really feel it. Regret will be an intellectual thing, like Christianity: a fine religion, but a practice, because one can only believe that the generous Bangala and the gentle, sweet-faced Loanda—despite their feathered idols—are loved by God. Why create such people if there is not hope for them? And why create him?

The track is dry here. The sun parts the leaves and—from the difference in terrain—Casement knows that he is coming close to the limits of Boma. He is wondering if this is a good place to rest the porters and distribute water when he hears one of his dogs, and then the other, barking angrily. He listens, but they do not stop and then he hears a yelp and a high-pitched bark—attacked?—and then the two dogs barking again. Casement pushes past a couple of porters, across to the left perimeter of the track, and breaks into a jog. The dogs do not let up, but now he is closer.

There is a European, tall and blond, and he's struggling, although Casement, because of the angle and the distraction of the dogs, does not first see what is causing this. And then Paddy, teeth bared, goes for the man's leg and a kick—the man's boots reach to his knees—sends the dog flying.

"Hey!" Casement shouts. "Hey!"

The man turns and Casement sees that he has Mbatchi, that he's struggling with him, but why?

"Are these your dogs?" the man shouts in French. His accent is Belgian.

"Yes. More importantly, that is my boy."

"Your boy?"

Although Mbatchi has stopped struggling, the man still has his forearm around the boy's neck. The dogs crouch, jaws ready, growling low.

"Call off your dogs," says the man.

"If you let my boy go, they will have no issue with you."

The man lets out a derisive laugh and releases Mbatchi, who takes careful, quick steps towards Casement.

"What would you want with a child?" Casement is shouting. "You've scared him half to death."

"He is a liar." The man's expression shows that he does not find that surprising. "He says he has no family around here."

"And he does not. This boy is Loanda, from Leopoldville."

The man shrugs. This is of no importance.

"And what would you want from his family?"

"You have been here a long time?" asks the man.

To him, Casement must look like a prophet with his long beard and torn pants, his burnt skin and now—as the porters begin to gather behind him, their loads set down along the track—as some sort of native himself. "What is it to you?"

"Things are changing," says the man. "You will see." And he steps into the trees.

Casement, hands on Mbatchi's shoulders, watches him leave. Casement hears the clank of rifles. There are others with him, maybe a hunting party? "Mbatchi," he says, turning the boy to face him, "are you all right?" But there are few elephants left here, or are they hunting for boys? "Did he hurt you?"

Why would they be hunting for boys? Casement takes Mbatchi's right hand and looks at it, checking the fingers, the pale nails, and then the other hand. Why does he do this? "You are all right now." He smoothes his palm over the boy's head and falls onto his knees, looking into Mbatchi's face. Mbatchi, who has been breathing hard, looking down at the ground, slowly raises his eyes. Casement pulls him into an embrace. What if he had no dogs? "I will keep you safe." What if he had been a moment too late? "You are all right. You are all right." And Mbatchi patiently waits through this as Casement finds his breath and calms his heart, until the boy finally responds. "Yes. Everything is good now. Yes. Mayala Swami, you can let me go."

Casement whistles for the dogs, who have not gone far. As the porters file back, one, a tall and muscled Bangala, fixes him with a look and says, "It is the rubber vine." Casement does not know what he means, but he trusts that look, and that all mystery will soon be explained.

"There are standards of behavior," says Casement, struggling to keep a civil tone of voice. Frissyn, who runs the station at Boma, is sitting behind his desk, where he is always sitting. Casement can't remember if he's ever seen him somewhere else—or standing. For all he knows, Frissyn could have no legs at all.

"Casement," says Frissyn, "these standards are low, as you know, and he didn't hurt the boy. Or is this another boy?"

"This is the one," says Casement. "He meant to kidnap him."

Mbatchi stands serenely by Casement's side. He says something to Casement. And Casement shakes his head dismissively—this is not the right time.

"What did the boy say?" Frissyn asks.

"It isn't important."

Which Mbatchi understands and gives Casement a look that communicates the contrary.

"He wanted to know," says Casement, "if there is ice."

"Here?" says the agent, incredulously.

Casement takes a can of sweetened milk from a crate stacked with other crates beside the agent's desk. "Put this on my account," he says. He tosses it to Mbatchi, whose glorious smile communicates that this consolation is prize enough.

"Frissyn," says Casement, "these men who have been showing up here need to be disciplined. There needs to be—"

"Disciplined? Most of them should have been drowned at birth. Who would come here if they could make their money somewhere else, except for you and the missionaries?"

Casement thinks this over—not for the first time—as he watches Mbatchi stabbing a hole in the top of the can with his pocket knife and then, after a proud look at Casement, stabbing a second hole to make the milk pour better.

"What about that Korseniewski?" says Frissyn. He's rifling through his drawer for the correct form to acknowledge Casement's delivery. "Someone told me he was a Polish nobleman. But what a strange duck! Did you meet him? How does someone like that end up here, unless they have something to hide?" He raises his eyes to Casement. "Ah."

"Ah, what?" says Casement.

"That look. Maybe you too have secrets."

"As do you." Casement smiles.

II
England

November 1890

There are several reasons why Sarita shouldn't be running. The first is that women shouldn't run. The second is that in her condition, even walking is supposed to be done with care, but these concerns are certainly trumped by the arrival of the morning paper, which must be intercepted before Herbert sees it. None of her shoes fit properly because of the swelling. Her feet thump on the thick rug and, oh, how quickly she loses her breath.

Margaret is dusting around the foot of the stairs—something that she should have finished with an hour ago—but the girl's looking a little pale and maybe she isn't well. The windows look sugar-glazed as the rain sheets against them and the artificial light, despite the glory of the French gasolier—a stack of lit orbs skirted under with crystal shards—still struggles against the daylight gloom. The door opens with a rush of damp air and the hard sound of rain—drops thudding on the stoop. There is Valentine taking the newspaper from the delivery boy, who makes his appearance as a pale hand emerging from a tent of oilcloth. Normally, the boy comes to the back door, but with the coal delivery—late—and the rain, he knows that—at this house, at any rate—prompt delivery of the paper trumps protocol. Valentine closes the door against the elements and begins to unfold the paper.

"Valentine," she says, "I'll take that."

"Miss Sanford," he protests, "the ink will transfer."

"It's Mrs. Ward," says Sarita, "and I'll take the paper now."

"Very well, Mrs. Ward."

He's unhappy. Should she expect otherwise? Servants are paid to have no sense of proportion—to devote their lives to making the silver sparkle, to take pride in their silent footsteps and invisibility, to make the appearance of hot food, pressed clothing, dust-free bannisters, and whatnot seem miraculous—to have one's goal be the affect of self-annihilation.

"I only need a minute, Valentine," she says, "I'm just checking the headlines."

Right. PARNELL MAKES NO DEFENSE—A SENSATIONAL OUTCOME OF THE O'SHEA DIVORCE SUIT. Poor Mr. Parnell, and poor Kitty O'Shea. She scans along—a lot of legal language that all of London is racing through—to get to the good bits: *In the Spring of 1883 Mrs. O'Shea took a house in Brighton. Capt. O'Shea would be away from home for days at a time, and when he was not there Parnell was. On these occasions Parnell called himself Charles Stewart. Once, while he and Mrs. O'Shea were in the drawing room with the door locked, Capt. O'Shea rang the front door bell. Parnell escaped through a rear window by a balcony and rope fire escape and, walking around to the front door, rang and asked to see Capt. O'Shea, making it appear that he had just arrived.* That's ridiculous. And is it really news? She wonders what Casement will make of this. He's an ardent supporter of Parnell, and sees him, as most people do, as the future of an Irish republic. So now it seems the Free State is going to founder on snippets of gossip and that is too bad, because, as an American who believes in revolution, she supports the Irish Free State. Although her father doesn't—bad for business—and Herbert doesn't, because he thinks that Englishness is a religion and as such is maintained by unquestioning faith: If something is against the Crown, how could he possibly support it? Sarita can't argue with anything as ridiculous as that so she doesn't. Casement, apparently finding any bad blood between him and Herbert unbearable, avoids that conversation.

So that's it for Parnell—nothing new. But here is Barings Bank—Lord Revelstoke's scandal, and therefore her father's—cozily jammed under the headline, right there on the front page. The Bank of England has agreed to bale out Barings Bank, so now the Rothschilds are involved, and no doubt her father's double-dealing in the back rooms of Argentinean brothels—in truth clubs, but people will still say brothels—will be much discussed. So thank you, Mr. Parnell, for your lack of judgment, and some gratitude to Revelstoke for the same, because it has relegated Herbert's scandal to somewhere in the body of the paper. The only thing better would be more Whitechapel murders—no one would care about the Rear Guard at all— but those gruesome killings happened two years ago.

"Right," she says out loud, though things are so undeniably wrong. Valentine waits on Sarita, stilled to a statue, in his affected patience. She opens to the second page, and there it is, the transcript of Stanley's lecture in New York: *I cannot understand why Barttelot would have gone on day after day crushing to death the helpless, docile humanity placed in his charge when the smallest reflection would have impressed him with the fact that he could not have marched or done anything in Africa without those men . . .* Now Stanley is a humanitarian? . . . *My criticism of the three surviving officers was provoked by the fact that they were three against one . . .* It would seem that Stanley is holding Herbert, Jameson, and Bonny responsible for Barttelot's behavior, that they did not throw over the officer in charge. Wouldn't that have been mutiny? Or is mutiny only for ships? Sarita hears Herbert's boots on the upstairs landing and thrusts the paper at Valentine. "Time to iron the paper," she says.

"Yes, ma'am," says Valentine, but he does not move. He distracts himself with neatly folding already neat folds. Valentine is playing for time. He wants Herbert to see him with the paper and is counting on a proud awkwardness on Sarita's part.

"Move, Valentine." She catches his eye. "These problems of conduct that currently only the two of us know about can soon become topics of frank discussion." Valentine is startled. His look says, *Surely you do not mean to mention the incident with Brock-Innes,* and Sarita's expression responds, *What else is there?*

She watches Valentine taking the exit for the steps to the kitchen. He shuts the door neatly behind him. And then there's Herbert at the head of the stairs, handsome in his tweed, smoothing his mustaches, and smiling at her. "I was looking for you to say goodbye, and here you are, conveniently at the door."

"Am I so thoughtful?"

"Other women in your condition would be in bed."

"Oh Herbert, the doctor thinks a little movement does good, and I still have two months left. I can't imagine spending all that time lying down." Margaret, who is finishing up the dusting of the outer railing, looks scandalized to witness such intimate talk. These English servants are absolutely the worst—even more proper than their employers. Herbert, who thinks he's utterly English, has no real idea of what being English entails.

"Anything in the paper?" he asks.

"Poor Mister Parnell is not testifying in the O'Shea divorce, which is tantamount to admitting guilt—so there goes Casement's Ireland."

"Roddie shouldn't be such a radical."

"But of course he is. He's one of the least conventional people I've ever met," she considers. "You're another."

"But not a radical. What else is happening in the world?"

"Didn't get a good look before Valentine whisked it away to be ironed."

"Rather wish they'd leave poor Kitty O'Shea alone," says Herbert. Sarita sights Margaret rolling her eyes heavenward. "This appetite for scandal is just not, well, acceptable."

"No, it's not."

"Do save the paper for me, dear," says Herbert. "Last few days, your father's run off with it, and that's been inconvenient."

Sarita draws forth an innocent, inquiring smile. "Constitutional?"

"In this weather? I'm meeting Hatton. I had a note from him with the evening post and he said it was important. I hope it's not more of that Stanley—"

"Margaret," says Sarita, "fetch an umbrella from the upstairs closet. I think this one's developing a tear." Sarita's hand plays at the handle of the maligned umbrella, stowed beside the door in the elephant-foot umbrella stand. Margaret heads up the stairs. She knows she's being sent away rather sent to fetch, but it ultimately does not matter.

"Stanley's been mudslinging," says Sarita in a whisper. "I'm sure that's why Hatton wants to speak to you. He's even slandering Barttelot and Jameson and Troup, who are dead and can't defend themselves. He didn't mention you by name but did refer to the surviving members of the Rear Guard. Rumor has it that Barttelot's family is going to file a slander suit against Stanley, so you shouldn't do anything right now. Let Barttelot's family get into it. That will keep you out of the paper, or at least make you less interesting."

"You've been keeping things from me," says Herbert.

Sarita knows an apology is expected, but Herbert prefers not to know certain things. "Your book is coming out. I didn't want you to be upset."

Herbert's eyes transcribe a thoughtful arc. "Anything else I should know?"

It's a sincere rather than sarcastic inquiry. But there is Margaret at the top of the stairs with the umbrella. "Barings Bank has defaulted and Lord Revelstoke is bankrupted," Sarita whispers as Margaret is making her descent. Sarita and Herbert share a look as he processes the information and she processes him.

"The umbrella, sir," says Margaret. Herbert takes it.

Sarita, smiling brightly, announces, "and so are we."

He nods at his wife and—as Margaret has opened the door for him— steps into the chilly damp air, taking care to open this upstairs umbrella before he enters that morning's deluge. Only once outside the door does Ward understand that *and so are we* refers to the state of the Sanford

170

finances and—as he has no finances of his own—his. Can they really have no money? As he stands on the street before the elegant façade of 6 Carleton Terrace—a property Sanford has gutted to brickwork, plastered to a blank brilliance, and filled with the flawlessly new, this seems inconceivable, but it must be true. And he also knows he must pick up a newspaper before he sees Hatton in order to know who he is today: wrapped in scandal, freshly poor.

Ward remembers the weight of Hatton's letter in his hand, how he'd approached Sarita as she sat, bundled in a blanket, on the deck of the *Saale*. How could it be that last November, he was still a single man with his life before him—a blank book with no limitations, something that he could sketch his future upon with only the bounds of his imagination to pose limits? And now, he is an unremarkable, penniless grunt with a wife to shelter and a child on the way and all the demands of the ordinary rising up like ghouls. But he's not penniless. He does have the book advance for *Five Years With the Congo Cannibals*, and a book tour. Could he go back to Africa and find work, send the money home? There was barely enough money in that even for a single man and the thought of supporting Sarita and whoever is due to join the family this January on a company man's salary seems impossible. How much does that even cost?

What does a lady need? And this child-on-the-way, what does it need?

Sarita has shown him her bare belly, coursed over with veins, stretched like a bladder, and he's watched the little leviathan swimming beneath the surface, seen the weight shift from right to left, put his hand on some roundish protrusion as Sarita—always so calm about this stuff, no matter how bizarre—wonders if he's palming the head or perhaps some buttocks. He wonders if all women are so willing to show themselves like this and he doubts it. He wonders if they could go back to Sark and rent that cottage again. Or just go back to Sark. Or just go back.

Later, that evening, as Sarita passes her father's study on the way to bed, she hears—startlingly—whistling. She pauses in the hallway, her hands cradling the hard bulk of her belly, listening to the puffing music of it and raps softly on the door. The whistling stops abruptly. She raps again.

"Yes?" her father calls out.

Sarita swings open the door and steps inside. She smiles at him, an eyebrow raised. "Hello, Father. What are you keeping from me?"

"From you? Whatever do you mean? Barings Bank has been bailed out by the Rothschilds. Lord Revelstoke has been dismissed. And we are . . ."

". . . I know," says Sarita, wrinkling her nose, "ruined."

Her father nods.

"And I know we're selling this house, which I always thought was a little too much anyway."

Her father nods.

"And most of the servants are being released from service."

Her father nods.

"And you're auctioning off a significant portion of your collection."

Her father nods.

"But that doesn't explain why you were whistling."

"A tune stuck inside my head," he responds.

Sarita sinks into the wingchair and stretches her legs in front of her. Her father has the lamp flame set high and the room is washed in sepia light. She studies her father, the fierce eyes burning a cold blue, the Roman nose, the hard set of his jaw, his tufting hair, and the dome of his head, which, despite what people have to say about Sargent's tendency to mottle the skin in an unbelievable way, looks very Sargentesque—a composite of blue and red and yellow and white shining light. Some of this is the way the light splashes from the candle—Father can't think without a sentimental candle, this man of sentimental habits: When he shaves (he won't let Valentine near him with a blade), he has to put a cigarette into his mouth and shave around that, even though he hasn't smoked cigarettes since Argentina. This father, the son of a Methodist minister, raised in the most austere of New Jersey households, took off for Cuba at sixteen years of age, was quickly fluent in Spanish, and in turning his own sinewy intellect to the creation of wealth. He is everything modern—a polyglot, a man who sees money not in stacks of gold but as currents of water flowing between great continental powers, a father who believes that the consignment of good female minds to child-rearing and husband-pampering is a waste of resources . . . but his sentimental candle makes him look more of the past—of Dickens—than of this age washed in the pulsing light of gasoliers. He's holding a pencil, suspended, by her gaze, in time. He has a crafty look, like an eagle. "Father," she says, tenting her fingers, her hands rested on the dome of her belly. "Why do I get the feeling that all these shameful sales and woeful dismissals are a ruse?"

"A ruse?"

Her father's desk is piled up with papers, all tidy. The inbox has a healthy representation of telegrams and she knows he empties that every couple of days. In the fireplace, the last of a stack of papers burns poorly. "This is not the study of a man who has been killed by poor returns in Argentina. I am looking at a man who has played some sort of trick and will, at one point, benefit from all of this financial disaster."

"Based on what?"

"All this neatness and communication could just be healthy activity to avoid depression. But Father, the whistling? Why do I get the feeling that you're wearing the hair shirt to hide your financial solvency from Lord Revelstoke and the others?"

"These English investors are far too conservative. Look at the Bank of England bailing out Barings. Don't they realize what capitalism is? So we live cautiously for a few years. Nothing is certain, not our failure, nor our success, but I've hung on to the Argentine railroad stock. I've even increased it. And our friends in South America—"

"Enough," says Sarita. "This is why people hate Americans, you know that?" And he does. It's making him laugh. "Have you told Mother?"

"Told her what?"

"That it isn't the end of the world."

"No one's been home for several days." Which means that Mother's taken residence with her pills and decoctions. "And when someone's home? I'll tell her something. But nothing is certain. We could very well be ruined."

"You are optimistic."

"I live in the future." He shrugs. "Where's your husband?"

"I'm not sure."

"Out drinking?"

"That's what I'd be doing."

"How's his scandal?"

"Eclipsed by yours. Thank you."

"Scotch?"

"Bourbon, if you have it."

He pours the glasses. She sips from hers and it warms her, but she knows she'll only finish half. Her stomach is so squeezed against her lungs that she really can't drink spirits anymore. Her father returns to whatever memo had been occupying him when she entered and she enjoys this. She can still sit in her father's study although she is a married woman and very pregnant. They can still chat like this. The fire sends out a pop and there's a pleasing show of sparks as the wood shifts. "You knew, didn't you, when you agreed to let me marry Herbert? You knew that we'd be broke and that he would survive it, that he wasn't accustomed to luxury, that he'd be ambivalent about marrying a rich woman anyway and would have too much pride to show me any disappointment in this fiscal decline."

"You married for love," says her father, looking up.

Sarita nods. One statement does not cancel out the other. "Reason makes love easier," she says. "Where are we going to live once this place is sold?" She wouldn't ask if she weren't pregnant.

"I think I'll take Mother back to New York," he says. "What is the state of your finances?"

"You know figures better than I do," says Sarita. "We have what Herbert made from the sale of *Five Years With the Congo Cannibals*. He was going to do a limited roster of speaking engagements because he wanted to be home for Christmas and because of the baby. But he could always do more."

"Do you want to keep Paz?"

"Of course I'll need a staff, but I'm not sure if Paz is a good fit, not if I'm scaling back. My hair is not a priority. I have to think about basic house-keeping and the baby." And she's seen how Paz throws her shoulders back when Herbert enters the room. In Buenos Aires, Paz's aunt was the mistress of a minister and would show up (although at the back door) in a cloud of fancy perfume, her bosom plump and straining like a wind-filled sail and her hair piled high in a pouf worthy of Marie Antoinette. And this woman was an inspiration to Paz, who no doubt dreamed of ministers and dukes and princes. But in the absence of this dream, the reality—Herbert in his shirtsleeves smoking a pipe in the drawing room—seemed to be filling the void. Sarita's hands pat her stomach, right where there was once a waistline. "Paz's English has much improved over the last year. She'll have no trouble finding a position. Maybe I'll take Mrs. Ogilvie, unless you want her." She's the cook and a nice matronly sort of person, someone the parlor maids like. She manages the kitchen budget well. Perhaps she'd do as a housekeeper. "Who do you want, Father?"

"I see no reason to get rid of Valentine," says father.

"He's a curious subject for such loyalty."

"He hasn't impregnated any parlor maids and that's good business."

How hilarious. Things have been so rough as of late that Sarita's for-gotten how she loves to be hunting from one funny thing to the next. "So only Valentine?"

"I don't feel attached to most of the staff here. We just hired them. I won't make any final decisions until the baby comes."

"Mother will want all the people with small hands," says Sarita, and they laugh.

Warrington, Lancashire, a depressing gray town packed into a wall of drab hills where a relentless drizzle pisses down on the muddy streets. Lucky for Ward, he's done transporting his things. He's staying that night in the upstairs room of the Black Hare, and the lecture is going to be in the tavern itself. The publican tells Ward that the majority of his audience will be miners and that he should be aware that these men do not wash up except on Christmas. Of course, the publican, a cheerful red-nosed, red-cheeked man who is screwing the glasses dry with a linen cloth, is not making fun of the miners but rather of Ward.

"Sir," says Ward, "I'm lecturing on the Congo." He points to the poster: *What I Saw in Savage Africa*, Illustrated by Limelight Illustrations . . . "Savage Africa is not known for its bathing facilities. I am a tolerant man."

"Then you can tolerate this," says the publican, and he pulls him a beer.

"Will you have one yourself?" asks Ward.

The man, judging him favorably, continues on with a short glass for himself. "Where would you like to set up the Magic Lantern?"

Ward looks around. "We can project onto this wall. I'll hang a sheet. The lantern will go at the end of the bar."

"How does it work?" asks the publican.

"It's very simple, actually." Ward notices that the miners have begun to file in, hats in hand, as if they're entering a church. "We have the two sacks ready—one of hydrogen, and one of oxygen. You feed the gas through these tubes. We light the flame and then inside there's a little block of quicklime that heats up nice and hot and gets bright. That quicklime throws the light. But I am going to need help with the slides."

The publican looks over at the miners, blackened with coal, the whites of their eyes catching the dim light. "There's Ben Field and his Jim is a bright lad. Jim'll do it." Jim, who doesn't look more than thirteen years old, is as covered in coal dust as his father.

"Jim, fancy learning something new?" says the publican, waving him over.

Ward explains the order of the slides, how to switch them out. He gets Jim a lemonade while the boy's washing his hands behind the bar.

Ward goes to work. Images start up like memories on the draped sheet—Bakongo witch doctors, Bwende belles, the Belgians with their guns and mustaches and order. He tells his stories and leaps around, roaring

176

like a lion, trumpeting like a bull elephant. The men shout and jeer, laugh, order more beers, and start lining them up along the bar for Ward. Jim, his eyes fired up with romance, beams a smile that burns as hotly as any little block of quicklime. Ward takes a second's break to gulp at one of the glasses of beer and, in the space allotted by this action, a chorus of coughing starts up as these men struggle to clear the lungs so that they can hear what happens next—a volley of poisoned arrows, the tattooed beauties, the yellow leopard eyes flickering behind the trunks of trees.

The show over, Ward tries to put a dent in the pints these men have bought for him, but he won't be able to finish. So they'll have to help. Ward tells story after story. And he asks for one of the miners to share a story with him. "When our stories get an ending, it usually isn't a happy one," a miner says. And they laugh, a low rumble that sends some into coughing, others into quiet introspection.

Ward works his way north, lecturing to ironworkers in Earlstown. He writes to Sarita, "I have buffeted the world a good deal, and have had some pretty rough times, but I think this lecture business in England is the dreariest experience of all my life." He misses Sarita and explores this new feeling—a loneliness that he could solve if he were near this woman.

Christmas Eve he's in Ardrossan, Scotland—a dreary coastal town where pig iron and coal are loaded onto ships, sent to Europe and North America, with the locals waving it off in a spirit of dour, religious, Scottish joylessness. Ward had been hoping to be proven wrong about Ardrossan. He's known some Scotts in his time, mostly in Australia and New Zealand— cheerful sheep people—and they were good for a drink and a laugh and a story. But here, at the Egglington Arms, he has been left to eat his steak in a room where the fire has died and a bare branch screeches against the pane as the wind circles the building, rattling casings, tearing at the roof, ruffling the hair on his forehead, as it squeezes through the cracks and makes a chill draft. Even his steak is bereft of companionship and occupies the center of the plate with neither sauce nor vegetable.

He's taken to writing Sarita every day. He has to be cheerful for her because he's sure that being without him in a house that's up for sale and a baby due in the next few weeks is cause for anxiety. He writes, "I am to lecture on Boxing Day in a church in the middle of a field where goats eat shoes and saucepans." His effort to cheer Sarita cheers him. He stays up writing, first his next book—his account of the events of the Rear Guard—and then back to the letter for Sarita so that at midnight he can be the first to wish her a Merry Christmas. Although he hasn't had a merry Christmas in years: One year, he and Casement got confused about what the date was and celebrated a day early and, after they figured it out, weren't sure if they wanted to celebrate again. Ward thinks back to the Christmas of two years ago, the one he celebrated in Yambuya with Jameson and Troup—that was their last Christmas.

On New Year's Day, Ward is in Belfast. He thinks of Casement as he walks along the narrow streets. A child stares at him until his older sister, also staring, smacks him on the head. The air is choked with smoke and there's a sense of deprivation that he can almost hear, like a low humming. He cannot associate Casement—straight-spined, sunburned, articulate Roddie—with this place. Casement does not have the difficult accent and his open demeanor doesn't seem to be a prevalent quality of the Irish of the North, or at least not the city folk. Quite a few people seem suspicious of Ward, although what he could possibly be up to—other than lecturing on Africa—who can say? The friendlier people have good humor and are full of questions. How big are elephants? Do the savages have many children? Does Ward have many children? How does he find Belfast? And some other questions that are probably very interesting, but that he can't parse out.

Did he really think that Ireland would be a nation of Casements— idealistic, poetry-writing adventurers with low-purring voices and philosophical personalities? Still, Ward engages the older gent at the hotel and tells him that his friend is Irish, from Ballymena. A Northern Irishman too, although the more Ward tries to follow this chain of conversation, the more he realizes that he doesn't understand the history of Ireland, nor even the present. He doesn't know anything about Parnell beyond Kitty O'Shea, and he'd rather not talk about this. Having suffered slights in the papers, he sympathizes. He doesn't want to be the man who only knows another by his scandal. Time to turn the conversation back to the Congo, to talk about cannibals and naked ladies and elephants, all safe and well-worn topics.

While the year is still new, he takes the ferry back to Liverpool—another former home of Casement's. Ward buys a ticket for the first available train to London, third class because that's where there's a seat for him. Then, from his third-class carriage, with his battered bundles and the borrowed brashness of having been with miners, and ironworkers, and ordinary people, he finds himself flagging down a growler. After—with his help—the coachman has loaded all of his things, Ward throws down his address.

"Carleton Terrace?" the driver repeats with disbelief.

"That's right," says Ward. "Number Six." He shuts his eyes, his legs still at sea from the crossing, or maybe from the rattling of the train, or maybe from the hard wheels of the jolting carriage as it grinds across the harder stones of London and into the upper class.

Sarita's contractions start shortly after lunch on the thirtieth of January. Ward will be a father. He remembers once when Janey, his mother's spaniel, had puppies and how excited he had been. He thinks that not only is he not quite as excited as he was then, but that he also shouldn't be thinking about whelping puppies and his own child as the same thing. Maybe he is not ready for fatherhood, but—and this is a relief—it really doesn't matter whether he's ready or not. His part in the current situation was done with nine months ago. He thinks of the curse of labor. He thinks it is damned unfair. But still, a doctor must be summoned and Ward is jogging down to Sanford's office to announce this when he notices his in-laws in the drawing room and he jogs backward to stand in the doorway.

"Mother," says Ward, as that's what she has asked to be called, "Sanford," as that's what he has asked to be called, "the baby is on its way."

His father-in-law sits frozen, the paper in his hands flicked open to its widest expanse. Mrs. Sanford blinks, stilled too, with Mrs. Ogilvie by her elbow, a pencil and paper in hand, apparently taking direction for some meal or shopping errand in the future. "The baby," says Sanford.

"Sarita's baby," says Ward. "Someone should call for the doctor."

Sanford tucks his paper into a hasty square and stands, presumably to find someone to fetch the doctor. Mrs. Sanford has not moved, but Mrs. Ogilvie ducks her head efficiently by the woman's ear and says, with complete conviction, "consommé."

"Shouldn't someone be with Sarita?" says Mrs. Sanford. "Where is Paz?"

Ward returns to Sarita's room to see her doubled over the windowsill, her head resting on the glass. He goes quickly to her, to help her back into a chair. "Herbert," she says, "don't be an idiot. If I wanted to be sitting in a chair, I would be sitting in a chair."

Ward is alarmed, but Paz waves him off. "Don't worry, Mister Ward," she says in a calm drawl, "very normal. She will get crazy." Paz mimics crazy with a sort of flapping, loose-claw hand gesture. "Is normal too." Paz stays on the far side of the bed from Sarita and she seems to know what she's doing. "The cold is nice for her head," says Paz. "She stays like that, is good. The doctor makes her get in the bed, she get very mad." Ward hears a growl and realizes that it's coming from Sarita.

"Where's the doctor?" he says, panicking.

"It's a long time, Mister Ward," says Paz. "Better for you with the others."

And just like that, he's booted into the hallway.

An hour later, a doctor arrives, although this is a young man—in his twenties—and his accent reveals him to be a Scot. He has black hair and an intense expression. He's come upstairs with his coat on—used to being in a hurry—with Margaret, dodged at the door, in hot pursuit. "Where is Doctor Danvers?" asks Sanford.

"He's been up all night and more with a difficult birth, someone in the peerage, no name I can share." The young doctor shrugs off his coat and tosses it to Margaret. "I am Doctor MacIntyre."

Ward and Sanford share a moment. "You look very young," says Sanford. "Have you done this sort of thing before?"

It is a silly question, but it's the exact silly question that Ward wanted to ask.

"This sort of thing, and this thing, and I had a good night's sleep, which is more than Doctor Danvers." Dr. MacIntyre gives Ward an appraising. "You're the father?"

"Yes, I am."

"Nice small head," he says. "And you?" he says, looking at Sanford.

"I'm her father," says Sanford.

Sanford's head is as big as an ice chest and sits almost directly on his shoulders, as if his neck has given up.

"It's going to be a while," says the doctor. "Have a drink. Get some rest. When something's happening, I'll let you know."

And when something is happening, there is no need of letting anyone know. The whole house can hear it. Ward paces like all fathers do, a *Punch* parody of self. Ward thinks of lovely Garnet, the cascading red hair, her joy at meeting him, her breathy whisper, "You're the luckiest man alive, but I bet you already know that." He'd had to visit at her house since American women of that class didn't go out when they were showing. She'd kicked off her slippers, put her narrow feet on Sarita's lap, and asked that Sarita rub them as her feet were numb and cold, late pregnancy circulation problems. Garnet confided, winking at Ward, that Sarita was the only person she could tolerate touching her. Sarita had added that Wallace too belonged in that number. "Him?" said Garnet. "He's the last person I want touching me. He's never coming near me again." Outrageous Garnet was positively the most alive girl Ward had ever met, other than Sarita. But now Garnet is dead and her baby did not survive, and—according to Sarita—that poor Wallace is drinking.

181

In the hallway, he can hear Paz's voice, soothing words that seem at odds with whatever response Sarita has—it's all in Spanish though. And then the doctor asks for more hot water. The door swings open, and for two seconds, Ward sees the sheet that is covering Sarita knotted beneath the doctor's chin, like a bib. The doctor's tools—smooth, ivory-handled forceps and large spoons—are spread across a chair. Paz calls into the hallway for the water, and Margaret—who has been at attention for hours—rushes off. Sanford stops Paz and says something to her and Paz, tiring, responds with more casualness than she really ought to, although what she's saying, Ward does not know. She opens the door again, and before it shuts once more upon the scene, he sees Paz unknot the sheet from behind the doctor's head, and pull it—as if she is a magician doing a trick, exposing Sarita's bare knees, reversing magic, showing how the rabbit really does get out of the hat. "The gentlemen want you to see," she says to the doctor.

"That's very enlightened," the doctor says, "and we will all be grateful." But the door shuts upon that scene and Ward sits for another two hours, unaware of his own physicality, breathing in a shallow state, focusing on Sanford's anxiety as a way of avoiding his own. Even Mother has managed to stay alert and the three sit in silent support—probably they are all wondering how they will survive if Sarita doesn't, what life could possibly look like without her.

Ward looks at Mother. Her paper skin is drawn tight across her well-formed cheekbones and fine nose. Occasionally her mouth twitches. Sanford raps his fingertips on his knee, his head bowed, and the hall clock shudders through a second's march, and then another, and then another, until a cacophony of righteous bonging introduces them to the next hour.

The baby is a girl, helpless and angry. Ward feels his whole life has been in anticipation of this moment and his conviction surprises him. He sits with Sarita, who is explaining to her mother how the baby was presenting face-up, whatever that means, and how that prolonged the labor. The doctor adds that Paz was the one who managed to get the baby turned, using the weight of the baby's head. "It's good for me to know," says the doctor. "You manipulate the mother, and gravity shifts the back of the baby's head to wherever you need it." Mother's making that anxious face that she saves for times when she thinks something being said is inappropriate, but isn't sure. Ward shakes the doctor's hand. Mother and Sanford escort him downstairs.

"Would you like to name her Garnet?" asks Ward.

"Garnet?" Sarita shakes her head. "That's best for redheads. And poor Garnet . . . No, girls have a hard enough time as it is. We should name her for a survivor."

"Then we should name her after your father."

"Charles?"

"Or Henry. Why not?" Herbert thinks. "We should name her after you."

"Sarita? We can't have two Saritas."

"Sarita Henry."

"Sarita Enriqueta," says Sarita. And there's nothing better than that. Of course, Ward is a survivor too, but there will be more children and they need his name and Sanford's first name, Herbert and Charles, for sons. But how many children can they possibly have? How could Sarita possibly get through this again?

III
London

May 1891

Casement is sitting at a table in a London café with his tea and a plate of cakes, which may or may not appeal to his cousin. Gee, now sixteen, was only a child when Casement left for the Congo, and that child had loved anything sweet. Could she really have outgrown it? He had written to her, as she'd made him promise, and now she knows all about him, although he is just discovering her. The bell above the door jangles and Casement raises his eyes, but it's not Gee, just a young man with dirty blond hair who brings a moment's interest.

The impermanence of love has been on Casement's mind. How convenient it would be to wake one morning and find the burden of it somehow vanished—alchemized into precious nothing. Also, how tragic. Although it might be nice to be relieved of his romantic nature, because he's losing patience with himself.

Waiting to board the ship, his trunk already loaded, he had looked around at the others, men either toughened or diminished by Africa, and wondered how they might perceive him. Tall, sunburned, intelligent, force-ful. Irrational. Sentimental. Lonely.

This is what had occupied him on the voyage back to England, in part because his sister Nina had somehow managed to find a husband. Some-where around the time that he and Ward were transporting the *Florida*, Nina—whom Casement thought had foresworn marriage since she was already in her thirties—became the wife of a George Henry Newman. The unlikeliness of the whole relationship was driven home when Gee had met him at the train station in Liverpool and advised him to avoid even mention of it. "They separated last year," she said, "but she still goes by Mrs. Newman."

Sure enough, on encountering Mrs. Newman in the flesh, she seemed entirely unaltered. Nina still tuts at him and straightens his tie, as she did when he was six years old. If she decides he's walking too slowly or not paying attention, he'll feel her grip on his wrist—a correction for careless behavior. Of the Casement siblings, he is the youngest and she the only surviving girl—the one who remembers burying little Annie, who had died of hydrocephaly at the age of four, and of the first infant Roger, whose all-too-short life is best not thought about, and now overshadowed by the second Roger, who has—thankfully—reached adulthood. And Nina never forgets those losses: hers is a ferocious, maternal love and Casement feels the force of it.

For much of his life, he has needed it.

The image of Nina at their father's funeral holds firm in his memory. When his father died, leaving them orphaned, Roger had only been twelve years old, and Nina a fully formed, seemingly adult eighteen. She'd nodded at him with a smile, as if people went to their father's funerals on a daily basis. At the edge of his father's grave, with the wind making a sad music of the branches and leaves, and the doleful urgings to faith of the long-nosed, uninspiring minister, he'd wanted to throw himself into Nina's arms. And the arms are still there, although the urge for this particular comfort is gone.

Casement sees Gee stomp past the teashop window, and then circle back. She finds him through the glass and breaks into a smile. The door bangs behind her, startling a patron, but Gee doesn't notice.

Casement gets up from his seat, as it's only polite, and Gee responds with a look of total horror.

"Cakes for you," says Casement.

"Which one's the best?"

"The only way to know for sure is to eat them all, and then decide." Casement smiles indulgently. "Where's my lunatic sister?"

"She'll be here. She had to drop by the bank," says Gee. She goes for the jam tart first. It's crumbly, and sticky, neither of which dissuade Gee from quickly dispensing with it. "It's supposed to be a surprise, but I can't keep secrets. Can you?"

"Depends what it is."

Gee picks up some shortbread, considering, then abandons it for a more exciting French-looking thing, shellacked with a clear sugar glaze. "That means you only tell the silly secrets, nothing good."

"That might be true, but what's yours?" He pours her some tea.

"Nina's bought tickets for us all to go see Stanley at Albert Hall."

"Why did she do that?" asks Casement.

"I don't know. She's your sister. But you'll have to pretend you want to go." Gee goes back for the shortbread. "Nina had a very hard time getting the tickets. The man at the box office said—although we now know he was lying—that they were sold out. Can you imagine that? Six thousand tickets? But then Nina said you knew Stanley, that the two of you were friends."

"And the man at the box office believed her?"

"No, actually, I don't think he did. But he could see she wasn't leaving without a fight and took a wise course of action." Gee picks up a chocolate thing covered in shredded coconut. She takes a bite, sets the cake down, and licks off the icing stuck to her finger. "I said, 'Nina, why would Roddie want to see Stanley when he's just spent all that time in Africa? Why don't

186

we take him to the theatre? Wouldn't he rather see a comedy?' and she said, 'Don't be silly, Gee. Of course he likes Africa best. Why else would he spend all that time there?'"

Stories like this make it seem that Nina is not intelligent, which she is, very. But she is also perverse and stubborn and outspoken and Casement is very happy to be back in her company, where not only is he not expected to make decisions, but also unable to.

Nina, Gee, and Casement eat at his favorite London restaurant. He orders his usual veal cutlet, and it is excellent. The bottle of claret is less excellent, but also exactly what was promised by the price. Gee eats her pudding, and then half of his. They have left plenty of time to get a cab, a good decision, as this takes a half hour. Nina wipes the seat off before she sits down. She carries an extra handkerchief with her for this particular task. He sees her sniffing as she sits, aware that there will be a bad smell somewhere and unwilling to miss it.

The cab brings them to Albert Hall with acceptable speed, although the cabby asks to stop several blocks away. All six thousand people seem to have shown up at the same time. "Horse is pulling to the left. I think it's the harness, but it might be a shoe. Anyway, you'll get there faster on foot," he says.

And Casement agrees. He pays quickly, before Nina starts trying to shave a few pence off the fare. Together, they join the mob of people, filing in with Nina leading the way. As usual, she's pushing her umbrella between the shoulder blades of the man in front of her and, when he angrily turns to look, Nina feigns complete ignorance. Gee, catching Casement's eye, starts giggling. These are the people who love him and whom he loves. Why is he returning to Africa?

It is an absolute trek to their seats and here, in *the gods*, peering down at Stanley, Casement feels quite out of body. But even from this great distance, one can see that Stanley is not well. He wears the strain of all his privations with a forced dignity, but—to Casement's learned eye—Stanley seems to be suffering from nerves more than fatigue and the lecture itself, all about pygmies and plants and wild jungle animals, seems to confirm Stanley's anxiety. He never mentions Emin Pasha, not once.

As they leave, Gee says, "It was in all the papers. Emin this, and Pasha that. And Stanley didn't say anything about him. Maybe Stanley didn't actually find Emin Pasha."

"Gee," Casement says, "Emin Pasha wasn't actually lost. Stanley had to 'save' Emin Pasha. The one he needed to 'find' was Livingstone."

Which is funny enough, but not quite as funny as when, after the final applause dies down and Nina rises to leave, she turns to Casement— her face set in a sneer—and says, "It should have been you down there, Roddie."

What on earth does she mean?

Thank God for Gee, for the company and bonhomie, which elevates Nina from a sort of humorous ordeal to an actual form of entertainment.

Ward is just back from America, is thrilled not to have missed Casement, but is only there for a couple of days before Casement leaves. Herbert-the-husband and, recently, father, now lives at his in-laws' in a very impressive house, although the house is, apparently, on the market.

Casement looks up at the face of the building, unable to reconcile this as Ward's home, even temporary. In the vestibule, the maid takes his coat and Casement stands in the expansive, unpopulated room where his only company is an ugly painting of a boy in velvet clothes with a yellow bird sitting improbably on his finger.

"There you are," says Ward, appearing at the end of the hallway. "I've been waiting for you."

"I'm actually a half hour early."

"What time is it?" Ward shakes his head at something. "Ugh," he exclaims, "probably time for tea."

"Is that what you do? Drink tea?"

"All day," says Ward. He comes to stand by Casement, shakes his hand. "And sometimes," he adds, looking to the boy with the bird, "I look at this painting."

They sit in the drawing room, where everything is new and rich and careful. Casement sips from the petal-thin bone china and chooses a mille-feuille from the assortment of cakes, which Gee might appreciate, but with Ward some hippo jerky would make more sense. Casement feels as if he and Ward are actors performing in a dull comedy. Or worse, that Ward is some sort of freak-show exhibit and his sipping from the cup while balanced on the wingchair, ankles crossed, seems the sort of setting and activity that a sideshow promoter would arrange for a dog-faced boy or an elephant man. This is not singing and malafu in a tent on the edge of the known world, but rather the death knell of opulence.

"Why so morose, Casement?"

"I wish you were coming back with me."

"Well," says Ward. He looks at his cup and then down at the rug, as if the secret to having it all might be contained somewhere in its lush pile. "Perhaps you'd like to meet the baby?"

Sarita brings in the baby, so small as to not be quite human. Casement reaches up to take her. It's instinct for him. He's always liked babies.

"You've got her," says Sarita, impressed.

Casement bounces gently, making funny, entertaining noises.

"I don't know if he actually wanted to hold her," says Ward. He looks over at his friend and his face crumples in disbelief.

They call the baby "Cricket," although Sarita's not sure about the nickname.

"What if she's bow-legged?" she says. "All the other children will call her 'Rickets.'"

Casement cannot help himself. He likes Sarita. He loves that little baby and he has to admit that Ward is all right. Ward seems a bit stunned, but not depressed.

At the door, as they make their goodbyes, Sarita throws back her shoulders and, squaring her gaze, says, "Don't worry, Mister Casement. We run him off the leash at least twice a day."

Casement is navigating the streets of London, exploring its open sidewalks, shadowed doorways, cramped skies marked off by sooted brick buildings. It's early in the evening and the restaurants are returning their patrons to the street. A boy pushes past him, hurrying to somewhere. Casement watches a man and his wife stepping into a cab. The husband helps her up and she takes his hand, even when seated and hidden from view, their tender connection holding as he enters after her. On the pavement an older woman looks about for a cab of her own. The boy makes haste to her. Casement is wondering why, and then he sees the boy grab her purse—a sharp tug and it's free—and the woman's moment of confusion as she struggles to understand what has just happened. There is the boy running, running straight towards him, but as she has yet to announce her violation, no one reacts. Casement waits until the boy is nearly upon him and then reaches, grabs his shoulders, lifts him with force but not violence, and holds him against the wall.

The boy drops the purse, and Casement the boy, and the boy gallops down the street, near skidding around the first corner that presents itself. Casement picks up the purse and makes his way to the woman, to a small gathering of people who are still trying to parse out what has just happened.

"I think this is yours," says Casement. He hands the woman her purse, which, although small, is uncommonly heavy—as if it's filled with gold coins.

"Oh, thank you, thank you," she says. Her small crowd disperses with a few cheery words, eager to be done with her. "How can I thank you?"

"You have. You're very welcome."

She looks around her, unwilling to release him. And now they are connected. How to escape?

"Please allow me to help you engage a taxi," says Casement. Politeness is there for when natural behavior might fail.

"Well, that's it then," she says. "Perhaps I can give you a ride somewhere?"

"I'm not sure we're headed in the same direction."

"No matter. It is the least I can do."

Casement was actually headed to the Turkish baths on Jermyn Street, and he strongly doubts that this woman, a Mrs. Beaker, is going anywhere near there. Sure enough, she's going to Knightsbridge, but he'll allow her a few streets of conversation before he asks to be dropped. What else can be done?

"Where are your people from?" she asks. This is a typical question.

"Liverpool," Casement replies. He's smiling. He's such a nice young man. "And Ballymena, in the north of Ireland."

"Oh, you're Irish. That explains it."

Casement is not sure what this explains. He smiles again, like a puppet.

"My cook is Irish, from Mayo."

Casement nods, but what is he assenting to?

"And what do you do?"

"I'm in the consular service. I'm currently on leave, visiting relatives."

"Well, you've done very well for yourself."

Casement imagines the boy still holding the purse, bringing it back to whatever modern-day Fagin there is to receive such things, taking the coins and distributing them among the poor. "I suppose I have," he says. "Would you mind if I got down here? It's very close to where I need to be."

In Africa, he is one of the English, but not in England. Places do that—throw you into some sort of relief against themselves. In Ireland he is both Northern Irish and Protestant. And within that, he is one of the people that believe in inheritance of the soul—the soul, regardless of Scottish roots and the Church of Ireland, is essentially Gaelic, and this separates him from the other British in Ireland. Although he's not, currently, in Ireland.

At the Turkish baths on Jermyn Street, he is that man who confidently divests himself of coats and shoes and shirts and socks, who has his feet buffed by oriental youths, and his back scrubbed raw by some anonymous, muscular hand—the self who wanders in off the street with an open, casual

191

expression and looks about in studied disinterest and, while trying to make up his mind and decide just what he wants to do, is pleasantly surprised by the attentions of another—curly-haired, stocky, smart.

There, with the water in constant trickle somewhere, the light dancing over the cool vaults of the Byzantine ceiling, one's eyes soothed with moisture, one's pores dilated, and the men lounging on the stone shelves, speaking in hushed whispers, a warm cough bouncing across the surface of the bath, the manic sparkle reflected in the vault of one's ribs—the little knot of muscle, his heart: a mad motor. And after, the hush of fifty men breathing the humid air and his shallow breath slowly rejoining, a soothing caress that dismisses all else.

This English self that buttons his shirt, this Irish self that puts on the coat, the hat, that picks up gloves and cane. And thus returned to the sidewalk, that self that should pick its steps back and back, walk in reverse—as time seems to wind backward to him—winding back to the time when none of it ever happened.

IV
Paris

January 1894

The Wards have been in Paris for two months and Sarita does not miss England. England is not a default country for her. She is not English and, although Spanish-speaking countries are all out of the question, primarily because they are inhabited by Spanish-speaking people, she has been longing for something a little more lively than the house in Harefield: Paris feels like a good compromise. She likes reducing her belongings to a couple of trunks. She likes the townhouse with its marble steps and sun-drenched back garden. She likes the gardener who listens to her stilted French with patience and humor and goes ahead and does whatever he wants to anyway.

Herbert mostly keeps her away from the Académie Julian's crowd, where he spends most of his time painting. He'd said, "Sarita, I don't think they're your sort of people."

"Why?" she asked. "Because of my fancy upbringing, my delicate manners?"

She knows that Herbert doesn't want her to ruin his image. He is playing the explorer and the less they see of the wife with her current fashion, well-tooled kidskin boots, and soft hands, the easier it is to keep it going. All the academies have to be a bit nutty, but this Académie Julian is the one that accepts women painters, who introduce a whole new set of scruples or lack thereof. These women arrive with their brushes and smocks and canvases, and God only knows what they leave with. They're in and out of bed with everyone. Even if Herbert returns every evening to their little apartment with its English habits and narrow views, in the morning when he leaves he arrives to a different set of values. Sarita can see the appeal of such adventure. One of Herbert's classmates, an Irish girl, is having an affair with a married Polish count—a Count Marciewicz. Or so he's heard. To Sarita, it sounds made up.

Sarita has managed to make friends and find things to do. Father has connections everywhere. One of his associates is a very wealthy banker who lives bordering the park on rue de Monceau and that connection had gotten her into a very fancy tea, where she'd spent a fascinating afternoon chatting with an elderly lady who spoke a sort of Shakespearean Spanish and had spent her whole life, to that point, in Istanbul. Money is not always dull.

Sarita has decided to drop by Herbert's studio and see how his work is progressing. She doesn't have a good reason to be in Montmartre, but perhaps a stroll to see the progress of Sacré-Coeur is reason enough. Cricket and baby Dimples are safe with Marte, who is—no doubt—making sure that they are kept as spotless and scentless as is possible for living things. Sarita sets out with Ticker the dog, a puppy of three or four months, who is fine but demands an anxiety-provoking level of exercise. She'll walk the few miles to Sacré-Coeur, have tea at one of the cafés, and then drop in on Herbert. It's a clear day, not too cold, not windy, with a vibrant sunshine. If she had a better sense of what she is trying to accomplish, it would be a good plan.

Ticker helps. He gives her the appearance of a sense of purpose. Together they wander up the twisting streets to Sacré-Coeur. They reach the church at noon. Paris spreads beneath them like a blanket. Ticker, unimpressed, blesses the church's bleached foundation with a raised leg. Sacré-Coeur, although started years earlier, is far from finished. From what Sarita can see, it will be, upon its completion, garish. The white stone is strangely luminescent—magical, but in a sugar-topped fairy-cake way. She prefers the airy darkness and attractive gloom of Notre Dame, with its pained children singing heavenly songs that are supposed to remind one of salvation but rather make you almost wistful for the comforting stillness of death. Sacré-Coeur is quite another thing, set up by the church to annoy the locals—artists and radicals—to cast its pure, white, sin-cleansing shadow over the windmills and brothels and absinthe cafés and studios of Montmartre.

Progress of Sacré-Coeur now observed, Sarita moves on to the second stage of the plan: sitting at a café.

She and Ticker take turns dragging each other down the hill until she finds a place that doesn't look too crowded. She decides on a seat inside. At a corner table, a woman sits with her Irish setter—a beautiful dog with a great, elegant head and impressive bearing. That dog, which, no doubt, has some noble name, sits still and upright, gently nodding to people as they pass, inspiring all sorts of admiration from the waiters, from young men, from the woman herself, who wears a crushed velvet jacket of the same rich burgundy as the dog's coat. Sarita orders her sandwich and tea. She watches the waiter appraise Ticker, who is either an overblown spaniel or an unsatisfactory setter. The whole time Sarita is eating her sandwich and gulping her tea, Ticker seems determined to garrote himself in some complex cat's cradle about the legs of the table.

"Well, Ticker," she said, "it wasn't a complete disaster. After all, you didn't bite anyone." But she's never bringing him to a café again. What was she thinking? Sarita had intended to stay longer, but now, walking past the Moulin de la Galette, she's set to arrive at the studio smack in the middle of the lunch hour.

The studio is in a shabby building on a side street and is painted cheerful shades—bright yellows and greens, although with no apparent yearning towards any aesthetic. She knocks on the door, then knocks again. There are weary footsteps. The door creaks open and an unshaven man—although it's not exactly a beard, more facial hirsuteness, like a monkey—presents himself.

"I'm looking for Herbert Ward," she says in French. "I'm his wife."

The man says nothing but, after a moment's assessment, tries to block her view with his shoulder. Sarita can still see the bare model, including his hairy buttocks, who is standing on a platform bathed in sunlight and underlit with shadow.

"Ehrbert Ward is not ehre, Madame," the man says, volunteering English. "Eh is taking a sandwich."

"Well, where's he taking it?"

"Madame?"

Another man appears at the door, relieving the first, and speaking French. "You must be Sarita."

"Yes," she says, surprised at the familiar tone. "And this is Ticker."

Across the street, barrels of something, probably beer, are being unloaded from the back of the cart.

"I am Jacques Petrie. I am a friend of your husband."

"Pleasure to meet you, Mister Petrie." This Mr. Petrie is a very handsome man and for a minute she can't remember why she's there. "I was taking a look at Sacré-Coeur," she gestures vaguely in its direction, "and walking the dog," she raises the leash for confirmation, "and thought I might drop in and say hello to my husband." She is waiting to see whether or not Mr. Petrie will accept this, because he's taking a moment, and his features are either droll, disbelieving, or just maintaining a practiced and unreadable expression, when there's a crash across the street. One of the barrels has slipped and landed on a workman's foot, and he's shouting, and the horses take off. Sarita feels the leash pull out of her hand. Ticker has bolted and is galloping down the street.

Sarita breaks into a run, aware that long after Ticker's fear has dissipated, he'll keep going. She watches him tear down the sidewalk of rue Fontaine and round the corner. And there is the gate to the cemetery. She's out of breath as she reaches it. Where is Ticker? She glimpses a few inches of feathered tail—going, gone—behind a marker. Sarita is out of breath, cursing her corset, and cursing Herbert—which may not be reasonable but certainly feels justified. She stands at the cemetery entrance, looking at forking paths and shadowed walkways, the spectral monuments and Catholic hush. She is cursing everything, herself included, in an audible, satisfying, unladylike Spanish.

"Madame Ward," comes a voice. It is Mr. Petrie, who has followed her.

"I've no hope of catching him," she says, her breath still rough, "he's possessed. But if we don't get him back, Herbert and the children will never forgive me."

She sees Ticker step out from behind an enormous mausoleum an improbable distance from where he'd initially disappeared. He seems nervous to return, fearing her anger, probably wondering if he's ready to relinquish his freedom. In Ticker's place, Sarita would feel much the same.

Mr. Petrie begins whistling in a soft, birdlike way. Ticker cocks his head and raises his ears, watching. Mr. Petrie steps closer, but not too close, and then, flat on the ground, lays himself out as if volunteering for a crucifixion. The dry leaves scutter past, the cawing crows give voice to the dead, and Ticker sits deliberating. The dog cannot resist. He trots tentatively towards Mr. Petrie, and then, as Ticker peers into the man's face, Petrie's arm shoots out and grabs the leash. Petrie gets up from the ground. He presents himself and Ticker, handing the leash to Sarita.

"Thank God," she says. "I honestly don't know what I would have done without you."

"It would have taken longer," says Petrie.

"Well, I hope there's some way I can return the favor." She resists brushing the leaves from his hair, which he seemed unwilling to do.

"Of course, there is not a need."

"No, of course . . ." Does he think she means to pay him?

"But maybe . . ." He was looking at the ground intently. Ticker follows his gaze downward. "You must say no."

"Must I? What is it?"

Petrie performs an elaborate series of shrugs and then, with an aura of complete resignation, says, "I need a woman's foot."

"How very interesting."

"You see, we have a model for this week, and she is beautiful in some ways, and sometimes the ugly ladies are better to paint—I mean it, more beautiful the ugly ones. But this woman . . . What has feet like this woman? They are grotesque."

"You can't make them better?"

"Feet are my weakness," he says. "I am no good at feet."

"Oh," she says, "I understand. You need a woman's foot. And I have two."

Petrie nods, thinking. "It is still no good. No women are allowed in the men's studio."

"Oh, well, is there somewhere else?"

"Only my room, which is not far."

Sarita knows she should never have entered into this conversation. She should never have tried to repay a favor. Ladies don't. Now she is stuck with either making Mr. Petrie out to be a rake, which he might be, or joining in with something highly irregular. Ticker looks from Petrie to her to Petrie. "I suppose if we don't take long," she hears herself say, "because I do want to see my husband." Her cheeks are burning. She wonders if Petrie knows what she's agreed to, because she isn't sure.

His room is on the second floor of an old house on rue Lepic. The light is good, but the floorboards gap, and the old couple arguing below might as well be in the same room. She's managed to get her shoe off—buttons, not laces—and, hidden behind a screen (what is it there for?) her stocking. "Do you need both feet, or just one?"

"Both, please."

Mr. Petrie has lost some of his friendliness, which is a relief. This is work for artists—women bared. She grapples off her other boot, rolls the hose down and hangs it beside its mate on the screen. She steps across the broad, gapping floorboards. What if her feet are grotesque? To Sarita, they seem completely acceptable, but what of Mr. Petrie's opinion? Clearly he is particular. He looks them over, his expression inscrutable.

"Can you stand like this," he mimes for her to bunch her skirt in her left hand, "and then like this," he slides a bucket over to her, gesturing for her to put her right foot onto it. The metal of the bucket is very cold against her bare foot.

He's been sketching for close to an hour, during which time Sarita has oscillated between boredom and anxiety. She wonders if that other man has told Herbert that she'd dropped by. She wonders if he's connected Mr. Petrie's disappearance with her exit. And then she wonders when Petrie will be done with his sketches so she can release her skirt and put her boots back on. Ticker has fallen asleep in the sunlight thrown by a curtainless window and she envies him. She is also hungry.

She imagines Herbert looking at Jacques Petrie's painting, at those familiar feet, stitched by the ankles to another woman.

When they return to Julian's, Herbert is still not there.

"This is not uncommon," says Petrie. "So many artists live here. If you are having a slow day, you can go visit the studio of another artist."

But Sarita isn't sure. She says goodbye to Mr. Petrie, whose frank demeanor she has found refreshingly unmannered—she would be happy as a woman artist, one of these painting comrades, if she could paint. But she is also happy as a mother and, most of the time, happy as wife to Herbert. And this is what she is thinking when, as she leaves, she raises her eyes to the second floor of the house on the opposite side of the street. A shutter has just been thrown open and a woman is standing in the window. She has a man's shirt thrown over her shoulders and her breasts, the type of soft rich flesh that Renoir paints so well, are exposed to the street. This woman is looking at Sarita—although why?—and smirking. Maybe she is the lover of Mr. Petrie, or some other artist, but Sarita does not care to find out. It doesn't matter. She's been envying Herbert's freedom and, one foot on the cold bucket, one on the dusty floorboard, skirt hiked in her cramping left hand, she has learned that she is free—not imprisoned in marriage: If marriage has bars and a lock, she holds the key.

V

Niger Protectorate

June 1894

Casement has signed on for some surveying work in the Niger Protectorate employed by Commissioner Claude MacDonald, and therefore England, and therefore not for Leopold, which is—therefore—not so bad. The stakes aren't as high for palm oil as they are for ivory. Palm oil doesn't involve killing anything and has replaced slavery in the region as a way of turning a profit. In West Africa, the small nuts are ground and distilled into a fat for cooking, but in England—all of Europe now—the grease lubricates the pistons and joints of Industry. Although here, marching along a native track with the chatter of porters, muted clank of equipment in baskets, and occasional bird screech as the only music, it's difficult to think that one is a part of the chugging, smoke-belching engine that is Europe.

Casement is moving through dangerous territory, that of the Anang, and wondering about the wisdom of traveling without weapons. He sips the last of the coffee and swirls the grounds in the bottom of the tin cup: Perhaps the future can be read there. Ofime, his linguister, had asked him several times if he was absolutely sure that he hadn't brought a gun, and this had made Casement snap—he hadn't appreciated being asked more than once and all that inquiry had made him nervous. Ofime did not feel responsible for Casement's outburst, nor was he insulted by all his shouting. Ofime has told Casement that his name means, "Don't be angry, wait all the time," which Casement has translated to, "It is good to be patient." Ofime is patient and Casement is patient, but on occasion it would also be good to have things where they're supposed to be, people behaving in a way that does not require patience.

Soon his stint with the Niger Protectorate will be over. He's looking forward to home leave. Hopefully brother Tom, currently bankrupted in Australia, will soon have his sea legs—or his bush legs—or whatever other legs one must have in order to stay beyond the range of creditors and Casement will be able to save some money, take a real holiday. He could even relocate to Liverpool, although it's hard to think of how he'd make a living. He could balance ledgers, like his uncle. Or he could write to his relatives in Ballycastle and see if they know of any openings, but all those people have been asking him about the consular service, as there's not much going for young men in the old country. He's a bit out of touch with Ireland. Since the death of Parnell and the latest defeat of the Home Rule Bill, he does not follow the machinations of the House of Lords. Parnell failed—even with Gladstone as his ally—and more failure fails to entertain. He's gotten into this with Ward, who has a hard time understanding how Casement can support the British in Africa and want an Irish Parliament—how these two things are not at odds with each other. Most ambitious Irishmen end up in England, or working with the English. It's an economic necessity. At least in Africa, England and Ireland are allied forces, working for the good.

Casement raises his umbrella against the sun, his only weapon and one, he fears, that is developing a tear. The porters are chattering anxiously. He sees Ofime patting the air as he moves past, as if he hopes to reassure them.

"Ofime, are we set to leave?" asks Casement.

"No. The Anang have refused permission."

"I already know that." Casement recognizes the insubordination. It is good to be patient. "Surely some diplomacy—"

"There is no diplomacy with the Anang without guns."

"Ofime . . ."

"Master, why are you arguing with me? Have I ever misrepresented anything? You don't want to kill us all. Not for your map. Put a big hole in this place. Or put a big gun so that the white man knows to bring one when he comes back here. If I tell the porters not to move forward, they will not move forward. But I want to tell them that it is because you have said that the Anang are too dangerous and that you want to take care of them. Why must you go here? Look. Over there. More Oil Rivers. And over there. More Oil Rivers. And in both directions, no Anang."

"It is not just for the map."

"You are the first man the Anang will kill. They are not scared of the English. They are too crazy and too barbaric."

Casement considers.

"Even if we turn back," says Ofime, "do you see that sky?"

"It's true, we will be marching in the rain," says Casement.

"We will not be marching. You will take that umbrella and instead of holding it above you to keep back the water, you will be sitting in it."

"All right, Ofime. All right. We'll go back." Ofime's head drops in relief. He nods to himself. He raises his eyes to Casement and he looks, to Casement, as if he wants to pinch him. "So I won't regret this?" asks Casement.

"No," says Ofime. "No, you won't."

"We're not being too cautious?"

Ofime solemnly shakes his head. He makes a joke with one of the porters and the mood lightens as, conversely, the first drops of rain start to fall.

Twelve hours later, the land has disappeared. Ofime was right; if Casement could sit in his umbrella he would. The trees extend their crabbed fingers above the surface and swift moving water carries broken timber and lost goods on its back. Below the surface, it makes weapons of stray branches. For hours Casement had waded with the water waist deep, then at his shoulders. The men had struggled with their loads, waiting for an improvement, but one that has not come. Ofime is somewhere towards the rear of the column and he hopes he is faring all right, but here—the shorter men are swimming. And then one of the Inokuns goes under. His basket begins to float off but is grabbed by one of his countrymen who, holding on to his own basket and to this other, sweeps his eyes over the area where the man has disappeared.

Casement sets loose his umbrella, freeing his hands. He's a strong swimmer and closes the distance, looking here and there. The man breaks through the water six feet from him and disappears. Casement cuts a hypotenuse to where he hopes the current will carry the man. His arms and legs are tiring as he fights the force of the water. That man could be here, but who knows how fast one travels with the current when not resisting it? He treads as much in place as possible and his leg strikes something—a body. Grappling through the murk, he manages to grab the man's slick, cold skin—his arm—and wrenches him up.

The two men are dragged along as all Casement's strength is being used to keep the man's head above the water. He manages to direct them towards a tree. He braces himself for the impact and there, forced against the narrow trunk, his arms and torso lacerated by the brittle twigs, catches his breath. The man, a boy really and probably only sixteen, looks in a panic at the water all around. He inserts himself into the tree, bracing against the current. Casement looses himself to the water, to other men clinging to baskets, those lucky enough to have caught hold of the makeshift rafts. He will have to send canoes to rescue those in trees in the morning.

Shivering and exhausted, Casement pulls himself onto the shore. The rain has halted but the air is still charged with it. Two men come to him and help him to stand. They walk him up the mud bank and to a grove of trees, where, at least, he'll be sheltered from the wind. He is happy to see Ofime sitting there.

"I thought I saw you drown," says Ofime.

"Close enough," says Casement.

Ofime says, "Do you have tobacco for me?"

Casement manages a chuckle. "That would be nice, wouldn't it, although how would we light it?"

Casement has returned to Calabar just in time for a party. His linen suit bags on his frame, attesting to the deprivations of the last few months. The MacDonalds' house feels like a stage set. The compromised building materials add to this feeling, as does the crowd of locals gathered about outside, sitting in casual groups upon the packed dirt that pretends to lawn, watching whoever has assembled on the not-so-graceful but breezy porches of the building. There is always a sense of the commemorative about such gatherings, although the gathering itself is what is being commemorated. Something about colonials and dislocation and superimposition makes Casement think that parties like this are so that each can confirm to the other that they really exist. Let's gather together the Europeans and have a conversation about civilized things! And Mrs. MacDonald had even sat them down at the front of the house, two rows—Miss Kingsley, the Mac-Donalds, and Bobby the dog seated in front, the rest in back—and had their picture taken. The *floomp* of the flash has frozen them on some plate of eternity and he wonders where this record will show up, what the future viewer will make of it. Will he be curious about what has brought that trader Mr. Lock, Shackleton, the doctor, Mr. Philipps, who is just stopping on his way back to the Bight of Benin, Mr. Harcourt, whose pallor and sweatiness indicate a true illness, he himself, and this Mary Kingsley—a spinster explorer—together with Sir Claude MacDonald, First Commissioner of the Niger Protectorate? And his wife? And Bobby the dog?

The photograph was followed by a five-course dinner—no jellies, no ices—and then liberal amounts of festive spirits. Here, in the Niger Protectorate, even the women drink. Or at least Lady MacDonald does, and he wonders if this is why she finds Sir Claude's remote posting acceptable. She is a tough lady and, as she tops up her gin, most often announces that it is one thing that protects her from malaria: the mosquitoes seem to intuit that her blood is poison.

The Niger Protectorate does have its pleasures, but he is ready to leave. How to describe the natives here, as they are different from his Bakongo and Bangala friends? He can only say that the Niger people seem ready for the English—they are suspicious. They lack innocence. The Congo has something Edenic about it—although a violent Eden and one that is being violated—but somehow the Niger Protectorate is a place like any other, although populated by Blacks and governed by witchcraft.

He has accomplished a good deal here in terms of his career. He is now, truly, a part of the British Consulate. Yes. He is the Acting Consul—emphasis on "acting." He has done a good job of convincing everyone that this is what he does, although the job itself is not well defined: The Acting Consul accomplishes whatever needs to be accomplished. On the top of Sir Claude's To-Do List: wiping out human sacrifice. In this, Casement sees the hand of the pro-gin, anti-ritual-murder Lady MacDonald. But he can be respectful of the natives in his pursuit to end a barbaric practice. He finds the shock and outrage that people like Lady MacDonald manage at the use of human sacrifice to be disingenuous.

Miss Kingsley is no stranger to the local juju. She has written books on witchcraft and, in London, people pack her lectures to hear about sorcery and the like. "So what you mean to tell me, Mister Casement, is that you support human sacrifice!"

"Miss Kingsley, I do not." She is teasing him. "But let's look at this calmly." He takes a thoughtful sip of lime-infused gin. "Even you civilized English have been known to enjoy a good hanging, and tell me that's not human sacrifice. It's all the same thing. Gather the people around, kill off one of your own, prove the power of your ruler, and terrify those who might dispute it."

"In the name of order—"

"Tax is in the name of order." Casement performs a sagacious nod. Miss Kingsley has been opposing the Hut Tax that the British government is eager to impose on the locals. She has been writing letters to the papers, speaking out in that high, reedy voice, her pale eyes all outrage and mettle, her shoulders pulled back, her mouth crumpled in an intelligent and unattractive manner. The natives might do better with a less singular champion, but she is, at least, articulate and vocal. The natives don't understand tax— don't understand why suddenly what was theirs now demands payment to another. Casement understands. As an Irishman, living on contested land is, if nothing else, familiar. And Casement, because of his Irish childhood, where his heroes were, although heroic, also losers, is a natural sympathizer with those in opposition to the Hut Tax, although now as Acting Consul, forced to at least act supportive of British policy.

Miss Kingsley laughs him off. "What's the point of us arguing? We're on the same side. And it's a small side. I'm just like you, not peddling religion. I have no weapons, other than rum and tobacco."

"You are not like me. You are my superior," he replies. "I am always working for others, compromising my own ideals. And honestly, I know I'm compromising, but beyond compromise, I'm not sure what my agenda is. You are a scholar—an anthropologist, a zoologist."

"You're flattering me, Mister Casement. I should be careful."

Miss Kingsley is the most engaging person Casement has spoken to in months—other than the missionaries—but the missionaries, with God on their side, are not so maligned. She has a very odd story. She is one of *the* Kingsleys and her uncle is a famous author: Charles Kingsley wrote *The Water Babies* and a number of other popular books, and Mary's own father—a physician who traveled the globe—wrote several volumes chronicling his journeys. But she, apparently, grew up at home, did not even leave to pursue an education. She says she was friendless. She says, "Hard to believe that, given my charm." But she *is* charming and all the self-deprecation—genuine—makes him like her all the more. This is Miss Kingsley's third trip to Africa and she's determined to penetrate farther into the jungle, farther into unexplored territory. Her boat leaves for Boma in the morning.

"Why the Congo?" asks Casement.

"Well, we've all seen the map."

"And that's an encouragement?"

"If it's a discouragement to others."

"If you don't like people, you can just stay at home and keep the door shut."

"I do like people. I like my linguister. I like my porters. I might even like you."

This is the first time that Casement is meeting her, although he'd been warned of her presence in the Congo her last trip through in 1893. She had outfitted herself in Loanda—picked up goods and porters—and headed off with no map and no desire of one. Casement had been told that sooner or later there would be the body of an Englishwoman to retrieve and send back to London, but Miss Kingsley's body had returned by its own efforts, which was a convenience to Casement, and an inconvenience to all the rest whom it proved wrong.

"You have to tell me more about the local legal system. I've heard you're very good."

Casement shakes his head. It's his turn to be self-deprecating. "There is no legal system. I make it up as I go along. I know a bit of surveying and project management, but this is my first consular position. Before I started, I thought it might be helpful to know something of the law, but of what law? English law? I'd be better off consulting the Bible—reading about King Solomon. It's ad hoc wisdom—or seeming wisdom—that helps. And I can't let them see that I'm making it up because these Niger tribes are not composed of stupid people. Honestly, they like watching the cases tried. Of course anything that's tied in with religion or luck or practices related to funerals and victory—all of that, the stuff that involves human sacrifice— they have a hard time letting go of. It's their way of life and they don't see what I'm doing there, saying that even though the Opobos have defeated the Quas, they cannot crucify a virgin girl at the crossroads. That interference, to them, defies logic. Why do I care? It is not my girl being killed. I do not know her, nor her people. The missionaries are doing their work and I am doing mine. The personhood of a human sacrifice is inexplicable to them without changing their moral code."

"How can we argue the personhood of a girl, when we treat donkeys better than men?" Miss Kingsley gives him a frank, questioning look. "I don't agree, Mister Casement. I believe these people to be every bit as moral as Christians."

"You and your juju, Miss Kingsley. If Christians lived as they claimed one ought to live, it would be a moral place. These natives are living as they claim one ought to live and it results in cannibalism, torture, and sacrifice."

"So you support hypocrisy?"

"Not all Christians are hypocrites."

Casement tops up Miss Kingsley's wine from the bottle on the sideboard. "My success is in my work with property disputes and domestic things. Is someone's goat grazing on someone else's land? Who was supposed to inherit the canoe upon the man's death? And sometimes I manage to bring reason to places where there is none. A woman was accused of turning into a crocodile and eating her neighbor's pig. Another man might have sent both parties away, but I was interested." He laughs. "I listened to the woman for close to an hour, and then the person who had lost the pig."

"And what was your conclusion?"

"My conclusion was that if she could have turned into a crocodile, she would have eaten that man's pig, and would probably have taken off his legs as well, just to inconvenience him." He remembers that case, how the woman accused of turning into the crocodile had shown up before him, carrying, to his amusement, the same umbrella that he had lost in the flood a month earlier.

"And you are sure she wasn't guilty?"

"As sure as I am that the woman accused the week earlier had not turned into a shark."

"And is that a 'yes'?"

"It is—as with just about everything—whatever you make of it."

VI

Goring on Thames

June 1895

Nostalgia drives Ward to punting. It brings him back to the Congo, his trip down to Boma, the rush of it, the empty banks suddenly rippling with bodies, some reeds revealed as spears. He'd paddled for his life and with men who knew the value of it—of breathing, of circulating blood, of seeing—since in their vicious existences, life could be snatched at any moment: Life was all they had. Msa had loved him, had let him live in a reduction to his noblest traits (bravery, fortitude, generosity), and for this, Ward had loved him back. What would Msa make of this trawl down the Thames, where instead of war horns and drums one has the warbling of wrens, the plaintive tweets of thrushes? It is nostalgia, but a twisted one, translated in his mind, as if his younger self can somehow be played at the same time as his current self, a recollection of life-affirming terror transcribed over this gentle journey.

Yet Ward is not unhappy, although mildly disappointed with himself for this contentment. He stands in perfect balance on the punt's platform, in charge of its progress. There's a bend in the river and he three-hands the pole straight down, draws it back up, sprinkling droplets into sunlight.

Sarita exhales, performing frustration. "Do you believe Paulson's story about the wheel being off?"

Ward considers. "Don't you?" He trusts Sarita's judgment on this. He's not much of a liar and Sarita's ability to sense falsehood in others sometimes makes him wonder if she herself is consistently honest.

"He reeked of beer," says Cecily, the nursemaid, shifting on her bench.

"And how would you know that?" says Sarita. "You must have been awfully close."

"Well, he did," says Cecily. "I think he got waylaid at a pub."

The two women are squeezed in tight on the first bench of the punt with little Dimples jammed between them. Cecily has baby Charlie on her lap and Sarita, a broad parasol that shades them all.

"Does it matter?" says Ward.

"James, do not think it's all right to make things up," says Sarita, addressing the second groom, enlisted as second punter for Ward's relief, and seated across from her at the front of the boat with Sarita Enriqueta—Cricket, now four years old—who will just not sit still.

"Mrs. Ward, I do not make things up," says James.

James—whose first name is also James—is Welsh, comes from some odd religious family, and is routinely the object of a lot of fun. Cecily giggles.

"I'd rather Paulson did lie," says Sarita. "Who wants to be the person who says, 'How dare you stop for a drink?' with the weather as it is: gorgeous."

Paulson is driving the cart with the belongings. Honestly, he should have been ahead of them at the inn by several hours. No doubt, he imagines himself on holiday as well. Today, they'll pull into Goring, and after that, they have one more day of punting, a night in Dorchester, some hired thing back to Oxford, the train to London, and a growler to Harefield.

"No, no, Miss," says James. Cricket is reaching over the edge for a floating stick, unappealing except in the danger of its acquisition.

"Get it, James," says Cricket.

"Please get it, James," corrects Cecily.

"No, James, don't get it all," says Sarita. "You don't have to do everything she wants. You just have to make sure she doesn't fall out, or start running around again." Two-year-old Dimples is satisfied with a small biscuit tin that she has clutched in her pale little fingers. Sarita strokes the sleeping baby's cheek. "All this talk of Paulson's poor behavior has made me want a glass of Champagne."

"James, you're up," says Ward.

This shift is now well rehearsed. Cecily settles the baby into Sarita's left arm and gets up, edging to the right as Ward places the pole lengthwise down the middle of the boat. He then—still in possession of a supernatural sense of balance—easily finds his way to the picnic basket. James gets into a crouch and makes his way, crablike, to the front. He makes a grab for the pole, presenting Cecily with a close-up of his backside. There are more giggles but James, flushed with anxiety, settles in, anchored by his short, strong legs. Once holding the pole, he transforms from this odd little Welshman, full of rules and problems, into something of a graceful athlete. He punts beautifully, this young man, and his steering is second to none. Of course, the skin on his hands is peeling, all that exposure to the sun, and his face is not serene, but rather in some sort of composed grimace. But he enjoys it, Ward is certain of that.

"Cricket," says Ward, "fish out a bottle of Champagne, will you?" Cricket lifts the lid of the basket and, full of mischief, pulls out a smaller bottle. "That's lemonade. I said Champagne."

"I don't like Champagne."

"That's what you say now, but in a few years—"

As Ward predicts, they all look to James, and he is disapproving, and Cecily starts giggling, quietly, but James will be seeing her shaking back.

Ward pops the Champagne open and it's warm. They had been dragging bottles in the water, in a nice net bag rigged for the purpose, but the bag is lost and with it the other bottle of Champagne, lying on the bottom of the Thames, no doubt, with many other Champagne bottles that have drifted down from Henley, post Regatta, although those bottles are certainly emptied—he's responsible for at least one of them. Ward pours a glass for Sarita and hands it to her. He pours one for himself.

The banks are slipping slowly by, and James drops and pushes, drops and pushes. The foxgloves are in ferocious bloom, bothered by bees. A cloying swan arcs his neck, dips, emerges, unfolds to his full-feathered span, showering a rainbow of fractured light across the river's surface. A wood pigeon with singing wings flaps to a branch overhead.

"Shoot it, Daddy," says Cricket. "Shoot it."

Little Cricket has the gift of violence. She loves to walk out with him, although she's so small that she quickly tires and he has to mostly carry her on his shoulders. She loves him picking the hares out of the fields, the clean crack and whistle of his gun, Ticker leaping through the grass to fetch. She loves to pat the warm soft fur of that new dead thing and once she dipped her little finger in the blood and tasted it. She'd met his eye and he'd thought that maybe this fierce little creature would also meet cannibals, would hear drums, would walk for miles and miles not sure of any worthy destination.

Harefield. That's where they live. Harefield. Although Sarita has wryly noted that if he keeps at it, soon they will be living in "Field."

Cricket takes the bottle of lemonade and sticks the top in her mouth, ready to grapple off the cap with her teeth.

"Cricket, don't," Ward says. He takes the bottle from her.

"Paulson does it."

"You've yet to acquire Paulson's talents. That one will come with age."

Ward sees little Dimples pry open the top of the biscuit tin and take out a dead butterfly, admire its powdery wings, and then place it back inside, lid pushed on with a creak. She shakes the tin gently.

"Think you'll whisper it back to life, sweetheart?" says Sarita. She does this to bother James—which it does—and to make Cecily laugh—which it does.

Sarita sights around the hotel lobby. At least they've made it to Gorley. The reception area is full of people, many of whom seem to be a part of the Ward party. Will they always be traveling in such a crowd? Cecily has the baby in her right arm and her left hand wrapped around Cricket's wrist. Dimples isn't inclined to run off: She's standing by her father, cooing at the biscuit tin. James had to stay behind with the punt. Seems like everyone has had the same idea: Henley for the Regatta, then a punt down to Gorley. So, there was nowhere to moor the boat and now they're short-handed. Sarita and Herbert both have an aversion to an excess of servants, but this is absurd. Herbert's struggling with the basket and wraps, and she's checking them in.

"But you do have our rooms?" asks Sarita.

"Madame, we do, and I apologize. As soon as we have a man free, he will be sent to find out precisely what happened to your mooring."

"We know what happened to the mooring. Someone took it. Can't you send a man now?"

"As soon as your belongings have been unloaded from the cart . . ."

He continues, but Sarita has become distracted by Cricket, who is struggling mightily to free herself from Cecily's grip. Sarita sees Cricket prying at Cecily's fingers with her left hand, then her open mouth and bared teeth.

Dimples's eyes widen.

"Sarita Enriqueta Ward!" says Sarita. "Don't you dare!" She returns her attention to the concierge. "I do apologize, but I need my man James immediately. I don't care if you leave our things in the street to be pilfered by derelicts."

Herbert is laughing now.

"Madame—"

"Where is Paulson?" Sarita asks Herbert. "I know he doesn't like carrying things, but for pity's sake."

"Sir—" says the concierge, appealing to Herbert.

"I'm sorry, but my wife seems to have everything under control."

"Do I really?" says Sarita.

"Don't you?"

"I'm not sure," says Sarita. She looks over at Cecily, who is jerking the poor baby around in an attempt to keep Cricket in place—Cricket whose heels are dug into the rug and has a look of pure rage on her face. Herbert lets the wraps and basket drop with a crash of crockery (is he drunk?) and dramatically presents himself to Cricket. Cecily lets her go, and the girl jumps into her father's arms.

"Problem solved?" asks Herbert.

"And a good thing too," says Sarita. "I thought my wheel was about to come off."

She sees the concierge looking dolefully at their abandoned belongings on the floor. A fashionable woman with a hummingbird hat edges away. Dimples looks at the hat with nervous horror. They are a circus. That's what she gets for marrying a circus performer. Although part of her does feel remorse for subjecting the other guests to this—people need their peace—but how is it that they don't have a man managing the moorings? Sarita has an image of whomever this moorings-man might be raising a pint glass with Paulson.

A boy with a silly, jaunty cap—hallmark of porters—appears at her elbow, and she gestures to the pile of rugs and the basket heaped on the floor. "I assume he has the keys?" she says to the concierge.

"Of course, Madame."

"Well, thank you for your kind attention."

"And Mrs. Ward, may I inquire . . ."

She waits. "Of course." Although the man doesn't seem to know what he is inquiring.

"Madame, do you know a 'Wardy'?"

"I'm sorry, but I don't understand the question."

"A telegram has arrived for 'Wardy.'"

"May I inquire, who is this telegram from?"

"It is from a Mister Harmsworth."

Sarita shakes her head. "It's for my husband. 'Wardy?' What is Alfred thinking? Doesn't he want you to get the telegram? And how did he know we were here?"

Herbert volunteers to take over the last of the check-in and she can't wait because Cricket needs the toilet as soon as possible. In New York, this hotel would have an elevator. Sarita follows the porter, who has nothing to port but the picnic basket and the key. She hopes he does not expect a tip because she hates dealing with that and also isn't sure that she has any appropriate coinage. She's carrying Charlie with Cecily bringing up the rear with the blankets, the girls in between, Cricket blocked from escape by the two women's skirts.

So, ascending with her three children, Sarita has a moment to process what has just happened. What is in that telegram? She thinks this through. The options are limited. It's something polar, no doubt. That's what's selling papers, unless Harmsworth's ladies' magazine has finally come through, although Herbert knows nothing about any women except for his girls—Dimples, Cricket, and her. And that's almost worse than knowing nothing because the three of them are hardly representative. Cricket just wants to kill everything. Dimples wants to bring it back to life. And what does she want? That Champagne has gone to her head; she's feeling fizzy and could use a quick trip to the toilet. The porter turns down the hallway with all of them processing close behind. He stops to unlock a door and they all pile in. Cecily has a coin for him, which he takes with a mild bow. Herbert must have given it to her. He's so clever about people, because of course Cecily likes to tip—thinks it's grand. The porter shuts the door behind him.

"Do you want me to take the baby, Madame?" Cecily asks.

"I'm fine holding him. Why don't you unpack the children's things?"

"They're not here yet, Mrs. Sanford."

"Yes, of course. They're at the pub with Paulson." She smiles. The door swings open and there is Herbert. He's holding the telegram in his hands, a hopeful look on his face.

"So where's Alfred sending you?"

"Russia."

"Russia?" It is polar. "Fine. Russia, and no farther, and I want you home inside of six months."

She does miss him when he's not around. Herbert is her best friend, and more than that. Communicating with him is somewhere in a realm between unspoken thoughts and actually engaging another person in discourse. When Herbert's there, he's most often in good cheer, and always pretending it regardless. He's kind to a fault, a loving father, a devoted husband when he's at home, and when he's not, how would she know? Herbert's letters are vivid and full of detail. He's a professional writer, so that would make sense. He does say that he misses her; certainly the letters seem sincere. He must get lonely because when he's at home, he can barely be in a room by himself for ten minutes without looking about for her. And even when she's not there, Ticker is a constant companion to him. It's as if Herbert has two modes—holding your hand, or thousands of miles away. Sarita has problems with both of these. Alfred Harmsworth. Damn Harmsworth. Thank God for Harmsworth.

She is again impressed by Harmsworth's cleverness. All the other ships in the Arctic Circle looking for the North Pole. The explorer Nansen, captain of the *Fram,* hasn't been heard from in over a year. Is he alive? Who knows? His plan, after all, was to be stuck in the ice and adrift and as he drifted in the ice, to keep his eye out for the Pole. Nansen is an explorer and, as such, if he's doing his job, there isn't anyone around to confirm his precise location, which gives you nothing to print. The reading public must make do with the point at which Nansen was lost to view, combined with his intended destination. Cricket had wondered how all these people were supposed to know when they'd reached the North Pole if no one had ever been there and no one knew what it looked like. First off, the Pole wasn't actually a pole. So why call it one? Well, they were scientists and poles meant a different thing to them. There was something magnetic involved (something Sarita herself didn't quite understand and couldn't explain) and the scientists would most definitely know when they were there. This explanation had somehow had the effect of convincing Cricket while at the same time filling Sarita with doubt. What was all the fuss about the North Pole?

Harmsworth has decided that rather than looking for the Pole itself, he will just send his ship, the *Windward,* as far north as possible in order to collect data. This objective, although less dramatic than reaching the

Pole, has some significant benefits. The scientific community is completely excited by this generous focus on research and, as Herbert wryly pointed out, if Harmsworth's just headed north rather than trying to discover the Pole, his expedition is bound to be successful.

"Alfred doesn't like losing," Herbert had said, "and with this expedition, he can't."

"Unless the boat sinks," Sarita responded.

"In which case, the bravery of the men will fire up the hearts of our good people and probably sell even more copies."

The *Windward* had sailed on the twelfth of July from Greenhithe with Herbert on it. Back in Harefield, Sarita and the children settled into their usual schedule with Cecily taking Dimples and Cricket to the park in the morning, most often with James, who had to carry hoops and dolls and balls and keep Cricket from running off. Maybe Cricket would turn out to be religious. Of course, this was hard to believe, but only the power of God seemed of sufficient might to control her and as God was the only thing that James possessed, one had to at least consider the possibility. Baby Charlie stayed home with Sarita in a cradle by her roll-top desk that she could rock with her foot. Parents weren't allowed to have favorites, but Charlie was such a good baby. He gurgled and cooed, took naps at regular hours, liked Cook as much as Nanny, and Cook liked him back and never complained about the odd proclivity that kept him about and not out with Cecily and the other children. And without a nanny of his own. Sarita liked being a mother. Why would she deprive herself of her children? Or at least Charlie. Look at him napping.

Sarita has flung open the window in invitation to the glorious day. The sun is streaming into the garden and the scent of the climbing rose hangs exorbitant and cloyingly sweet. She's finished the household accounts with Mrs. Ogilvie and the maintenance bills with Mr. Garrity, bills easily vanquished by the rising profits of Father's latest shenanigans. She's started to help Father with his correspondence in order to free him up for meetings—some things need to stay within the family—and so she doesn't have as much time as she once did. She likes this excuse to stay at home and just sent money to the local chapter of the Anti-Slavery Society, of which she had once been the secretary. Having cut back on her social obligations also cut back on such things as her dressmakers' costs and trips to the haberdashers.

No, she has no use for the dressmaker, nor as much use for Paulson who, in Herbert's absence, spends half his time in London as second groom to her parents, which he prefers. Paulson considers himself a Londoner, although why, who can say? Cecily knows for a fact that Paulson is from Yorkshire, the son of a bricklayer, and grew up in a small town not far from but not overly close to Sheffield. Charlie cries in his sleep, gasps a little, and then returns to some baby dream with a smile. Sarita rocks the cradle with her foot.

This latest piece of information from Father is an instruction to the family solicitor concerning a rather large deposit into her bank account. Could they really be worth that much? She looks around at the décor of the little study—an odd combination of juju masks and spears, stained glass and stuffed birds, a fashionable miniature putica and sketchy French paintings. These last she'd saved from being auctioned off in the Carleton Terrace liquidation: They were recent and not worth much anyway, but she—like some critics—found them really inspiring. Sarita sets the letter down and rests her chin in her hand.

It is crowded in this little room, and everywhere in the house. They will have to move at some point and she will have to tell Herbert that they're rich again and he'll get that agonized look that has to do with fluctuating between joy that the children are so well provided for and misery that he hasn't been the one to pull it off. And she'll have to admit she's rich again and hire more people, when all she really wants is what she has: Paulson, James, Cecily, Garrity, Kate the housemaid, and Mrs. Ogilvie, who's the housekeeper, but still insists that she's the cook because "It isn't Christian to be putting on airs."

Who knows? Maybe having only five upstairs rooms and Georgian plumbing is Christian too; it is also inconvenient. Herbert has taken over the whole southern end of the drawing room for his easel, even though he's claimed the room next to the nursery for his artistic pursuits. Or maybe that's for writing. Regardless, that room doesn't have the long windows that Herbert needs to paint. And paint he must, although, this being England, long windows and southern exposure don't guarantee you sunlight. In a way, she wishes they had returned to Paris this past winter. They'd meant to, but Herbert had fallen in with Seymour Lucas, a painter with a distinctly English perspective, who felt that Julian's Studio was some sort of radical hotbed of Continental dissipation. It was as if Lucas didn't know that Herbert was studying with Bouguereau and Robert-Fleury. Bouguereau painted naked women and children whose gorgeous glowing flesh was reduced to perfected marble, but there was always something overtly erotic about his work. It was as if he had meant to cool some of this by chilling women's skin and putting wings on naked children, but this just made the seductive quality of the pieces all the more perverted. And as for Robert-Fleury—well, he didn't have the saving grace of Bouguereau's overt pleasures: He was just standard Neoclassical establishment. Why would Lucas have a problem with him?

Herbert has no problem painting the common man—that's his natural inclination. But years of sketching and a tendency towards outline—the two-dimensional side of the two-dimensional—make him shy away from techniques determined to replicate light and movement, that underscore ephemera, that celebrate the fact that these subjects are fading, have already faded, are gone.

Ward has been living on the *Windward* for the last month. He gets his articles in to Harmsworth, but that doesn't fill the days. He keeps busy doing whatever needs to be done, painting boats, oiling gear, counting stores. His tiny cot is in a storeroom filled with photographic equipment and oilskins and pepper pots. And tomorrow the *Windward* will sail and he will be left onshore, left to return to his wife and family. He takes a bottle of vodka from his trunk and heads for the deck. All is quiet. Some of the crew are onshore with their own families, and some may have gone to sleep early. But who can sleep with such a journey looming? He sees a familiar figure lying on the hay bales. The flare of a match illuminates the man's face as he studies a book. It's the captain, Jackson.

"Jackson," says Ward, "what are you up to?"

"I'm committing the sky to memory as one is not always in the position to consult a book."

"Fascinating," says Ward. "Well, there's Ursa Major." He points.

"That's Ursa Minor," says Jackson. "And Cassiopeia. And the tip of Draco." Jackson's arm arcs across the sky. "My last trip, Siberia, we survived because of three things. Celestial navigation. Dogs. And the third thing?"

"I'm guessing vodka," says Ward, handing over the bottle. And he's right. Jackson is coolheaded, as befits his occupation, but even he is having a case of nerves.

Two years ago, Ward had been in Christiania covering the departure of the *Fram*, which was making a run on the North Pole. As the *Fram* departed the harbor, Ward, following in a small boat, saw Nansen's wife standing on a rock in front of the explorer's house. She wore a white dress to be visible to her husband as the boat passed and the white dress and rock and waves hitting it made her seem like a specter. "Do you think Nansen's still alive?"

Jackson laughs. "Nansen is still there, and I'll be the one to the rescue him."

The following morning, Ward watches as the *Windward* disappears from view, his coat flapping in the brute wind. Alone on the pier, he tries to cheer himself. Self-pity is not in his nature—or if it is, it shouldn't be. Perhaps there will be other adventures, ones in which he will perform a role, not simply record for history. But for now, his sketchbook is filled with pictures of the *Windward*, the thoughts and fears recorded not his but rather those of Jackson. He feels as if he is yet one of the Wards of Wigmore Street: a preserver, an animator—a taxidermist!—although it is Jackson who is very much alive, and he who feels (he can't help it) as if life is over.

VII

London

January 1900

Casement has been shuttling back and forth from Africa for the last five years. He's currently consul at Lorenço Marques in Portuguese East Africa, which sounds a lot more fun and exotic than it actually is. Home leave is most welcome, and the *leave* part of it he wholly understands, although the *home* part is still a bit of a mystery. Where is his home, really?

This is Casement's second leave of the last six months. During the first, his doctor in London had informed him that he was in poor shape, due to a combination of weakened kidneys, arthritis, water on the knee, and a compelling need for another piles operation. Faced with all this, Casement had decided to head back to Africa, where his first act upon arrival had been a dramatic collapse in Durban. So now he is back: four months, doctor's orders. Four months is a long time and beds from the North of Ireland to the South of England have been made ready.

Soon Ward will arrive to whisk him away to the first of his destinations of recuperation. Surgery accomplished, Casement is packing up in his cheap hotel. Nina is put out by the thought that he's spending money on accommodation, money he doesn't have, but he did pick up the check, as always, when he last had lunch with her. His brothers are also short on cash and Casement, as a result, is short on cash. It would seem that the only person who has any money is Ward.

The room is cheap. The translation offered by the mirror—a distancing and palliative inaccuracy—still testifies to its shabbiness. And Casement too is shabby, gaunt, and sallow, the yellowness that comes from a pale complexion punished by sun, then suddenly robbed of it. He's nervous, his heart uneasy in his chest—fluttering like a schoolgirl's, because Ward robs him of his composure. He can feel that soaring, involuntary hope as he anticipates Ward's company, can predict the ensuing low spirits when Ward leaves. The recovery. Everything collapse and recovery. Casement carries his bag down the stairs. He chooses a seat along the same wall as the entrance, a place where he will see Ward before Ward sees him.

Ward is late by a half hour and seems to have been running when he bursts through the door. Casement watches him go up to the reception desk and rap with his knuckles, as the clerk has stepped away. Ward has gained some weight and lost some hair but Casement can see the younger Ward somehow superimposed upon the older—the glossy hair, the loose posture, his eager spirit.

"Ward," he calls across the lobby.

Ward turns, his elbow still resting on the desk. "There he is! Roddie Casement himself!" Ward has obviously been drinking. He rushes to grab Casement's hand and shakes it so vigorously that Casement can feel the pull of tendons in his shoulder. "Sorry I'm late. I had a lunch meeting with some of Sanford's associates, and one of them wouldn't shut up."

"Do you do that frequently?"

"Lunch? Once a day."

"I meant—"

"I know what you meant." Ward manages to wrestle his features into a sage expression. "I'm not bad at business. I'm just much, much better at pleasure!"

"So where are we going?"

"We're going back to the club," says Ward. "There's three-quarters of a bottle of Champagne sitting in a bucket of ice at my table."

"You just left it?"

"The club's right around the corner," says Ward. "Give me your bag."

"I can carry my bag."

"We're in a hurry and you just got out of hospital." Ward grabs the case. "We have to get there before they clear the table."

Ward had wanted to book a room for Casement at the club, but non-members are not allowed to stay. Always the gentleman, Ward has booked them both into Sarita's favored hotel, which will likely be an improvement over anything Casement has ever experienced. And, as Ward explains, he'll be happy to dodge the recreational supervision that is the mainstay entertainment of the other members. The club is an old one, entrenched in its ways, established and establishment.

"And they let you in?"

"After that to-do with Stanley, it seems a miracle, but one that's easily explained. Several members are, apparently, on the hook with Sanford and Sanford doesn't see the point of having leverage without using it, so here I am, obliging. And they make a good bread pudding."

"How much is that costing you per serving?"

Ward laughs, embarrassed, but in a way that's a relief for him. "It's also for the children."

"Do they belong to the club?"

"Very funny. And no, but it's in their future. Or at least the boys. I don't know what's going to happen to the girls. Cricket is still ferocious, and Dimples is still odd. If they're lucky, they'll take after their mother."

"And how is she?"

"A source of awe, as always. I wish I had her brains, but I'm probably happier with whatever God gave me. And how are you, Casement?"

"Recovering well."

They have reached the steps of the club. Ward is embracing Casement's battered bag and his hair, blown athwart the suggestion of a heavy pomade, is somewhat vertical—saluting at intervals in the wind. They exchange a look.

"Unbelievable," says Ward.

"What?" Casement is smiling broadly.

"All of this didn't seem nearly as ridiculous before you showed up."

Casement is finishing up the last of a slice of beef pie—his lunch—although his appetite has been weak.

"So," says Ward, "what have you been up to?"

"Me?" Casement shrugged. "I was in Lorenço Marques with malaria for company, and now I'm here."

"But why would they send you to Portuguese East Africa?"

"I am not the first British consul in Lorenço Marques."

Ward tips up the last of his Champagne and waves to the waiter. "You're a spy, aren't you?

"A spy?"

"You're watching the Boers and the Germans. You're a spy and I'm a businessman." The waiter arrives. "Whiskey," Ward says, placing his order. "And, for different reasons, I'm watching the Boers and the Germans too—the markets, you know."

"Ward, are you really a businessman?"

Ward shrugs. "I'm mostly in Lambourn and on a beautiful day, with a good horse, there really is nothing like Berkshire. I come to London every couple of weeks. And I do my painting and get a piece a year into the Royal Academy."

"That is certainly something."

"Oh, please, Casement, not you too. I don't want people to hold my hand and tell me how well I'm doing. I have children. I too have use for that kind of language." Ward leans on his elbows, fixing Casement with his gaze. "The business gives me much-needed time away from home. I have my studio in the Woronzow Road and I'm working on some sculpture and that excites me, but as long as I'm in England, I'm Sanford's puppet. He spends half his time in Argentina, which is good—of course—for all of this," he gestures in a loose way, "but makes me necessary. In a better world, Sarita would take care of the banking. She has a fantastic mind for maths, and this bizarre ability to understand people. It's impossible to keep a secret from her. I've never even tried. But she's home with the kids, and I'm here, at a club, where they would have loved to blackball me but didn't have the guts because Sanford's holding all their money."

"You could put Sarita in men's clothes, give her false mustaches."

"I've thought of that, but she actually likes being in the middle of nowhere with the children. But we're going to move as soon as we can."

"To France?"

"That's the idea."

"And Sarita's all right with that?"

"She's behind it. She wants me to focus on the art."

"Why does she want you to do that?"

"Because," Ward presents an incredulous look, "it makes me happy."

After some whiskey, it was time to order dinner, and after the carp/roast beef/bread pudding meal, Ward had felt like taking a walk, and then he wanted to catch a cab to a theatre to watch some dancing, and then he wanted a nightcap. They should have stopped at the walk.

The dancing girls had not all been girls and when Casement pointed this out—drawing Ward's attention to the size of the statuesque blonde's hands—Ward had been shocked. Maybe that's what the nightcap was supposed to counteract, but one nightcap—a fragrant brandy—has morphed into three.

"Another?" says Ward.

"Not for me," says Casement.

"Well then," says Ward to his empty glass. He picks it up and tilts it around, but the glass is absolutely drained.

The path to the elevator stretches across a lobby populated with men standing with their wives. Ward must have been one of their number on his last visit to this hotel, but the prospect of dodging through it all is now making him perturbed. "Roddie, let's take the stairs." As the two men start their ascent, Casement is unsteady and Ward, for all intents and purposes, legless. Of course they're on the third floor, which is going to be a challenge. After the first flight of stairs, it becomes obvious that Casement will have to help Ward to his room. Ward seems inclined to try his key in every door that presents itself and Casement has to keep gently pushing him to keep him going.

"Why don't we just try this room?" says Ward.

"Because it's not yours."

"But it could be."

"Give me the key," says Casement, and Ward does. The corridor forks and Casement steers Ward to the left. Finally, they have reached their destination. "Here you go, Wardy," says Casement, opening the door. He places the key on top of the dresser. "And a good night. I have no doubt that we will both sleep well."

"Casement, Casement, don't leave. I have missed you so."

Casement hesitates at the door. He begins to laugh.

"You're the best friend I have. My Roddie Casement. My friend. All those years that have passed mean nothing to me when I think of us, in the Congo. Don't go yet."

"All right. I'll stay a minute."

Ward collapses into a seated position on the bed. "And you have to help me get my shoes off." Ward extends his foot, like a child, and Casement pulls at the laces and then wrenches the shoe free. He gestures for Ward to raise his other foot, and Ward does. That task now accomplished, Ward says, "And now my jacket."

"That is ambitious. You'll need to stand."

Ward registers this with a hearty if imprecise nod. He rises to his feet, begins fumbling with his buttons himself, then turns so that Casement can release him. Something in the orchestration of the moves feels well rehearsed and Casement wonders if he's filling in for Sarita.

"A good tug and I'll be out," says Ward.

Casement tugs at the jacket, but the jacket is snug around the upper arms. Another tug and Casement, who is not sturdy himself, has toppled both men to the ground. That's a lot of noise and he's hoping that they haven't woken people up. He stifles laughter, as does Ward, as if they're schoolboys. They're sitting propped against the door with Ward on the floor before him, as if they were rowing, but with Ward leaned right against Casement's chest and Casement feels that hope—a mistaken, drunken hope—flickering in his heart.

"Ward, get up. Wardy." There's no answer. There's a snuffle. Has he passed out? "Ward, get up. Are you there?" Ward has fallen asleep with the miraculous urgency of the drunk. He's actually snoring, a dead weight, but warm. Casement can smell the salty sweat on Ward's clothes, see his scalp beneath the thinning hair, feel Ward's very breathing in his arms. He'll wake him in a few moments, but he's sleeping so peacefully, it seems a shame to disturb him. He rests his cheek on Ward's shoulder and feels Ward's heat coming through the starched cotton. He'll just sit there for a short time, just a short, short time. There's nothing wrong in it.

The next morning comes and goes unattended. Casement wakes up in bed at noon to a tapping on the door: Ward, the heel of his hand pressed to his forehead, has no recollection of anything after the first brandy. "I was lying flat on the floor just inside my room. I did manage to get my shoes off." The next train for Lambourn leaves at three. They'll have time for lunch if they don't dawdle. "Do you think they'll give me rashers, even though it's lunchtime? It's exactly what I need."

There are no rashers available and the waiter's look makes clear to Casement that this is an irregular request. Ward responds with a look of equal and extravagantly enacted disdain. Predictably, Ward sleeps most of the way to the station and the entire journey to Berkshire. He has his sea legs back by the time he reaches Lambourn, which is good, because the three older children have decided to meet them at the station. It is an unseasonably mild day, windless, and with uninterrupted sun. Sarita has sent a cart because the children like riding in the open, as does Ward, and there are some things to be picked up in town. Cricket, Dimples, and Charlie pile in with the luggage in the back and Ward, sprawled and using a full sack of potatoes as his pillow, lies down between them. The children giggle, tickling his face with a piece of straw as he attempts to get the last nap in, while Casement—up on the bench beside the driver—turns around to grab their little hands as they poke at his back and tug the bottom of his jacket.

This house is no tent on the banks of the Congo. Lambourn Place is a sprawling Tudor manor that encases a series of older dwellings—like Russian dolls—all the way back to 1489; the earliest home, Rogers Manor, was built by Alfred the Great. It is hard not to be agog at such a spectacle of brickwork and history. "We're only renters," Ward had said. But what a rent it has to be.

His room is down its own corridor, but if Casement wants something more private, he has only to ask. Sarita chose the room both for the décor and the warmth. The fireplace throws a lot of heat and this room is less penetrated by drafts, which are a perennial problem at Lambourn Place, although lack of space is not. Casement has assured Ward that he does have enough privacy: Any further and he'd think they didn't want to see him, and even if they did, he probably wouldn't be able to find his way to their company.

The previous night, Casement had sunk into a profound sleep. His dreams were strange and full of sounds, sensations, blunted realities. He heard footsteps pacing outside the door and—at one moment—he thought the footfalls had actually passed into his room, that there was someone standing beside his bed. Malaria, he thought, ghost-fevers. Casement slept late, until ten. He'd been woken up by the girls chatting outside his door, Cricket saying, "He's not going to like it," and Dimples's reply, "Why not?" He'd opened the door in his robe and bare feet. *Good mornings* were exchanged. Dimples was holding a pillowcase like a sack. She opened it and there, twitching languidly at the bottom, was a small green snake.

"I do like it," Casement said. "It is a beautiful thing. I have seen many snakes and this is by far the sweetest and most appealing." Dimples was victorious. Later, he'd heard her telling Sarita that Mr. Casement had liked the snake, heard Sarita's delight to know it.

Lunch will be served in about an hour, and until then, Casement can enjoy his book in this room, which is the "drawing room" but might as easily be called the "third living room," as there are many such rooms, although not all have furniture. Ward is out riding. That is what he does in Lambourn, if the weather permits. He is inordinately fond of his horse, "The Monkey," and—if his accounts are accurate—spends half his life suspended mid-vault over hedgerows, another third or so thundering across Berkshire, a bit shooting (and hitting) various representatives of the local wildlife, and whatever is left eating, sleeping (the horse, too, needs sleep), and working on his oils. Ward had tried to convince Casement to go for a ride that morning as it was clear, although very cold. He could always borrow the reliable Snowball from Cricket, although his feet might drag. Casement had reminded Ward that recovering from this particular surgery and riding were not compatible. Instead, he is reading *Mon Frère Yves* by Pierre Loti, ostensibly about a friendship between two men—one a rough Breton soldier and the other an officer.

Sarita pauses at the doorway. How still Casement looks, and fragile. It's hard to believe that this man is single-handedly trying to overthrow King Leopold and save thousands of Congolese from slavery. She watches at the entrance until it feels a violation. "Hello," she says. Casement, deep into his reading, is startled. He's instinctively lowered the book and is holding it to the right side of the chair, out of view.

"Roddie, what are you reading?" she asks, raising her eyebrows.

"Ah," says Casement. "Just some French literature."

"Anything interesting?"

"It's a bit slow."

"Well, then I'm not bothering you."

"Not at all."

Sarita can see him scanning her face. As of late, she has been alternating between ferocious vibrancy and quivering nausea. Right now, she must be pale. She takes a seat across from him and reaches for the book, which he hands to her. She turns the pages idly. "If we go to France, I'm going to have to do better with my French. I keep lapsing into Spanish and everyone thinks I'm odd."

"Maybe you are."

"Well, I definitely am. But how are you? How's the 'recuperation'?"

"If this is illness, I don't care to get better."

"How are you sleeping?"

"You know, it's strange," he says. "I could have sworn that I heard someone in the hallway last night, walking around, opening and shutting doors. Could it have been one of the children?"

"Not over there," says Sarita. She widens her eyes dramatically. "But we do have a ghost, Sir John Hippisley the last of the Lambourn Hippisleys. He defrauded the church and townspeople of quite a bit of money and it's rumored that he murdered a servant. But I wouldn't worry about him. They say he's quite remorseful. And no one's seen him, although Ticker has been known to start growling when there's nothing there."

"Well, Sir John is welcome to my company, as long as he doesn't need anything."

She senses that Casement wants to talk but is not sure how to proceed. He's one of those men who assume one knows all there is to know about him, and as a result she knows very little. "You are recuperating," she says, "or perhaps your consular work has made you crave solitude?"

"Not solitude as much as this sort of company."

He is so very polite and charming. What if she were to resist? "So where to, after you've tired of your friends? Is it back to Lorenço Marques?"

"I hope not. That was a ridiculous posting. The only reason I was there was that a great number of other British subjects were also there—and without good reason. I believe that the English go to Portuguese East Africa with the express intention of having problems. They go to be extorted by the local officials, or have their crates stolen, or to come down with malaria."

"What does that have to do with you?"

"Everything. I'm the man standing at the edge of the world who says, 'Go home before this place kills you.' And if they're smart, they listen."

"And finally someone said that to you."

"And I'm smart, so I listened, and here I am. I'm hoping my next posting is Cape Town, a lovely place—crystalline light, an arctic-splashed breeze."

"And a war."

"Looks like it," says Casement.

"Herbert says you're a spy."

"Not very good at keeping secrets, is he?"

"He's not, but I am. So you should be all right." Sarita sees Casement look inwardly, disappear into his thoughts, and then resurface. "Just imagine, Roddie, you and Herbert knowing each other all these years. And you're still friends."

"Yes," says Casement. "Still friends."

"You know I've another child on the way."

"I'd wondered, or maybe hoped. A house full of children is a blessing. I'm a bachelor who actually means it when I say it."

"And I believe you, which is why I want to name the child after you. 'Roger Casement Ward.'"

Casement is speechless.

"Herbert said that you'd want your name for your own child, but I told him that men like you didn't marry. And he said," she drops her voice to mimic Ward, "'Men like me don't marry either, and we all know how that ended up.'" Sarita laughs and holds Casement's cautious, searching gaze.

"Thank you," he says.

Sarita dismisses his solemn gratitude, waving it off with a flick of her hand. "I've always liked your name."

"Roger?"

"No, Casement. Casement sounds noble and dignified." She pats her waist, which is still narrow. "He'll be Roger Casement Ward, and we'll call him Roddie, because we miss you when you're not around."

"But what if it's a girl?"

"I'm sure it's a boy. I know it's impolite to talk about such things at this early date, but I wanted to tell you directly rather than include it in a letter. Herbert has always thought of you as a brother." Sarita watches her statement hit its mark. "You have been like family to all of us, and now you will be."

VIII
Cape Town

March 1900

At the moment, it's hard to believe there's a war going on. Brother Tom has enlisted and is off in the Free State menacing Boers with the Irish Horse. And Casement? He's at the Grand Hotel, in the tearoom waiting for a gin and tonic with its promise of ice. Casement's score is light chatter and chamber music, countered only with the bleat of fishmongers' horns as they round the corner of Adderley Street—no flash and pop of rifles, no groaning of injured men, no screaming horses. Right now, the only violence he sees, through the window, is on Strand: a young black boy is being smacked repeatedly on the side of his head by a well-fed Englishman. He hits the boy with the heel of his hand and boy's head jerks, returns, and then is smacked again. But that is not the war, and since it is not, then perhaps it is peace.

In the corner of the tearoom an amateur quartet saws their way through some music—Boccherini?—that has great energy and little else to recommend it. One could say the same of the war. Casement's drink arrives, startling him. "I'll have another gin and tonic," he tells the waiter.

"Another, sir?"

"That last one took nearly half an hour. So by the time I'm done with this, I'll have a fresh one waiting." Casement smiles.

"I do apologize," says the waiter. "We had trouble with the ice."

Casement is still, ostensibly, a consul, but as of late there have been greater problems than English nationals falling ill. He recalls that woman in Lorenço Marques who collapsed on his couch—choosing to enact her distress rather than tell him—and stayed there for an entire month. He grew accustomed to her and on occasion was the one who held the glass to her lips. And then she was gone. What was her name? It's not as if they ever had a real conversation, although she was a sort of company. He's considering returning to his rooms when the specter of a woman, he knows her, appears on the far side of the room: It is Miss Kingsley. He hasn't seen her in six years, not since the MacDonalds' party in Calabar. Casement waves at her and her face registers recognition with a shock of delight. She crosses the room in her inelegant, purposeful stride.

"Mister Casement, don't you show up in the most ridiculous of places!"

Casement rises in greeting. "As do you, Miss Kingsley. You must join me."

"I will," she says, pulling the chair out. She allows him to push it in but senses that she's doing this for his sake rather than her own.

"What's that?" she says, looking at his drink.

"A gin and tonic. Yours is on its way."

"Really?"

"I must have had a moment of clairvoyance."

"Funny you should say that," says Miss Kingsley, "because that woman over there offered to read my palm." Across the room are two older ladies who look so similar that they must be sisters.

"And what did she find?" asks Casement.

"I didn't let her look."

"You don't believe in that sort of thing?"

"On the contrary, Mister Casement, I do. And I would rather not know."

He remembers that she has no use for Christianity but can't recall exactly what she's replaced it with. "Well, Miss Kingsley, what brings you here?"

"This ugly war."

"I didn't know you were a soldier."

"I'm not." Miss Kingsley's right eyebrow shoots up with wry humor. "I'm a nurse."

"I didn't know that either."

"It is a recent development, unless you count former experience dosing aged relatives with beef tea."

Miss Kingsley is in Simons Town working in a hospital that caters to Boer prisoners, injured soldiers, and those women and children sickened in the camps. Casement listens, nodding ineffectively. This war demands that you forget that the Boers are anything but soldiers mobilized around territorial concerns and mining interests. The fact of their farming, their families, their religion—even their race—is an inconvenience that hums unheeded at every meeting he's attended. Or perhaps he's the only one who hears it.

"It is an outrage, a violation of human rights. They're calling them 'concentration camps,' as if it makes it any better. But they're women and children, picked off the fields and held as hostages. The conditions are horrific. We're killing off the Boers with a combination of starvation and enteric fever."

"It's the same tactic that the Belgians use to bring in workers to collect rubber. They round up the wives and children and keep them in pens. One works to pay off the ransom."

"How do they create a justification for that?" Miss Kingsley's drink arrives and she takes an impressive, joyless gulp.

"Ah," Casement exhales. He shakes his head and looks Miss Kingsley square in the face. "They don't." The humor takes its strain as a principle.

Miss Kingsley does not look well. She is thin and overworked. Her knuckles are cracked and despite the girlish vitality of her carriage and gesture, he sees the streaks of gray in her hair. She reaches out and puts her hand on his—a pat—and then withdraws it. Together, the two wander a narrow circuit of thought, as if they are the only people of reason alive.

"But really, Mister Casement, why are you here?"

"I have knowledge of Delgoa Bay. That was my last appointment. That's the Orange Free State's closest seaport."

"Why don't they shut it down, then? And end this war?"

"And stop the fun? Truth is it wouldn't take that much. All you'd need to do is blow up the railroad in Komatipoort. It's how the arms get to the interior."

Miss Kingsley narrows her eyes dramatically. "Do you want to know a secret, Mister Casement?"

"If you're going to tell me a secret, you should call me Roddie."

"Roddie. I really don't care who wins the war—I just want it to be over."

"And who's your money on?"

"Oh, England, of course. And call me Mary." She pushes her chair back from the table and crosses her ankles, looking out across the room as if the truth lies in the offing. "England seems determined to empty its back alleys into this country."

"And its colonies." The two fall quiet. Casement was present at the British defeat in Colenso, there to hear the priest's reedy voice declaiming in Latin over the bowed heads of those Irish soldiers—boys—falling to their knees to receive the blessing. Turned out to be Last Rites, for not a single man came back. One horse did return to camp and her eyes were wild, her flank streaked with her rider's blood. She was hard to subdue and kept sidestepping and swinging her head until someone managed to grab the bridle. "Mary, as you know, I'm Irish."

She gives a meaningful nod. "You know that some of the Irish are playing for the other team?"

"I've heard that."

"And what side do you have your money on, Roddie?"

"England, but we've underestimated the Boers. The Boers like the fringes of civilization, like digging in the dry dirt and then thank their

Calvinist God for his meager gifts. They know their territory, and they're fast. They disappear from the landscape and once they've done that, they're hard to shoot." Casement shakes his head. "And we can't trust the Germans. That's who we're really fighting. We don't know what the Kaiser's thinking, but it definitely involves a clever, long-range plan."

"The Kaiser's sneaky, like Leopold." Miss Kingsley's disdain arranges her features, settling like a wad of tobacco in her cheek.

"When are you going to get back to the Congo?" he asks her.

"When this bloody war is over." She takes another mouthful of gin and tonic, reducing the glass by a third. "I have friends there," she says earnestly. "You must too."

"Many."

"When this war is over . . ." Her voice trails off and her eyes seem to be scanning a distant memory, or perhaps an unrealized possibility. "If we survive it."

As if on cue, one of the women in black—the soothsayer—is making her way to their table. She stops at the perimeter, her eyes burrowing down on Casement. He can see her sister rushing to settle their account, to stop this intrusion.

"Madame," says Casement. He rises from the table out of habit, but also since his full height offers some security. She reaches out and he, not feeling as if he has a choice, extends his hand, which she grabs. He expects her to flip it and expose the palm, but she doesn't. She clutches his hand, her eyes tearing quickly as she looks deeply into his, a visage of profound sorrow slowly overcoming her. "You will die young," she says. "It will be violent and tragic, on your fifty-second birthday."

Her sister has finally reached them and, placing her hands on the woman's shoulders, slowly turns her away. The woman seems to be held in a trance. The sister looks to Casement and says, "I am so sorry." He has no protest because he himself has known this, somehow, in his marrow. He does not regret this intrusion because it has reduced his loneliness.

He turns to Miss Kingsley, who is looking at him calmly, and he knows, somehow, that she too will die young. He senses things, although void of detail, and therefore easily ignored. He would ask this clairvoyant more questions, but she is now on the opposite side of the room, her shoulders collapsed, still being guided by the sister, exhausted by her knowledge of the future of men without comprehension as to why these lives should be so compromised.

The Boer War, in its death throes, drags on with no clear battle lines. Casement has been sent to Brussels to talk to King Leopold as the focus of the Foreign Office is back on trade.

Casement's charge is to urge the monarch to lift taxes on exported goods, but thus far Leopold has avoided this topic. The previous day, Casement had shown up for a meeting only to be ushered in to lunch. Present were the King's wife Marie-Henriette, the uncomprehending Princess Clementine, and her mincing suitor, Prince Victor Napoleon of France. Conversation struggled along, with Princess Clementine asking politely about Casement's life—childhood, youth, career—that in its telling sounded made up, even to Casement. He found the whole encounter offensive. Leopold, sensing his failure to charm, had extended a second invitation to meet.

Casement has spent the whole morning in his hotel room rehearsing lines, trying to figure out how to bring up the treatment of the natives in a casual way, without calling attention to his host's being a murderer. He already wore his good shirt to the lunch yesterday but decides to put it back on, as the clean one is a bit yellow. This will be his last opportunity to make an impression as he doubts Leopold will be willing to meet a third time. Casement takes a moment to appreciate the fact that he has become someone who discusses the fates of nations with monarchs.

After fifteen minutes of waiting in the echoing entrance of the King's residence, Casement is led up the long left arm of a pair of staircases, shuttled down a portrait-hung hall, and left on the wrong side of a heavy oak door.

Leopold is in there, muttering with someone. Heavy footsteps thump across carpet and, finally, the door swings open. An attendant presents Casement with an oily bow, gesturing for him to enter. This is an overheated chamber. Leopold, backed into a corner and coiled like a snake, presents Casement with narrowed eyes. Casement takes the chair opposite. He clears his throat, noting, in his peripheral vision, the candelabrum of gorgeous ebony Africans bearing the weight of candle cups in gold. He can already feel the sweat trickling down his ribs.

King Leopold has never been to the Congo and shows no interest in making the journey. But he thinks he understands everything to a degree that Casement cannot fathom, finding him distracted by an assortment of local realities. "Mister Casement, we are improving the lot of the natives by introducing them to the civilizing influences of work. I don't have to tell you what degraded lives these people led in the past."

Casement attempts a relaxed attitude, but the back of the chair makes it impossible. "Your Highness, with all respect, the lives of these natives— charges who are under our protection—are still degraded."

"Well, patience. I have learned to be a patient man."

"Your Highness, the value of one's labor is a lesson that is best supported with compensation for one's labor."

"Then we are in agreement."

How to maneuver? Usually Casement is struggling to control his temper, but right now it would seem that all his energy is being drawn away by disbelief. "If the natives felt the benefit of ownership—a stake in property— they might better care for their resources—"

"You are suggesting a tax on property."

"Am I?"

"And was that successful in the Niger Protectorate?"

The Hut Tax was seen for what it was—a foreign power extracting money for property that had once been free—and there were riots. Casement initially supported the tax because it seemed a harbinger of modernization that would benefit everyone. "I no longer support it."

"Ah, you have changed your mind. But I think strong, consistent leadership is what's needed now." Leopold tents his fingers thoughtfully. "I have not forgotten the Paris Commune. None of Europe has. I am wary of rebellion, discord. Violence. And here I am with a workforce of two million. My people, like the wretched natives, need work. The Congo provides it."

"Respectfully, one would hope that Belgium, with so great a workforce, would have more professional managers to provide to the Congo."

Leopold shakes his head sympathetically. "What to tell their wives when they come back? The climate . . . Truly, Mister Casement, you are an exceptional man that you could spend long years in such a place and present yourself to me so whole. Africa, the Congo in particular, creates perversions of people."

"And of free trade," Casement counters, which is a stretch as far as segues go, but a safer topic. Is Leopold having him followed? His mind flickers back to the young man on the pier two nights previous, his rough French, and rougher hands.

"I too admire free trade," Leopold says, "and that is why I support it."

"All that is imported into the Congo is rifles and ammunition, used to subdue the local population."

"No, that is not true."

"Respectfully, that is true. The rubber workers are not paid."

"The workers are paid. Although sometimes they incur debts in the course of their employment, so unfortunate—although perhaps, given time with a civilizing influence, the natives will learn to better manage their resources."

Casement could kill him. He could rise from his stiff little chair, step around the inlaid table, find the monarch's neck beneath the curtain of beard, and hold tight for as long as it took. Why not? They are alone in the room. He could do it, sacrifice himself to the greater good. But unfortunately for the Congo, Casement is no martyr. And he is not a fanatic, but a diplomat. "You do understand that the poor treatment of the natives will result in sanctions."

"Mister Casement," says Leopold, "you must know that the natives of the Belgian Congo are my subjects, and therefore their welfare is my responsibility. My business, if you will."

"The various anti-slavery societies will intervene."

"These are the societies that gave me complete control of the region."

This last statement is true. Maybe Casement can harness public opinion against Leopold and get him out of the Congo. The Foreign Office will probably be in favor and might even back him.

Leopold leans forward. "Do you believe that the British will actually support free trade?"

"I do."

"As in Ireland?"

Leopold's intelligence is good.

"Mister Casement, I know of the Irish Famine as it happened right after the one in Belgium. But the one in Ireland, if I recall, in part resulted from manipulated markets. England decided to restore free trade and export great quantities of food just in time to see the Irish starve."

"I am aware of this," says Casement, but is not sure how else to follow it up. Leopold sits back in his chair, but Casement can hear his thought as if he's actually speaking it: "And still you put your faith in England."

IX
Paris

November 1902

Ward takes the tongs and positions more coal on the fire. His studio is drafty, exacerbated by the high ceilings, which he needs, because he can't get a sense of a piece unless there's some air around it. Casement is in Paris, now at the Foreign Office to pick up some funds. His brothers are off in Australia and South Africa and must be working—you don't go that far to do nothing—but Casement is always sending them, and his sister, money. And then when it's gone, asking Ward to help him out.

Ward needs to get back to his sculpting. Casement will be showing up in the next hour to initiate the slow march to inebriation. Casement likes this piece, a witch doctor, but is an unreliable critic. He likes everything.

Ward has got the figure up on its right foot, balanced on the ball, with his left arm extended up over his head holding an idol. The pose is extreme and François, the model, has protested vigorously. François has said that no black man stands like this—even the savage African. And Ward had agreed—he'd never seen any man in such a pose. He'd been inspired at the ballet. If a ballerina could do this without falling over, a bronze statue could pull it off as well.

Right now, Rodin is all the rage. Sarita adores Rodin, something about his ability to create tension in bronze. Of course, this bothers Ward. She never says anything quite so articulate about his work. So how does one create tension in bronze? Take a witch doctor and stand him on one toe like a ballerina.

Now he's being hard on himself. Dupuy had dropped in to see his progress, and had very nice things to say about the savage beauty, the glorious male physique. Et cetera. This same man had shuddered, physically repulsed by François who, in his usual way, was smoking a bad cigar, squatted on his bare heels by the door. Ward should make a statue of that. François would hold the pose just fine, wouldn't complain of feeling ridiculous. But *The Witchdoctor* is going to be a good statue, might actually win something. So what if it doesn't have the frenetic emotion of Rodin? Is that Ward's fault? Rodin is, after all, sculpting literary greats like Balzac, while he, Ward, is in the business of animating demented Juju priests.

He steps back. The musculature is really good, and that's his knowledge after all—the body. And the African. He's not sure how to depict angst because he's not particularly susceptible, nor even interested. And people like his work—important people—and *An Aruwimi Type*, that first head, had received a Mention Honorable at the Salon. Ward has, apparently, made it. Although sometimes, and this is the true insecurity, he feels that he has entered into the Ward family business: taxidermy. As he resurrects this witch doctor from the drawings and memories of the long-dead past, he feels that there is something stuffed about him, this dancing Bangala, as if—beneath the surface—one would find straw and wood shavings and oakum, as if the noble bronze would be tainted with the whiff of formaldehyde.

In these moments, when he feels lost and unsure, he remembers Jameson. *Art is a gentleman's pursuit*, he'd said. And Ward, insecure at the time, had demoted his life's passion to a hobby, like tying flies or scissoring silhouettes from card stock. And now that he's a gentleman, the art is no longer a hobby but a pursuit. He's chasing it and it's dodging his best shots, slipping out of sight, or vaporizing when he feels as if he might have it in his grasp.

Casement shows up and Ward, who had resolved to work another hour and let Casement read his book, immediately caves. They reach the café and Ward opens the door. There's a suitable table by the window and as they sit, the first of the rain blows in, a horizontal handful of drops that tap against the pane.

"How was Italy?" asks Ward.

"Like a dream."

"And you're going back there?"

"I'll have a couple of weeks in Sicily before I head to Lisbon and then—"

"Ah!" Ward groans. "I'd do anything to go with you."

"It's not the same, Ward. The Congo is quite changed."

"As are we." The waiter comes to the table and Ward orders two brandies. "How was the Argentine?"

"I was there for almost six months, you know, being Sanford's marionette. I learned a little Spanish. And the countryside is spectacular. I got some good watercolors of the mountains." He had been altered by this last trip but every word Ward hopes to bring to the conversation—*beauty, grandeur*—is so overused as to have no currency. He'd felt lonely for the first time in years and it was a lovely sensation, like a long bath after weeks spent hiking in the jungle. "I went with some Indians up the mountain and no one had anything to say to me, and I had nothing to say to them."

"I find that hard to believe."

"That is because I save up my conversation all year to spend on you. Usually, it's just me making shadow puppets for children. Or listening to Sarita talk about moving to England and moving back and moving to the country, telling everyone where they need to be and what they need to do. She should have been a general."

"Really?"

"She's a right Napoleon. Only Napoleon had his Waterloo and Sarita has never lost a battle in her life."

Brandies in hand, they drink a silent toast to this wife of his.

"Tell me about your illness," says Casement.

"Tell me about yours," Ward responds.

"Which one?" Casement smiles. "I have become arthritic and my back seizes up. The doctor seems most concerned about the intestinal thing, which he calls a 'loosening of the lower bowels.'"

"If you can just get your back into some sort of agreement with your backside, you'll be all right."

"Very funny, Ward. And how are you?"

"I had a touch of fever in Argentina." Ward shrugs. "Wasn't my first fever and chances are it won't be my last."

"Sarita said you were down for months and that it was rheumatic, possibly causing heart damage."

"You could say that. Or you could just say that we're getting older and this, unfortunately, is what age looks like." Ward rakes his fingers comically through his thinning hair.

Casement is considering applying for a position in Lisbon. He is worried that he won't survive another appointment in the Congo. The situation has gotten worse. Casement tells Ward of the practice of cutting hands, how even children can be found maimed in this way.

"Awful stuff," says Ward. "When you finish your report, I'm sure the government will step in."

Casement's Congo has no beauty, no grandeur. Casement's Congo has nothing but disfigured children and starving women and flyblown corpses. Casement goes on, his eyes flickering and his head twitching.

"Be careful that you don't get in trouble."

"Me?" There's Casement's indulgent smile. "Remember, Ward, I'm the responsible one."

"It just sounds like you're getting on the wrong side of some very powerful people." They take a moment's quiet, where they both upend their glasses. Casement must be struggling to find his levity. He takes a couple of deep breaths, signaling a conscious change of mood.

"Is this your favorite café?"

"It's all right," says Ward, "about midway between the apartment and my studio. And it's a bit more colorful than my other watering hole, has a reputation for attracting artists and writers and, as of late, Irish radicals."

"Then it's a good place for me," says Casement.

"Not really. You must know about Maude Gonne. And if you don't know her, then you'll have heard of the husband."

"John MacBride?"

"Then you do know him?"

"Not personally, but we were both recently in South Africa."

"Very funny, Casement." MacBride is a treasonous lunatic who sided with the Boers and managed to raise up an entire regiment of anarchists: the Irish Transvaal Brigade. He's also the subject of a lot of local gossip.

"MacBride is not technically Irish," says Casement, his eyes smiling.

"MacBride not Irish—because he's a British subject?" asks Ward.

"MacBride is actually a citizen of the Orange Free State, not a British subject at all. He changed his citizenship."

"Are you saying he's African? Don't split hairs, Casement. We all know that he changed his citizenship to avoid being tried as a traitor. He did it to avoid hanging."

"That's very likely," says Casement. "But, Ward, the Boer War was a messy thing. No one comes out of that unsullied."

"Well, the English are less sullied," Ward says with conviction. "And remember whose side you're on. Stand with the winners. Who would you rather be, Napoleon or the Duke of the Wellington?"

"I would have to say the Duke of Wellington."

"Who was English."

"Actually, he was Irish."

"But his troops were English."

"The significant troops in that engagement were Irish too."

"Well, I'm English," says Ward. "And I'm ordering another round."

Casement is in his room at the Ward's Paris house. Due to limited space, he's sure he's replaced someone or something, but Sarita manages to keep that hidden, skilled in all manner of politeness. He holds the letter from his publisher, which states, "I think I ought to say at once that I do not look forward to a remunerative sale." It is a rejection. Fisher Unwin doesn't see how political Irish poems, travel pieces mostly about Africa but some of Italy, and deeply personal work that skirts love can possibly fit in one work. Of course, he is right.

Casement has not mentioned this to Ward as Ward would be sympathetic and that would be too much humiliation to bear. He should burn this letter, and he looks over at the beckoning coal fire, but can't seem to do it. He'll fold the paper back into its envelope and when he reopens it, maybe it will have changed its mind. There's a tapping at the door and, when he turns, he sees little Herbie at the threshold of his room.

"Hello, Herbie," says Casement. "How long were you standing there?"

"A very long time."

"Why didn't you let me know?"

"I just did."

"Do you want to come in?"

Herbie takes the invitation and walks purposely over to Casement and, as is his habit, crawls into his lap. Herbie is four years old, a golden creature like his father, but more temperamentally like his mother.

"Mummy says I can't ask you why you're not married."

"Why not?"

"She says it's rude."

"Is it?"

"I don't think so." As Herbie ponders this, he picks up Casement's hand and begins trying to bend back his nails, one at a time. "I know you have a dog. But you can't bring him here because he's sick."

"Not exactly sick." John is in Lisbon, not allowed into England or Ireland because of strict quarantine rules. Casement will have to pick him up on his way back to Africa.

Sarita passes the door and, seeing Herbie, returns. "Herbie, I told you not to bother your uncle Roddie."

"He's not bothering me."

"You're too kind to the children. And Herbie will talk your ear off."

"Now that would be strange," says Casement, a stage whisper for Herbie.

"Herbie," says Sarita, "Anna's looking for you. It's time for your bath."

Herbie gives Casement a droll look, unimpressed by the need for ablutions. "I'd rather—"

"Not of interest, Herbie. Come on."

Herbie slides down over Casement's knees like a blanket slipping from a couch. He sits momentarily collapsed against Casement's shins before he collects himself. And then, one slow foot in front of the other, he makes his way to the door.

"Say good night," says Sarita.

Herbie is considering this. Instead, he says, "Uncle Roddie, why don't you have a family?"

"I—"

"Not your sister. Your own family."

"Uncle Roddie does have a family." Sarita draws her back straight. "He has us. We're his family."

This answer is short of satisfactory, as is made clear by the child's expression. Herbie makes his leave, wishing Casement a good night, but Sarita lingers by the door. Together, Casement and Sarita enjoy some polite, truthful silence. In other corners of the house, the girls can be heard arguing and Charlie yelling at them to shut up. And then Ward saying that they should all be in bed. "Roddie," she says, now addressing him. "You need to take a break. I know you're headed back to the Congo but you really should consider alternatives. You're not a young man anymore and you have to think about your health. You don't look well."

"I must go back, one last time."

"Herbert said that you're taking statements from the natives and compiling a report?"

"That's right."

"It's not your responsibility to save these people."

"It is the right thing to do."

Sarita holds up her hand. "The right thing to do is to value your life. To hold your well-being in such low regard could well be suicide. And remember, suicide is a sin." Although Sarita seems to believe in nothing but common sense.

"It could be martyrdom," he says, playing.

"Saint Roger? Spare me."

"It's better in Irish."

"What would that be?"

"Saint Ruairí."

"It's still ridiculous. You're ridiculous. And all this nonsense about Ireland—"

"What nonsense about Ireland?"

"Fine, Roddie. Go save the Congo. That will take care of everything because you'll be too dead to create more trouble."

Casement studies Sarita.

"Oh, I'm sorry." She raises her eyebrows a few quick times. "An outburst, no doubt in bad taste. But heavens, Roddie, some times these excesses of good taste become a sort of bad taste. Herbert and I have become so . . ." She's waving her hand around as if to grab the right word.

"Wealthy?"

"Boring."

"You and Herbert are hardly boring."

"Kind of you to say. And I suppose Herbert is an artist. And what am I? The wife of an artist?"

"You are having forward-thinking thoughts, Sarita."

"Perhaps. Why not? But I'm no suffragette. Who cares about politics?"

"You're a very exciting lady raising her children in a foreign country."

"True," she says, "but when you're not from anywhere in particular, you're not exactly foreign. Or you're always foreign."

As soon as Sarita gets one problem resolved, another takes its place. Perhaps this is just existence. At least she does not want for food, and she says that actually having been hungry, although hunger—want in general—is buried in such a remote room of memory as to seem up for debate. She is grateful for all she has, but being wealthy presents its own peculiar challenges, for example, managing the education of your children. For the boys, it's pretty straightforward—bite the bullet and send them off to school. For girls, however . . .

Miss Bass, the governess, is English. Both Sarita and Herbert had thought it a good idea as it seems likely that the girls are going to marry Englishmen, and Miss Bass could prepare them for the London season. Someone needs to, although it's still a long way away. Cricket is only eleven, but so recently she was only six. Sarita can impart her common sense, but what's wanted from girls is something else entirely. She doesn't know what this is, and neither does Herbert. When Sarita had relayed Miss Bass's concern over graceless Cricket's coordination, Herbert had pointed out that Cricket's hand/eye was spot on. The girl is a magnificent shot, the best of the Ward children. Charlie isn't bad, but he hesitates. Herbie finds winning overrated and is thus crippled by contentment. Has Dimples ever even held a gun? Who knows? But Cricket—she should be a sniper. Clay pigeons explode. Grouse fall to the ground. Rabbits speeding through the parting grass are hit, trip, expire. Unfortunately, such skills don't win one a husband, unless, perhaps, Cricket manages to bag some man in the same way Herbert used to bag elephants.

And there's Cricket, finally, standing at the door.

"Mama, you wanted to see me?"

"Come sit down." Sarita pushes the chair beside her at the small, marble-topped table. "Would you like some tea? I can ring for another cup."

"No, thank you." Cricket takes the seat and maintains an unusually correct posture.

"Cricket, could you please—"

"Miss Bass hates me. She does. She only likes Dimples. It's always, 'Frances, can you read out that passage?' 'Frances, what nice embroidery.' 'Frances, why are you so much better than your sister?'"

Sarita gives her daughter a cautioning look. "You were assigned to write an essay on *Jane Eyre*."

"I did."

"Cricket, it's obvious that you didn't touch the book. Unless by accident. Or to kill a fly with it."

"That's not true—"

Sarita raises her hand. She brandishes the essay and quotes, "If Jane Eyre had just been more fun, she wouldn't have had to be a governess." Sarita stifles a smile.

Cricket is, a rare occurrence, silent.

"What I can't figure out"—Sarita waves the paper at her daughter—"is how your work can be so full of extra scribbles and crossings out when it's obvious that no improvements have been made at all."

"I won't read it."

"You will."

"It's a stupid book."

"Sarita Enriqueta Ward, you are reading *Jane Eyre* by Friday, and completing a proper essay, or there's no tennis weekend for you. I have no problem telling the Loutins that you failed to do your work and, as a result, have to decline the invitation."

"That's not fair."

"Actually, that defines fair."

Cricket rolls her eyes from one side to the other, involved in some hard thinking.

Sarita exhales dramatically and levels her most reasonable look at her daughter. "Don't you have some reading to do?"

Cricket pushes away from the table, grinding the chair legs across the floor. She walks to the door, dragging her feet, her shoulders dramatically slumped. She turns at the transom, forefinger raised. "That's one for Miss Bass, but next time . . ."

"Next time you'll do your reading when asked."

Sarita taps her papers together into a neat stack. The room has grown cold and she wonders what Herbert is up to, probably reading a magazine, or sketching—which he sometimes does in bed.

In the girls' room, Frances is sound asleep with her arms crossed over her, *like a vampire,* as Cricket likes to say. At least the girl is reading something, even if it is Stoker. Cricket too is asleep. Sarita goes over to the nightstand and picks up *Jane Eyre.* If the bookmark is accurate, Cricket has read five pages.

The hallway offers up its stillness, the clock the silence between ticks. Is this day already finished? The weeks seem carved to nothing with Herbert's travels and sculpting and all the back and forth, and the children, who, yes, have a decent staff to manage them. A staff that needs decent management. Along with the other staff. The move to the country, whenever that happens, will need even more—gardeners, handymen, housemaids. Maybe even a night watchman.

She sits at her dresser and undoes the clasp on an earring—nice diamond studs, purchased by Ward in Buenos Aires, although the diamonds are from South Africa. She sends it pinging on the silver tray, and then its mate. She looks back at herself, her reflection keeping company.

Joubert had sent a card over last week to say that a rather charming painting had shown up and would she care to see it? And of course this is one of the benefits of being shockingly rich: people send cards over when paintings become available. This particular dealer has a good eye for what she likes. He is one of those men who—how does one put it?—has a sympathetic connection with women. The first time she'd entered his gallery, there'd been a Renoir sitting at the back, waiting to be packed up and shipped off, and she'd been drawn to it. Her presence in the gallery was something of an accident. She'd scheduled a meeting with the real estate agent and had the time wrong. When she showed up at two in the afternoon, the agent was still with another client in some fancy part of the city, probably standing in his pointed pumps with his nervous fingers tapping at some well-executed architectural detail. Sarita seldom had an unplanned hour out of the house and she took it as an opportunity to stick her head into a few galleries—places that she hadn't been into since she was in Paris with her father more than a decade earlier.

Boy with Cat was an odd painting, particularly for Renoir. The boy, naked, is standing angled away from the viewer, arms languidly embracing a cat. The cat is up on some sort of bureau, although it might be the back of a piano, but it was impossible to tell because the whole of it was draped in a floral patterned silk. The cat's face is pure pleasure, the boy's inscrutable. One of his legs is crossed in front the other, resting on the ball of the foot, causing a spiraling of the form. Sarita guessed the boy to be about twelve years old.

"Madame, that one has been purchased," said Joubert. "But we will enjoy it while we can, before it again disappears into someone's drawing room for twenty or thirty years." He smiled. "Do you like it?"

"I find it interesting."

"It is a mysterious painting."

"Mysterious?" Sarita stepped back. "It's about loss of innocence. The boy's ambivalent about growing up, about leaving the world of women. That's why his legs are crossed, why he's hugging the cat."

"You are a critic?"

"I am a mother."

Joubert had served her tea and together they had looked at the various oils and watercolors, not with an eye to sales or purchases, but rather to merely enjoy. And yes, Joubert remembered her father. "He bought every new thing, even if he did not like it, just because it was new."

Her father still favored Romantic landscapes and he might have had a good selection of contemporary works, but they were usually assigned to places such as a guest bedroom or above eye level on the wall by the staircase.

The picture about which Joubert had written to her was a smallish oil in the Impressionist style. The woman in the painting was at her dresser, her right arm raised to unpin hair, presenting her back, and her reflection was so murky—shattered by angle and rough brushstroke—as to reveal nothing. Her white dress and black choker were in dynamic, choppy stroke, but the woman's skin was a soft pink, glowing and smooth, as if lifted from Boucher or Fragonard.

"What do you think?" Joubert had asked.

"Don't know where I'd put it," she replied.

"You are in the market for a new house."

"True." She leaned in close, then stepped back. "All these women in front of the mirror. You must have at least five such paintings just in your gallery."

"I have twelve, but this is the best, a contemporary putica."

"It's not a putica, Joubert. There's nothing titillating about it." Surely even Joubert could see that. "Men are always painting women at the mirror because they want to catch what we're thinking. The mirror doesn't mimic Venus's pond but presents woman's innermost being."

"Would it surprise you to know, Mrs. Ward, that the painter is a woman?"

"No."

"No?"

"Because she reveals nothing. Look at the mirror—completely obscured. You'll never know anything about women, that's what the painting says."

Despite Sarita's confident analysis of the painting, she'd been unsure if she liked it. By the time she came around, the work had already been purchased by another, as a gift for his wife.

Joubert's shop is a far cry from Herbert's studio. Herbert has unpacked all of his spears and skins and heads and juju masks—crates of them—and arranged them all around his studio as if it were an exhibit at the Exposition. Into this, he sets his sculpture, perhaps to assist in the full imagining of the Congo in the middle of Montmartre. How bizarre. And he has enlisted the help of several of the area's negroes to help him do it. Ostensibly the dearth of black people in London is one of the biggest motivators to living in Paris and sure enough, there is François, and there is Martine. Sarita had been present when Herbert had explained what African savagery looked like to François, who was more than a little skeptical. Ward had explained what the idol was for, what sorts of spells witch doctors cast, and the kind of ceremony that he was trying to bring to life.

"That was a long time ago," François had responded with his face composed in tremendous patience.

And Herbert has to tolerate François because of all the men who had shown up for the modeling work, it is François who had the best physique. He is a laborer and as a result has the sort of diet and level of physical activity that translates well into a naked witch doctor. The piece is coming together well—nice molding of the legs and torso, a feat of bronze muscle. Herbert could call the piece "Parisian Laborer Connecting with His Ancient Past," which would at least explain the statue's resigned and pleasureless expression. The thought of this is making her smile as Herbert, done with his late evening brandy, enters the room.

X

The Anversille

March 1903

Casement boarded the *Anversille* in Lisbon. The last port of call was Tenerife and it is only a matter of days before he reaches Boma. At least he is now reunited with his dog. Poor old John. He pants in the heat, making the most of the draft that comes in beneath the cabin door. His smile is always affable, even as it shows off his powerful jaws.

There is such an odd assortment of people going to the Congo these days, or perhaps they are the same people as in the past and his changed perspective is what alters the composition. The adventurers seem more mercenary, the missionaries more naïve, and he less robust. Although the work is important and he will have to find strength. He's writing a report for the Foreign Office on the use of slavery in the region, and the possible ramifications of such a document, should he execute it well, weigh heavily. He could save a lot of people. Or he could exert great effort and manage nothing. How are these things decided?

Casement has been under the weather since Lisbon. Despite this, he managed some gambling there and even met a young man—Aghostino—who still flickers in his mind's eye. Casement gave him money, said that he would be back through Lisbon and that they would meet again. After all, it was possible. Casement would be finished with the Congo after this report was done. His best and most likely posting is, at this stage, Lisbon.

It's late, but sleep is not coming. He has a book in his second suitcase, O'Grady's *History of Ireland: The Heroic Period,* and, as he's read it several times, maybe that will send him off. He pulls the case out from under the bed. The rusted clasps on this one had crumbled as he boarded at Tenerife and the case has been tied shut with a rope. Although he knows for a fact that a sailor is responsible for this knot—Casement watched him do it—this is definitely no "sailor's knot." Much as he prods at it, even poking into the seams with a pencil point, the knot holds fast. Perhaps it is a Gordian knot and everyone knows what that needs: a blade. Unfortunately, Casement's pocketknife too has fallen victim to the same rust as the clasps and it is only now, as he finds himself in need, that he remembers his intention of purchasing a new one at the last port of call.

"Move, John," says Casement and John, who is lying to block the door, pulls himself up on his bowed front legs, gets the hind legs under, presents his great head to be patted and scratched. Casement shuts the door behind him. Outside the cabin, a breeze worries the damp air. All is quiet. Down the deck, he can see two Kroo boys leaned up on the rails, one gesturing through some funny story with loose, sweeping hands, the other slighter, more reserved in his movements, laughing and shaking his head in disbelief. As Casement approaches, the boys quiet themselves, but they relax as he is recognized.

"Pleasant evening," says Casement.

"Yes," the boys pleasantly concur.

"Would either of you have a knife?"

"A knife?" one says. "Yes, I have knife."

Suddenly Casement isn't sure what they're talking about. "There is a rope I need to cut."

"Yes. A rope you need to cut."

Although Casement assumes that his words are being repeated out of a sort misplaced politeness, something in the exchange feels comic, or possibly erotic—but the harmless eroticism of schoolboys.

"Shall I cut your rope for you?" asks the reserved, slight boy. A boy, certainly, but maybe nearing twenty.

"Yes, please do," says Casement. "That would be much appreciated." Cut my rope.

The two head back to his cabin. Belowdecks, he hears an expletive ejected into the night and in response, an avalanche of drunken laughing.

"Someone has lost at cards?" suggests Casement.

"Yes. I think maybe that is what happened."

Casement opens the door and John slips out, trotting past and down the deck, retracing their steps. His nails tick on the boards. "He won't go far," says Casement.

"Unless he can swim," says the boy.

Is this logic or a joke? Casement smiles—a response appropriate to either. "There is the knot," says Casement, indicating the suitcase, which is on the bed.

The boy takes the knife from his pocket. He slips it loose from the leather sheath and slices at the rope in two places so that it falls from the suitcase. The boy opens the suitcase, not to invade privacy but to be helpful—to finish a task.

"Thank you very much," says Casement. "Can I offer you a drink?"

The boy's eyes flicker to the doorway and he smiles sweetly.

"Or will your friend be missing you?"

"He will not miss me," says the boy, "if I am not too long."

So they'll have a drink and whatever else because he's heading upriver again. And even if this is just a drink with a pleasant boy with beautiful, coffee-colored eyes and a gentle manner so sensitive and light that it almost dizzies him with its unassuming power, it will be cherished. Because things are no doubt about to get very dicey. He's going upriver in search of atrocity, butchery, horror. The boy picks up Casement's compass. He presses the top, which flips the lid open.

"Do you know what that is?"

"A watch?" The boy looks, not understanding the device's language.

"It's a compass. It lets you know where you're going."

"You don't know?"

"Don't know what?" asks Casement.

"Don't you know where you are going?" More gentle teasing. This boy might easily be nineteen, the age that Casement was when he first traveled to the Congo. Who was that young man—that boy—encased within him, ringed in as trees ring in their younger selves?

"Know where I'm going? Not always," says Casement. "What's the fun in that?"

Sometimes he wakes up weeping. As he quiets himself, John panting at the bedside, he'll feel his heart pounding away—a muscle slick with something not quite wholesome. He'll calm himself by remembering that he is not the infamous Sir Hector MacDonald, dead in his Paris hotel room, that it is not he who is being court-martialed for indecent acts. He thinks over MacDonald's horror of loneliness, of that brave man—revered for his courage as a soldier—holding the gun, considering his options. Did MacDonald's mind wander back to his days in Ceylon with the warm breeze shaking the tops of the palms, the sand like scented powder beneath his feet, the spices afloat giving even the air one breathed a potent charge? MacDonald is rumored to have interfered with a number of the native boys. He is also rumored to have had no tolerance for the colonials, who went for the easy kill when they saw their interests compromised.

And you, Roger Casement, are now taking on the King of the Belgians and all of his supporters. He thinks of Sarita Ward's admonition, "The truly brave are often the truly stupid. They just don't understand danger." This was a mother's common sense after Herbie broke his arm trying to climb down from a tree that the much-taunted Roddie had been unwilling to follow him into. And there is Casement, going up the Congo alone, while other clever chaps are patting him on the back, wishing him luck. Here's a drink for you, brave Roddie, and we do hope we see you again, that when you make your way downriver you're not in a box.

Chumbiri would waste his spirit even if he were in good health, not subsisting on a diet of mysterious "custard" that the cook, Hairy Bill, has presented to him two out of three meals since he arrived in early June. Custard. It does have eggs. And perhaps it causes hirsuteness since he and Hairy Bill (whose name must be something else, but whose appearance seals the moniker) are by far the shaggiest men in the region. The knock on the wall at the entrance, since a curtain serves as door, makes him think, *More custard!*

"Yes!" says Casement. "Enter!"

It is Hairy Bill, who looks apologetic, even though he is not bearing the usual bowl.

"Hello," says Casement. "Do you need me?"

"There's a young man to see you. Loanda. He says he is your friend."

"I hope he is."

"Loanda?"

"My friend. I can always use another friend, Hairy Bill. And I could also use some fish."

Another apologetic look and a smile. "If there is fish to be bought, I will get it for you. But you know the men around here have to sell all food stuffs to the Force Publique, even at the cheap rate, because if they don't, their wives are taken."

"I shouldn't have said anything." Just the day before, Casement had volunteered to pay three times the Belgian rate for some goat meat and this suggestion had brought the village chief to him, begging him to stop trying to buy it, as this would tempt his men to sell it, and he wanted his children back—and these were being held hostage. "Forget about the fish. Send me the friend."

Hairy Bill nods and excuses himself through the curtain, like a stage actor making his exit. The curtain is pushed aside once more and standing there is a familiar figure, who he at first does not recognize as he must have grown nearly a foot in the last few years.

"Mayala Swami. Do you not know me?" He is speaking good, missionary English.

"I do." Casement's eyes fill with tears. "You are Mbatchi, son to Luemba."

John, sensing Casement's happiness, raises his head.

"Maybe you are looking for a cook?"

"I already have a cook. And there's no food anyway."

"Maybe you need someone to water your dog?"

"Well, I can always use that."

Mbatchi is now twenty-four and Casement admonishes him for coming upstream. He should have stayed in Boma or Kinshasa, where his English and missionary connections might keep him safe. But Mbatchi has come looking for Casement. His immediate family are nearly all dead—the beloved father Luemba, his brothers. Of his mother, he can find no trace. She was last a hostage of the Force Publique while his brothers and father worked the rubber to try to keep her safe, but now they are dead and without them, she has disappeared. He has one sister that he thinks might have escaped north. Mbatchi will act as interpreter, as diplomat. Casement knows some Loanda, which has been helpful, but not nearly enough to get the full story. And people have a hard time believing that he is actually on their side. John's appearance does not make him a convincing goodwill ambassador.

"Why are you still here?" asks Mbatchi. "Why are you not farther upriver?"

"I need a boat that isn't State owned. I can't use any of the Free State's transportation because they just take you to what they want you to see."

"You need a missionary boat."

"Mbatchi, do you know someone?"

"I know Jesus." He smiles. "And some of his friends."

The *Henry Reed* belongs to the American Baptist Missionary Union. Casement's friends are Loanda and Bolobo natives, and American Baptists—strange allies for strange times. Crawling upriver, Casement thinks of Conrad. As Casement puts together a committee of powerful, potentially helpful friends in his head, Conrad is there. He is married now, has a son, and lives on a farm in Sussex. Casement has read Conrad's Congo story—which, although it includes the stink of hippo meat, somehow remains above the actual rot. Conrad is more concerned with the concepts of civilization and horror, how man is tugged backward as much as forward, how barbarism is contagious. Conrad's story is *Heart of Darkness* and it is about the "heart of darkness"—focusing on the atavistic—whereas Casement's current project works to introduce the possibility of civilization, to bring a little hope into the mix, although there is little hope on display. Casement's report might be called "Causes of the Heart of Darkness" or "Some Manifestations of Evil" or "Looking Back to the Good Old Days When One's Biggest Fear Was Cannibals." He is not looking into the heart of darkness but rather at its face. He takes detailed notes with the help of at least one and sometimes three interpreters—recording depositions. He chronicles the loss of life, the maiming of children. This is not digested material, this is *the facts* with names and dates, for these are people, not characters: One should not choose to see them or not see them. Regardless, any attention to the Congo, even fictional, is of dire importance.

Casement outpaces his depression by escaping into profound world pity. He is drowning in sympathy, empathy, sliding into self-loathing, bursting to the surface with anger. He is at sea. He sees Mbatchi's concern, his calm with which he is hoping to infect his Mayala Swami. Mbatchi stands at the prow and waves to the helmsman, a shout back and forth, a nod to Casement. They have arrived at some destination, some suppurating ulcer on the wall of this intestine that is the Congo.

"Mayala Swami," says Mbatchi, "you should take your medicine."

"I already have," says Casement. He manages a smile.

"Okay," says Mbatchi. He has just learned this from one of the American Baptists and is inordinately fond of the saying, most likely because it sounds as if it could exist in Loanda.

By nine o'clock there is a line of people waiting to see him. Mbatchi says that some of them have marched twenty miles to deliver their story, leaving their rubber quotas unfulfilled, risking death at the hands of the Force Publique.

"Tell them that the line continues over there, in the shade. I'll make sure that we take their story in the order in which people have arrived, but I don't want anyone in the sun. And please take a bucket of water and go up and down the line. There are children and they must have a drink in this heat." Casement, to calm himself, takes several deep breaths.

"John too needs a drink," says Mbatchi.

"And John too," says Casement, trying to force relaxation.

A man stands before him, gray at the temples, nervous. "Please sit," says Casement in Bolobo. There is an upturned bucket provided as a chair and the man glances at it, then looks nervously at Casement. The man will not sit. "Please tell me your name." The man looks to the Bolobo translator, who nods in the affirmative. This causes a flood of Bolobo from the man, the gist of which is that he thinks it would be reckless to attach his name to what he has to say. He says he has no guarantee that this is not a trap made by the Belgians to determine who these people are who do not want to work for them. There is some heated back-and-forth, some mention of relatives, some mention of something else—is that the word for boat? No, canoe, he thinks. Casement knows the word for canoe, so it must be some part of a canoe.

The interpreter has been instructed to be patient, not to interrupt, and to let the men and women finish their statements so they know that their voices will be heard. But it takes so long to hear the same argument over and over. Finally, the man turns and lifts the back of his loin covering. Casement has thought himself readied as this action often punctuates the proceedings, but the deep grooves of the chicotte, one of which is a fresh welt, make him dizzy. It's the blood. Lately he has found himself unable to look at the redness of blood. Even John, his ear cut on thorns, has caused a fainting episode. Casement looks down quickly at the tops of his shoes, his head spinning, and tries to focus on the words in his notebook, which are now swimming on the page in spidery pencil.

"I am so sorry," says Casement in Bolobo. "Take his statement," he says to the interpreter. "Where is Mbatchi?"

Mbatchi sets down the bucket of water that he has been using to water the line of people. He comes quickly to Casement and squats, his hands on Casement's knees. Casement exhales roughly. He gestures at the man. "This man needs salve."

"After he gives his story," says Mbatchi, "I will give him the medicine."

"Thank you, Mbatchi," says Casement. He nods to the interpreter and the man, still standing, finally begins his story. *He has traveled far into the jungle in search of rubber. His companion was taken by a leopard. In fear he returned with less than his quota of rubber. For this he was whipped. He is an old man. His wife is held so that he will bring the rubber in.* This is the story of many people. How to make it unique for each one? Originally, Casement had thought the names ought to be withheld for the very reason that these people wish to remain anonymous, but the suffering is unique. The people are unique. He does not want his readers to be fascinated by man's slide into atavism. His readers should weep, should see themselves in this aging man who has been physically tortured, who cannot see the end of his suffering.

The man is led away by Mbatchi, who will treat his wounds. "What was that word?" Casement asks the interpreter. "It has something to do with a canoe, I think."

"The side of the canoe," says the interpreter, "for the cutting of hands."

His interpreter has taken the Bolobo and turned it to French. Now if there were only an interpreter to take it from the French and into comprehension. The line of people is snaking beyond view, so for now he must move forward.

The next man appears to be in good health, although his face is vexed in sorrow.

"What is your story?" asks Casement.

"My son," says the man.

Casement understands these words.

"Is he dead?" asks Casement. He knows this Bolobo all too well.

The man beckons at the group of people and a child steps out, nervously making his way to his father. The boy is undernourished but a sweet-faced thing, maybe eight years old.

Casement smiles in a consciously kind way. "How can I help?"

"They cut his hands," says the father.

Casement sees then that the boy has two stumps in place of hands. No hands. Both hands removed. There is something about this that his mind struggles to not accept, as if his eyes are presenting invalid information. But this is real. He is looking at a child with no hands. He knows how they were removed: with a knife or a machete by a white man or some alien black mercenary. "Brave boy," says Casement in English. The interpreter steps in quickly with some appropriate response, and unsteadily, Casement gets up. "Cinq minutes," he says to the interpreter. He catches Mbatchi eyeing him as he stumbles to the hut. He hears that word or words—the term for *side of a canoe*—and the interpreter explaining to Mbatchi why the boy was brought there, why they cut his hands. *Because a man had escaped who was wanted for stealing the rubber and they needed proof of his capture and the boy was found nearby. They put his arms on the side of a canoe to steady him as they took his hands. Why did they take both? Because he struggled.* More words follow as Casement manages to make a distance between them and him. Someone has started weeping. Is it the father or Casement?

Casement pushes into his hut and lets the curtain fall behind him. He sits on the side of his cot. There's a gentle tap at the door but he knows his privacy will not be respected. Mbatchi enters quietly. "Mayala Swami—"

"Five minutes is all I need. Is that too much to ask for?"

Mbatchi considers this. Even if the interpreter is the one taking the story, Casement will need to put it on paper, to get all the necessary details before the interpreter begins to conflate things. "Yes. I know you're sad, but sadness is useless now. You are also angry."

Wise boy. "True."

"I am also angry. I can write, but no one will listen."

"I'm not sure people will listen to me," says Casement.

"Yes, they will," says Mbatchi. He takes the bottle of malafu and pours a glass. "Take your medicine," he says.

XI
London

January 1904

Casement is staying at Ward's house in London and he has the whole place to himself as the Wards are currently in Paris. There is a manservant, Paulson, a groom by trade, but who is capable of preparing simple meals and keeping the house suitably provisioned. If Paulson were a different sort of chap, this would be a different sort of idle, but he's not. Casement, free from distraction, has his mind focused on this meeting with Edward Morel and Alice Green.

Alice Green is a historian, the widow of a historian, and Irish too. Alice, it turns out, is wealthy and very much into supporting radical causes, in this case the publication of the *West African Mail*, devoted to exposing the use of slavery in the Congo. Morel is to be the editor. So we have publisher, editor, content advisor (that's him), and now if they can work out the small issue of a readership interested in the fate of Congolese natives, he'll be doing very, very well. And there is Paulson standing in the doorway of the drawing room.

"Sir," says Paulson.

"Hello, Paulson," says Casement.

"I just wanted to inquire whether you would be needing me later this evening?"

Casement scans the room. "Actually, I'm expecting people. So it would be much appreciated if you could top up the coal, and bring in some glasses and a jug of water. And perhaps some sherry."

Paulson slackens his posture and leans in the doorway. "Are you entertaining a lady, sir?"

"Well, yes," says Casement, casually, before he processes exactly what Paulson is asking him. "Not that sort of lady." Casement laughs, and adds, "And a man." Although not that sort of man.

"Right," says Paulson.

But he's not entertaining in the strict sense of the word, unless recounting tales of violence has the ability to entertain. And Edward Morel, at least according to Alice Green, is not the sort to be entertained, but rather inspired, as is she. Casement should have told Paulson that he was "inspiring" some people. Would Paulson have asked if he were planning to "inspire" a woman? Is this how the vernacular grows? In current parlance, men like him are referred to as musical. Musical. As in, "He's a hard-working consul and talented diplomat and we had high hopes for him until he revealed himself as musical." Of course, no one has said such a thing, but he is conscious of the fact that someone could. He holds off on assignations until he's in big, anonymous cities. He's tried to keep his picture out of the English newspapers lest someone recognize him. But his name, as of late, is everywhere.

Paulson comes into the room with the glasses, sherry, and a crystal water jug. He tops up the coalscuttle. He arranges the fire and places the tongs back on the stand. "To be prepared, sir, what time are you expecting your visitors?"

Paulson has made plans. "I'm quite capable of receiving them myself." Ironic, that, to be meeting about slavery *and* involved in a conversation where two grown men discuss whether or not one can answer a door. "No. You are on your own. Thank you, Paulson."

"Well, sir, I will be retiring to my quarters."

That Paulson. Casement is certain he's headed out as he's changed into a fancy pair of brogues, not the kind of footwear you put on for the final day's journey down the back stairs. Casement knows the shoes to be Ward's as he remembers Ward wearing them on several occasions, but he can't make himself care, and he's pretty sure Ward would ignore it too—if, in the first place, he remembered that the shoes were his.

Morel is Ward's friend, known from the London circuit of people concerned with happenings in Africa. It's a small group, really, and a strange one. There's Arthur Conan Doyle, who was before the mast in his doctoring days, and, of course, Conrad. These two men have certainly introduced Africa, or at least a sense of adventure, into London drawing rooms in very vivid ways. Mary Kingsley was one of this number. Her writings on the Congo were bestsellers, and her lectures standing room only, although some of them were delivered in barns and other such venues where women were permitted. Mary had introduced Casement to Alice, but she is dead three years now, having succumbed to enteric fever while nursing in Simons Town.

The bell sounds at eight. Casement makes the journey down the hallway and opens the door. Alice Green presents her profile, as she's looking down the street. Snow has begun its benediction on the coal-streaked buildings.

"Finally," says Alice. She stomps her feet and comes inside. "Where's the butler?"

"Out." Casement helps her with her coat.

"And the maid?"

"Shows up in the morning as she's staying with her parents while the Wards are in Paris." Having divested Alice of her coat, Casement is not sure what to do with it. Alice takes it back and throws it on the chair by the front door.

"Where's Morel?"

"I'm sure he's on his way."

"I should hope so. You have half an hour. I need to get home before I end up stranded here."

Morel shows up ten minutes later. He's walked the five miles from his rooms. "There were no cabs, which was no problem, because I couldn't have afforded one."

"Why didn't you tell me? I could have collected you," says Alice.

"I missed the two o'clock post. Besides, I do my best thinking when I'm walking."

Alice waves off the sherry as if it's poison, as she prefers whiskey. Morel sticks to water.

"No time for chitchat," says Alice, "I want a budget."

"That depends on the circulation and the number of pages," says Morel.

"And that depends on the content," says Alice. "So, what have you got for us, Roddie?"

Casement considers. Where to start? The pool of human suffering expands in all directions, a widening, unstoppable vortex filling the air with the metallic stench of blood. It is unbelievable even to him who has witnessed, so how to make others believe? How to best appeal to their sense of morality?

"Don't think too hard, Roddie. We don't have time for that. You're not delivering a speech. You're giving us some facts. And Morel here will boil it down further and give it context."

Morel has a small notebook into which he is scribbling some figures with a gnawed-at pencil. Casement can hear him speaking the figures to himself in French. Morel, like Casement, had started off as clerk at Elder Dempster in Liverpool. And this company, which delivered Casement to the Congo, had sent Morel to the serpent's den in Antwerp as his French was native, and even his clerking à *la Français*.

"Morel, what have you got?" says Alice.

"Nothing yet." Morel doesn't look up from his calculations. "Different budgets create different publications, so perhaps it would be helpful to have some figures for our benefactor to look over."

"That's one variable," says Alice. "And the other is content."

"And that," says Casement, "is infinite."

This drawing room with its decorous trappings and sweet heat, the light collecting in the grooves of the cut-crystal jug, the paintings thrown into shadow, Alice's face carved out by the darkness, and Morel creating music with the scrape of his pencil—is this truly the crucible of reform? Is this how people are saved? Morel is a Quaker, has made peace his life's work, has a wife who is his soldier as much as spouse. Casement is happy to place him in charge of the Congo Reform Association.

And Alice Green, her wit aggressively sharpened on the whetstone of her sex, sees suffering both farther afield and closer to home. She's from Kells, County Meath. When she and Casement are not picking apart the tangle of power that has the Congo so ensnared, their conversation wanders. She has renewed Casement's interest in the Irish language and in the heathen origins of the true Ireland, before Cromwell, before Patrick. She's selected him for something, he knows it, even though she has not yet shared the specifics.

Casement is on a train heading to Sussex, speedily propelled and also trapped in this cold yet airless carriage, trapped with his thoughts. He leans his head against the windowpane and feels the soothing vibration of the train's progress, the glass cool against his cheek. Conrad will have something to say. Conrad always has something to say. This is not a war to be waged with weapons—if it were, the winners would already be decided. Is the pen mightier than the sword? He rolls his eyes at some invisible witness. Is he back in Ballycastle, engaging in schoolboy debate? This is what such worn questions bring to mind. Well, is it? Is the pen mightier? And all the boys—grouped in teams—duck their heads together and scribble, foment pompous arguments, perform juvenile orations, exercise rhetoric, and nothing is at stake except a bonus hour on the sports field or an extra helping of pudding at dinner. *Is the pen mightier than the sword?* is a question created to pit pen against pen, not Irish diplomats against Belgian sovereigns.

Is compassion mightier than the sword? is a better question. But he already knows the answer to that: no. Compassion is not mightier than the sword. Compassion is an indulgence, or a condition—somehow profoundly powerful in its experience yet diminishing to naught in its deployment. Unless it can be alchemized into something artful—a persuasive essay, a paragraph with the capacity to enrage the public, to make them weep. Yes, weep and then act.

Again.

Is the pen mightier than the sword?

The train arrives in Hythe and Casement asks the way to Conrad's house. It is a three-mile walk along winding country roads. The wind rolls up the Downs, flinging heavy damp and light fog. He'll walk quickly and the walk is probably good for him, good to loosen up his back and get the blood circulating. The crouch over his desk, the lurch and pitch of his sleep, the cramping of his bowels: That has been the last couple of weeks. Although he has managed to find company—a young lad with red hair, a dour expression, poor posture, yet complete unbridled boldness, which was all the more welcome for the surprise of it. And then there was the other, black-haired, blue-eyed, resigned yet merry, as if they were two soldiers in a drawn-out battle not of their choosing who had decided to make the best of it.

On the other side of the lane a farmer walks towards him, leading a horse. The horse is bearing light bundles of wood and the man is happily chatting with it. Casement wonders at the light load, the contented talk, and imagines a dark cottage, a small fire weakly licking the cold, the dour wife who has sent this man wandering the Downs with his horse. This report! He has begun compulsively filling in narratives for everyone. Casement nods at the farmer as they pass and the farmer calls out to him, *Good day to you,* in a low rumble, and the horse seems to raise its whiskery chin in greeting.

He wonders how John is fairing in Lisbon. Soon Casement will be there too—or at least the possibility of it has been introduced, as Parkinson, the current consul, is again threatening (or promising) to retire and Casement's hardship service, along with his poor health, make him an obvious choice for the position. And he and John will be reunited.

Casement pauses at the gate. Inside, the writer moves behind the window, disappears behind a wall, reappears in the other window. And then the wife appears. And then the child. This is how families are assembled.

Conrad looks up and, seeing him, is quickly out the front door. "Casement," he says, "you have the look of a wanderer."

True enough. He's even holding a crooked walking stick that he'd found along the road, one that must have slipped from the horse's bundle. "And you have the look of a man living in a cottage with his wife and son."

Conrad smiles with subtle shrug. He looks over his shoulder and shrugs again as if it has all been an accident of little importance. They meet halfway up the path and shake hands. "No family?" asks Conrad.

"I borrow one when it's needed."

The parlor is a low, wide room with a broad oak beam running the width of it. The walls are thick, and the windows thick-paned. Conrad is subletting the place from Ford Maddox Ford. There are paintings by the eponymous uncle Ford Maddox Brown, a couple of small Rosettis, a desk by William Morris. It is an odd location for Conrad, made even stranger by the presence of the pleasant wife and the bright-eyed Borys. Although Conrad seems to find it to his liking. Or, perhaps a truer observation, as much to his liking as something else would be. There are quite a few writers in the vicinity and Conrad tells Casement that he isn't lonely.

"Or not as lonely as I'd like to be, but it is very good to see you."

Casement and Conrad lapse into easy conversation. Ivory was bad, but rubber presents greater hardship for the native, and since the advent of the rubber tree—cultivated in places like Malaysia—rubber vines don't offer an easy profit.

"Slave labor helps in this regard," says Casement. "This is why rubber is worse than ivory."

Conrad lifts his shoulders. "Ivory is better to write about, although the plight of these natives working the rubber is affecting." Conrad gives his head a rapid shake. "I'm not sure why you think I can help."

"I'm collaborating with some people to form a society, the Congo Relief Association. Perhaps you could influence some of your friends to join."

"Who is organizing this?"

"Currently Alice Stopford Green. Do you know her?"

"She was married to that historian from Oxford."

"And is an historian in her own right. And there's Edward Morel, who edits the *West African Mail.*"

"What is your involvement?"

"I just finished up the report and now I'm trying to get people to pay attention to it, but support is . . . well, complicated by many things."

"Such as?"

"For example, although saving Congo natives from slavery would seem to be a good thing to do, not everyone is behind it. Some see it as an attack on the Catholics and as the vast majority of the missionaries—whose accounts are forming the bulk of commentary—are Baptists and other Protestants, powerful Catholics are seeing the whole movement as an attack on King Leopold's good work. Catholics make easy targets."

"But isn't Alice Stopford Green a Roman Catholic?"

"Irish and Protestant."

"And you?"

"The same."

"Your life is complicated."

"Yes, it is." He leans back and strokes his beard, amused to see that Conrad has replicated the gesture, although he doesn't seem to notice. "What I need is a sympathetic newspaper with a large circulation. Maybe you can help with that?"

"Currently I've been submitting work to the *Daily Mail.* And I do like the editor, but I'm not sure he's interested in humanitarian issues."

"*Daily Mail.* That's Alfred Harmsworth."

"Do you know him?"

"No. He is a good friend of a good friend of mine."

"Maybe he can put a word in," says Conrad. "And I will too. But I'm not overly optimistic. Currently it's balloons that excite him."

"But he has shown interest in Africa."

Conrad seems skeptical.

"During the Boer War. Harmsworth refused to publish unverified accounts of English victories and ended up being labeled as pro-German for destroying morale."

"Of course." Conrad's mind finds the track. "But that wasn't really about Africa. Harmsworth has some theory about Germany's ascendancy. It's all about Germany and England. To Harmsworth, Africa doesn't exist in a real way."

"Just as a rugby field for other powers?"

Conrad nods. "I'll try him," he says, "but Harmsworth's fond of sensation."

Casement feels the panic rising as his patience dissolves. "Children are being tortured."

"Unfortunately," says Conrad, philosophically, topping up Casement's glass, "that is hardly the stuff of news."

XII

The Pennsylvania

September 1904

The sun has finally broken through after three long days of damp chill, horizontal rain, and rough seas. Sarita, wrapped in an oilskin, had been enjoying her quick, on-deck strolls in peace, but now the weather is mild and all those people have been released from their cabins. Sarita hopes her black dress will put them off, because she is jealous of this solitude. Her sister Ettie has been dead one year today, of influenza, leaving James and the three children. Ettie, dead. It's not as if she and her sister had communicated much over the last five years, so how does Ettie's absence even register? But it is sad. Poor Ettie, who, after trying to find a way to avoid her husband for years, finally figured it out.

It was Ettie's death that sent Mother into decline, as if all the work of mourning for that long dead daughter, buried in a pine box in New Orleans, had somehow been undone. The grief for Ettie compounded with this revenant sorrow had caused something to snap, although Mother had first borne her grief with an oppressive, performing silence. Mother had survived Ettie by six months. The cause of her death? No one really bothered to address that beyond a vague reference to her suffering from "nerves," since women in their sixties were often dead for no particular reason. Sarita had known it was grief, was embarrassed at her own resentment that her presence in her mother's life had not been enough to make life worthwhile, and then let it go. She was a mother and once there were children, one abandoned the role of child, had to acknowledge that aging parents too were a variety of child. Still, her independence and success as wife and mother had somehow made her less lovable than the passive, stuck-in-a-loveless-marriage Ettie. When her father had asked that Sarita be the one to accompany the casket back to New Jersey for burial, she was resentful, even though she is the only child left to do it. And where is her father? In South America, making deals.

Half of her feels that he should be the one on the boat with the body— he owes her mother that at least. Half of her feels that her father's presence would be hypocrisy too perfect to bear. All these actions distract from the real grief, which is an odd, cold, terrifying thing composed in parts of stunning absence, maudlin pining, and the sensation that her mother's vacating the role of matron has forced her to occupy it. Sarita now has a deeper understanding of her own mortality.

Soon it will be time for lunch. Sarita is waiting for the boy to finish tucking a blanket around some old man, supervised by a woman who must be the daughter, who controls all the action as if the boy is a marionette. She pantomimes with her hands paddling the air. Why not fix your father's blanket yourself? Or leave him to the cold? The man doesn't look particularly animated and—a casual look here—that open mouth could just as easily illustrate a postmortem gawp as an orifice well adjusted for the intake of oxygen. *Heart attack, please,* Sarita wishes for herself. She wishes it for all of them—Father, Herbert. Why can't we all disappear with a little crackle of energy and some dissipating wisps of smoke? The boy is done and Sarita gets his attention with a raised parasol.

"Yes, Madame," says the boy.

"Do you know Mister Ward? Mustaches, blond hair?"

"Yes, Mrs. Ward, of course."

Herbert's always friendly with boys on ships, remembering that boy who, all those years ago, took passage to New Zealand. And she's kind to this boy because he's roughly Charlie's age. "Could you please tell him that I'm going to have lunch in our rooms, but that he shouldn't be obligated to join?"

"Yes, Mrs. Ward."

She watches the boy step away in a funny, jerky gait. Maybe his shoes are too small.

The ship had hardly steamed out of Plymouth before Herbert reconnected with a Mr. Grimes, known from his last trip to Panama, and the two have disappeared into the world of cigars and whiskey and men. Herbert always runs into people he knows. Or turns complete strangers into people he knows. She'll make one last promenade along the deck to pass time in case Herbert wants to join her but, to be honest, she'd rather be left to her letter-writing; there are still some people—Father's friends, all of them—who have yet to be informed of Mother's final retreat from society.

There, at the railing, is a woman who seems not altogether unfamiliar. Something in her posture—the aggressive thrust of shoulders and lengthened neck—is known to Sarita. Before this elegant, contrived creature has made a full turn to face her, Sarita has figured it out. It's Paz.

How long has it been since Sarita has seen Paz? Paz left her service shortly after Cricket's birth, and Cricket is now fifteen years old. Paz is wearing a yellow silk walking suit and her hat is elegant, feathered, yet small enough to not overpower her features: the pronounced nose with flaring nostrils, the arched eyebrows, the liquid, almond eyes. Perhaps her mouth has grown a little harder with the passage of years, but Paz's dramatic beauty still commands. In her expensive clothing, she is certainly turning heads on deck.

Sarita is almost upon her when Paz registers who she is. Part of this is, perhaps, that Paz is unaccustomed to being approached, but whatever work the years has performed on Paz, an equal measure has extruded across Sarita's own features. Sarita lets a moment expire before she says anything. She extends her hand.

"Paz, how long has it been?"

"Madame," Paz says. She takes Sarita's hand and squeezes with the correct pressure. A number of adjustments are being made to Paz's expression, little moments of honesty that surface, quickly veiled by composure.

"You must call me Sarita," Sarita says, although she's not sure why. It's clear that Paz, as attested to by her outfit—the latest couture—is no longer a lady's maid, but Sarita senses that she's wandered into a realm that has yet to be covered by contemporary etiquette.

"I trust that Mister Ward is in good health?" says Paz, in heavily accented English.

"Quite well," Sarita responds, then, dropping into Spanish, adds, "the dress is for my mother. If you're not busy, maybe you could join me for some lunch or a little coffee in my rooms?"

Once the two women are seated across from each other on the stiff little couches in the stiff little drawing room, Mother in the next room enacting a stiffness all her own, Sarita is not sure what to say. The obvious is to ask Paz how she's doing, and how she's occupying herself, but her set of skills might not be a good topic for conversation. Pointing out Paz's finery is no doubt also the wrong thing to do, but the only alternative seems to be this awkward silence. "That is a lovely color on you, Paz. You were always trying to get me to wear yellow," she adds, "but it is an atrocious color on me, washes me out and makes me look dead. It might be a good option for my burial, or at least appropriate."

"Black is what looks best on you," Paz replies, tilting her head to better gauge. She's relaxed her face into a smile, "although mourning does not."

"It's been tiring."

"And how is Sarita Enriqueta?"

"We call her Cricket, and she's poorly behaved and a lot of fun."

"And I heard there was another daughter?"

"Dimples. She's twelve. And I have three sons. The youngest is six."

Paz smiles politely as she does the math in her head. Sarita was forty-two when Roddie was born.

"I am blessed with children," Sarita says.

"And they are blessed with you," Paz responds. The coffee arrives. The girl, in some prolonged state of "training," is unsteady with the tray and the jittering of the crockery increases as she's presented with the spectacle of Paz in her yellow dress. Paz gives the maid a patient, condescending smile, maintaining silence until she leaves the room.

"And are you well?" asks Sarita.

"Happy within reason," Paz replies. She smoothes her skirt, which responds with a soft rustle, then turns the full strength of her dark brown eyes upon her former mistress. "I once had ambition of a kind that I would never realize. And now I don't."

One evening, Paz comes by for a glass of wine before dinner and the presence of Herbert adds a much appreciated levity. Herbert recounts the entire event of Cricket's birth, complete with an enactment of Paz's pulling the sheet from around the Scottish doctor's neck.

"Herbert," says Sarita, "that's not polite conversation."

"But it's only Paz here, and she's family. Well, like family. Besides, she's seen it all, hasn't she?"

There's a good chance Paz has. Oh, the horror of Herbert. But no doubt this insensitivity is a form of sensitivity.

"That Doctor McIntyre became very successful," says Herbert. "We were lucky to get him when we could afford him. He certainly thought highly of you," he adds, nodding to Paz.

The following day, as she's taking her on-deck constitutional, Sarita sees a man who closely resembles Dr. McIntyre. How strange. Should she say hello? But why would she do that? He's an obstetrician. Maybe he wouldn't recognize her face, which is a joke, of course, and one that sounds more like Herbert's humor than her own. She positions herself in the shade, behind a pillar. The more she watches the man, the more she's convinced that it is indeed the good doctor himself. And then, surprise, Paz appears at the far end of the deck, now in a habit of deep rose. Paz draws to him—definitely McIntyre—cautiously taking his elbow. Perhaps this is not so much a surprise as an explanation. Sarita sees it now, all the blanks filled in, even that of Mrs. McIntyre, back in England, aware or unaware of the nature of this journey, but certainly at farther distance to the good doctor than Paz.

XIII
Ireland

October 1904

Casement skirts the cottage, passing inches from a narrow window ledge, and wonders if he's made a mistake. The clochan should be right here. He ducks beneath the clothesline and its flapping drawers. He's having a hard time summoning that romantic frame of mind that will let him truly appreciate what it might have been to be a monk trying to come closer to God through this feat of exile. Sure enough, the clochan is no more than a fortified badger hole and when he peeks in through the broken roof, his feeling is more of disappointment. Had he expected the monk to still be there? Casement is thinking like a child, although he just turned forty last month.

Casement has a couple of weeks on the island of Inishmaan, which is as far to the west as Ireland can manage. This is at the recommendation of Alice, who thinks he should indulge his recent interest in the Irish language, and seems to have no shortage of activities to occupy his time. He's come in the shoes of Synge, and all those Irishmen who had their language stolen somewhere in the past and now have to go retrieve it. He'd be happy listening in on people's conversations, but that requires getting two people together in the same place, when the majority of the time the men are working alone in the fields, hanging in their required locations like planets in the sky. And the women, well, they are often grouped together about the hearths and washing, but what's his excuse to find their company? How would he enter their houses?

Casement tracks back up the curving path. There is Dún Chonchúir, the great cheese-wheel of it, sitting on the windswept mound, hairy with grass. An escaped sheep crops growth drunkenly by the entrance, sidestepping when Casement comes near. Inside the quiet is the kind you can almost touch. A set of stone steps leads up to the top of the fort and to a view of the island, and from the island out to the sea. The blanket of fields rolls out to the flatlands, out to the pounded, gray brim of sand. A few currachs dot the water. Birds wheel and drop.

Casement wanders past fields marked off by wobbling walls of flat rocks. They don't use mortar here because the walls would be toppled in the first gale, which is practical, but gives a sense of impermanence, or at least struggle. He's just gone through a gap into a field, then into another, but there's no exit other than that so recently serving as entrance. Casement, pacing around like a fool, has gained the attention of the farmer, who was busy at his rows but is now standing with his knuckles resting on his hips. He takes his hat from his head and puts it back and Casement wonders what this action has accomplished.

"Dia dhuit," says Casement.

"English, are you?" says the farmer.

"No," says Casement. "I'm from up North."

"Ah," says the farmer.

Which says a lot, but makes self-defense impossible.

"Where are you needing to go?" asks the farmer.

"Nowhere in particular."

"The pub's just down the road," the farmer offers. Suddenly this seems like a good idea. That he's not actually lost doesn't seem worth arguing. He listens out of politeness, then follows out of inertia. Besides, it looks like rain.

The wind picks up and palms the surface of the island. A brisk breeze rattles at the karst, sings through the walls, makes Inishmaan feel as if it is alive, shivering. A breath of wet chill blows over and the first handful of raindrops rattles on the packed dirt. He has barely time to pull his scarf up to his ears when the rain drifts over like a windblown drape.

The weather changes minute to minute here, as does his mood. The rain does not last.

Two girls walk towards him on the path, their arms linked. In this sparsely populated place, he knows he'll be recognized. And the girls look familiar to him. One, dark, is chattering ferociously. The other, light-haired and with heavy cheekbones, listens, pausing to adjust the bundle of sticks tucked under one arm. They wear the big skirts. They have the shawls wrapped across and knotted at the back.

"Dia dhuit," he says, as they meet.

The girls smile in return. The blonde says something that translates as *Where's your wife?* But he's not sure if he's translated correctly, and even if he has, how to respond? The other, wild-eyed, says something else— something he has not been taught—and the girls erupt in laughter.

Casement had thought this trip would bring him closer to ordinary people, but everywhere he is met with respectful reserve. He thinks of the farmer in his field. Beyond pleasantries, he hadn't known what to say to him, and if he had, the man could not afford the time to hear it. Would that farmer want to hear about the latest political developments? Does he know that Gladstone himself supported the Home Rule Bill? The Irish State could be a reality and discussing it is not lofty talk. But this farmer spends his day digging in a field. He has a wife. He has children. Some live, some die. Those are buried in the dirt. And the potatoes come out. Casement is not sure what he wants from this man, these farmers, other than some abstracted approval. Although why he wants this *is* a sentimental thing. Lofty.

The pub is a low-ceilinged, flagstone room with a narrow bar on one side and some benches set around. A turf fire sends its warming smoke into the air, fortified with coal that he senses from the prickling of his nose and the heat. Inside there are four men along the bar, the smell of damp wool and their plain, unwashed selves steaming in the air. Casement takes a seat by the fire and waits for Flaherty to appear. Flaherty owns this place and is the closest thing Casement has to a friend on Inishmaan. And there he is, smiling in a way both welcoming and judgmental. He raises his ginger eyebrows to Casement. Casement responds, "Just a pint." Casement should have used his Irish because he could have used his Irish, but Flaherty has traveled, has confident English, and enjoys speaking it.

Up at the bar, they seem to be talking about the best way to cook fish, which is not what he'd thought they'd be talking about, but there it is. The conversation then peters out entirely, which is what happens here. The men are content to sit with their own quiet pints, side by side.

The shoulders at the bar swivel to and back as Flaherty sets down Casement's glass, and his own, which is only three-quarters filled. "A rough crossing today," he says. He means to the mainland. Casement takes a slurp from his beer. They chat about this and that, about the boy who drowned last month, of how the currach slid into a deep trough of sea, of the wave that shattered it with a thousand brutal pounds of water, of how the boy's body washed up on the mainland. "He was a handsome boy," says Flaherty, "and when he washed up a week later, he was untouched, still pink, as if he might wake up. Of course he didn't." He nods with a look of accomplishment. "I know you learned types like the fairies."

"Sometimes I get the feeling that you're making things up," says Casement.

"And what about your stories of the witch doctors and cannibals? People cutting off the hands of the black fellows?"

"It is a terrible world we live in." Although the world right now seems very small and manageable, his wool pants slowly steaming dry.

"That's why I came back," say Flaherty. They raise their glasses in a wry toast and drink. "My bit of traveling makes me special. Most of us have never even been to Galway, although once we get going, we can't seem to stop and often end up in Canada."

"Were you there?"

"I was." He glances around the walls of his business to explain. "I spent time in Connemara too. My wife's people are from Screeb. That's how it's done, of course, or the children get a bit simple." Flaherty tugs his face into a droll look, giving a backward nod to the bar. "Once, must have been ten years ago, I was cutting the turf and, what do you know, I found a body in there. I sliced it in two with the slong." He raises his hands as if he's holding a paddle. "Boom." He drops them. "Right across the middle of him. Nearly stopped my heart. So we dug him out and he some sort of bog man chief from the old days. He had a necklace and a cape, and some red hair. His hands were blackened, but other than that, looked as if he'd just curled his fingers the day before. His teeth were all there, which is more than I can say for them at the bar. A lot of him was just skin, leathery you know, clinging to the ribs."

There are Flahertys in America. There are Flahertys in Canada. There are quite a few on Inishmaan, and there's a cousin in Galway, and an aunt who married and moved to Mayo and hasn't been heard from since the 1860s, who might have emigrated or just died because Mayo was hard hit by the Great Hunger and has but a scanty population.

Flaherty is like that after the first pint: talks less of fairies, more of evictions. One of the men at the bar pulls himself to standing, and then, with wobbling steps, heads for the door. Flaherty's eyes follow him. "Him with the black hair," he starts in a whisper, "is older than he looks." The door slams behind him. "At the height of the Famine, he was fourteen. His family scraped together what little they had and sent him off to Galway so he could make it to America, find a way to make a living, and save them all. And he'd never been off the island. He's not a stupid man now, and was probably sharper then, but still, he was just a boy. He had a younger brother that he was close to. And he had two sisters, one just a baby. And a grandmother along with the parents." Flaherty consults his glass, but it's empty. "So off he goes to Galway, waving goodbye to the family. He took the one pair of shoes still left among them. And of course the story doesn't end well. He gets to Galway with that look of total ignorance written on his features and shortly thereafter someone comes along pretending to have a boat ticket and just like that relieves him of his money. He didn't come back for five years. He was too ashamed. He took to wandering, worked on one of them walls for the government until he realized that carrying the rocks was making him more hungry than the food it could buy, and also that the wall was for nothing, just going up the mountain. So he left the west and went east, stealing what he could. He sold the shoes. He came back five years later, when the worst of the Famine was over but everyone was still on their knees from it." Flaherty sets the hollow glass down. "His family were all dead, the parents, the brother. Cottage was still there. Someone had shown up for an eviction, but apparently the Famine had done it for them. So, in our man goes and there are none of his loved ones around, just the skeleton and skin of his dog, lying before the fireplace. The dog must have outlived everyone. It's possible. Hunger did a lot, but the cholera made quick work, and that leaves the dogs alone." Flaherty's eyes flicker up towards the bar. He lowers his head near to Casement's. "That story was kept secret for a long time. We all thought he'd been to America. Why not? He'll tell it when he's had some whiskey, just one set of ears at a time, and the next day he doesn't remember having done it. So he thinks we still don't know, but we all do, each of us, and told by his own lips."

Casement takes his supper there and it's late when he makes his way back up the street to the cottage. The black sky is stretched to full capacity. The wind makes a soft lullaby among the grasses. A night bird calls in some confusion and then shuts up. There's the crunch of his leather soles on packed dirt.

Casement is supposed to return to Lisbon to take up the consulate, but he's not eager to go back. He feels his true purpose is here in Ireland. Maybe the Foreign Office will let him extend his leave. After all, his doctor has warned him that he is most likely going to need another surgery. How he will pay for all of this, he is not sure. What little money he does have, he can't seem to keep from giving to others. Of course, this is all under the guise of loans, but you only loan money to people with no other means of coming by it, so how can any of these people—by definition—ever pay him back? And Nina too is coming up short each month, so what little can be scraped together goes to her.

He has written to Ward.

He has written asking him for money.

He has not yet heard back.

Politics. That's what Ward calls it. *Don't talk about politics, Roddie,* or *Why would I be thinking about Ireland?* And this last classic statement, *Casement, you're practically English. You were just a boy when you left home, and you're not even Catholic.* Ward, who manages matchless sympathy for the natives of the Congo, has nothing but derision for the Irish, or rather Irishness, which he sees as some degraded form of Englishness. And it's not only Ward. Others too make a big production of saying that he is as good as English, and what does one do about that? There he is, Roger Casement, British consul, honorary Englishman. To deepen the joke, now he's received the Order of Saint Michael and Saint George. That makes him Sir Roger Casement. That is funny and he finds a smile for himself. He hadn't wanted this bauble. He didn't need this thing about the neck to remind him of all his efforts on behalf of the less fortunate. He hadn't wanted to accept it, but others had urged him to. Even his Republican friends had desired that he take this honor, take whatever you can from the English, make the quick grab and tally it later.

Casement is back in Ballycastle visiting cousins and will soon head to Belfast. Why is it that visiting family can so undermine one's sense of self? The walls of the room he occupied as a child close in on him, having shrunk as he matured into adulthood. He looks through the battered footlocker at his old belongings—exercise books, Latin primers, yellowed clippings from the *Freeman.* A lark's nest—in with the papers—attests to some long-ago interest in birds. And here's an old poem in the stilted writing of his child hand. A poem! All those things he would choose to leave stilled in the past begin flying around like unsettled moths. There is his loneliness, his spotty education. There is his unwanted self, living with an uncle who feels bad not only that you've lost your father and mother but also that you had such parents in the first place. There is his father's angry assertion that with family it was duty to support each other, not charity, and his mother's veiled expression as she processed his statement, her packing the family's meager belongings yet again. There are his brothers brawling in the London streets, coming home bloodied and dirty. And at her end, Mother presenting the full belly of a woman with child, but it was just a ghost sack of toxins at work as the drink killed her.

Casement escapes the house and heads to the shore. This is old behavior. His long strides towards the sea feel a function of muscle memory, his pacing makes him wonder if he could be stepping in place with the planet revolving beneath him.

He stands on the cliffs, feeling the wind's insistent nudging, watching the waves shoulder the unyielding granite. These great rocks cooked in the cauldron of prehistory make him feel the simultaneous joy and terror of insignificance. A sadness starts to spread through his limbs, which he realizes is actually a larger, abstract sympathy. He turns his back to the cliff edge to see that same terrible wind now delicately riffling the grass in liquid shadow, creating pools of deep green light. Scudding clouds flock past the sun. He feels at one with all of it: the sheep, the grass, the cliffs, tree arms winding up the wind, splash of light, water roar. There is an urge to fling himself into the sea, to leave the matter of his days. Would he be the foam whispered by the waves? Or merely a man floating facedown, a bloated corpse torn at by fish? But this is mere fancy. There is so much to do that he has little time to dig around in his own sorrows. The maw of his ontological angst has become, thank God, something of an indulgence, and one he doesn't care to feed.

Casement turns the corner to Ardigh. Frank Biggers is expecting him and, if nothing else, the excuse of helping out with the Feis will provide accommodation free of charge for the next few days. His funds are wrung to naught, just a few pounds left of the money that Ward finally sent after his concern for his friend at last outweighed his disapproval. He makes the steps of the Biggers' house and rings the bell.

It's Tommie that answers the door. He's in his shirtsleeves and is, as always, bearing that droll expression. "There you are, Casement. Where are your things?"

Casement raises his battered leather case in response.

"That all? Frank thinks you're staying all week."

"I am."

"You travel light."

"*He Traveled Light* will be on my tombstone."

Tommie takes the bag and Casement passes him into the hall. "I'll bring this up," says Tommie. "Go see Frank. He's having some trouble with a kilt."

"What sort of trouble?"

"If I knew that, I'd be able to help." Tommie is ostensibly Frank Biggers' chauffeur, but he's not a particularly confident driver. He does look very well in a cap.

"Is Alice here?" Casement asks.

"Yes, but she's working on a pamphlet and has said no one's to disturb her."

From the kitchen, Casement can hear boys singing a traditional ballad. Two of the voices sound quite good, but one is flat and the flat one strains itself into a higher note, cracking on the way. And then there's laughter, lots of it. He moves down the hall. Sunlight pours through the long parlor windows, curtains hitched and sashed out of its way. A few chairs have been pushed to edges of the room and there is Biggers, on his knees, pulling an enormous tartan sheet into pleats.

"Roddie," says Biggers. "How long have you been here?"

"About a minute," says Casement.

"You must help me," says Biggers.

"The pleats go in the back and there's a long bit that comes over your shoulder and you tuck into a belt. And you don't wear anything underneath."

"Everyone knows that. But how're you supposed to get it on?"

"Better question: Why are you supposed to get it on?" Casement smiles.

"Ah, to you, this looks like a piece of fabric, but to me"—Biggers gestures dramatically across the tartan landscape—"this is the future of Ireland."

Frank Biggers has done more to promote Irish culture among the youth than anyone else in Belfast. He's into singing and dancing, heraldry and grave rubbing, Gaelic sports and dressing up, and all of this is best done with a large number of enthusiasts. Biggers has mobilized a crowd of boys from twelve to twenty-two—his *Neophytes*—and given them something to do: sports, singing, camping, a place to meet, a purpose. He's explained what being Irish might look like, and that embracing the Gaelic self provides a sufficient register of material that one can shed the Englishness entirely. And Biggers is fun, which boys like.

Casement needs fun and Biggers helps with that. Exposing atrocity means articulating atrocity—being that voice of ugly truth, and that is not fun. Fighting injustice is so often mobilizing people to stop other people, rather than getting them to act on their own creative impulse. And there is Biggers to wrap it up with the things that he enjoys—plays, spectacles, an anachronistic embracing of culture—and as his enjoyment is infectious, why not?

Although, here's a boy of fourteen in a long Elizabethan gown and it's hard to figure out where exactly this fits in to the larger goal of Ireland's independence.

"Gordon," says Bigger when he sees him, "what seems to be the problem?"

"Mister Biggers, sir, I can't get the back done up and no one will help me." Gordon is laughing. "They say I could be prettier."

"Nonsense," says Biggers. "Millar Gordon, Sir Roger Casement."

The boy reaches his hand and they shake.

"Gordons of Ballymoney?" asks Casement.

"Yes, sir."

"I think I played bridge with your father a few weeks back."

"Possibly my uncle," says the boy. He pulls the dress back up as it's slipping off his shoulders.

"I'll get the buttons," says Alice, walking up the hallway. "Come over here." Alice makes quick work of the buttons and Gordon thanks her, asking if she'll help him out when he's done rehearsing. And then he's gone.

"This is total mayhem, Biggers," says Alice. "I'm never staying with you again."

"You shouldn't try to work here," Biggers responds.

"True, but it does all come together," says Alice. "This pamphlet is to discourage Irish boys from enlisting in English conflicts. In a couple of years that boy running around in a dress will be running around with a rifle. And then coming home in a box." She thinks to herself for a minute. "Roddie, I need you to take a look, because it's mostly about the Boer War."

Casement's heart stops. And then starts with great fervor. This is it.

Perhaps he's written to the papers, put his name on various things, but he knows the pamphlet will be seen as seditious, another level entirely.

Alice knows it too. Her face is uncharacteristically composed.

"Why not?" he says. "I'm not much good at kilts."

Later, he finds himself sitting on the back porch in the evening's stillness with Alice and a gin and tonic. The day's sporting events have ended. The prizes have all been awarded, best telling of a story in Irish and best hank of Irish yarn, best written copy in Gaelic of the Lord's Prayer.

"Roddie, you seem sad," says Alice. "Are you disappointed that you didn't get a prize?" She looks at him with sharp eyes.

"What better prize than the gift of your company?"

"Where to start?" Alice responds. "For one thing, I'd rather you weren't running off to Lisbon, or wherever else you're headed. You're needed here."

"I'm needed wherever they'll pay me."

Alice fusses with her skirt and settles, hen-like, back into her chair. "Not all payment is made in coin, Sir Roger."

"I certainly don't need another honor from the King."

"Don't be obtuse. You're walking around with a title and people respect that. They think, 'If Sir Roger Casement is on our side, we stand a chance.'"

"There is still the minor matter of my employment."

"If you stop giving all your money away, you should be able to get by on your pension."

"Alice, people are counting on me—"

"Ireland," says Alice, "is counting on you."

"Well, then," says Casement, "she must need all the help she can get." A breeze picks up, sending leaves flipping across the grass. The lawns at Ardigh reach out to the line of trees, washed by light to a tempered mauve. Alice chuckles. She reaches her glass over to Casement and they clink in some silent toast, a toast to nothing, or maybe to all there is.

XIV

Paris

November 1905

The cook is again glowering. "Is there really no fish available?" Sarita wonders if it's worth holding her ground.

"This is not the season for fish, Madame."

"I'm sure there's fish at the market. I've seen it."

"It is not the best."

"Fine." Sarita's not sure what coda the cook, Madame Villiers, lives by, but whatever it is, she will not be moved. So, good for her. The French have triumphed. No fish. "You said Monsieur Joubert sent some cheese?"

"And a crate of winter pears," adds Villiers. The battle won, she'll desert the field and retreat to the kitchen where, no doubt, she will continue to plot and strategize, to fortify her battlements so as to never, ever give an inch. But Villiers does cook well. Sarita values her, especially after the last cook, who thought everything, even scrambled eggs, began with goose fat.

"Are the pears ripe?" asks Sarita.

"They should be eaten within the next few days, Madame."

Joubert has a house in Normandy—good for pears and cheese—and, as Sarita is becoming a very good customer, he is wise to be generous. She and Herbert have bought a country house in Rolleboise, about halfway between Paris and Rouen, and Sarita is in the middle of a massive decorating project. Pears had come up in a recent conversation at Joubert's gallery; Sarita and Joubert were standing before a painting with a girl up a ladder picking the fruit. Sarita had found the picture cloying and said so, but it had introduced the subject of gardening and Joubert, it turns out, is an avid gardener, although Sarita can't imagine him digging around in the dirt or picking up shears. She's pretty sure he has a fleet of boys to do the actual labor, but he is an amazing source of information. Joubert has encouraged her to plant the Passe Crassane, which ripen off the tree, their stems sealed carefully with wax, and present their full-flavored selves long after the other pears have given over to preserves or rot.

Rolleboise is slowly making strides towards being habitable, but it will be a few months before the family can move from Paris and right now planting trees is something of a fantasy. November has proffered a couple of days of sunshine, but mostly sports its gray shroud in a vile gesture towards winter. She'd been hoping to sit outside with her notes from the draper, but now the patch of sky visible to her through the drawing-room window is deepening to purple. Ticker suddenly appears at her side, a bit droolly, his eyes wide with fear, and just as Sarita considers this, a massive boom of thunder sounds from the back garden.

"Oh Ticker, it's just thunder."

There's a sudden gust and here are the raindrops, pounding tinny on the paving stones. The gutters start to thrum.

"And rain and wind." All of which this dog hates. Ticker has begun to wake her by scratching at the door when he's afraid, which is ridiculous because even the children have never done that, except for Roddie on a few occasions when he had a particularly vivid nightmare. The children have always had nannies, but there's Ticker, who won't settle for anyone but her. She wonders if he'd be better off with a nanny of his own. She imagines the advertisement. "Dog's nanny needed, references required." And why not? She already feels as if she's hiring half of Martes-la-Jolie to run the new country house. What's another warm body?

The front door swings open with a wet draft and Sarita hears her husband, laughing, stamping his feet. He's early, and he's not alone. She steps into the hallway. Evangeline is taking the coats and hats, which are damp with rain, and the men divest them upon the girl until she seems to have disappeared beneath a mountain of wet wool.

"Herbert, you're home early, and who's followed you in?" But she's already figured it out.

"Look, Sarita. Alfred Harmsworth."

"Don't you mean Lord Northcliffe?" says Sarita. It's a new honor and this is the first time Sarita's had a chance to try it out in person. "What a pleasant surprise. I didn't even know you were in Paris."

"Mrs. Ward," he says. "How are you?"

"Very well." She needs to send down to the kitchen for the pears and there should be some cake. "I do hope you'll join us for dinner."

"Unfortunately, I already have plans, but I can stay till six."

"That's enough time for a drink," says Ward.

"There's a fire in the drawing room," says Sarita. "Pull up a chair, kick your boots up." Now that he's got the baronetcy, Sarita's sure people are presenting their most polite selves, but the opposite is what's needed from friends. And Harmsworth is still, after all, a man with a job.

Whiskey is poured, although Sarita has tea. She might have had a sherry, but the draper is coming by shortly and all the numbers—window measurements, yardage, and expense—are best met with a clear head. Harmsworth approaches the piano and pulls out the bench. He pretends to flip up coat tails and dramatically takes his seat, lifting the lid to expose the keys, arching his fingers above the ivory. "Aren't you going to ask me why I'm in Paris?" he asks. He plays a questioning line of music.

"You're always in Paris," says Herbert. "You practically live at the Ritz."

"Wrong answer," says Harmsworth. He bangs twice and loud on the keys.

"There's some new motor car something or other," tries Sarita.

"Close," says Harmsworth. He alternates between two sweet, high keys.

"I thought you were all about balloons now," says Herbert.

"Even closer." He looks from Sarita to Herbert to Ticker, and lets his gaze rest on the dog for a dramatic moment. "You've never witnessed anything like it."

"Well, if I've never witnessed anything like it, how am I supposed to guess what it is?" says Herbert.

Sarita laughs. "Do you want us to read about it?"

"No. You can see it for yourself. This Monday, in Bagatelle Field, Santos-Dumont is going to fly through the air in a machine."

"Another glider? Don't those people keep killing themselves?" asks Herbert.

Sarita sips her tea. She would like to keep up with the news, but she doesn't have time. Maybe after they're settled in Rolleboise.

"This is not a glider, not a balloon. This is a genuine *aero-plane*," Harmsworth purrs the word, "equipped with an engine and the ability to steer."

"Didn't somebody already do that? It was those Americans, the Wright Brothers. It's been done," says Herbert. "And Santos-Dumont managed something last month, didn't he?"

"He managed to get off the ground in a heavier-than-air flying machine with the power of an engine."

Herbert's dismissive. "So it's already happened."

"And that was news, and this is news because it's being done again and done better. And it will happen again and again and again." Harmsworth shuts the lid of the piano and turns on the bench to face them. "Get ready for air travel."

"Not in my lifetime," says Herbert.

"In your lifetime, Wardy, and in the next five years."

Sarita would like to go see the experiment on Monday, but unfortunately the engineer is dropping by with plans. The new property is right on the banks of the Seine—gorgeous—but there's some sort of issue with the embankment and erosion. Herbert might deal with this, but he's completely useless on these matters. He seems to think that contractors show up at the house to be charmed with witty conversation and everything takes twice as long. But first she must deal with the issue of the drapes. She flips the flap of her leather binder and pulls out the notes—the feathery, fussy script of the draper, her own blunt pencil filling the margin with question marks and queries. On second look, the estimate for the long curtains in the dining room seems fine. Why did she have a problem with it? Oh, and why is Evangeline blocking the light?

"Yes?" Sarita says.

"Would Madame care for some tea?"

"Ah, that's a good idea." What is wrong with Evangeline? She's looking a little washed-out, a bit red around the eyes. Sarita slides her glasses down her nose and peers up at the girl. "Something's the matter. Please don't waste my time, or yours, denying it."

Evangeline dips her head quickly in assent. "Would Madame consider asking the seamstress to provide me with another uniform? This one is . . ."

It's bursting at the seams, now that she takes a good look. "Sit down."

"Madame—"

"Sit."

Evangeline sits.

It's that boy delivering the flowers, Sarita's sure of it. He is exceptionally handsome, charming, probably "delivering flowers" all up and down the street. Sarita has even seen Cricket eyeing him—spoilt, ferocious, anarchic Cricket—who is barely sixteen. Lucky for this mother, the class divide is very, very wide, even for a strong swimmer like her daughter.

"First of all, the draper does drapes, not uniforms. Second, you don't need a uniform. You need to go home. I'll give you some money. I'll check with Mister Ward to see what an appropriate amount might be." There's a silence that Sarita eventually breaks by tapping her pencil on the tabletop. "You were going to bring me tea."

"Yes, Madame." Evangeline stands up. "Thank you, Madame."

"Don't thank me." For one thing she's just been let go. "You've enough on your plate, but I could use some help with a suitable replacement."

Deep breath, Sarita. It's more than a personal inconvenience. Dig up a little human sympathy. What will happen to the girl? Worst-case scenario, she goes home and tells the truth to her very religious family, gets dumped on the street, and turns to whatever employment opportunities exist there. Best-case scenario, she makes up some story about her fiancé (or husband) dying tragically in Vietnam or Senegal or Cameroon that is believed by the family (religious or not) and Sarita hears from the girl a couple of times a year—pleasantries, fond memories—and there's a final plea for money right before the earnest entreaty to God to continue his fond protection over all the Wards now and forever. Amen.

Harmsworth is convinced that Germany is hatching something. He points to the Entente Cordiale to show that the world leaders share his opinion. Why else would France and England form such a friendship? What is in it for the French? What is in it for the English, for that matter, who at least share no borders with Germany—no borders with anyone, excepting the minor complications of Scotland and Ireland. The English, apparently, have finally gotten over the Norman Invasion, although it's taken nearly a thousand years. Well, if they're going to have a war, do it soon and make it quick. And win it before Charlie and Herbie and Roddie, who would make a terrible soldier, find themselves in uniform.

Ward is standing on the front step in the cold, clear morning in his hat and coat. It's a Monday and there will be traffic, which is probably why Harmsworth has arranged to collect them at the inhospitable hour of seven in the morning, although Bagatelle is only a few miles away. He can hear Sarita calling out in French to the nanny, saying that Herbie needs the fur-lined mittens and what is the point of having them if they're lost? Charlie steps out the front door, his features composed.

"What do you think, Charlie?"

"I think if Herbie has a cold, we should leave him behind."

"He'd be very disappointed."

"Boys often are."

It's not clear whether Charlie is delivering this from a sympathetic viewpoint, or whether he considers himself past all that as he's reached the advanced age of twelve. Regardless, Charlie should claim whatever maturity he can as he's off to Eton next fall, something that Sarita engineered for him, and now can't seem to make peace with. It might do Charlie some good to be away from his mother. She's protective of him and his generally abrasive, pugilistic way actually makes her coddle him more as she worries about him not being likable. He is a fantastic thug, this Charlie, and will no doubt do well at school. He challenged the gardener's son to a boxing match the week before and gave him a black eye and the boy was two years older and three inches taller. Well, Charlie has a low center of gravity. One might say that about his build, and also about his personality. He reminds Ward of his father-in-law.

Ward hears some loud, enthusiastic honking, an off-stage horse screech followed by a clatter of hooves and some colorful French, and then there's the motor car, a large German thing that Harmsworth is very, very fond of. The driver, Bradford, is stylish in goggles and some sort of leather coat and in the back, waving, in some extreme goggles of his own, is Harmsworth himself.

"Are you ready?" shouts Harmsworth as he draws near.

"Ready for what?"

"For air travel," Harmsworth shouts over the now sputtering, idling engine.

"Not really," says Ward. "It's far too early."

The front door swings open and Herbie, bundled in a muffler with the evasive mittens jammed onto his fists, is propelled out the door. Sarita steps onto the porch. She's carrying Roddie, who's five and too old to be held, but that's not a battle worth having. "I want you to stay away from the flying machine. For God's sake, don't get under it. Or into it," she says.

"Be careful!" She's waving. "Have a wonderful time!" Although these two admonitions seem to be at odds with each other.

Ward delivers some reciprocal waving, hardly necessary, since they'll be home by lunch. "I'm in back with you, am I?" he asks Harmsworth.

"Yes, yes. And the boys are up front with the driver." Harmsworth is wearing an ankle-length fur coat and matching hat.

Ward looks at his own wool and shifts on the seat. "I feel underdressed," he says.

The car starts and there's a jerk forward where Ward feels tugged back—this is his normal reaction to innovation—and soon they are speeding along, a disruptive spectacle. Startled horses, leaping pedestrians, disgruntled deliverymen pass by in quick succession—a proliferation of brief faces and gestures and words that recede so quickly, so quickly, as if time itself—the length of seconds—is being altered by this motor car. Harmsworth drums his fingers along the fine leather backing the front seat in approval of all his smooth progress and the mayhem it occasions.

"What do you think?" says Harmsworth, shouting in the wind.

"I think I should get some goggles," Ward replies.

Bagatelle Field is populated at this early hour, a small but concentrated crowd that parts like the Nile as Harmsworth's car, horn blaring in a helpful, determined way, suggests this accommodation. Herbie is now standing with his elbows resting atop the windscreen, chatting with the chauffeur in French, then remembering to use his proper, unfortunately slang-free English. Charlie is silent. Ward can practically hear the gears turning in the boy's brain. He must be really enjoying himself as this tends to turn him grim.

Bradford pulls the car at a sharp, arbitrary angle and kills the engine. "Sir?" says Bradford, looking to the backseat, although Ward isn't sure what he's asking.

"Right," says Harmsworth.

There's a moment where the only spectacle is a wall of backs, people's coats, rough sorts and fancy sorts all jammed together.

"I can't see anything," says Herbie.

"Maybe Lord Northcliffe will let you stand on the seat," says Ward.

"Absolutely not," says Harmsworth. "We're press. Out of the car!"

Bradford gets the door and soon they are following Harmsworth through the gathered people, who seem to realize that any man capable of wearing such a coat—which, from the back, makes him look like an enormous, furry penguin—must be, if nothing else, important.

The flying machine does not look airworthy, nor even a capable go-cart. It looks like something the children might create in the garden from a collection of pastry boxes. Ward's lack of faith is completely canceled out by Harmsworth's enthusiasm. He assembles his writers, who gather around him with nerves on edge, pencils ready. Harmsworth has a reputation for biting people's heads off, but that's certainly not the man Ward knows, and few people know Harmsworth as well as Ward.

There's Herbie just where his mother told him not to go, under the machine. But she must have meant when it was off the ground, and now he's on his way back. Charlie, overcoming his reserve, asks Harmsworth, "Lord Northcliffe, could I please meet the pilot?" to which Harmsworth replies, "Let's wait and see if he actually does something." Charlie smiles and nods: He too has high standards.

The last time Santos-Dumont had tried this, last month, he had managed to get the machine off the ground for a distance of sixty meters. This is, of course, exciting as anything heavier than air being elevated, particularly with a man in it, is exciting, but it doesn't really have a practical application. It's not as if men need to elevate themselves; for such a short distance, one would think a series of leaps would do the job adequately. But there's some practical element at work here. Harmsworth has a nose for this and it can't be abstract or merely recreational for him to be this wound up. Scientific innovation, that's one thing and maybe it's new, but not news. Harmsworth works his writers. He sends one to the end of the field, another over to the man working the moving picture camera, and a third to observe the pilot close-up in these final moments.

Santos-Dumont marches up to the machine and takes the ladder in purposeful, focused strides. "And he's off the ground!" says Ward.

"Don't be silly, Father," says Herbie.

The pilot gets into the machine and, to Ward's understanding, appears to be facing the wrong way. Gliders have the pilot at the wings with a tail sticking out in back, as if the pilot's sitting on a big bird, and that makes sense. Shouldn't flying machines look like birds? This flying machine is sort of like an elephant head with boxy ears: the pilot sits at the wings looking down the length of a clumsy trunk. The whole thing looks clumsy. Were Ward to go shooting off the ground, he'd want something a tad more substantial around him, but that's the point, isn't it? *Substantial* will never leave the surface of the earth. Harmsworth is staring at the machine with such concentration that one would think he meant to levitate it with the power of his mind. Ward could use a drink—a little brandy to stave off the chill, but he hasn't thought to bring any. He's also forgotten gloves. Herbie sniffles beside him.

"Why don't you wipe your nose?" Ward asks.

"I can't get my hankie out of my pocket with my mittens on and Mama made me promise not to take them off."

Ward laughs and wipes Herbie's nose with his own handkerchief. "There." Charlie would never let him do this, even when he was six, but Herbie, at ten, doesn't mind.

"Thank you," he says.

"Charlie," says Ward.

"What, Father?" he replies.

When did Charlie start sounding so mature? "Maybe one day you'll fly a machine like this."

"Yes, Father," Charlie says. He's being overly polite, as if having his father present is somehow an imposition. Ward makes a funny face at Herbie, mouths *Yes, Father* in that dyspeptic way that best approximates Charlie's condescension.

Now there are men wheeling the plane around. Someone is running up the track with a windsock, making calculations. At least it isn't raining. Look at Harmsworth, nodding at some truth that has crystallized out of his liquid imagination. Theirs is an odd friendship. At heart, they are just two school chums from Milne, two neighbors who used to chuck rocks at passing carriages and, on occasion, lift penny candy from the corner store. And now Harmsworth is a Viscount, and Ward is a millionaire. So why shouldn't this machine start flying through the air? Stranger things have, obviously, occurred.

The engine starts up, first with a flat flapping, then a rattle, then a clunk—has it died?—but then there's a rich growl, as if the plane has cleared its throat. The engine now has the familiar, confidence-inspiring chug. Ward suppresses a cheer. Men are now running alongside the plane in jackets and ties, dressed for occasion, not weather, and Santos-Dumont is standing upright, leaning into the next second. The machine speeds along, and onward some more, and Ward momentarily forgets that it's actually designed for a different purpose than running along a track. Faster goes the machine, and a little faster, then, with an insistent jerk, the machine begins to ascend. The wheels have left the ground. The machine has escaped the surface of the earth. This awkward structure of boxes and bits of wood is motoring through the air. Ward hears himself utter, "I don't believe my eyes." For the first time he actually understands the failed transaction that gives meaning to that sentence. There's a man being propelled through the air, standing in this machine. Ward loses the image as he unpacks it, because the crowd has moved, racing towards the plane. He finds himself walking with the crowd, following Harmsworth, whose coat, if nothing else, makes him easy to pick out. Herbie and Charlie are lost in the crush of people, unable to resist running ahead. Ward cautions himself not to worry. They're boys—he shouldn't know where they are. There is Harmsworth, with two writers. Ward catches up.

"Two hundred and twenty meters," says Harmsworth, "and six meters off the ground! And in less than twenty-two seconds!"

"Sir," says one of the writers, "should that be the headline?"

"No, you idiot!" says Harmsworth. "The headline, the headline, you fool, will be, 'England Is No Longer an Island.'"

"Sir?"

"Write the damned article and don't send it anywhere until I've approved it." Harmsworth looks around. "And where is Parker?"

"Interviewing the pilot, sir."

"Which is where you should be, or at least talking to the man with the moving-picture camera. You'll want to see what he's captured whenever it's available."

"Yes, sir."

"What are you waiting for?" Harmsworth pulls a cigar out of his pocket and sticks it in his mouth. He chews at it, perhaps forgetting that it's not lit.

"Well, you straightened him out," says Ward.

"He's just the first in a long line." Harmsworth looks up and down the length of the field, impressively agitated. "Ah, Wardy, don't you see? Doesn't anyone see? It's only a matter of time before they fit that thing with a gun. And do the math. Last month, that machine only made it twenty meters. Today, it's two hundred and twenty meters. England has got to catch up quickly and develop an appropriate line of defense. How long do you think before these aeroplanes are crossing the Channel?"

"Crossing the Channel?"

"Wake up, Herbert. It's the twentieth century."

She can hear Dimples and Cricket arguing and is going to tell them to stop but then decides against it. Why shouldn't they argue? In the next room Herbie and Roddie are sound asleep. Herbie has the covers pulled over his head and Roddie is snoring lightly. Herbie must have given him his cold. Well, next year with Charlie gone, Sarita can make over the room for Herbie. But wait—she won't have to do that. The move to Rolleboise will mean plenty of room for everyone.

It's late, but Charlie's lamp is still lit. She knocks lightly on the door.

"Enter," he says.

Sarita swings open the door and sees him sitting bolt upright on his bed, dressed in pajamas. There's a book splayed, facedown, on the pillow but Charlie is occupied without it or other distractions.

"You should go to sleep soon. That was a long day," says Sarita.

"I will."

What is he thinking? "I hope you're not concerned about going away to school."

"Not really." He cocks his head to one side and meets Sarita's gaze. "I know that Herbie says he'll be a pilot, but he'll never do it. He'll be too scared." Charlie has that intense look on his face, the one where sometimes he starts crying even though he isn't unhappy.

"Charlie," says Sarita, "someone has to be a pilot. Why not you?"

"Do you think I'll be a great man, like Santos-Dumont?"

"Absolutely," says Sarita. "I'll be sure and let the birds know to keep out of your way."

"Mama—"

Sarita raises her hands, guilty. "I was being flippant. I know you're very serious. The birds will get out of your way. And I will get out of your way. And everyone else, Charlie, will get out of your way. You are a special boy. You work hard. Anything you really want I have no doubt that you will get."

This is an easy statement to deliver since she truly believes it. However, she cannot believe she's letting this boy go away to school. She can't believe she's letting this boy go. As she wanders back along the corridor, she's tearing up. If she allowed herself, she could sob now, but she doesn't. Self-indulgence like that is good for no one. She steps inside the young boys' room. Roddie rolls over onto his side and settles into sleep. Maybe she'll stay for a few minutes, just a few. She'll watch his sleep-puckered mouth, the curls damped at his ears, the rise and fall of the blanket, the quiver of his breath set off by dreaming.

Casement is visiting and all routine has been disrupted. Sarita is happy to have him because this recent spat had completely depressed Herbert in a way that shocked her. Casement really is the closest thing Herbert has to a brother and, as Herbert is no longer in touch with the Wards, is actually all the family he has. Sarita had told him to just give Casement the money, had said it didn't matter if Roddie gave it to Irish widows or—what was that ridiculous school where they were teaching children how to speak Irish? Saint Edna's? Something like that. Regardless, it was hard to have an opinion about any of it because it just seemed so unimportant. She did wonder who would want their children learning Irish. No one but potato farmers had spoken it in probably hundreds of years and why revive it? Why not bring back the Plague while you're at it? But she'd counseled Herbert to give the money because it didn't make sense not to. So finally Herbert had arranged a transfer of funds and, sure enough, here is Casement visiting, although he'll soon be back in Brazil, his latest posting.

It's getting late. Dinner took twice as long as usual and the children are still awake, because they haven't seen their uncle Roddie in a while and they do love him. Sarita has sent Marie to bed not only because the girl was yawning but because Herbert and Casement have had a fair share to drink, will most likely drink more, and Sarita doesn't want the maid circulating the details.

"Tell me a ghost story, Uncle Roddie," says Herbie.

"A ghost story. Won't that frighten you?"

"I certainly hope so," he replies.

"Oh, be quiet, Herbie," says Cricket.

"She's only saying that because she gets scared," Herbie responds. "She makes Dimples go and stand outside the door of the water closet and talk to her when she's in there."

"She does," says Dimples. Charlie starts laughing.

"Herbie, you're a toad," says Cricket. "Mother?"

"You want me to quiet him? Cricket, I'm a big admirer of a good ghost story."

"Mama tells really good ones," says Dimples. "They're from Argentina, so no one else has ever heard them. There's that one about the maid who was killed by the son of a gentlemen."

"A ridiculous story," says Ward.

"Every word of it true," says Sarita. "Go on, Roddie, give us a story. Surely this is easy work for an Irishman."

"All right," says Casement. He draws his eyebrows together dramatically, the gears of his imagination grinding almost audibly. "In the days of stage coaches, there was once a man who stopped at a country inn. The innkeeper said that all the rooms were taken, and that he would have to sleep elsewhere, but the man protested that there was no other place and that any bed would be acceptable. He would pay well. To this the innkeeper's wife replied that there was one room, although they never let it out anymore—"

"Because there's a ghost in the closet. I don't want that story," says Herbie. "I want a true story."

"I thought that was pretty good," says Ward.

"But it's Dickens, Daddy. I want a real one."

Casement smiles indulgently. "All right. This one is set after the Great Famine when a great many people in Ireland died. A landowner had come to a cottage where a woman was just hanging on. She had lost her husband to the typhoid, and five of her six children. She only had the wee baby left and was struggling on through the cold with whatever food she could beg. This landowner demanded his rent, and when the woman could not pay it, he threw her out and boarded over the door, telling her that she better not come back until she was willing to earn her keep. So the woman moved off down the frozen road in her bare feet and rags, clutching her baby, and she raised her finger to the landowner and delivered a curse, but he did not understand it because it was in Irish."

"But what was it?" asks Herbie.

"I'm really not sure," says Casement. "My Irish isn't good enough."

"But it was bad?"

"For pity's sake, Herbie," says Cricket, "let Uncle Roddie finish the story."

"So the woman," continues Casement, "disappeared down the road. The potatoes came back, and so did some of the villagers who had left in those years, but that woman, she never returned. The landowner, who been a young man at the time of the Famine, found himself a bride."

"A Protestant, I'm sure," Sarita says, unable to keep that to herself.

"A Protestant to be sure, like myself, only without the beard."

"Don't make it funny," Herbie protests.

"All right. The wedding is on a sunny day with such gentle weather that one forgets it's Ireland, and the party is held outside, as is the banquet. The dancing goes into the evening, but as the sun the sets, a fierce wind starts up. The guests leave, and the bridegroom and his new wife retreat into their house."

"Is this for children?" says Cricket.

"I will make it so," says Casement. "The bride is still in her gown and, as tradition dictates, the groom lifts her and carries her across the threshold and, feeling young and strong, begins to carry her up the stairs all the way to the bed chamber, but as he does this, he begins to hear a whisper, a hush of a woman's voice, in his ear. He asks his bride—"

"Elizabeth," says Cricket. "The bride's name is Elizabeth."

"He whispers to Elizabeth, 'Did you hear that?'"

Sarita sees that Herbie is distracted. Why does he keep looking at the curtain?

"And Elizabeth says nothing," says Casement. "So he asks her again, 'Did you not hear that?' and he wonders if the veil is muffling the sound because she is not answering. So they reach the bedroom and he rests the lovely bride on the bed and, as tradition dictates, he lifts the veil to give her a kiss, and there, THERE is not the lovely Elizabeth but the maggot-eaten face of the woman—"

"Not yet!" Herbie shouts. And Sarita screams because a little ghost girl all in white has burst from behind the curtain. And when Sarita screams, the little girl, her face glowing pale, bursts into tears and runs to her. Everyone screams, including Casement, and Sarita is there with the little girl crying and crying, getting flour all over her skirt. It's Roddie, in one of Dimples's old dresses and someone—Herbie—has covered the poor boy in flour.

Herbert and Casement are completely convulsed with laughter. Even Charlie has lost his usual reserve.

"He was supposed to wait until Uncle Roddie was done with his story," Herbie complains.

"I got too scared," says Roddie, his arms still around his mother's waist, his voice broken with crying. "It's dark behind the curtain."

"Herbie," says Cricket, who screamed loudest and is now angry. "You're an idiot." She looks to Sarita. "Punish him."

Herbie is unfazed. "I'll take whatever you dish out, Mother. It was completely worth it."

"Roddie," says Sarita, "look at you, you sweet thing. And completely terrifying."

"Was I really scary?" says Roddie, calming.

"I thought for sure this house was haunted," says Casement.

"You should be an actor," says Sarita. "What a great performance!"

"I was good, wasn't I?" says Roddie.

This is a moment to preserve, Sarita thinks. This is how she would like them to stay, even if she's covered in flour and Roddie's in the dress. And there is Casement, lighthearted, laughing too, reaching for the whiskey. But she doesn't quite trust him—something in her gut flutters ever so slightly to see him there, but she can't articulate it, so she can't communicate it, certainly not to Herbert, but somehow not even to herself.

XV
Rolleboise

April 1909

Time is passing too quickly. Could her daughters really be of marriageable age? Dimples has caught the eye of Eric Clare Phipps, a career diplomat, and he has started sending her notes. Dimples is besotted. And the man? Quite unsuitable—not only twice her age, but too recently widowed from his previous wife. Which is why Sarita and Herbert had been disposed towards kindness in the first place. Phipps seemed sad and the girls, lively Cricket and pleasant Dimples, were a distraction for him, apparently more distracting than Sarita had intended. Phipps is thirty-three years old, which is twice the age of Dimples plus an added year.

The whole thing is odd. Phipps isn't Dimples's only suitor. Why would she settle on him? Maybe she doesn't attract quite the numbers that Cricket does, but the young men courting Dimples are nearly always sincere. She's not as much fun as Cricket, although quite beautiful in a dreamy, deranged sort of way. Men get serious about girls like that, girls who aren't always trying to arm wrestle, drive cars when they don't know how, calling stupid boys stupid—that's all Cricket. And Cricket is sincerely looking out for her sister, worried about Dimples marrying an old man, getting saddled with the weepy widower looking to bury his sorrows and whatever else into this very young girl.

At any rate, Sarita is not prepared for this latest development, which has her out on the terrace with Ticker, flopped on his side in the sun, and her children. The Seine flows prettily as a gentle wind carries up the cantankerous chat of ducks and geese. Pear blossoms scent the air and the legendary dappled light dapples her as it inspires a slew of painters. But who can care? She is shut out of the drawing room where Herbert and Phipps are deciding her daughter's future. She should be in there. Herbert is likely to agree to anything, as Phipps is *a good sort of chap*. That's what landed this man in her midst in the first place.

"Mother, for God's sake, say something," says Cricket. "Watching you is a torture."

"What is there to say?" Sarita drops her voice as she sets her gaze on Roddie and Herbie, who are pitching nutshells over the terrace railing. "He's already been married. Dimples should have someone with the same sort of knowledge as she does."

"I know what you're talking about, Mother, and I know you're not that naïve. Men know everything, always have."

Sarita shares a patient look with her risqué daughter.

"Well, it's true. If we weren't so cosseted, chaperoned all the time, hung on to like prize heifers until the opportune moment, we might have more of a chance of standing up to our husbands, which is why I'm never getting married."

"Cricket, for once this is not actually about you. It's about your sister."

"What?" says Herbie, suddenly interested. "Is Dimples getting married? She's not marrying Phipps, is she? He's old enough to be her father."

"He's not that old," says Sarita. Is she already steeling herself?

"He's old enough to be her uncle." Cricket flicks her eyebrows a couple of times. "And too old to be her lover."

Herbie bursts out laughing. Now Roddie is interested too. He doesn't know what a "lover" is and has the openmouthed look that he gets when he's trying to figure things out, although he's spoken over so much, as the youngest often are, that he doesn't bother to ask. Herbie wraps his arms around himself and presents his back, his own hands groping at his shoulders in a parody of an embracing couple.

"Herbie, stop that immediately." Where has Dimples gone? She must be listening at the drawing-room door. Sarita pulls herself out of the chair, ready to find her, but there she is at the threshold of the house, smiling in a slightly unhinged way. Behind Dimples she sees Herbert, who is making that *what now* face. And there is Phipps looking less dour. Of course, Sarita had formerly attributed the cast of his features to grief, but now she knows that's wrong.

Herbie wraps his hands around his mother's elbow and tugs gently. Sarita, not thinking, bends her head. He whispers, "Do you think he killed his first wife?"

"Yes?" says Sarita, and her affirmation is meant to read as a question for Herbert and Phipps, but Herbie knows she's playing—what else can one do?—and delivers a few conspiratorial giggles. And there's Dimples, looking like the cat that ate the canary, since she doesn't realize she's the canary.

Sarita and Herbert don't get to talk until evening, although she realizes that she's avoided him throughout the day, the same way that one avoids opening letters that are suspected to bear bad news. She has been sitting in an armchair with a novel opened to the same page for the last half hour or thereabouts when she notices Herbert at the door.

"Am I bothering you?" he asks.

"I don't know," she responds. "You haven't said anything yet." Not caring to mark her place, she closes the book.

She moves her feet and Herbert takes a seat on the hassock. He leans forward, elbows on knees. He has an earnest look. She doesn't usually see him at this angle and it really is surprising how bald he's becoming.

"Did you know that your father put Phipps up to it?"

"Father?"

"He met Phipps in London last August, not that long after the first Mrs. Phipps passed away. Sanford told Phipps that it was best to get back in the saddle, that he wasn't a young man and didn't have time to play with."

"And Phipps told all this to you?"

"I'm paraphrasing."

"Probably why it sounds so close to what Father might actually say."

"So what do we do?" Herbert shrugs. "Dimples is too young, but Phipps isn't a bad sort and he has all the right baubles."

Herbert's right. Phipps is solidly in the peerage, as were both his parents. He's also secretary to Sir Francis Bertie, ambassador to France, and has been in the diplomatic service for ten years. He is an obvious catch and if Dimples were a set of statistics in search of another, Sarita would see the value of the union. "What does he gain?" she asks.

"Dimples speaks French and English, is nicely turned out, and Phipps would like to keep your father close for undisclosed financial reasons. Phipps finds Dimples's disposition soothing, which, I gather, was not the case with his first wife."

"Maybe he did kill her."

"I see Herbie's gotten to you."

"What do they have to say to each other?"

"Dimples has never had much to say," says Herbert. "Phipps is probably worn out with talking by the time he gets home from work, since he's a diplomat."

"So in the evening, the two of them can sit in silence, staring into the space in front of them?"

"I don't understand the attraction either," says Herbert. "It's love. You're not supposed to."

"What draws people to people?" Sarita looks at Herbert and some revenant passion is recalled with a momentary thrill, but settles quickly, like the aging Ticker when he adjusts himself on his cushion. Herbert too seems struggling to recall.

"It was your conversation that drew me to you, your sense of humor," he says. "You didn't seem to need me and I found that challenging."

"Challenging?" Sarita laughs. "Other men would think 'pretty' more appropriate."

"And what was it you liked about me?"

Sarita arches her eyebrows. "Me? I liked your hair."

The clock in Ward's study has stopped and he should set it, but if your clock has stopped, how is one supposed to know the time? And, of course, his pocket watch is where it always is when he's in Rolleboise—hanging off the bottom of his easel. So it could be time for dinner now, but who can know? Outside, down the lawn, he sees Ticker wander over to the flower beds and sniff around, then, joyfully, flip onto his back for some enthusiastic rolling. Père Fabrice must have just done some composting. And now Père Fabrice will be giving a dog a bath.

Casement is in Rolleboise for the next couple of weeks. Sarita has voiced concern over his health, as would anyone. His weight is down and he's developed a tremor. He says he's just worn out, that it's nothing that some cool air and fresh food won't fix, and so Sarita has seen to it that there's a lot of fish on the menu. Also salads. This is what she's convinced is healthy. But there's also a cheese course that makes an appearance after lunch as well as dinner. Sarita says, "Roddie needs some meat on his bones." Unfortunately, the benefits of all this cheese are also showing up on Ward. But Casement said it was nothing that serious—despite recent deprivations and the reoccurring malaria, he hadn't picked up a bug. *Just nerves,* Casement says. But nerves are everything, aren't they? So, fresh food, fresh air, and calm. Being in Rolleboise on a lovely spring day, it's hard to think of anything that the light and soft breeze can't cure.

Casement's latest appointment is Brazil and he says it's abominable, that there aren't any true natives, just some sort of odd mishmash of negroes and Indians and Italians, some Spaniards too, who all fall under the term "Brazilian." Brazil, where officials are stabbed beneath the window for demanding compliance with the law, where overburdened mules are beaten mercilessly, where the reek of coffee struggles against that of sewage in the hot, wet air. Everyone is sick, about to be sick, or in an uphill struggle to recover. Africa, according to Casement, is the better place. Just better. Better workers, more interesting, something that feels pure. Brazil is corrupted to the extent that the original composition has been so adulterated as to no longer exist. Casement, obviously, dislikes the place as it's not his beloved Ireland and doesn't benefit, like the Congo, from having been the setting for his coming into manhood.

Ward is worried that Casement is falling out of favor with the Foreign Office. He is a great humanitarian, but that's not exactly what the FO is all about. Casement is supposed to manage local populations and help British nationals, and who can be sure which team Casement is rooting for? He's certainly down on England but is undeniably in the employ of the English government. Casement can't expect the FO to throw plum appointments at him and underwrite endless home leaves if he's actually in league against them. It's all very tricky, especially with Casement short on funds as this latest appointment pays next to nothing. Ward has offered more money, even though he knows it's not going to Casement's living expenses nor to defray the cost of purchasing books nor to ensure a longer visit to his old friend Ward, but rather being laundered through Casement's penury and sent on to Irish radicals.

And what a strange lot they are: socialists who support Larkin, neurasthenic poets, bookish women with sensible shoes—suffragettes. Ward, of course, knows that women are intelligent—he lives with Sarita and admires both his daughters—but what business do women have determining national leaders, or the fate of the world?

Ward moves to the window, sees Casement striding up the front path, back from his evening stroll along the Seine. If it's not yet time for dinner, it's definitely time for a drink.

* * *

Dinner is served late. Apparently, the oysters were off, something determined by Marie, who was supposed to be serving, but is instead indisposed in her room. As Sarita noted, the girl should not have been sneaking oysters, but in truth they are all grateful she did, and she'll probably never do it again.

Instead of the lithe Marie, they have Villiers serving the soup, her great bosom banging into the back of Ward's head as she ladles it out. Up the table, Casement is trying his hand at radicalizing Cricket. She must seem an easy mark, but she isn't. She may like the occasional bohemian for his long hair but is quite intolerant of any opinion that might threaten the status quo—*her* status quo of fancy holidays, dressmakers, and the ballet.

"Wouldn't you rather be allowed to vote?" Casement asks.

"If you put it like that, it seems obvious. But I don't know anything about politics."

"She doesn't know very much at all," says Herbie.

Little Roddie has already eaten with the nanny but Herbie, thrilled to have his "Uncle Roddie" visiting, has begged his way to the table.

"My voting is one thing, but would you really want Dimples voting?" Cricket says.

"You'd have to vote for a person, Dimples," says Herbie. "You can't vote for Ticker and you can't vote for fruit fool and I think that's all you're interested in."

Herbie seems to have forgotten about Phipps, who is, after all, easily forgotten.

"I should like to vote," Dimples responds. "I could at least cancel out whatever Herbie has in mind."

"Sarita, what do you think?" asks Casement.

"Me?" There's Sarita composing her thoughts. Her spoon hovers above the soup. "I don't think women voting is such a bad idea, but we're all so busy that we don't have time to read the papers. We'd have to consult our husbands, and if that's the case, what's the point? Why even bother?"

"Men are the ones who have to fight the wars anyway," says Herbie.

"Bravo, Herbie," Herbert says.

"Herbie in battle?" says Cricket. "God save us."

"Because he'll need to," adds Dimples.

Discussion then circles around less contentious topics. Is Herbie excited to join his brother at Eton (very), does Cricket have any interesting romantic prospects (four romantic prospects, none very interesting), what is Dimples reading (Collins, *Moonstone*), and some question that sends Herbie off on an enactment of Longfellow's "Hiawatha" that involves standing on his chair and enlisting a vegetable fork as paddle. Apparently, Sanford has agreed to send Herbie a genuine Indian canoe if he can memorize it, which he might do, but who will know if he's making it up?

Cricket, seated to Casement's right, has corralled him into a private conversation, leaving Ward to Sarita.

"Herbert," she says, "we need to talk about the apple orchard." Ward hates the thought of digging up anything. Sarita's being opportunistic because Casement is there and Ward won't want to come across as the grouch. "Père Fabrice says there's a new variety that we can get from Predon's gardener."

Ward nods in a bland way. "Casement," he says up the table, "filling my daughter's head with ideas?"

"Actually, the inverse," Casement replies. "Your daughter is very informative."

Ward—and all others—are surprised to hear it. "We're talking about the state of Europe," says Cricket.

"So what have you got for us?" asks Ward.

Cricket produces a smug smile. "Alsace Lorraine is sort of like Ireland," she says. "The Irish are angry and the French are angry too." Cricket seems bored, even though she's the one speaking. "The French sit around talking about how nasty the Germans are, and the Irish say the same thing about the English."

"Not all the Irish," says Ward.

"And not all the French," says Sarita.

"Still," says Cricket, "things could get very messy. There could be another war, right here in France."

"Really?" says Sarita.

Cricket takes up a spoonful of apple pudding and puts it in her mouth. She thinks for a moment. "I don't know how far back you want to go, but first everyone is annoyed at Napoleon, so France is in the dog house, and then there's the Franco-Prussian War, and France loses, so people feel sorry for France and are a bit nicer, but they're still friends with Germany. And then there's the Boer War, and England doesn't like Germany anymore, so they make friends with France. That's the Entente Cordiale. And the French want Alsace Lorraine back because it's French, but the Germans really want it because it has coal and Germans like factories. And nearly everyone's related—the Tsar and the Kaiser and the King—so of course they pretend that they're best friends, but they all must hate each other." She rests her spoon on her plate and smiles.

"Well, I am impressed," says Sarita. "We should send you to Eton."

"Me?" says Cricket. "Oh, please. Pocked-up boys in monkey suits whacking each other with sticks? No, thank you."

"I didn't realize that you were so concerned with the state of European diplomacy," says Ward.

Cricket delivers one of her attractive, probably mirror-rehearsed sneers. "Last time Lord Northcliffe was here, that's all we talked about. He kept asking, 'What are the French thinking?' and I kept saying, 'Why do you care?'"

Harmsworth was actually asking the right person. Young men determine the fate of nations and no one spends more time with young men than Cricket. It's only been forty years since the Germans were marching on Paris, so to revisit that is not so difficult. Although Ward thinks the greater problem is these home-grown radicals—youths with open collars and long hair who lurk around Montmartre and who Cricket currently favors, or at least that's what he suspects. She's been going to Paris an awful lot to see friends, to buy things, to go—four times in the last few months—to the dentist. It's all very suspicious. And he's mentioned it to Sarita, but ever since Dimples's engagement, his wife's decided that suitable partners are actually the real problem.

* * *

Casement has returned to Brazil and routine is now restored. Herbert and Sarita sit in the drawing room, he with the newspaper, she at the escritoire working on a letter for Charlie. He's succeeding at everything—rugby, wrestling, rhetoric—but there's something desperate about Charlie's indiscriminate domination. She senses self-doubt in his letters, although to anyone else it would look like hubris. She's told Ward that he needs to send letters to Charlie as well, and he's tried, but after a couple of sentences, he's at a loss.

"What are you telling him?" Ward asks.

"Oh, I don't know. All the things he's missed."

Ward looks around. His eyes rest on the clock that ticks pointedly in the corner. "What would that be?"

Sarita props her chin on her hand. As an artist, Herbert has a very specialized sense of observation that seems to miss at least half of what's happening. "Well, Roddie has mastered the bicycle that Harmsworth sent, and would very much like to be a boxer, like his older brother. Herbie has gone moony over Claudine Etienne, even though she's sixteen years old. Ticker is still chasing rabbits, although not very well. And then I speculate on how old the dog is, and he must be thirteen. Is that possible?"

"Isn't Charlie too busy to read all of that?"

Sarita rests her pen. "No, he's not. Sometimes, Herbert, it's as if you don't know him."

"Well, that's Charlie's thing, isn't it? He's hard to know. I know that, and it means I know him. What's in his letter to you?"

Sarita hesitates. She and Charlie share confidences. "He would like to know if he can take flying lessons. He says that Northcliffe knows someone."

"That's ridiculous."

"Good. It's too dangerous."

"On the other hand, he is fourteen. Almost a man."

"Charlie? Almost a man?"

"You coddle him. It's mothers that have turned this generation of young men into louche, lazy hangers about."

"If you weren't *hanging about* Montmartre you wouldn't see the other people who are likewise *hanging about*." She looks at Herbert with narrowed eyes. "Don't think I don't know what you're talking about. The French may want this war with Germany, but I don't."

"I don't want it any more than you do. But if it happens, we're going to need soldiers, not sons."

"If that's the case, we're going to have to send Cricket. She's the one who knows her way around a rifle." Sarita manages a smile, but she can feel the strain of it and is sure she does not look pretty. "What does Northcliffe have to say?"

Ward consults the front page. "Well, if he thinks there's going to be a war, he hasn't written about it."

"Sometimes I think you want a war, that you're hoping for one, just because you want something to happen."

"That's not true, but I do sometimes wonder if bringing our children up in the lap of luxury might have robbed them of something."

"And you think war would provide them with it?"

"That's not what I'm saying." Herbert pauses.

"You know, Herbert, Charlie knows how you feel and it affects him."

Ward sighs and the sight of him deflated is, if nothing else, novel. "I do think that having an adventurous life helped me become the man I am."

"You speak with such authority."

"Sarita, I have seen battle."

"Herbert, having the occasional savage toss a spear in your direction is not the same thing as serving in an army. I've seen war, real war, up close. Or at least its effects."

"The American Civil War ended when you were five years old."

Sarita looks serious, patient. She pushes away from the desk. "My earliest memory is of being at a railroad station at the end of the war. I'm guessing it was New Jersey. My parents were shipping boxes or working out tickets or some such thing. We moved so much in those years that I'm not sure where we were going. I wandered off into a group of soldiers. They were everywhere in those days."

She remembers the one soldier, whom she now thinks couldn't have been much older than Charlie. He was missing his leg from the knee down and the stump was wrapped in bandages soaked with blackening blood. She could smell a sweet rot that was misplaced on someone still alive. The soldier saw her looking and called to her, and she was frightened, but he had a young face and she felt bad for him. So she went to him, and he asked her name and how old she was. He was from Boston and had a sister. He also had a dog. She asked him why he didn't have a leg. And he said that he did. He said, *I'll whistle to it, and let's see if it doesn't come hopping back to where it belongs.* So the two had stayed side by side, the youth whistling, and Sarita whistling too, until her terrified mother found her and dragged her off.

"There were a lot soldiers missing limbs, and a lot of bodies, and those were boys, Charlie's age, not men, Herbert. Boys."

Herbert returns to his paper, agreeing to disagree. And it's her duty as wife not to pursue it further, to just let things go, to let him be the superior mind in the marriage as is good and natural. She takes a deep breath and returns to her letter but she's lost the easy accumulation of words. She would like to tell Herbert about the young man missing a leg, but she can't bear to hear him distort this into a tale of noble youth and sacrifice, of this boy—soon dead, no doubt, of gangrene—finding a moment of playfulness with a little girl. There is nothing redeeming about the story. And when she sometimes wakes with a start in the night, she knows the cause is often that her thoughts have shaped this boy from distant memory and set him to motion in her dreams. She can hear his soft whistle and the leg hopping on the boards of the platform, hidden by the rough walls of the wooden shed. The leg sounds in thuds, growing louder and louder. She waits at the boy's side. The sound draws closer and the boy smiles at her and then she wakes up, realizing that the pounding is just the beating of her heart.

XVI
The Putumayo

October 1910

In Iquitos, the murky air is charged with something fearful and vultures—actual vultures—collect at the street corners, fighting over bits of sinew, or waddling after weakened dogs as they circuit the town.

Casement is a champion of hopeless causes, a Saint Jude whose presence signals true desperation without any of the palliative hope. Even his witnessing of his own life seems a harbinger of certain doom. But for now, he is headed to the plaza, where the young men collect, much as they did in Brazil. With his conquistador's beard and his *soles*, he's popular, although sometimes mistaken for a priest. There are young men sitting by the fountain, their arms linked with girls and with each other. Casement sits on the low wall listening to the water trickle and lights a cigarette without difficulty—the breeze has stilled to nothing.

Here is a young man possibly attracted by the smell of good tobacco, but hopefully more. He's smooth-skinned and sleek-haired, more Indian than anything. He has a very sweet expression, such gentle eyes.

"Buenas noches," says Casement. He will manage a little conversation. Despite his limited vocabulary, his Spanish is surprisingly fit for certain subjects. It's time to extend a cigarette, then an invitation for a drink. And whatever else. Tomorrow he's headed up the Amazon and into the Putumayo to investigate the state of the Indians, and he knows it won't be good. Casement has become involved in a roundabout way. Apparently, the *blancos* hire Barbadians to work as overseers and these Barbadians are British subjects. The Barbadians have been kept laboring long after their contracts expire, and—because of the system of payment and provisioning—are often deep in debt with their employers and unable to free themselves. So here is Casement. And there is the river.

The boat should have left at dawn, but some mechanical issue has delayed them and they left Nauta in the full heat of day. Casement stands, holding the rail, and watches as the arms of the riverbank close behind him. Here is an endless gloaming, as if the river itself were holding her breath. One can hear the rattle of monkeys in the trees, the air batted by the sweep of wings, the leaves onshore shifted by the passage of some earthbound thing, the heart-chug of the steamer as she plows onward, upward. The mosquitoes descend in burning clouds, piercing his skin with a toxic fire. In the evenings he sometimes sees bright lights flicker at the shore, but it is only the reflection of the boat torches catching in the eyes of caimans. A telltale splash lets you know that one has slipped into the water, is mapping its way around the boat.

Casement maintains his reserve with the other Commission members. To him, they are tourists. They see only what is pleasant. For Fox, it is the exotic foliage—palm fronds the size of sails that called to mind the work of Jules Verne, or creeping vines weighted with brightly colored blooms that, even in maturity, hold their petals in close, secretive folds. For Gielgud, the massive chorizos of rubber that appear, wrung from the jungle, keep his spirits high. Barnes is still curious about the plantations. He hasn't seen anything that looks like cultivation yet but is sure that he soon will as the fruits of some sort of successful agriculture are filling the storage huts from La Chorrera to Indostan. The effects of industry—if not the actual process—keeps Seymour Bell, a note-taker, taking his notes. Tizon, a businessman, surprises with his hesitant yearning to justice.

The Indians guard their expressions, speak in hushed voices. Most are near starvation. Many are whip-scarred. The only Huitotos and Boras who seemed to be thriving are a few young women. In every place the *Liberal* stops along the river, there are guaranteed to be a group of at least five girls with combed hair and shining skin, usually in some manner of loose-fitting gown, a phenomenon that at first read as modesty but that now Casement recognizes as the entitlement of some *blanco* to the girls' naked beauty. Farther up the river they go. Soon they will reach Occidente, and after that Ultimo Retiros. Next they will trek inland to Entre Rios. He already knows of the horrors that await him upriver.

In Occidente, the other Commission members had gone on some sort of fact-gathering hike to find the rubber plantations, which Casement knows aren't there. There is no cultivation. All around is evidence of slavery, in the well-constructed bridges that span the Igaraparana, in the chorizos of rubber in the storage huts, in the stocks on display in the clearings of the settlements, and in the deep weals on the legs and buttocks of the Indian laborers. Of course there is no plantation. Where is the means of paying the workers? Why are all the workers half-starved? Why are there armed *capitans* whose sole purpose is to pursue the Indians through the jungle when they try to escape?

Casement still has not found his way to the center of it all. The pilot of the *Liberal,* Jose, has provided some distraction. He has a kind face and his friends are often laughing at what he says, so Casement assumes he has a good sense of humor. He watches Jose bathing in the river, and sees the boy catch him and deliver a shy smile. Later, Casement, wandering the lower decks, is attracted by chatter and the smell of something fresh sizzling in hot oil. The boys are frying piranhas that they must have caught off the side of the boat. There is a predictable and humorous exchange, pantomimed, about the ferocious appearance of the fish, about how this toothy thing is now dinner for Jose, and that Casement—smile, nod, hand gesture—should try it. He takes a small bite as this small fish, despite its appetites, provides little to staunch another.

"Good," he says. And the boys laugh, which means that he is very welcome to eat anything any time with these Indians (although Jose is tall, which means he is of mixed blood) and that they are pleased to be his friend.

Jose spends most of his time sounding for depth and checking for snags in the coffee-black Amazon water. The two spend long hours, side by side.

In Ultimo Retiros, Casement has to leave Jose, leave the boat, leave the Igaraparana and all the creatures hidden beneath her reflecting surface—piranhas and caimans and anacondas and paiche fish the length of the boat—and at this loss, he feels the weight of the forest. The music of panic is the soaring wail of insects flashing close and then closer to his ear.

In preparation for his inland trek, Jose brings Casement to a termite nest at the side of a tree. He slices it open with his machete and plunges his hands into it. He grinds the termites between the heels of his hands and smears the crushed insects onto Casement's neck. There is a smell of acid wood. With his left hand, Jose makes a frenetic gesture, bringing it close to his face. Crushed termites repel mosquitoes and this remedy, along with a return to his heavy wool trousers, will be somewhat helpful, although neither precaution is much welcome in the heat.

Jose keeps waving. Casement loses him to a bend in the path.

Here, the ground is uneven. Wet leaves lie over tree roots or sucking mud. Much of the time, his eyes are bound to the earth, to the step ahead. A wall of flat wood means a paddle tree has sunk the great palm of its root deep in the mud. The branches reach up, holding the tarp of sky, still branches, not the waving arms of Irish trees but the fierce, unmoving gesture of the Amazon. Here time holds each second, his fingers clenched into an unyielding fist.

Feeling a pair of eyes watching him, he jerks to see nothing. Sometimes there are tamarins, but always moving quickly away.

Casement does not know how malnourished Indians can carry loads of seventy pounds along these paths. Even in the Congo the porters bear no more than sixty-five pounds. And those are larger men. The thought that the Congo could represent a higher standard of justice to any place anywhere seems impossible, as are many things. Even empathy feels a luxury of nonessential thought as he struggles to keep upright on the muddy path. The Indians maintain a quick jerking step akin to donkeys, the gait of man endeavoring to outpace death. A log translates itself before Casement's suffering eyes to be a corpse. A train of ants course through an eye socket. Here is someone who had been working to stay alive and then thought better of it.

How long has he been marching? The mud slows everything, making time difficult to track. Casement has already slid into a ravine and had to be rescued with a rope. Now he trips on a root and falls to the ground. He feels steady hands at his elbow, helping him upright, and is shocked to see the tiny woman that is his helper. "Gracias," he says and executes a little bow—a gesture that usually carries across cultures. She squeezes his hand, whispering at him earnestly. A benediction? A curse? She takes her basket up so that it rests on her back, fixing the strap across her forehead as is the way of portage here. And there's that jerking step as she outpaces him and whatever else is stalking the rutted walkways of the Putumayo.

Soon after, a ridge presents itself and along the ridge Casement sees first one Indian, and then another, and one after another the men and women assemble until there is no unpopulated space along the ridge. There have to be sixty Indians lined up, shoulder to shoulder, and then just as quickly as they have assembled, they disappear, one by one.

"We are close," calls Villa, a *blanco*, from the head of the column. He has been marching with them since Puerto Peruano. He walks with a boy on each side for support. Around him, six girls in white gowns hover about like earthbound fairies.

Casement's heart is thudding in his ears, a sound that ravels and disentangles with and from the beating drums. Tizon raises his eyebrows in a way that signals resignation. "Sounds like O'Donnell has prepared a carnival for us," he says.

Casement produces some strained cheer. "Could be fun."

"Perhaps if it's your first time," says Tizon. "Say no to the ayahuasca. The Bora believe that the spirit world and real world are happening at the same time.

After drinking ayahuasca, you will too. A little coca is all right, and the masato, but also consider moderation. The headache after masato is a revelation."

Exhausted from the journey, troubled by his weak eyes, Casement fairly stumbles into the clearing at Entre Rios. The drumming is loud here and Bora Indians are pouring in from the edges of the jungle, naked but for feathers in their ears, or paint along their legs. One has a white feathery thing pasted in his hair—it looks like frayed cattail punks. A gourd with fresh water is thrust into his hands. He sees Tizon take a mouthful from his, and then pour some water into his hand, with which he washes his face. Tizon looks willfully bored, but Casement sees his own nervous wonder reflected in Fox's face, and in Seymour's. Gielgud and Barnes must be farther back in the column.

The drumming grows louder and now there are women singing too, chanting, the repetition strangely soothing. Now a group of Bora men are crawling in his direction. They writhe and slide over each other, rolling across the dirt, washing themselves with dust as they draw closer. Their mouths are foamed with saliva, as if they're rabid. He looks quickly over at Tizon, who has maintained his droll expression. And then there is a *blanco* on a small wiry pony, riding up behind the Indians. He jumps from the pony and sweeps his arms wide, calling out in Bora. The response reverberates from all corners of the clearing. A number of young Indians, their hands waving through the air before them, gather around this man. He wades through the writhing Indians, who roll out of his way, addressing Casement and the others. It's in Bora, but has to be a greeting.

"Good afternoon," says Casement, which—although it is afternoon and is the only available greeting—seems ridiculous.

"Welcome to my kingdom," the man responds, which is both ridiculous and appropriate. This is Andres O'Donnell, the chief operator of Entre Rios.

O'Donnell's appearance does not betray much in the way of his Irish roots. He is of a slightly pinker cast than most other *blancos*, but only O'Donnell's grandfather was Irish and he the sort of Irishman that leaves and settles and multiplies in another land, in his case, Spain. O'Donnell, having inherited his grandfather's wandering spirit, if little else, had left home at seventeen, traveled here and there and, eventually, here. He is fluent in Bora and Huitoto and runs one of the most productive camps in the entire operation of the Peruvian Amazon Company.

"Pound for pound, give me a Bora over any other worker," he says. He gestures for Casement to sit beside him on a long bench. Dinner is being brought in: roasted pork and some dish with chilies that he'd first mistaken for kernels of corn. "I hope you're not too tired," O'Donnell adds. "We're likely to be up all night."

The masato smells like sour milk and beer, and tastes as if that's what it is, although that particular combination is not one Casement has ever sampled. He drinks a light tea of coca leaves as well, declining the preferred technique of the Indians, which involves sticking the tip of a five-foot pipe up your nose and having your friend blow in a powder from the other end. Casement is tired and his eyes are burning, presenting a blur of visions. Perhaps it has been unwise to drink the masato, or maybe his coca tea hides another stimulant. Now they have moved (when did they move?) from the long table and are seated around the perimeter of a circular hut. There is a massive drum made from a hollowed log suspended from the ceiling and a young man with a long spike through his nose is banging at it with two leather-covered beaters. The sound hits his ears like the pounding of a great heart. As the dancers enter, Casement feels a flutter in his chest, as if he has captured a bird in the cage of his ribs, and then this fluttering thing—his soul—escapes to hover up at the roof's high point, gathered together with the souls of all the Indians. He must have asked a question because O'Donnell is telling him that 500 Bora will show up for this dance, that they take the coca, which is why they are able to carry such heavy loads over great distances, that they eat each other but not white men because they find *blancos* disgusting and could not imagine ingesting them. O'Donnell's face is backlit by blue smoke and all the words are distorted by the aphasia-inducing liquid air. He feels that he is collapsing backward, but then he is outside and a girl has him by the hand and is leading him through the doorway of a hut.

*   *   *

He awakes with a poultice over his face, stringy dampened bark. He is lying on a comfortable mat, conscious of his different body parts, fingers, feet, aware of their mass yet knowing that he is not fully that, not fully the body he occupies. He feels his tongue lying heavy and thick in his mouth. There is someone in the room with him, breathing lightly, shifting on nervous feet. He peels the poultice from his eyes and sees, through the safety of his own mosquito net, an angelic girl who has her enormous nut-colored eyes trained on him. She raises her hands to the corners of her eyes and he mimics the gesture. His eyes are free of pain and feel cool. He can see clearly.

"Everything is here," O'Donnell informs him over a breakfast of fried yucca and fish. "The cure for every illness, a medicine for every ailment." The angelic girl has her little hands resting on O'Donnell's shoulder and is speaking quickly in his ear, nodding at Casement with earnest concern. "She says that she had your translator tell you that she was there to do anything you wanted and you said you didn't want anything from her, unless she could fix your eyes. So she did."

Casement remembers none of the exchange. "She is speaking the truth and please thank her on behalf of my eyes."

O'Donnell responds with a gesture, harsh, dismissing the girl.

The gentle Boras with their bright skin and warm eyes, straight and strong, are perhaps the most beautiful of God's creatures. Were Ward here, he would have endless inspiration. He would rejoice to model these graceful beings in bronze. And what company he would make. Ward could hunt jaguar through the jungle, palaver with the witch doctors, collect new spears, although the weapons here are admittedly less artistically wrought than their African counterparts.

When Casement clears his mind to consider, he sees Ward sitting in a chair with a pipe, reading a newspaper, chatting with Sarita, who is in her element at the drawing table with stacks of correspondence and reading glasses. How hard it is to conjure that golden man from the Boma days, his bronzed skin and tensed posture, his alertness as if every sense functioned at its acme.

PART THREE

I

Paris

May 1911

Casement has escaped to the bracing chill of the balcony. Having reached the advanced age of forty-seven and still a bachelor, he has become the prey of a set of women who too have remained beyond the reach of marriage, the sort of women whose fantasies are mired in the mundane, who dream about clean collars and tidy teas and losing their birth name. He reaches into his pocket and produces a cigar—gift of Ward—but, patting himself down, realizes with grim certainty that he has left his matches in his overcoat.

"There you are," says Ward, shutting the door behind him.

"How did you find me?" says Casement.

"The miracle of glass." Ward gestures to the door that divides—in its eight panes—the finery of the guests, the gilding of the room, the falseness of the chandelier lighting. "Would you care for me to light that for you?"

Casement looks at his cigar and nods.

"You shouldn't be so dismissive of her, Roddie."

"Of who?"

"You know who. You could save a great many Indians, several Congolese, and even yourself if you married her. And she wouldn't want much from you—just a pleasant face over the rim of her teacup."

"A man's bathrobe hanging on the peg?"

"Or something hanging on yours." Ward winks.

It is—quite literally—beyond imagining. The sound of a glass shattering on tile reaches from inside, then laughter. Casement glances over his shoulder, but there's nothing much to see. "I'm too set in my ways to ever get married. I think you've known that for a long time." Which is true. Casement can't remember Ward ever asking him about why he'd remained a bachelor and, although he can't be sure, Casement thinks this stems from Ward's conflictedness about the domesticity of his life, although he wouldn't sacrifice the family, nor security, nor Sarita, whom he complains about, but whom he can't bear to be separated from—even by a wall—if it can be helped. Casement's freedom acts as an alternate existence for Ward. There's Ward in the Putumayo, working for the Foreign Office. There's Ward being knighted. There's Ward looking for adventure at the end of the evening rather than piling into the carriage with the wife and children. "When is this party of yours going to be over? I look like a giraffe in this monkey suit."

"Pick one animal, Casement. And it's not my party. It's for Dimples—who's getting married soon—and for Cricket, who isn't. And it's for Sarita, who didn't want to have a party, but when the girls wouldn't stop nagging, begged me to get it over with as soon as possible." Ward finds his own cigar and lights it. He's looking down at the street with some concentration, although the one slow passing taxi and its sad hoofbeats and rattling wheels doesn't justify his attention.

"You're awfully quiet," says Casement.

"I want to ask how you are but am concerned that I'll find out all about those two Indians that you brought to London and how much they like pudding, and then something about Cesar Arana, and then something about Home Rule and Ulster. And all I really want to know is how you're doing."

"That is how I'm doing."

"No, Casement, that is how the world is doing."

"We're even," says Casement. "You talk endlessly about Germany."

"When Germany invades, my house is in the direct path. France could, yet again, be overrun by Huns."

"It could be worse," says Casement.

"How?" Ward has his elbows leaned on the balcony and, as he turns, Casement can see his jacket buttons tugged to capacity across his belly.

"The Germans are an enlightened people."

"Don't say that too loud around here. Someone will string you up." Ward shakes his head. "I don't think they were 'enlightening' Alsace Lorraine."

"True, but the Germans weren't running concentration camps in the Orange Free State."

"And they lost. Look, I'm not in favor of all that—going after the women and children—but sometimes you need to do what it takes."

"What it takes?" Casement, despite the implied challenge in his question, actually believes this.

"That's not controversial, Casement. War is never pretty. And someone is always going to disagree with your methods. In general, the English are honorable."

"I remember a young man in the Congo who told me that he hated England and all things English. And that same man is now living in France."

"Good enough," says Ward, and he claps a hand on Casement's shoulder. "The French, why not? But the Germans? Never!"

Close on four, the party finally breaks up. Taxis are lined along the curb and slowly they turn to circuit the still streets where the only sounds are grinding wheels and conversation muted by lateness or leavened by Champagne. Cricket, wobbly on her feet, shuffles up to Casement and leans on him, standing as straight as she can manage.

"Everything all right?" asks Casement.

"No," she says. "Percy Granger is marrying Celia Louise Hobson."

"Do you like him?"

"I don't feel anything about him at all, but I really loathe Celia."

The Ward carriage pulls up and Sarita, fussing with the boys, appears on the sidewalk. She's a commanding presence in her pale blue gown—lean, formidable. Charlie looks like a fireplug in his suit. He doesn't seem to have a neck, which must help him with his boxing. Apparently, he's pummeled all of Eton into submission. According to Ward, Charlie is being groomed to take over the Sanford Empire. Ward is excited for that, can't wait for his boy to be done with his education, and is already thinking of a series of sculptures to occupy the still-as-yet-occupied time. Dimples stands, melancholy and sweet, lit by the streetlight. She looks as if she might begin singing some sentimental air. Ward is concerned at her innocence—nervous at the upcoming nuptials—although Cricket is of the opinion that Dimples knows a lot more than she lets on, that her reserve actually springs from her need to keep secrets.

"You were supposed to go home with Roddie at midnight," Sarita is saying to Herbie. "And why do you smell like cigarettes?"

"Everyone's smoking in there. It's just on my clothes."

Charlie is the first into the carriage, and then Casement gives Cricket a steadying arm, saves her from pitching backward. He helps Dimples in next, and then Herbie, who presents his hand for assistance, batting eyelids. The boy does smell like cigarettes. Sarita is next. Ward hops up front with the driver.

"Herbert, you don't have to sit up there," says Sarita, calling out.

"I need the fresh air," says Ward.

"Can Cricket have some fresh air too?" shouts Herbie. "I'm sitting next to her and she doesn't look very well."

Casement, laughing, closes the carriage door.

"Roddie, there's plenty of room in here, although I don't think Herbie's made it seem very attractive," Sarita says.

"I would rather walk," says Casement. "It's a lovely clear night. It will do wonders for my head."

* * *

334

Paris is a dead city. Truth be told, Casement doesn't much like France beyond the Wards. France is a nation in decline. Deaths outnumber births, and exports? Well. What does France really do? If you're going to look for a winner, look to Germany, who doesn't need any Entente Cordiale to make her feel safe. There's your model. Industry. Organization. Mobility among the classes. Germany, France—England too—could benefit from a bit of the Kaiser's clear thinking. Germany is a good model for Ireland, although Casement does harbor concerns that Ireland's future leaders might not see it that way. But once thrown off, the English yoke will need to be replaced with something.

Casement takes the turn off the wide boulevard, tracking back from the Place de l'Opéra, heading west. The cafés will be closed at this hour, but there will be people milling around. There's always someone looking. If he would ever speak to anyone on the subject, he'd be an amazing source of advice. In Iquitos and Para, try the fountain. In Montevideo and Bridgetown, try the docks. In London, the bath is the best place because even if no one is interested you can always get a look. And a bath. And in Paris, well, the moral laxity of the French is in your favor. In a café, a perfectly respectable lady will be drinking tea with her sister while on the balcony, highly rouged girls sport with businessmen, and alert boys scan for clientele. Most people would be truly astounded at how many inverts there are. And who they are. He thinks back to Montevideo—a successful dock crawl—and the Norwegian sailor who approached him. That was a burly blond man with hot blood, not someone that Casement would have thought to go after without encouragement.

And then there's Millar back home, who (could it really be four years ago?) made it clear that he was interested in whatever "Sir Roger" was up for, even though he didn't present—and still didn't—as being remotely musical. Millar. At seventeen, he was a boy of such pent-up passion that probably anything would have ignited him: Casement, a postcard, a loaf of bread. He said he'd admired Sir Roger for years. Now he is a bank clerk, still living with his mother. And this Mrs. Gordon, so smitten with Sir

Roger's friendship, even has a room made up for Casement—waiting—in her lovely house at Myrtlefield Park.

Maybe he should head back to the Wards' townhouse. He doubts that Millar is prowling the streets of Belfast, but this is part of the problem. Casement is sadly anticipating that day when Millar—like a Greek—says he's moving on, done with his apprenticeship, an *eromenos* to Casement's *erastes*.

There's a little life at the end of the street, a group of three young men collected beneath a weak wash of light pouring from the streetlamp. Casement's fancy clothes in this particular neighborhood will communicate all that needs to be said. There's a smile for him, and then another young man turns, moving his cap back from his forehead. There will be steps in his direction as he finds his way along the footpath. There will be a retreat from the light. He feels his adrenaline pick up and maybe, right now, Paris is not so bad after all.

Casement stands stoically by the drawing-room window. How are they supposed to talk about anything else? Ward takes a gulp of tea and sets the cup rattling hard into the saucer.

"Please don't fuss," says Casement. "It looks worse than it is."

"You know that's not true," says Ward. "Black eyes take a day to really display their finery. I don't know why you don't want to report it." Casement's eye is more red than black, but threatening to bloom into something truly impressive.

"It's a waste of time," says Casement. "I'm leaving for London tomorrow and who knows when we'll get together again? I don't want to spend my last day in France sitting with detectives. And I didn't get a good look at him. He was tall and dark and wearing a cap. That could be anyone." Casement is looking out at the cold sunlit morning. He's turned in such a way that Ward can no longer see the eye, as if he could hide it. Or the importance of it.

"And this happened near the Opera House? I think people should know. A gentleman should be able to walk, no matter the hour, and have every expectation of personal safety," says Ward. He stands from the couch and walks purposefully from one side of the room to the other. Sarita tracks his progress. She's sunk into her usual chair and must be tired out from the previous evening's festivities, as she's failing to muster the requisite outrage. She sips her tea, looking at Casement with narrowed eyes.

"How much money did he get?" she asks.

"About eighty francs. And my watch."

"And where exactly were you?" she continues.

Casement, with some effort, smiles. "On the pavement."

Casement has been waiting at the Belfast ferry terminal for an hour. Millar is not usually this late, although he has been later as of late and has even canceled meetings set well in advance, meetings that he would never have thought to miss when they first got together. Although, Millar is solicitous, happy to run errands, organize accounts, arrange figures. Casement adjusts himself on the wooden bench. If Casement had need of a personal bank clerk, Millar would be there, one hundred percent. But lately he has been a distracted creature and, honestly, what does Casement have to offer?

And then Millar presents himself at the entrance. Casement watches. Millar's jacket is buttoned incorrectly, so the collar's askew. He's looking all around, mouth agape and nose wrinkled, but Casement doesn't wave. He feels two currents playing through him at this moment. One is that heart flutter that he always gets when he sees Millar, the sense of incredible luck that he could be here in Belfast and have someone waiting for him, to have something that approaches the conventional. The other is a dull ache, the anticipation of grief, which is unfortunately the gift of middle-age wisdom. And that's why he doesn't wave, because for this minute at least he knows where Millar is, knows that Millar is looking for him.

"Mister Gordon!" shouts Casement, and Millar looks over. There's that smile and it could be that Casement is overthinking things, as is his nature.

Millar pushes through a couple of idlers, extends his hand. "Sorry, Sir Roger. All of Belfast's a disaster today." He sees Millar notice his eye, acknowledged only with subtle nod. They shake hands. "The streets are jammed."

"Business as usual?" Casement picks up his case and the two make for the entrance of the terminal.

"Have you not looked at the newspaper?"

"I have yesterday's *Daily Mail*."

"The *Titanic* was launched this morning, so we should move quickly. Things are going to get very hectic around here."

"That's right." Casement remembers. "Did you go see it?"

"Me and all of Belfast. They're saying there were over a hundred thousand people there. Do you know that it took twenty-two tons of soap and tallow to get her down the slipway?"

"That's a lot of tallow. Did you get a good look?"

"The ship's four stories high and hard to miss."

"I suppose it will be difficult to get a taxi?"

"Not difficult, impossible. Good thing I have my own transportation."

Casement gives Millar an indulgent nod weighted with foreboding. It's Casement who bought him the motorbike in the first place, because it's what Millar wanted, and he had cash then—cash, which shows up miraculously every now and then, and is quickly consumed, like summer strawberries. "What about my case?"

"That's easy. Goes on your knees."

"And how does it stay there?" Casement needs both his hands to grip the bar at the back of the seat to keep himself from pitching off.

"With any luck, I won't have to make any abrupt stops."

On the street corner, the motorbike does not seem quite so terrifying, although it does look small to transport all it's needed to. "Maybe I can call Biggers."

"He's out of town." He arches an eyebrow. "Apparently some graves in Londonderry needed rubbing."

It's Derry, but Millar has a hard time keeping that straight. Millar gets on first and rocks the bike off its stand. He gives a ready look to Casement, who gets astride and then squeezes the case between him and Millar. The case seems to have been invented to prevent the touching of bodies. Millar kicks the motorbike into life. "Don't go too fast," says Casement.

Millar responds with his usual statement, "When I lean, try to lean with me."

Belfast should feel like home, but it doesn't. No place does, really. Rumor has it the bill is going to be on the table next April. Home Rule could be a reality in the next three years and English sovereignty a thing of history. To say the North is adamantly opposed to an Irish State is something of an understatement, although the faction in favor—Biggers, Hobson, Alice, himself—are at least organized. Things are getting heated. He's cautioned himself to stay calm in these discussions as such behavior is usually better for his cause in the long run, but he is a man of many passions, all of which, unfortunately, look better on the young. On people his age passions don't seem virile, rather the opposite—hysterical.

Still, there are some things he can discuss calmly. No, he doesn't want to be ruled by the Pope any more than Henry VIII. And no, he doesn't want to find himself beholden to some toothless Mayo sheep farmer. Keep the North as is. Linen and shipbuilding and good Protestant work ethics have brought wealth to the region. The successes of the North are exactly what make a free Irish State such a viable thing—the leavening in the bread. What needs to be articulated is an Irishness that appeals to Ulster ledgers. He can't keep pointing to dancing girls and soda bread and boys at the hurling and expect Ulster Scots to leap on board. Lean. Lean. Lean. Millar is taking this corner too slowly and Casement is worried the motorbike will topple. There is a wobble and Casement feels a wash of adrenaline as he predicts the fall, but then Millar grinds into a different gear, there's a jump of speed, and the bike rights itself.

At the house on Myrtlefield Park, all is quiet. Casement sets his bag inside the door, rakes his hands through his hair, looks around.

"No one here," says Millar. "I gave Margaret the day off because her sister just had a baby."

"And Mrs. Gordon?"

"In Ballymoney at a funeral."

"No one close, I hope."

"Not to me, or to her. Mother just likes funerals." Millar widens his eyes with the mock horror that usually accompanies all references to his mother. "Tea, Sir Roger?"

Casement smiles. Millar is presenting a casual self that's a touch too relaxed. Casement follows him down the hallway to the kitchen, taking in the slightly pigeon-toed gait, the low hairline that no matter how he keeps his hair always touches his collar. Casement is quiet. Millar will soon recognize this, if he hasn't already. It would be like Millar to intentionally ignore this so as not to get into a discussion. Millar goes about filling the kettle, holds his hand over the stove to check the heat, then puts the kettle on.

Casement leans on the doorframe and Millar leans against the counter, folding his arms across his chest, crossing an ankle. "Are you tired?" he finally offers.

"No, I'm fine."

"How are the Wards?"

"I always enjoy spending time with them."

"And your friend Herbert?"

Once, Millar had nursed an envy here, had asked for details about their time in Africa, had suspected that there was more to this history, a suspicion that Casement had nurtured to give an alternate past, perhaps. Or merely to heat desire. "Still capable of charming any man, woman, or beast."

"Or combination thereof?"

Casement smiles again.

"And your eye?"

"Still working. I think it gives me a masculine edge, helps when I'm addressing the workers of this great soon-to-be nation." Will Millar ask how he got it? He doubts it. And Casement won't ask about the lady's parasol he saw leaned inside the door, definitely not the stiff black affair that Mrs. Gordon uses to shield herself from the sun's cheery rays.

"Quite the brute," says Millar.

Things are looking up. "And I suppose you're an angel."

"I'm no angel, Sir Roger. You know that."

Sarita is headed to Aldershot with Herbie, whom she's checked out of Eton for the night to watch Charlie box. The carriage is first class and, as a result, reeks of first-class cigar smoke, and also something that she can't quite place. Cat urine comes to mind, but it's probably the afterglow of some modern perfume. She'd been thinking of ordering a light snack, but the thought of eating anything with her olfactory senses so assaulted does not seem advisable. Herbie probably wants something, even though it's only an hour's journey. He's at that age—fourteen years—and has changed since the last time she saw him, just a matter of weeks earlier. His cheekbones are higher and he's developing her reedy build, her deep-set eyes, her discerning intellect. "Mother," he says, "why are we taking the train if Grandfather is going in the motorcar?"

"Paulson is a terrible driver. I don't think it's safe."

"Everyone's been complaining about Paulson for years. He wasn't a good groom. He took some of Father's shirts when he was watching the house in London. And he got the Fordham's maid pregnant."

"It was the Fordham's governess. And you're not supposed to know about that."

"Why doesn't Grandfather just fire him?"

"You don't just fire people who have been working for the family for years." And besides, if Father did that, Paulson would no doubt show up at Rolleboise with his hat in his hands and next thing Herbert would have created a position for him and soon all the maids would be complaining about Paulson's advances, as he's not the lad he once was. Sarita performs the folding of hands in her lap. "Loyalty is a virtue, Herbie."

"Is that what you're going to say when Paulson drives Grandfather into a ditch?"

Herbie is playing with her. She knows it. He's so clever, that boy. He's probably figured out the real reason why they're on the train. Now that

Mother's dead, Father has taken a companion, and this new addition is currently his companion in the motorcar. Father had actually asked Sarita if the arrangement was acceptable to her, if she had a problem with it, but the truth is she'd been sending Paz money since Dr. MacIntyre's death. Paz was no longer lady's maid material and she had nothing to her name but four trunks of last season's gowns. Even the jewelry that she'd thought good was just paste. What she'd said in the letter actually was "basta bisuteria, como yo," or *just paste, like me*. And never having lied to her father about anything, Sarita had laid it out, just like that. Father taking Paz as mistress made sense. He was old, of course, but Paz was no longer a girl. What was Father's response? "Sarita, you are both pragmatic and kind."

Herbie is watching her think, his lips pursed and eyes squinted, the gears of that Sanford mind grinding all pretense into substance. "And why are we staying at The Goring?"

So Herbie does know. But so long as he doesn't know that she knows that he knows, it will all be acceptable. "You don't need a reason to stay at The Goring." She sounds like Cricket, who might not need a reason to stay at The Goring, but this sensible mother does. At some point they will have to figure out how to give all access to the London house.

"Will Charlie be joining us?"

"He might." If he's not in hospital. Charlie is competing in the Public School Competition representing Eton. She doesn't know where he finds the time to do this and would rather he found something less dangerous for sport, but here her opinion matters little. Herbert is suddenly interested in his eldest son. He can't make this fight as he booked a Volunteer Force bivouac for the same weekend, but he sends support. Sarita's father is so pleased with this fantasy of self that has become a flesh-and-blood grandson that whatever protests she has as mother are not worth considering. And she understands it. She hears herself, "I'd rather you weren't standing in front of all those people in your shorts," "Doesn't it hurt?" and, this one bon mot, which Herbie finds endless use for, "Charlie, you'll ruin your nose." Any time she asks anyone not to do something, Herbie asks if she's afraid the person in question will ruin his or her nose. For example, "Cricket, you should not go riding with Alain Breson," is met with Herbie's "Afraid she'll ruin her nose?"

Neither of her sons has an adequate sense of self-preservation. Last term at Eton Herbie had been sanctioned for the most stupid of offenses. Apparently, as the stew was particularly awful, he'd taken his bowl up to the high table and said, before the whole student body, "Please, sir, can I have some less?" Herbie had told her that the whole thing was worth it. He'd become some sort of hero and claimed to have no regrets, although she doubted he'd felt that way when he was being birched.

"Can I have some oysters?" asks Herbie.

"Oysters on the train to Aldershot?"

"Fish pie?"

"You are asking for food poisoning. Steak and kidney pie, if they have it." She raps her knuckles on the window as the porter passes. "Or some sandwiches." She's not sure that the dining cart will be open off hours, but they must have something to eat.

"What time is Charlie's fight?" asks Herbie.

"It starts at two o'clock." The porter passes again and she raps, again too late. "And no, we don't have time to find a good lunch venue. We can always eat at the teashop at the station. You can have all the oysters you want when we get back to the hotel."

Dimples has just finished decorating her new townhouse in Paris and that's where Roddie and Cricket are staying this weekend. Phipps is nice enough, but Dimples is having some trouble settling in and Roddie has been spending most weekends with her. Everyone anticipated that Roddie was going to miss Dimples—the two have always been close—but his grief at her moving out was a shock to all. And then, a week later, Ticker failed to wake up for his morning beef tea. This had been a blow to her as well, but not a surprise. As Herbert argued, that dog, out of canine devotion to her, had willed himself to the unprecedented age of seventeen and made a very reasonable exit. But Roddie was unmoved. He kept looking at the place by the newel post where Ticker's cushion (and therefore Ticker) had been for years with a look of such horror that Sarita had suggested he use the back stairs until he was completely recovered.

Roddie is too sensitive. Ostensibly, he's going to Broadstairs next year, which should prepare him for Eton, but he's so easily persuaded to tears that she doesn't know how the other boys will react. Herbert's solution? Tell Roddie not to cry. Toughen him up. Last week Herbert had mentioned sending the boy to Africa. She pictures little Roddie, although he's now eleven, standing on a beach with his case and hat, a few black men milling around, a grinding sun, an elephant, and Roddie's face composed in that stunned halibut look that he gets right before falling to pieces. Sarita thinks the boy's best served by kindness, but she's a mother, and her opinion is biased, useless, ignored. Distraction is probably good for him, and Cricket has managed to get tickets for them to some nutty—no doubt distracting—Russian ballet, even though all the seats were sold out a month ago. Cricket has been running with an artistic crowd, not a good idea for someone who's logged several seasons, and seems content to log several more. What if she finds herself with someone unsuitable? When Sarita had brought this up with Herbert, his response had been, *I was an artist and that wasn't a problem.* Which was unhelpful, but also difficult to argue with.

"You just missed the porter again," says Herbie. He gets up and with his knuckles gently raps on her forehead. "Hello, Mama, are you in there?"

The gymnasium on Queens Avenue has the look of a prison. At the entrance, an anxious boy jumps up and down on the balls of his feet, strange behavior, but no doubt related to some athletic endeavor. Sarita washes in through the doors with all the other people. She'd been concerned that there would be no women, but quite a few are here for the tournament, a lot of young girls surreptitiously pinching cheeks and turning to face the world with the composed, serene, false expression so prized in society. She wonders if one of them is here for Charlie, who, despite his blockiness, projects a ferocious masculinity that is not quite handsome but very effective. He's admitted to having an involvement with a local girl who works in a teashop, but says he's being careful. How strange that in her short life she has gone from someone who could have been that girl to a mother warning her son not to become entangled.

"Mother, should I go find Grandfather?"

"Not yet, I don't think he's arrived," says Sarita.

Paz enters the gymnasium alone and glides along, quickly recognized from her posture, taking steps to the top tier. A pair of soldiers in uniform turn to look as she passes, and they are ignored, as is Sarita, who has been sighted out the left side of Paz's vision.

"Let's sit here," says Sarita. These stupid hard seats are not sympathetic to women's fashion and she'll be spending the next hour or so leaned up along its supports like a plank. Sarita sees her father enter the gymnasium. He props himself on his cane, setting it before himself like the third leg of a tripod, and scans the seats. "Go say hello to your grandfather."

"Can I get some sweets?" Herbie is digging around in his pockets, which are yielding a surprising amount of coinage.

"Please do," says Sarita. "Butterscotch would be nice." Her stomach is unsettled. Why is she here? She doesn't want to watch some brute attacking her son. And these sporting terms: terrible. Right to the kidneys. Left hook. Apparently it was safer before they started using gloves because the bones of the hand are more delicate than those of the head and boys had to soften their blows. All this random knowledge she's picked up. She'd thought punch-drunk was what happened to people drinking cocktails made with cheap gin and now she knows the term refers to brain damage sustained in matches just like this.

Herbie comes running up the steps, two at a time, and takes his seat. He's got a bag of sweets in his hand, and some tucked into his cheek. Herbie has never seen a chipmunk, so she won't say he looks like one, because he'll just make fun of her for being a foreigner.

"I did ask for butterscotch, but they didn't have any, so it's just bull's-eyes." Herbie offers the bag and she takes one, which is suspiciously sticky. "It's about to start. Look, there's Charlie."

And there he is in an undershirt and some shorts with a fancy sash around his waist. She breathes through her nose. Charlie's shoulders are bigger than the other boy's and he has that angry look, but she knows it just means he's concentrating. There are a number of grown men milling in the ring, coaches, umpires, whatever aging masculinity exults in youth-on-youth destruction. Perhaps they're going over the rules. But for the umpire, the men retreat from the ring, leaving Charlie and the other boy eyeing each other, fists raised. Then a bell rings. Sarita watches the boys circle, but when the first fist flies out—was it Charlie?—she looks to her lap. "Is he all right?"

"Why don't you watch?" She can hear Herbie breaking the sweets to bits with his teeth. "Good lord!" says Herbie. There's an audible smacking noise and hearty cheers. She hears her father, "That's my boy!" from the front.

"What's happening?" There's the squeaking of the shoes and that strange chorus of "heps" and "ohs" that come from the spectators. She hears a girl's voice, "Come on, Charlie," and is tempted to look, to see if it's the girl who works at the teashop, or a real contender for Charlie's affection. She takes a quick peek and is too late. In the ring Charlie dodges a punch, not looking terribly concerned, but then the other boy lands something—that must be one of those kidney hits—and she returns to looking at the forget-me-not print of her skirt. And then it's just thud and thud, and that shoe-squeaking, and she wants it be over.

"Eton, Eton, Eton," Herbie yells, but no one joins in. And then there's a heavy smack and a loud whump—someone's hit the floor—followed by cheering.

"Unbelievable!" shouts Herbie. He's laughing and standing up, applauding.

"What happened?" says Sarita.

"Charlie knocked him out. That Charterhouse boy didn't stand a chance."

"Oh!" says Sarita, and she gets up, also clapping. The other boy is toddling in a tiny circle, roused now, shaking it off. Charlie, composed, is surveying the stands, maybe looking for his next victim. Sarita gives a

346

little bird-wing wave and he sees her. No smile, but that's Charlie, as if he's pummeled the other boy because she asked him to. "So he won."

"And now he advances," says Herbie.

"He advances?" She sighs.

Herbie laughs at her. "Did you want him to lose?"

Sarita reaches for the bag of sweets. "Not if it ruined his nose."

The boy from Bedford also doesn't see the second round, although Charlie, tiring, allows the next contender—at this point in the proceedings a wide-eyed, nervous thing—into the third round, but not the fourth. Having run out of boys to box, Charlie is a champion. And this is important for a number of reasons that Sarita finds unimportant, including Eton's having boycotted the event for the last several years. Who could care? Sarita is waiting for the crowd to thin a bit before she congratulates her boy, but there's Father shaking hands alongside Charlie. Why does he think he deserves to do that? And there's Herbie hopping and jumping around, boxing Charlie's arm, although Charlie doesn't seem to notice. Charlie's arm is roughly the circumference of Herbie's leg. And finally he sees her.

"Mother!" he says, and the crowd magically parts to let her through. "What did you think?"

"That was possibly the worst hour and a half of my life," she responds.

"But I won!" he says.

"You are a champion, but you are not a mother"—she leans in to whisper in his ear—"and hopefully not yet a father."

To which he laughs, a booming laugh, indulgent, and she realizes that Charlie has become enough of a man to treat his mother with gentle, affectionate patience.

II
London

May 1914

The Ulster Volunteer Force with Ulster money has gone to Germany and purchased 25,000 top-of-the-line rifles, arming themselves. And their enemy? The English who say they aren't English and the Irish who claim them as kin.

This is the response in the North to the prospect of Home Rule. Soon, the Irish State could be a reality and the response of Ulster is to organize, arm, bristle.

Despite the rifles, there have been no shots fired. Apparently, English troops in the North are also on the fence as to whether or not Ulstermen are Englishmen and haven't shot anyone. The standing English troops in the North have rebelled with their refusal to violence, but it is a rebellion without consequence. Casement has a feeling that the rest of Ireland will not be so lucky.

In the South, the Irish Volunteers need rifles.

Purchasing guns in Germany seems a reasonable way to proceed and, as no other option has presented itself, that's what they're trying to do. At any rate, when the time comes, English troops cannot be relied upon to enforce Home Rule.

He has spent the afternoon listening to all sorts of palaver—understandable—as all of them, Figgis, Childers, Alice, Mary Spring Rice, have been trying to figure out what this plan means, if it's feasible. How will Redmond feel about this overture to Germany, considering that England is on the brink of war and Home Rule still on the table? How does anyone feel? How can Casement reconcile his life of seeking peaceful means with organizing the purchase of weapons?

In January Casement had been in Galway with Thomas O'Malley, professor at the university and staunch Sinn Féiner. O'Malley had been approached by a German journalist, who was writing an article on the poverty in Connemara. Casement had done a good job of raising funds for the region, had organized a system of school lunches for the children, which was good for two reasons; firstly, it brought young minds into schools where Irish—and the Irish perspective—was taught, and secondly, it fed them as they were all the children of hard-hit farmers or people who had once been farmers and were now destitute without the palliative activity of labor. It was arranged that O'Malley would drive the German journalist and Casement out to Connemara to tour the schools.

Casement was known to the journalist, an Oskar Schweringer, who had read his articles in the *Irish Times* and *Irish Independent* from when he'd been lobbying to bring the Hamburg-Amerika line to Queenstown, or Cobh. This was after Cunard had discontinued service to Ireland and Casement had reasoned that it was impossible for Ireland to have an economic presence if ships were not docking in her harbors. He'd argued well, yet futilely, as the British easily blocked the move.

From talking to Schweringer, you'd think that the Germans were as incensed as the Irish by this transparent action driven by what could only be English greed. Schweringer's outrage was suspicious, as was his supposed interest in kelp farming, something that he said had sparked his devotion to Connemara. But whether or not Schweringer was sincere—a Hibernophiliac kelp enthusiast versus a German spy—he was indisputably a journalist committed, for whatever reason, to publicizing the desperate need of Connemara. He listened attentively to all of Casement's arguments, which, as of late, had been feeling worn, but with this Schweringer, attentive as a terrier at a badger hole, sounded distilled to flawless truth. Maybe Schweringer was a German agent, but that at least meant that the Germans had an interest in Ireland and one that involved getting the English out.

It was clear that Schweringer knew to voice a hatred of the English but also clear that he had no idea what an Irishman felt in this regard. And that was another worn proclamation, one that Casement had not bothered to share. How could this German man, never enslaved by another nation, understand the subtle, dehumanizing way a conqueror justified his actions? Casement had been born into this anger, had watched his older brothers beaten on the streets of London. He had sat through dinners listening to Englishmen joke about their "Irishness" as a romantic, poetic, irrational thing—what made men sing when drunk. He'd bitten his tongue, not pointing out that a romantic, poetic, singing thing—in essence, the soul—was all one had left after being robbed, enslaved, and forced by starvation to abandon one's country. Also, that this "irrational" and therefore savage Irish ethos was used to shore up the sense of English civility and reason, which is what allowed the English to unleash their criminal abuse across the globe and persuade themselves that all their victims were somehow raised up in the process. And why had such an eloquent man stayed silent, given that? Because defending one's self in such a context was emasculating, and as an entire nation of men had been so humiliated, all one had left was forbearance and dignity. Although dignity—this silence—was not seen as Irish.

Driving around the west of Ireland, Schweringer—who had done his reading for this mission—had gone on about the Penal Laws. On seeing a donkey—picturesque with its baskets of peat and emaciated child—he had remembered, with comic outrage, that the Irish had been disallowed from owning an animal worth more than five pounds, this to keep horses that could be used for military purposes out of Irish hands.

"That's where you're wrong. The English wanted us all on donkeys so that we'd look silly," O'Malley had interjected. "Also, so that they could look down on us." O'Malley, committed as he was to the Connemara project, had begun responding to Schweringer in this manner as his suspicions of Schweringer had crystallized into outright certainty that he was escorting a German spy through the peat bogs of Connemara, which was ridiculous. But what could one do?

After they deposited Schweringer back at his Galway hotel, O'Malley and Casement had strolled up the canal for a drink. O'Malley had said, "I don't really trust the Germans."

And Casement had said, "They're the only ones who can beat the English." And then he'd added something about German industry, discussed the possibility of Belfast wealth expanding southward, but all the while he'd felt of two minds. On the one hand, he was a humanitarian, and entertaining an alliance with Germany was in opposition to his instinct to peace. On the other, the Germans wanted Ireland on their side, and the Irish might actually be in league with the winners.

As it currently stands, they are not entering into any agreement with Germany, although some sort of Entente Cordiale might be wise. If Germany has her war and wins, which seems a distinct possibility, it would be desirable to have an understanding in place for Irish Independence.

All the others have left and now it is just Alice and Casement. Alice insists on the dining room despite the discomfort of the chairs, although perhaps this might be why she likes it, perhaps enacting a disdain for comfort as a way of performing her gender-defying strength. But Casement's old problem, the piles, is aggravated and he has to keep getting up.

They are trying to break down the glorious gunrunning plan into a series of small, effective actions. As it stands, Darrell Figgis is to purchase the weapons in Hamburg. Erskine Childers and his wife, Molly, will then transport the guns to Howth on their yacht *Asgard*, with Mary Spring Rice along for the ride. Erskine Childers is a writer, famous for *The Riddle of the Sands*, a veteran of the Boer War. His wife, Molly, an American, although crippled, is good with a boat. And Mary Spring Rice? You do need someone to help load rifles. Women might draw less suspicion to the cargo, although perhaps more by their presence as yachtsmen in the North Sea. As he thinks it through, the venture seems either doomed or bound for glory. Or both, as is the case with so much of Irish history. This plan might not be the best to ensure Home Rule, but currently it is the only plan, and as such he should support it. Although his mind still darts here and there, hoping to create one less bizarre.

The official meeting adjourned at half six. Darrell Figgis had finally left at eight, when it was clear that Alice was not going to offer dinner or pass around the whiskey. Figgis, from the Figgis tea merchants, has done himself up as a Bohemian, writing poetry, growing a scant but lengthy red beard, and swanning around in shabby clothes. He's running the business end of things and one would assume that he should be present as the planning proceeds. But Alice can't think around him. Figgis is sharp but changes topics constantly and can't bear silence. He is brave and organized, willing to risk the trip to Germany, and maybe that should have been enough to let him stay on.

Casement and Alice sit together at one corner of the table. There's a cold joint of lamb with some of last night's mint jelly and savory pudding, just in case they feel like eating. He has little appetite and Alice is preoccupied. He watches her unspool all kinds of scribble across the page, darting to the margins to pencil in occasional notes. She consults her work, scratching her head with the pencil tip. "If I give 750 pounds, do you think you can double it?"

Alice is counting on the donors who supported the Congo campaign; although, illiterate, starving children in Connemara are somehow a harder sell than Congo rubber workers. "Well, I do know who to ask. Maybe. Maybe I can do it."

"In two weeks?"

"In two weeks, or not at all," says Casement. "Alice, are you proposing we run a revolution on 1,500 pounds?"

"Revolution? No. That's just a rough estimate of cost based on how many rifles Esrkine's guessing we can fit in the *Asgard*'s hold."

"You're budgeting a pound a rifle?" asks Casement.

"Something like that," says Alice.

"Don't forget the ammunition," Casement adds. "So less than a pound per rifle. Any rifle at that price will be, at best, a relic of the Boer War."

"Are you having second thoughts?"

"Second thoughts. And third thoughts," says Casement. "But not enough to back off."

If they land the guns—regardless of quality—it will bring much-needed credibility to the Irish Volunteers. The Ulster Volunteers are no doubt drilling in the hills of Antrim. And what are their brothers to the south doing? Running at scarecrows, impaling them with broomsticks.

"Who's our man on the Supreme Council?" asks Alice. They're going to need a high-level Irish Republican Brotherhood person to approve this.

"Most likely Bulmer Hobson," says Casement. "If it creates belief in an Irish Republic, Hobson will be for it." Hobson will hope that having armed Irish Volunteers can possibly cancel out armed Ulster Volunteers: Try to make it so that no shots are fired at all. But at some point even Hobson will have to accept that with this many guns, some are bound to go off.

Alice creates a column of figures and taps at the edges of the paper.

Casement strips a bit of the lamb off the joint, drags it through the jelly and into his mouth. That one bite activates his hunger. He puts some food on his plate, even the savory pudding, which tastes of salty lard.

"Roddie, we need real money," says Alice, "and for that, we need America. So this is something that needs to be planned. I'll book passage as soon as can be managed."

"That makes sense," says Casement. "How long will you be in America?"

"Me? We're not sending a woman to the United States." She screws up her face. "We'll send Sir Roger Casement. He's a knight and Americans love that." She delivers that conspirator's smile that makes so much more sense now that they're actually conspiring. "We'll send you to New York and you can go shake some hands, empty some pockets."

"And then what?" asks Casement.

"And then we go back to Germany and buy more weapons."

Casement spends this long night winding himself in his sheets, first a swaddled baby, then a dead man. The drop into stupor finally succeeds, the membrane dividing wakefulness from coma is breached, the black clouds of sleep work their gentle suffocation . . . now.

No more! He coughs inward and his lids fly up. At first he does not recognize the room. His heart drubs against his ribs as a cold wash of adrenaline spreads to the tips of his fingers, the backs of his knees. Sleep is over. He wonders what has woken him this time. The wind is rattling the pane but bad weather is most often soothing for him. Perhaps a bad dream. He closes his eyes to find it, and sees Millar, feels a second surge of panic. Get up. Get up. Find a drink. Use the water closet. The term would be *drifted apart*—he and Millar have drifted apart. But that's not accurate. They were both neck deep in whatever they shared, swimming along, and Millar has outpaced him by several lengths and is widening the distance. They are friends. The room is cold. Casement sits up and swings his legs off the bed. He groans just to hear some human sound in the darkness. He feels for the slippers on the floor and his feet find them, the slippers belonging to Alice's historian husband. How long has he been dead? Why keep the slippers? Does she keep them for him? He puts them on—a perfect fit—and thinks, *I am wearing the slippers of a dead man.*

In the hallway, he can hear Alice's robust snoring. There's a rough drag outward, the smart inhalation, the three epiglottal hacks to finish the intake of breath. And then she goes again. He's stayed in this house a dozen times at least but still gets turned around at night, although he does not miss chamber pots—always thought walking out of a shimbek to stand in the honest air preferable, the sound of one's urine spattering onto the ground somehow more satisfying than trying to contain oneself into a bowl that was then slid under one's bed to be left percolating until the following morning. He pauses at the end of the hallway. There will be a door to the left, but right now moonlight is pouring through the window of the second guest room and through the open door he sees the brightness. The somber beauty of this draws him and as he moves to the window, he is momentarily stopped by what he thinks is a blanket folded and left upon the floorboards. He toes it carefully, but it is just a square marked off by the gentle lunar light and he would like to lift it, to somehow unfold it, to wrap himself in this pale, cold shroud. Why not go to America? Why not pack his bags again?

Sarita's sure he's seen her and is pretending he hasn't. What is Casement up to? It's been a year and a half since he stayed in Rolleboise, but he's aged more than that. Well, he won't lose her now. Narrow skirts mean smaller strides but she can shuffle quickly and does so, feeling like one of those Bavarian dolls with the hinged legs that move in step. She pushes along the pavement, nudging people out of the way. He's a quick walker too, although Sarita's shortening the distance. Still, she's about to miss him as he's rounding the corner. "Roddie!" she shouts, and people turn, no doubt surprised to see this well-dressed, well-heeled lady standing there, yelling.

Casement stops, his head nodding forward with resignation, and he turns, a smile already on his face. It's so good to see him, even though he was trying to escape. He returns along the pavement and she takes his elbow, leads him around, urging him along. "Let's go."

"Sarita, where are we going?"

"I'm bringing you to lunch, although by the look of things, I really should be taking you to buy a new pair of shoes." There's a hole on the top of his shoe, the leather worn through, and she's sure the soles are in even worse shape.

"I'm not sure I have the time."

"For lunch? You need to eat."

355

"I have an appointment."

"And now you have two. Don't be rude, Roddie. I know you're accustomed to turning ladies away, but I am married, and there's no need to worry." She's trapped him with intimacy. She watches the comic slumping of the shoulders. "So, Sir Roger, where do you want to go?"

"We could go to my usual, the soup kitchen, but I'm worried you might catch something."

"Like what?" Sarita widens her eyes.

"I don't know," says Casement, "smallpox? Typhus?"

"I think you need a steak."

"I don't have the money. And I'm not having ladies pull out their purses to support me. Tongues will wag." He raises his eyebrows a few times. He's acting out fun and, as a result, is starting to feel it.

"There's a place around the corner where Herbert has an account. No money will be displayed."

"Very well. It's bad enough that I'm out with a married lady. I can't afford to be embroiled in scandal."

The restaurant isn't too fussy a place and the service is brusque and oil free. Herbert has a liking for it as it's walking distance from the Sanford offices and also because the portions are enormous, although watching Casement polish off his steak—agonizingly slowly, however, as gobbling would be impolite—she wants to order him another, which is what she would do for little Roddie, who's having trouble at Eton and seems more and more starved each time she comes to visit. Thank God Herbie's there to keep him company, although this is his last year and he can't wait to get out. And Charlie, fine as well, excelling at Christ Church, ready to break it off with the Oxford shopkeeper's daughter, but unsure of how to do it without her making a fuss. And he's been "touring in the motorcar" with the sister of a close friend, whom he'd like to get to know better, although it seems that they are already very friendly.

"There's also someone else, if you can believe it: the exotic Pandora, whose parents sent her from India so she could be conversant in the ways of the English. Courtesy of Charlie, she's learning very quickly." Oh, there's a big laugh for them both. "Charlie is having difficulty juggling them all and can't seem to make a decision. Do you know what he said to me? 'Mother, I just wish this damned war would get started because that would take care of everything.' "

She's laughed at this many times already, but sharing it with Casement is a special pleasure. She's already written to Casement that Cricket, who's his favorite, is due to have her first child in a matter of months, but hearing about it from Sarita: the vomiting, Cricket's yelling at poor Colville Barclay—in front of all—never to touch her again, her insistence on mushrooms when they're out of season . . . it's all a tonic to him. She can see that. Dimples has gotten into the spiritualist thing, although Sarita thought that had gone out with the last century. Dimples has friends over and they sit around the board, moving a glass. Apparently, Casement's father had also believed in that.

"So he was actually a Catholic," says Sarita, which is the funny thing to say.

Sarita has, of course, visited the boys, but she's in London to go to the heart specialist with her father, who thought it improper to go with Paz. Sarita had pointed out to him that at this point in his life Paz was not only being passed off as his nurse but had actually come to occupy the role.

"Your father has been a wonderful host to me more than once," says Casement. "Please extend my best when you next see him."

"Done," she says. "Roddie, you've asked about everyone but Herbert."

"I've never known him to be anything but well."

"You make him sound so dull," she teases.

"So how is Mister Ward?"

"You can ask him yourself. He's off the ferry this afternoon and should be here by four. We'll have dinner. At the soup kitchen, your treat."

"Here's the tragedy: I'm going to miss him. I have a train to catch."

To look at Casement's face, it is a sorrow of epic proportion. "Where are you going?"

There's a moment as if he is not sure. "Scotland."

"Scotland? Why there?" Sarita watches Casement, who seems to be equally surprised at his choice of destination. "You're being very mysterious." Is it consul work? She remembers his time in intelligence and wonders if the looming war has dragged him back in this direction. "Or perhaps you can't say."

"I will make it to Rolleboise as soon as I can," he says.

"Maybe next time I see you, you'll be a world-famous hero." She watches him as he tracks some rogue thought through his memory. He's quiet for some time and then, remembering he's in company, manages a smile that has a wince contained within it. "That's your other appointment," says Sarita in a tone she saves for her boys, for when they lack confidence, "an appointment with destiny." She smiles her casual, brave smile, but as always this is a cover-up for the very insecurities that she shares with her sons and now Casement, her anxiety that all will not be well, that heartsick contraction that makes her think of the uncertain future with respect and fatalism and only the faith that it's likely that she, at least, will survive as that is what she's good at.

Outside the restaurant, back on the pavement, Casement seems to be casting about for what to say. He is uncommonly distraught. "I am so sorry I missed Herbert," he says, finally.

"Herbert will be quite jealous we had lunch." She glances over at the long panes of the restaurant, gleaming and reflective, and sees Casement and her captured there—his tall stoop, her girlish stance. "Let's make a plan for next spring. You always love the spring in France."

"I do." Casement takes her extended hand and squeezes it. His grip is firm, yet his hand feels cold through her glove, the bones too pronounced. "Goodbye, Sarita."

"Roddie," she says, leaving her hand in his. "Say it again."

"Why?" he asks.

But to look at him makes her think he knows. "So it won't sound so final."

"Lovely to see you," he says. "Let's get together as soon as we can manage."

"All right, Roddie. À bientôt."

Sarita releases him, watches his agitated gait as he expands the distance between them. She makes a note to remember this particular moment— Casement walking on, the sun washing cold on the long windowpanes, the clip and drag of a slow-moving horse towing a slow-moving cart, a tentative spring sky. She feels a grip—a chill—and wonders why of all things she's feeling this: the pull of grief.

III

New York

July 1914

At six o'clock, he is still waiting for Adler Christensen to show up. This is Adler's place, joyless and plain. Adler would say *honest*. The bar has shadowy corners in which patrons lurk, silently draining glasses, uninterrupted by such distractions as company or conversation. Or sunlight—that splashing excess of American heat that glories in its stinking brilliance, more and more, as July draws to a close. Casement is on his second gin and tonic, even though he knows he should take it slow. This latest bout of malaria has made it hard to eat, which has brought down his weight, which has made him an easy drunk.

Here in America he has raised close to $5,000 but does not have control of it, as the Americans are quick with introductions and invitations, but know to hang on to their accounts. He does his dog-and-pony show, and the profits disappear into some coffers that are being held on behalf of an independent Ireland. Irish Americans are still Americans, quick to remind you that they're the risk-takers, the successful ones, the people who have embraced the twentieth century and, much as they share brotherhood with their picturesque, backward brethren, they'll take the lead, thank you very much. They like Casement well enough, although the moment he gets in the full swing of his passions, he can see the looks exchanged: *the man's unstable*, they seem to say. He has cash pushed into his hand as if he is a gentleman with an allowance, is told where to show up and how long to stay.

Casement is an activist, an organizer, a man who will change the face of Ireland.

Casement is a man waiting for another man to meet him, one whose spirits are diminishing as his spirits (rattle of ice in glass) are diminishing.

"Another, sir?" says the barkeep.

"What time is it?"

"Just inches past five. A good time for a drink."

"As you advise." Casement manages a smile. He's been asking the time every few minutes. The barkeep raises his eyes, attention drawn to the door, and Casement follows his gaze. There is Adler.

Adler looks nervous and could use a wash. His blond hair is dark with grease and why do his eyes pick around the room like that? He seems to be concerned at the possibility of a fight, or angling for one. It's the same look Casement remembers from the first time he saw Adler in Montevideo ten years ago. Casement—down on the pier—had returned the glance, then felt unsure, that this man might be looking for the kind of money earned through a straight beating. Adler had followed him, laid a hand on his shoulder, and said, *Aren't you interested?*

Then, as now, he is a little in awe of Adler.

Adler is Norwegian and speaks an American-inflected English, both slang and accent. He's a stray dog and has shown up broke in as many cities as Casement has made an appearance with a full wallet. That they should meet is understandable, but that Adler's transit should cross him again, here in New York, seems like fate. As much of Casement's time is spent cooling his heels, company is good. He was waiting to find out if the guns made it to Ireland, and just today they have been safely landed in Howth, transported to the city center with great pomp and circumstance—no doubt Hobson's idea to capitalize on the moment. But soldiers had opened fire on spectators at Bachelor's Walk, and that's the spectacle—innocent blood, martyrs. And that's the rallying cry. Urgency attaches to civilians shot down on the streets of Dublin, so now Casement waits for the money to start pouring in. He waits to see what this new war means to the Americans, who have fought a war with England but now waffle on whether or not to back Germany, or perhaps just to thank the cold sea for buffering them from all that gunpowder and bloodshed. He waits and waits and waits.

"Sir Roger," says Adler, moving him up the bar with his elbow. "No Champagne? I thought we were celebrating."

"We are," says Casement. "But the landed guns haven't yet accomplished anything, except for killing some bystanders in Dublin." Adler gives him that look, *Can't you ever enjoy yourself?* And he can't. "And now Austria has declared war on Serbia."

"Serbia?" Adler shrugs.

"You find Serbia dull?"

"Not dull, just not interesting."

"And how do you feel about Russia?"

"How does anyone feel about Russia? It's full of Russians—condescending drunks."

Casement has to laugh. "You've just described yourself very well, my dear Adler."

"Often true, but right now I am sober." Adler waves over the bartender. "What is he drinking?" he asks with lazy gesturing to Casement.

"Gin and tonic," says the barkeep.

"Well, I'll have that, but no tonic please." Adler looks around, still twitchy. He really wants that drink and is impatiently rapping his fingers on the counter. He manages a patient look for Casement and claps a heavy hand on Casement's shoulder. "Your face is crumpled like a grandma's. What is bothering you?"

"The Prussians will soon march on Belgium."

Adler is unmoved, confused, and disbelieving, as if all these facts of all these countries are some variety of gossip that fails to entertain, that flit about without gaining mass. Russia. Prussia. Serbia. And now Belgium?

"When Germany marches on Belgium, the Irish will side with the Belgians," says Casement.

"Why?"

"Because Belgium is a Catholic country."

"For the Pope?" Adler is being purposefully obtuse. He does this for his own entertainment. His drink arrives, placed with a cheery knock on the surface of the bar. The glass is smudged, and Casement would have asked for another, but Adler downs the gin like he's a pirate. He looks at the empty glass thoughtfully and rests it on the bar, raising a finger to the barkeep for another. "I don't understand any of it. The news is changing every day. Why bother?"

"You're not interested in what's happening in Europe?" says Casement. He means to sound incredulous but can't muster that right now.

"No one understands this war. And religion? No one understands God. It's true. Sir Roger, do you understand any of this? Don't lie to me."

I'm not one of your little boys. That's what Adler implies now with a sly, sideways glance through his smiling blue eyes. His face is cherubic or florid, round cheeks, fleshy lips, a relaxed dissipation that Casement knows has been identified by Devoy—who is running the American show—and everyone else whom Casement has introduced to Adler. Or introduced Adler to, as he is now Casement's amanuensis. Devoy doesn't trust Adler— calls him "that Christensen"—but Devoy doesn't trust anyone. Devoy is an old-style Fenian rebel living in exile. He's spent a lot of time in prisons and breaking people out of prisons, which has led him to believe that everyone has a price. And honestly, looking at Adler, who is already at his second drink and most likely picturing the next, it's easy to see why Devoy would think Adler's price within reach of anyone who might want to purchase him.

"Where were you today, Adler?"

"I had a meeting."

"Business?"

"In some ways, yes. Listen," and Adler turns to him. He's going to ask for more money. "I need some money."

"I'll get your drink," says Casement.

"It is not for me. And you will ask who it's for, but Sir Roger, I don't think you want to know." Here Adler tries to compose his features in some sort of apologetic, boyish cast, but he's betrayed by a coldness in his eyes.

"Are you being blackmailed?"

"Yes," says Adler, "if marriage can be called that."

Casement has put away another gin and tonic. Together, he and Adler move along the New York streets, ready for a change of location and some food. At this very corner of Broadway is the same rooming house that he stayed in as a young man in the room above Glave. Glave had been flitting about arranging payment for a story set in the Yukon. And Ward was in New York too, so long ago. All of this is being lost, rained upon by the years, drained of color, returning only in stuttered memories that float to the surface as brightly colored streamers before fading and sinking through the deep. And he could meet it with despair, but the fact is that Casement is walking down the pavement with Adler. At least, he is not alone.

Adler, despite his affectations of boredom and disinterest, has a clever mind. He breaks things down into small, workable chips of action. Oh, Casement has always been good at the lofty thought, but once presented to Adler, this becomes a contact at the docks, a folder of information, a ticket to Norway. Once Adler fixes his various problems, including this wife—a youthful error—they can focus on the work at hand. And even Devoy must admit that Adler, with his years at sea, his Norwegian papers, his casual grasp of numerous languages, will be helpful in getting Casement to Germany to purchase the arms. The looming war has made all movement suspicious. Had he managed to get to Germany in preceding weeks, he might have been all right, but the Americans are predicting that England will declare war on Germany within the next two weeks, that by the middle of August, the world will be embroiled in the likes of a war it has never previously encountered, the war that Ward has been articulating for years fed on the facts and lists and figures and spies of his old friend Harmsworth.

*   *   *

Adler is sitting on the bed, naked, his knees wide, rolling a cigarette. He twists the cigarette paper to seal it and scratches the inside of his left thigh, casually rearranges his testicles. "Pass the matches, Sir Roger," he says. He gives Casement an appraising look as Casement searches through his pockets and finds the matches, reaches from the desk chair across to Adler. "I don't like it when you're quiet like that. I don't think the sight of me has the power to silence you as it once did." Adler laughs to himself and fires up the cigarette.

"I've been talking all day," says Casement.

"But that look." Adler mimics him and it is the expression of a stunned goose.

Casement is being quiet. He does not want a fight and doesn't trust himself to discuss anything calmly. "I didn't know you had a wife."

Adler's eyebrows shoot up. What new ridiculousness is this? He's momentarily distracted by the sound of furniture being dragged around in the next room but comes back to Casement. "She isn't here."

"No. But she needs money."

"Only because I won't abandon her."

Such kindness. "Why marry her at all?"

"You are jealous?" Adler laughs. He points at Casement with his cigarette that is poking through two fingers of a fist. "You should see this woman. She's half Indian, a Redskin, but more red-hearted. A wild thing. I could call the asylum to pick her up. She tried to kill me once in my sleep. I woke up and she was standing at the side of the bed with a knife, all that black hair pouring over her shoulders, down her back. She was like a thing from hell. I had to take the pillow and belt her from the side, knock her down. She would have murdered me there."

"And cut out your heart and eaten it?"

"She would have sliced me open, and then found nothing inside." Adler takes another drag. "I am only good to you, Sir Roger. For everyone else, I am a devil."

*   *   *

As predicted, England declares war on Germany. Casement and Devoy have made plans. Devoy's eyes follow Casement as he moves about the room and when Casement meets Devoy's gaze he catches the assessment: Devoy has no faith in him.

"This is a plan I made with Patrick Pearse two months ago and I don't want you to fuck it up."

"John," says Casement, "I'm a diplomat. We're not planning a prison break. We're negotiating with Germans, creating allies, creating a future for Ireland that will hold in the new world order."

"Fancy talk."

"Which has its place." Casement is standing by the window. The sky is a crackling, harsh, American blue. There, on the corner of Fifty-Second Street, is a beggar on a wheeled palette, the right age to have lost his legs in the American Civil War. He's pulling himself up the pavement by making steps with his hands and there's a sign around his neck, but Casement can't make out what it says from here on the second floor. Devoy, at the table, his legs kicked out in front of him, has composed his whole self in disdain.

"If anything seems off, we're bringing you back to New York. And when you hear that call, you'd better heed it."

"If you don't believe in this plan, who will?"

Devoy nods to himself. He's no idiot. He's taking in Casement's height, the posture, the elegant brow. Casement has shaved off his beard in preparation for the journey and does not feel himself, but looks quite the dandy. His movements are being followed at this point and the beard gives him away—the beard that makes him a conquistador, that makes him a Don Quixote. He has also been washing his face in buttermilk to try to lighten his complexion. Adler finds this hilarious, even volunteered to buy it once, saying some ludicrous thing about the need for Casement to stay pretty. But the $2,500 budgeted for his trip is nothing to laugh at. Neither are the tickets for both him and Adler to travel to Berlin, via Norway. And the letter of introduction from the ambassador Von Bernstroff, also no joking matter.

Devoy is still looking at him, perhaps admiring his milky, youthful skin. "Thing is, Casement, you don't seem to understand just how much needs to be worked out."

"John," says Casement, "we can trust the Germans."

"Roddie, we can't trust anyone. Look what's happened to the Irish Volunteers."

Too true. As if it wasn't enough that Ulster has faced off against the Nationalists, now the Irish Volunteers have faced off against each other. Redmond has pledged Irish troops to fight for the English on the Continent, against the Germans. The thinking seems to be that England, in gratitude for all those Irish lives, is going to be in a generous state of mind come the end of the war. But these are the English, and their treachery has been proven. So there is the cause of his sleeplessness of the last three nights and Devoy is looking less the old rebel, and just old. "I'm aware," says Casement. "We've been split down the middle."

"Not down the middle," says Devoy. "A hundred and seventy thousand Irish troops have gone with Redmond over to the English, and we're left with little over ten thousand."

"I know the figures—"

"And still nothing on paper from the Germans saying that they'll back us once this bloody war is over."

"You've said this all before," says Casement.

"And I'll keep saying it until I get a reasonable response from you that convinces me that you understand what's at stake in Berlin."

Of course the Germans want unrest in Ireland. That's fewer English troops on the Continent. Casement's negotiating might be no more than that fly biting at the English flank, but he will strive to fulfill his two objectives. The first is to create an Irish Brigade from the Irish soldiers already in German prisons. The second is to secure the arms for the Irish to rise up, which—now that England is distracted by Germany—has found its moment. The Irish are playing at the same game as the Germans.

*   *   *

A last dinner in New York brings out an interesting crowd of potential donors. Casement has held forth on a number of things that evening— lectured on the benefits of the Prussian industrial model and the ascendency of Germany in the new world order as his soup grew cold, carefully navigated a conversation with a high-up in the Police Force where equal rights for the Irish had degenerated into a screed against "niggers" still pouring North from the crippled South.

With relief, Casement had released this man to a like-minded fellow on the other side of the table. Adler, who had been seated at the far side of the room by the kitchen, had come over with his drink—his friendliness suggested it wasn't his first, nor even his third—and pulled a chair to sit by Casement. Adler is now engaged chatting with the man seated at Casement's right, an old Fenian born in County Clare, and now the owner of a shoe factory in Worcester, Massachusetts. The man is smoking a cigar and this activity has drawn attention to the fact that he's missing the top digit of his right index finger.

"This?" says the man, waggling the finger, which means that Adler must have asked after it. "Shot off at Antietam."

"By a Confederate?" asks Adler.

"I certainly hope so," he says, smiling. "I was, after all, fighting for the North."

"And then you settled in Worcester?" asks Casement, politely.

"No. Then I went west to fight the Indians. We won that one too." He rests the cigar in the ashtray and, with his shorn-off digit, taps the table three times. "And we'll win this one. God wills it."

Later that night, bags packed, Casement and Adler sit in the still of the room. There is an inch of whiskey left in the bottle, and Casement knows that Adler is incapable of leaving a bottle in that state, even though his glass is full. Casement could sleep. Adler does not mind drinking alone, but the next day's journey has Casement rattled, so he might as well stay up.

"Who is Wolf Tone?" asks Adler.

"He's an Irish hero. Why?"

"Someone was saying at dinner that you're like Wolf Tone." Adler is smirking. "Maybe he liked boys?"

"I don't think so," says Casement, enacting patience. "About a hundred years ago, Wolf Tone went to the French for help for Ireland."

"The French?"

"They had just had a revolution and were feeling sympathetic. And also, France is a Catholic country." There's religion again and, of course, Wolf Tone was not a religious man and, if he had been, was from a Protestant family, but let's not complicate things. "So Tone went to Paris and the French were quite taken with him, and pledged some ships."

"But it doesn't work?"

"So you know the story?"

"I know the Irish are still in mud up to their knees hating the English."

"Wolf Tone was really conquered by the weather. There was a storm and ships couldn't land, things were delayed. Yes, it didn't work."

"And what happened to this Tone? Did they hang him?"

"No," says Casement. "They wanted to. It's what they do to criminals, but Tone argued that he was a soldier and as such should face the firing squad."

"So they shot him?"

"No," says Casement. "They insisted he be hanged, but someone smuggled him a razor and he cut his own throat. It took him three days to die, but he won that one."

Adler wheels the bottom of his glass in a small orbit. He says, "I don't understand this Irish winning."

Casement delivers the wry laugh. He'll have to toast that little wisdom, so he tips a little more into Adler's glass and stains the bottom of his with the dregs of the bottle. Their glasses clink. Cheers, cheers man, cheers to Irish victory.

Cheers to Norway.

Cheers to Germany.

369

IV
Rolleboise

September 1914

September is the time for harvesting the pears and, as all the able-bodied men have enlisted, Sarita herself has gone to the orchard with a basket. The air seems alive with its own good will and every leaf, every blade of grass, expresses itself in excruciating prettiness—each one a perfect exercise of light and shadow. Roddie is atop a ladder down the row. Herbie, ostensibly enthusiastic about pitching in, has shown up with a net *just in case a swallowtail shows up,* and one must have, because he's disappeared. Herbie really has no idea how to work and going to Eton has validated this innocence by introducing him to an entire class of people who are likewise uninformed.

Beatrice has taken over some of the garden work, which she prefers to polishing bannisters, and why not? Why not be in the sunshine in this glorious weather? She's scything the lawn in front of the house, as the mower doesn't work without a horse and all the horses have been taken, along with Charlie. The morning they'd all left, Sarita had seen the unhitched mower abandoned to its sorrow, but the horse's leather lawn shoes, strewn comically about, communicated the loss most poignantly. *Guess Blackbird won't need them where he's going,* that's what Herbie had said. The thought of poor little Blackbird towing a canon is almost enough to get Sarita's mind off Charlie.

Charlie, who is due to start training at Weston-Super-Mare in the next few weeks.

The pears at this time of year are full, heavy in one's hand, cool to the skin, and dripping with perfume. The branches almost drag, overloaded with fruit. Pears. Misshapen globes, swollen dugs. The sound of workers moving a piano from a house across the river carries on the wind. There's an occasional jangle of the keys, which, at first, she'd thought was some modern piece, composed of banging and intellect. But perhaps moving a piano on such a gorgeous August day is modern and that's her music—discordant keys, men shouting, and both from such a distance as to render anonymous. Or perhaps it's not workers moving a piano. The sound registers so minimally that it could be anything.

She pulls off two more pears. What's to be done with them all? If the boys who show up to pick them are all heading to the front, then what are the chances that the men who organize their sale are still here? She picks another and, not that she's hungry, takes a bite. Juice drips everywhere and she wipes her chin with the back of her hand. Roddie shouts in some sort of aggravated state and calls to her, "Mama, it's a bee."

"Wave it off gently," she says. "The bee won't kill you, but falling off that ladder might." School starts in another week and Roddie is on edge, a case of adolescent nerves.

Everyone's on edge. It would be nice to solve one problem—any problem. Maybe she can eat all the pears, just stay in the orchard, and move from tree to tree, until each one is unburdened. Blackbird has a fondness for pears. And also for apples. She closes her eyes against the thought and, when she opens them, is surprised to see a very dirty child, maybe six years old, standing in front of her. He's been crying, she can see that. He has big cheeks, a bow mouth, and such a scowl on him that he looks like an old man.

"Bonjour," she says. "Do you like pears?" She puts the one she's been eating in her apron and takes another. She extends the pear to the child, who snatches it, is about to take a bite, but thinks of better of it. "Take another," she says, reaching towards him again. He puts the one he's got in his right hand and reaches again with his left. So he's left-handed. "You could say thank you," she says, but the little boy has already started edging backward, not dropping his gaze. He backs all the way through the hedges—which must be where he came from. Once lost to view, she can hear him crashing through the branches, with quick little footsteps.

"Mama," says Roddie again, "I think you should see this."

"What?" Sarita says. She puts the basket down. Roddie is already coming backward down the ladder as fast as he can. He somehow looks pale, even though he's sunburned. Sarita wipes her sticky hands on her apron and goes up the slippery rungs, placing the arch of her leather soles carefully, holding tight to the rails.

"Look in the direction of the river," Roddie says.

Where the property slopes down to the river, there's a bend in the road, just visible from where she's standing. And now she can see what Roddie wanted her to look at. The road is packed, like morning traffic in Paris, cars and trucks and—is that a wagon?—moving very slowly.

"Roddie, get Herbie," she says. But Herbie is already there, standing with his net.

"Mother," says Herbie, "I think it's time to head back to the house."

Herbert has his back to them as they trudge up the lawn, the long grass drunk with summer tangling round their ankles. At first she can't see what he's doing, but then the Union Jack makes it slow descent down the flagpole. They haven't had an English newspaper in weeks, and the French accounts are careful with what they present. It would seem that things are bad. Herbert sees them and waves. It's his cheerful wave, but as his face is in a rictus of affliction, he appears to be warding them off. Still, they collect by the naked flagpole. There is birdsong and response and the smell of blossoms.

"How much time do we have?" she asks.

"Twenty-four hours. Actually, less than that. We should be on the road first thing tomorrow morning." Herbert takes the flag in his hands and seems to be entertaining some English mawkishness, but he catches himself and drapes the flag casually over his shoulder. "I used to know how to fold a flag," he says.

"I know how," says Roddie solemnly.

So that's what Roddie has learned at Broadstairs. He doesn't seem terribly well equipped for anything and he's due to start Eton next week. And there's Herbie, armed with his butterfly net. "Perhaps they're exaggerating," she says.

"The Germans are fifty miles away. They'll be in Paris by nightfall." Herbert sights down the mantle of lawn polished to brilliance with sunlight. "We may never see Rolleboise again."

He's going to scare the children. That's the problem with Herbert. He can be completely sentimental, yet so lacking in sensitivity. "Surely—"

"Sarita. Listen. The British base is moving to Le Mans. Colonel Burroughs was just here. The Germans are advancing rapidly and the roads are clogged—have been, all day. Père Fabrice left an hour ago to evacuate his family and Georges is gone too."

"He left us?" Sarita feels the first wash of panic. Georges was the only one remaining who could drive the car, the rest—including Charlie—all having enlisted. "What do we do now?"

"I'm not sure." Herbert's voice falters. "I'll have to find someone to drive us. There are five seats in the car. We'll just fit. Villiers has voiced a desire to accompany us. She's trying to get to her sister's in Bordeaux, but perhaps that can't be managed. If I can't find anyone to drive, maybe I can get a horse and carriage. Although, given the situation, people aren't much moved by money."

Sarita realizes that she has covered her mouth with her hands, as women do in melodramas. "You have to fetch Georges back."

"It's too late, Sarita. Georges is not a possibility. He's bringing his parents to his aunt's house in Tours. He did leave me the names of some men in the village. Beatrice set off on her bicycle to find them, but she just got back."

"And?"

"And she was barely down the drive before someone knocked her down and stole the bike."

"She'll have to walk."

Herbert nods, clearly retracing a path of thought already wandered. "What are the chances that those men are still there?" He is strangely calm, thinking and thinking. "Maybe I can figure out the car." Although he's terrified of cars, doesn't even like being a passenger. "Or maybe you?" This to Sarita, who he's always thought has the better sense of mechanics than him, but her knowledge is limited to things like getting the radiator unstuck and organizing the purchase of gardening equipment.

"Is there petrol?" asks Herbie.

"There is," says Herbert. "Do you have an idea?"

Wonderful. Now they're consulting the children. Sarita places her hand on Roddie's shoulder and delivers a falsely confident smile.

"I know I'm not allowed to drive the Hotchkiss," says Herbie.

"Because you'll kill yourself," says Sarita.

"Herbie, can you drive?" asks Herbert.

"He can," says Roddie. "He drove all the way back from Paris last July. Georges wanted to take a nap, so he let Herbie try and we only ended up in a ditch once."

"Was it a big ditch?" asks Sarita. And, of course, is ignored.

"The Hotchkiss is hard to handle," says Herbie, "but I can do it."

"The roads are already stalled," says Sarita. "And those people are desperate. Is it safe?"

"We should probably take back roads. Herbie, why don't you look at the maps?"

Herbie nods and begins walking quickly to the house. "Farther," he says, "where are we going?"

"We are going to La Rochelle."

"La Rochelle?" Sarita feels the second wash of panic. "Herbert, that's three hundred miles away."

"Probably longer on secondary roads. Sarita, ships haven't been running from the north for weeks."

"Can we at least telegram ahead to secure a berth?"

Herbert's face assumes a look of tragic patience. "No, Sarita, we cannot. We are at war and are being invaded by Germany. I doubt there's anyone in La Rochelle much interested in taking a reservation."

Why have they waited this long? They should have sent Roddie to England weeks ago, and Herbie. Although if they'd done that, they'd be walking to La Rochelle. "What should I do?" she asks.

"Whatever you think should be done, provided that we're ready to leave by eight o'clock tomorrow morning."

Inside the house, all is still. The summer light floods the windows without cheer, making the drawing room seem enchanted. The house is so hollowed out with quiet that Sarita feels as if she's haunting it. The scent of furniture polish holds in the air, that and vinegar, which is what they use to clean the mirrors. The hall clock ticks and in the dining room Sarita sees Villiers holding a tray of crystal goblets, but standing stock-still.

"Villiers!" There's a panicked tinkling, but Villiers manages to set the tray down without breaking anything. "What are you doing?"

"I am putting the washed glasses back in the cabinet."

"Do it later, if there's time. I need you to collect all the silver. Grab a blanket."

"Why not pack it in the cases?"

"We're not taking it with us. There's no room." There's so much to do that Sarita can't move in one direction before feeling herself pulled in another. "Herbie!" she calls. Both Herbie and Roddie appear instantly, which means they were just outside the door. "Herbie," she says, "I need you to dig a hole."

"Why?"

"Because we're burying the silver."

"Like pirates?" asks Roddie. "Can I bury the silver?"

"You're needed elsewhere. Although where exactly? And doing what? I want you to take a pillowcase off one of the upstairs beds and put my jewelry in it, and look around and get anything else that's valuable. And then you should pack some clothes. Or maybe Beatrice can do that. Where's Beatrice?"

"She's scything the lawn," says Herbie.

Sarita follows Herbie out onto the verandah and, sure enough, there is Beatrice slicing the grass into submission, shearing and shearing, in a dangerous frenzy. "Beatrice!" She looks up. "Forget about the lawn. Just leave the scythe. You're needed in the house."

In the coat closet, Sarita finds her carpetbag, which she usually uses for overnight visits to Dimples and the baby, who are, thank God, in England, as is Cricket. She'll need to send the daughters a telegram but doubts she'll have the chance before La Rochelle. Is she crazy to be packing the accounts? Deeds, those are worth something, aren't they? Or maybe she should be in the wine cellar, because that's an item that won't lose its value. And Herbert has certainly spent enough money stocking it. She drops the bag, looking around at the desk, at the cabinet, at the rug—which is valuable. Should she do something with the rugs? Probably not, but the paintings—they should at least be hidden, but where won't the Germans look? Maybe in the root cellar? Or perhaps in the attic of Père Fabrice's cottage? Who's free to do that? She looks out the window and sees Herbie wandering around with the shovel.

"Herbie!" she shouts.

Herbie turns around, mouth opened in way that does not inspire confidence.

"By the flower beds, so it doesn't look like you just dug it up."

Herbie nods, wanders over to a likely patch, and breaks the surface of the soil.

"Not there, Herbie. Anywhere but there."

"Why not?" he yells.

"That's where Ticker's buried."

Herbie breaks into a smile and moves a few feet over.

Beatrice, in her house apron, is standing at the door.

"Beatrice," says Sarita, "I need you to bring the paintings to the foot of the stairs there and stack them. And then I guess we'll wrap them in blankets and bring them to Père Fabrice's cottage." Sarita hopes that there's room in his attic, but if there's not, she's certainly capable of tossing the stuff out the window. Or will that arouse suspicion?

"Madame," says Beatrice, "all the paintings?"

"Just the valuable ones," says Sarita.

"Madame?"

"The ones you don't like." Which is funny, funny to both of them.

Roddie comes down the stairs with the pillowcase. He looks inside it but seems lost. "Mama, this is all I could find." He extends the pillowcase. "I don't know where all your necklaces are, or the tiara with the sapphires."

"The good stuff, Roddie, is in the vault in Paris." And of course what Roddie has there, diamond studs, some gold, that funny butterfly hairclip with citrine and garnet, is just what one wears to lunch at the neighbors. This activity does seem ridiculous, futile, but one has to do something. "Why don't you pack some clothes for you and Herbie, and don't forget some warmer things for the ship." If they can get on a ship. Move. Move. Move. Don't think. Don't panic.

The papers are now stuffed into the carpetbag, giving some satisfaction. Although it does strike her as ironic that the most valuable of these papers is the deed to the house. She makes her way up the staircase and into her bedroom. Roddie has closed all the drawers of the jewelry case, neatly arranged her brushes at right angles to the table edge. Now he's working on the collection of the silver as Villiers has to put together lunch and, while she's at it, some food that doesn't take up too much space for tomorrow's journey. And they need water. They're running out of space as the petrol is already filling the luggage rack. Herbie's pointed out that they're going to need extra tires. Back roads, extra weight, and the anticipated heat make punctures probable. So Herbert has taken the task of packing the car and a steady mountain of items is massing in the garage that may or not make the final cut. There's a moment of silence and she savors it.

The windows are still open and an energetic breeze fills the room, plays at the chandelier, setting the crystals to soft music. The wind billows the curtains, then sucks them flush to the wall. That chandelier was very expensive, despite its modest size. Maybe they should take it down, bring it with them. Or the one by the stairs, although she remembers the size of the crate in which that arrived, the miracle of it surviving the journey from Baccarat undamaged. The crate required a cart to itself, a cart that moved at a crawl all the way from the train station, softly easing in and out of ruts, the horse at a steady, steady pace. Caring about luxury things is a luxury. There's a thought she's never had, because she's never been in possession of such items and at risk at the same time.

The paintings are wrapped and stored in the cottage attic, and the jewelry is in the vault in Paris, nice and handy for the Germans when they're looking for it, but she's glad to be leaving France. She should be in England, all of them should be together, at least while Charlie is still there.

Beatrice volunteers to keep an eye on the house as she has nowhere to go but her family in Vernon, who also have nowhere to go, although what Beatrice can accomplish for security—little, doll-like Beatrice—who can guess? At least Burroughs will send a man ahead of the Germans to check that the house has been cleared.

"When they tell you it's time to leave, you need to go. We don't know how accurate these accounts coming out of Belgium are, but I would rather you not be alone when the Germans arrive." Sarita hugs Beatrice, who bursts into tears.

"I should have married him."

"Married who?"

"Marcel."

Marcel is the second groom, who's been gone for weeks. "Beatrice, did he ask you?"

"Yes."

"And did you want to?"

"Not then." She shakes her head, loosing a mass of blond hair on the left side. "But now, yes."

They're all doing it, *the last look at Villa Sarita*, all but Villiers, who is already sitting in the car. Villiers remembers the last time the Germans came through and has no misgivings about leaving. Roddie gets in next, squeezing up beside Villiers, and then Sarita, who looks immediately exhausted, as if she's been holding it in. It is six in the morning and Ward has not slept. Neither has Sarita. Herbie stands with the crank at the front of the car. He puts the crank in.

"Herbie, do you know what you're doing?"

"I've never started it. I know how, but Georges says it's tricky." Ward comes around to the front of the car, giving a tug on a tank of water that looks a bit loose but is actually secure. Herbie manages to get the crank around once, but then it sticks. He pushes it again and gets it to six o'clock, but then it sticks again.

"So what do I do?" Ward asks. He's never asked Herbie how to do anything.

"You crank it, but you can't really grab it. You have to sort of wrap your fingers around one side."

"All right," says Ward. It's really tough, takes a lot of strength, and looking at Herbie, the slenderest of the children, he can see why he's not up to it. Herbie is only sixteen, has yet to fill out, and might never, as he seems to have inherited his mother's bird bones. The poor boy's nervous, that's clear. He's got the brave smile going, a tick also inherited from his mother. "Here we go." Ward moves the crank one revolution, and feels a click—something's happening—and then he repeats the action a couple of times, then faster, and there's a clicking and a rumble.

Ward jerks out the crank and he and Herbie exchange a look. The Hotchkiss is alive. The running board is completely loaded up with petrol and Herbie has to climb over it. He settles himself into the seat and looks at the controls, reaches for the pedals, which involves sliding to the edge of the bench. He holds the gearshift and looks around him. Herbert hands him Georges' goggles. At any other time, this would be funny, but this is Ward's family who is now in the hands of Herbie. Sarita hands Ward a cushion and Ward folds it and tucks it in behind Herbie's back.

"Much better," says Herbie. He releases the brake and sets the car in gear, making some careful maneuver with the pedals. The car creaks forward and then they're moving. Moving at five miles an hour. They continue at this speed, slowly, slowly, with Herbie holding an almost painful concentration. A leisurely bird passes them, banking to the left across their path. They make the first bend in the driveway.

"By the time we get to La Rochelle, the war will over," says Roddie.

"Don't listen to him, Herbie," says Sarita. "This is fast enough."

Ward sees Herbie slump his shoulders ever so slightly. Ward doesn't even know the language for cars.

"Right," says Herbie. "Here we go. Second gear."

There's a terrible grinding noise, then a lag. He thinks the engine is going to quit, but Herbie does something and the car leaps forward. Now they're really going. A final turn and Rolleboise disappears from view. Soon they are coasting down the hill into town. In Vernon, the café is being boarded up. Mathou, the proprietor, watches, hammer in hand, to see them leave and his face says everything: You are here when things are pretty, and when they're not, you're back in England. Mathou does not raise his hand in greeting. He does not smile. On any normal day, the market would be noisy with tables buckling under produce and women shuttling along with full baskets, but the space is empty. On the packed dirt, a child on a tricycle makes figures of eight.

Ward spreads the map across his knees.

"We should go right, to connect with the Tours road."

"Father, are you absolutely sure?" says Herbie.

"Do you want me to look?" asks Sarita from the back. There's an edge in her voice.

"I think it's pretty clear that we need to take the right," Ward replies.

"Should I stop the car?" asks Herbie.

And they're only in Vernon. With any luck, they'll make La Rochelle by midnight.

It's the second flat tire of the morning. This jack seems about as substantial as an eggbeater. Herbie's got the hang of it—at least the concept—but the elbow grease is all Ward as it's dangerous and they can't afford that Herbie get injured. Sarita and Villiers have wandered away from the road since flat tires make good rest stops. Roddie has been instructed to stay as near them as is acceptable and is keeping guard with his rabbit rifle. The idea is that he shoots over the head of anyone who comes too close, or shoots to announce the presence of someone, or something like that. No one's sure, but there has already been one group of men chasing them down the road, and they outpaced them, but if they hadn't, they'd be on foot right now, relieved of car, valuables, food, water.

"We can't afford another flat," says Ward.

"Not without killing each other," says Herbie.

"Any ideas?"

"Yes," says Herbie. "Make Villiers walk."

Jack sufficiently cranked, the car is tipped up. Now Ward has to get the tire off. Some of the newer models have removable wheels, which will definitely be the case with the next car Ward purchases. But until then, he'll have to grapple with the tire lever.

"The Routes Nationales will be better maintained," says Herbie.

"Maybe when we're closer." This is the same tire that they replaced an hour ago. "How much farther do we have?"

"Distance-wise, we're halfway, but if there are more people to the south—"

"I doubt it," says Ward. "We should be ahead of the majority of the refugees."

They get back into the car and Villiers hands around some sandwiches—pâté, ham, a sharp cheese. This could be a picnic. There is some wine, but

Ward takes none and Herbie just a mouthful. The road rolls out its pale and looping reaches for mile after mile. People are walking, pushing handcarts, carrying sacks over their shoulders like storybook characters. They keep their faces angled to the ground, grim, enacting their hopelessness.

They pass a cart pulled by dogs, which marks the couple as Belgians. The cart isn't much bigger than a wheelbarrow, packed solid and covered in a blanket. Sarita makes Herbie stop the car because she wants to give the dogs water, and then, seeing the ridiculousness of this, gives the man a bottle of wine. He's from Dinant, which was hard hit. He produces a picture that at first Ward thinks is of him, only without mustaches. He says it's his brother. Has Ward seen him? And no, Ward has not, not this man. Another man, a Belgian, has told him that he might have seen the brother several days ago. And one man from the town says he thinks the brother was shot as a sniper, but isn't sure. There were so many men executed. The man's French is rough, and he seems to want to provide details, but keeps glancing over at Sarita as if the presence of a lady prevents honesty. He's heard that England is taking Belgian refugees, but he would prefer to stay in France. France is closer to home, but if it falls to the Germans, they'll all be starved if they're not lined up against a wall and shot. The whole time the man is talking, his wife says nothing. Ward would like to ask if they have children, but where are they? The woman stares at Roddie without blinking. Sarita gives them the leftover sandwiches, but there's no more to be done for these people. They are the lucky ones, picturesque with their dogs and cart, the ones you stop for and give wine and sandwiches. Herbie puts the car in gear and soon the distance expands between them.

Sarita says, "It's so strange that everyone's headed in the same direction."

Up ahead, there's a wagon pulled by a horse, which is surprising until Ward sees the age of the animal, and the age of the man up by the horse's head, whispering to it, tugging it along. An old woman wrapped in a shawl, despite the heat, follows behind. The wagon wobbles through a rut, displacing the mattress that rests atop all the other belongings, and she raises her hands as if to catch it. But the mattress stays put and the three—old woman, old horse, old man—continue moving southward. The composition seems allegorical, but what would it serve to illustrate? The progress of old age? The flight of reason? The death of tradition? He never liked bald illustration anyway. He admired Turner—the light, the movement—but, as he's matured, that wildness seems out of reach. He will create a frenetic watercolor every now and then, but the body is so much with him that it dominates his vision.

Herbie navigates southward, taking turn after turn as the day slowly exhausts itself. The boy has exhibited an impressive sense of direction.

"You're like a homing pigeon," says Ward.

"Only I'm not going home," says Herbie. He moves his head around, making his neck crack. Roddie has fallen asleep, his head cushioned on Villiers' expansive chest. Sarita, lost in her own thoughts, has her eyes trained on the passing landscape. He wonders if she's thinking about Belgium, about the civilians being pulled from their houses, lined up in the town squares, and shot. Is she wondering if that could be them? Is she wondering if another flat tire will put them within reach of the invading Germans?

"Do you think we have enough petrol?" asks Ward.

"We should," says Herbie. "I really don't know."

They reach the limits of La Rochelle in utter darkness, guided by a battery-operated torch as neither Herbie nor Ward has been able to figure out the gas-operated lamps on the Hotchkiss. Villiers has earned her keep with her knowledge of Bordeaux. The roads leading to La Rochelle are all familiar to her and, when unsure, she has had the right accent to ask directions. So now it's just getting to the quay. And then another step to get them across the Channel. Herbie has stopped speaking as all his energy is being used to operate the car. Ward cannot remember a time when the boy was quiet. They join the file of cars—overloaded and occupied with disheveled, silent passengers—slowly heading to the harbor.

"How much farther?" says Sarita.

"It is no more than a mile," says Villiers. "If it is acceptable, I will get down now."

"Of course," says Sarita, and there's embracing and Villiers has tears, but Sarita is too tired to engage in such a display of emotion. She gives Villiers a wad of cash and takes an address. "Who knows what it will be like when we get back to Rolleboise?" she says. "Imagine what the clean-up is going to be."

Villiers nods, relaxed, yet grimacing, as if the promise of some sort of domestic task has restored her faith in the future. The goodbyes are light, because the drama is not over. "I'm going to walk to the pier and see if I can work something out," says Ward. "It shouldn't be that hard to track down the consul."

"How will we find you?" asks Sarita.

"I'll find you. It doesn't look like you'll be going anywhere." Ward gets out of the car, which appears to be parked—just parked—in the road with the other cars. He strolls down the street as if he is taking in the pleasant evening air. On any other night the waterfront would be a different sort of lively with women trailing parasols and taking tisanes with their companions at the quayside cafés. Maybe sailors would be collected in groups at street corners, flogging their lonely selves. And there are women, and there are sailors, but a silence pervades everything. Silence asserts itself between terse statements that might otherwise be conversation. The future may always be uncertain, but paradoxically, the future holds an irrefutable certainty: We know that we don't know what will happen. This grim absurdity diminishes all chatter. There is no joy and even a dog trotting down the footpath stops to sniff in a perfunctory way, raising its leg to the bricks without merriness, its tail at half-mast.

Ward stops a policeman and inquires politely for the location of the British Consul. It's down on the port, as is everything. Any other day, the office would have shut down at five, but here it is near midnight and the lights are blazing. Ward walks into the office, listens to a French woman weeping and weeping, and the consul's patient response that if the woman was indeed married to an Englishman, she would need to be accompanied by that Englishman in order to be considered for evacuation to England.

"You, sir," says the consul, sighting Ward. He's desperate to get out of the conversation with the woman and Ward's English self certainly seems like a good escape. The man's French sounds native. But for the old Etonian tie, Ward would have thought him a local. "You must wait here," he says to the woman and walks her to the door, placing her on the footpath like a cat. "Looking for a berth?" says the consul.

"Yes, I am."

"Just you?"

"My wife and two sons."

"You know, there's nothing for the next two weeks. I can try to get you into a hotel."

"Ah," says Ward. "That will not work. I have a son due to start at Eton." The consul smiles, conquered. "And the other son?"

"Just graduated. Needs to be at Cambridge."

"I'll see what I can do, but you should find a place for tonight. Where are you coming from?"

"Outside of Vernon."

"And you live there?"

"I have a lovely house on the Seine. I'm an artist."

"I know who you are," says the consul. "Your daughter married Phipps."

"That's right. Herbert Ward." Ward extends his hand to grip the consul's.

"Do you want a drink?"

"That would be delightful."

The consul's name is Sterling and he has not slept in two days. La Rochelle has been transformed since the middle of August, but this latest wave of refugees has pushed its resources to the limit. "It's hard to see where this is all heading," says Sterling. "La Rochelle was supposed to be a nice relaxed appointment—a form of retirement really, a reward." Sterling chuckles.

"I have a good friend in the consular service," says Ward. "Maybe you know him?"

"Quite possible. There aren't that many of us, but we tend to be very, very far apart."

"Roger Casement," says Ward, smiling.

"Ah, Sir Roger," says Sterling. His eyes trace over Ward's features. "A good friend?"

"Like a brother. We were in the Congo together."

Sterling's face is hard to read, as if he's stopped himself from saying something. He raises his eyes to Ward's, smiling in a reserved yet warm manner. "Have you heard from him lately?"

And then there's Roddie at the door, passing the French lady, who is protesting something. "Father," he says, "Mother wants you to come quickly."

Ward gestures to his son, "And this is Roger Casement Ward, due to start at Eton next week. This is Consul Sterling. What's the hurry?"

"Mother got us onto some ship. They're already loading the car."

"How did she do that?" asks Sterling.

"I don't know," says Roddie. "It was all in Spanish."

"The *Orduña*," says Sterling. "Your wife must be a clever woman."

"And forceful, particularly when speaking Spanish." Ward shakes Sterling's hand. "You were going to say something."

"No. I was going to apologize for not being more help, but it appears you don't need me, not with a fine son like this, and a wife who can work miracles."

"My other son drove us all the way from Rolleboise, and he's only sixteen," says Ward.

"A brilliant, wonderful family. Good luck to you all."

"And best of luck to you," says Ward, still convinced that Sterling was going to tell him something but, for whatever reason, had changed his mind.

V
Christiania

October 1914

The picture is of a ship sailing through a fjord and hangs on a nail above the desk. Casement adjusts the frame so that it is level. He thinks of Ward, although it takes a moment to connect this picture of a ship and his old friend. The memory sorts itself. Ward had written a piece about an explorer for Harmsworth, which had brought him to Christiania some time in the 1890s. He wonders if Ward too stayed at the Grand Hotel, or even in this room with the view of the park and the street and the people walking dogs, catching trams, busy on their business. From this vantage-point, he feels disconnected from the pool of humanity. But to look at the Norwegians—who move quickly, circuiting the footpaths and broad streets—they seem propelled on their various trajectories with the express intention of not contacting another person. This is what Adler has told him about Norwegians—self-sufficient, truthful, reserved, harsh people. Adler is not this way, but on reaching Christiania has enacted the relief that one always has when returning to one's tribe, that sense of belonging, but also the anxiety of being held to the standards that one has left behind. Left for

387

a reason. Here, he supplies Adler's dialogue, *Yes, Sir Roger, go ahead and articulate it as it's probably true, but is it worth knowing?*

Through the window, Casement sees a familiar figure appear on the pavement, or maybe it's not familiar. That could be Adler, but as this is Christiania, there are many large-framed blond men, and from this angle, even height is impossible to determine.

Too much time in close quarters aboard the *Oskar II* has made Adler antsy. At the Grand they have separate rooms, and Casement's, as is should be, is more grand. And Adler, as he's home and probably has people to visit, is already out, although Casement does not know where.

He should get some breakfast, at least coffee, although he's not hungry. Leaving the hotel room makes him nervous. There are people looking for him. He is traveling under the name of James E. Landy and has taken to wearing an American pin in his lapel, as if "Landy the American" would do this. Four days short of Christiania, the *Oskar II* had been intercepted by the British Atlantic blockade. Casement had taken the papers he was bringing to Germany and given them to Adler to conceal, and Adler still has those papers as Casement is worried that he'll be picked up on the street, or that his room might be searched.

He decides to get some coffee in the lobby, which will tide him over until lunch. By the front desk, he manages to find a copy of the *Daily Telegraph*. He has a boy bring coffee to his chair, which he has chosen for being out of sight of the front door, a place where he can calmly catch up on world events. The Germans are spilling into France and the French villagers are getting out of the way. The Wards must have evacuated Rolleboise in the hubbub of early September but, with the reversals at the Marne, could have returned home. The trenches have been dug and the quick win for the Germans is a dream deferred. Charlie is now old enough to enlist and, being combative by nature, must be in training somewhere in England. One must hope the war ends before Charlie finds himself on some front, carrying a rifle. How is Ward handling all of this? He wishes he could get in touch with him, but it's not possible. He might have to wait a year. It all depends on how long the war lasts.

"You're awake." It's Adler, throwing a shadow over the top of the paper.

"Of course I'm up. It's noon."

"Then it's time for lunch," says Adler. He allows a moment to pass, volunteering nothing. "Come on, Sir Roger. You might have no appetite, but I am hungry."

Casement watches Adler over a plate of fiskebolle and barley bread. Adler's already done with his fish stew and is yelling at the waiter to bring something—gin? It sounds like gin but could be a segment of some other word. He doesn't know how words and syllables sort themselves in Norwegian. He often thinks he understands what is being said, as the language seems to mimic English sounds, but when he tries to add the bits into some sort of comprehensible whole, there is nothing.

But gin is always gin, at least with Adler. "It's too early to start drinking," says Casement.

"What makes you think I'm just starting?" Adler balls up his napkin and throws it at Casement. "And you should have a drink. You should see your face. Your expression is like a raisin."

"You think a drink would help that?"

"It would not hurt."

Adler has made no mention of where he spent the morning, and perhaps it was with family, but there's something in his demeanor that makes Casement think he's hiding something.

"You are resisting my charm, Sir Roger."

"And you mine," says Casement. "Where were you?"

"You sound like my wife."

"Do I? I wouldn't know, never having met her."

Adler laughs out loud, looks at the other tables, but no one has even looked up. Everyone at this restaurant seems to be involved in a grim Scandinavian meditation.

The gin arrives, two glasses of the stuff, and Adler sets one glass down in front of Casement. Adler, with an upturned palm, makes a series of quick gestures to encourage Casement to his drink. He takes a sip. "You know, Adler, asking where your friend has spent the morning falls well within the bounds of casual conversation. I'd assumed you were with a friend or family member. But knowing you as I do, it would seem that something is afoot."

Casement watches as Adler clicks through some escalating thought process. He opens a collar button with one strong thumb-flicking gesture. "I have made contact with English intelligence." Adler lifts his own glass and subjects it to a brutal draining. "They wanted information. They are following you."

Casement feels the panic rise. At the next table, a man with long mustaches, and a cane that should belong to a more feeble owner, hooks his gaze briefly before turning away. "Who is following me?"

"You were recognized on the boat and they intercepted a telegram to my father. This morning, when I went down for breakfast, there was a man—English—waiting for me in the hotel lobby."

"And you went with this man?"

"Of course. I wanted to know what he knew." Adler leans back in his chair, crossing one leg over the other dramatically. "Aren't you interested?"

"What did you tell them?"

"Nothing they didn't know already"—Adler delivers a quick nod—"but I learned something."

"And?"

"I learned that I have very good taste in friends, because you, Sir Roger, are quite valuable." If the English wanted to grab him, why haven't they done it? But they can't, can they? Norway is neutral and the English have no power here. Adler sends an aggressive finger pointing in his direction. "There's a price on your head. Don't you want to know what it is?"

"How much am I worth?"

"Hah!" says Adler. "Five thousand pounds. Yes. Five thousand. So you'd better be nice to me. And I'm your ticket out of here, because as long as I'm with you, they know everything about you that I know. Or they think they do."

Everything? "What are you playing at, Adler?"

"Whatever is fun." Adler delivers his smirk. "The Kaiser will tell you everything, and you will tell me everything, and I will tell Findlay everything. As long as I am with you, you're quite safe."

"Who is this Findlay?"

"British minister."

Casement looks over to where the man with the cane had just been sitting, and he is gone. Would it be better if he were still there? Would that not be more unsettling? "We must leave Christiania immediately."

"Not possible for several reasons. First, there is no boat, and that is a problem. Second, I have a meeting with the British legation tomorrow."

Casement rises from the table, knocking the edge. Adler reaches for Casement's gin and grabs it before it spills.

"Sit, sit. Do not call attention. We must look to be very friendly with each other." Adler is still holding the glass of gin and takes a casual sip, having claimed it. Casement settles back into his seat. "I need you to be clearheaded. What do I tell these people?"

"What do you tell them? You tell them nothing."

Adler scratches his chin. He needs to shave and his nails make a rasping noise along his jawline. He is waiting for Casement to see the value of these English vipers, to process the usefulness of the connection.

"You will tell them," says Casement, "nothing of the Irish Brigade. You will tell them that my mission in Berlin is purely diplomatic, that should Germany prevail, that I seek an agreement that the welfare of the Irish people, who have no quarrel with Germany, be protected."

"Surely we can do better than that," says Adler. "A U-boat, perhaps, that could be targeted. Or some 'pipes' that are being transported somewhere. Then we can hit the English navy."

"Adler, this is not a game." But from Adler's expression, it is very clear that to him, this is a game, and regardless of Germany's participation, and England's, and even Ireland's, he has no intention of losing.

Casement spends the afternoon writing letters in his room. There is the ship sailing through the fjord, again at an angle, again adjusted. He writes to Devoy about the treachery of this Findlay. It is an outrage that one cannot travel in a neutral country without being threatened by so-called diplomats, who are such thugs as to put a price on a man's life. He realizes that some of this outrage is concern over Nina, who is still in Ballycastle and should have been sent to the safety of America. There are papers in Biggers's house that need to be moved or destroyed, but since the telegrams are all intercepted by the English, he will have to accomplish this through some contacts in New York. He is having difficulty focusing on what needs to be said, and begins penning an article on the improbity of Findlay, of these English diplomats who use their posts as ways of expanding the reach of English oppression. But he certainly cannot publish this now, because it would give too much away. And where would he publish it anyway?

Adler had not understood his anger at the British legation.

"What makes you think the Germans are any better?" he had said, but that must have been the nastiness of the first flush of gin. Adler had said that Casement sounded like an Englishman. He'd laughed at the idea that any great principles were being assaulted, or defended. Had Casement not read the accounts coming out of Belgium? In the village of Aerschot, the villagers who had not escaped were locked in the church with no food. The women were separated from the men and housed for the pleasure of the German soldiers. And the men? Something like three survived out of eighty. The bodies of Belgian civilians are found stacked in the villages unlucky enough to be situated in the path of the German advance, and the victims are often children.

Adler does not read—unless he has to—so this story was fed to him by that Findlay of the English legation.

Of course it is a lie, an elaborate tale crafted of the believable to sway Adler to the English cause. Findlay is mistaken if he thinks that Adler can be so easily manipulated, because he's not weak, although he has no allegiance to ideas. Adler thinks moral rectitude is a character flaw that exposes you to all kinds of exploitation. He's right, but the fact that he feels one can choose against doing the right thing can be alarming. Or amusing, depending on Casement's mood. Adler is someone who has already seen so much abuse in his life that he does not recognize, nor always understand, kindness. Adler left home at twelve because he thought that his father, a violent drunk, might kill him. Wandering the docks, he was taken onboard a ship, and there mistreated in every way possible. That scared boy is still the core of Adler, still the heart of that drinking, grasping, brutal man. No, Adler is not weak, but he has been defined by the basest survival. If the English think that spinning tales of German evil will turn Adler one way or another, they are mistaken. His only loyalty is to himself and, now, Casement.

VI
London

Sarita's back at her father's house on Eaton Square with its measured sweep of the street and gleaming façade, the careful birds, the precise and tasteful flutter of leaves, the lack of natural clutter. Cricket calls the Sanford house the "white sepulcher." Somewhat dead, it is peaceful and right now the world is in such a state of riot that she'll take the quiet. At least the food is reliable: good coffee and fresh fruit at breakfast, an unfussy lunch, dinner. It really doesn't matter what she's eating, just as long as she's not responsible for the organization of it. All she needs to do is show up in the right room at the right time, as if she's a child of twelve. Father likes having her around, but he prefers his grandsons: rugged Charlie and clever Herbie and meticulous Roddie. And it's strange to be so displaced in her father's affection, but it would be even stranger to still command it.

Widely accepted is that Charlie is the favorite and that he's closest to Roddie, but her father relaxes around Herbie, finds his jokes funny and his fondness for poetry of interest, although they don't like the same poets. Herbie loathes Kipling and is the only person she knows who feels this way.

Herbie likes the modern poets that Sarita has never heard of and has little hope of ever hearing of, unless she accidentally overhears Herbie in an argument with his grandfather about who is worth reading, or with Charlie over the purpose of reading poetry in the first place. She wonders if Casement is still working at his lines. There's the possibility that he's some sort of secret agent, but she's not sure what spying involves, other than lurking around street corners and standing in the shadows, listening in on conversations. But Casement always stands out and aren't spies supposed to blend in?

In the next few weeks, she'll be relocating. The estate agent has found Sarita a house in Weston-Super-Mare, furnished, although she's insisted on buying a new mattress for herself as she can't abide the thought of lying on someone else's. There are many rental properties in this part of Somerset as the place is a resort. Families typically spend a few weeks there in the summer, taking in the cool air and enjoying the beach, although Charlie will, apparently, be using the ample sand and broad reaches of flat land to learn how to dig trenches and play at being a soldier.

And after Charlie's training? Well, after that, the war had better be over and they can return to Rolleboise and bring the Villa Sarita back to its normal state. She can't imagine the appalling mess that Herbert has made of the house, having turned it into a hospital. It's official, sanctioned by the Union des Femmes de France, which is some branch of the French Red Cross, although it sounds like a club that caters to gentlemen. Villiers has said in a letter to her that the downstairs furniture has been stored in the barn as there are no horses and that the living room is now filled with rows of cots. The hall closet—where the coats once hung—has been fitted with shelves and stocked with medicine. Sarita should be in Rolleboise helping, but there is so much else to do. She has just returned from New York where Cricket has had another baby—a sweet little boy, but Cricket is depressed and moaning the state of her complexion and the fact that half her hair has fallen out. Hair grows back. If Sarita were a different sort of mother, she would have reminded Cricket that she was lucky to come out of childbirth alive.

Herbert had come to see her off at the port in a paranoiac state brought on by the specter of U-boats intent on destruction. Why would Germany sink a passenger boat full of well-heeled Americans? Surely the fact that America has resolutely stayed out of the war would prevent the Germans from doing anything so provoking. But Herbert had gripped her shoulders and looked into her face with a look of such abject despair that he'd made her worried. That's where Roddie gets it from. Everyone has been blaming her mother for the boy's nerves and odd obsessive behavior, but it's all Herbert. And now he won't let her return to Rolleboise because if the Germans move south, she won't be safe and he's adamant that her presence *in her own house* would be inappropriate. That had been an argument for the books, Herbert saying that it was improper to have his wife in a house full of convalescing soldiers and what would she do? Empty bedpans? Perhaps he had a point, but what she would like to know is what *he's* doing there. Herbert is an explorer and an artist and an expert in South American finance. Is he emptying bedpans?

It's all well and good to be fussing like this, to have the humor and good sense leavening the situation, but the truth is she's been living with a black dread that eats at her guts like a cancer. She's lost weight and the lace at the neckline of her dress gaps, the skin under her chin looks loose, and her hair is thinning. And that must be where Cricket gets it from.

Sarita had been hoping to complete this latest ridiculous task: the ordering of more somber, war-appropriate clothing, but it seems that she will have to make do with what she has. Her regular London dressmaker—another patriot—has volunteered to make uniforms and is supervising some factory in Kent, but she had referred Sarita to a seamstress, a tiny Jewish lady, who accidentally showed up on the front doorstep and had to be rescued from an intense and xenophobic berating delivered by one of the maids. This Mrs. Beldenstein was a nice enough woman with decent English, clearly skilled, but the whole time she'd been taking measurements and showing fabric samples, she kept breaking into fits of weeping. When it came to the actual ordering of garments, the woman was in a state of collapse. Sarita had to ring for the maid to bring some sherry. Apparently

Mrs. Beldenstein's son, only sixteen, had enlisted under a false name. Who knows where he is? Sarita had reminded her that, yes, they are taking those younger than enlistment age, but no one is to serve until they are nineteen. By the time this woman's son is of service age, the war will be over.

After calming her down, Sarita wasn't sure that she trusted the woman to make a straight seam, even less produce a few uninteresting dresses in navy wool. So she'd ordered undergarments—that she didn't need—and some dressing gowns for the babies as this woman does some nice embroidery. And now she is waiting for Herbie, who was supposed to be home half an hour ago. Of course, he's decided to defer Cambridge until the war is over, and now has to go meet friends to get some laughs as opposed to pretending to learn things with friends to accomplish much the same.

Sarita pours herself a glass of the sherry as the maid did bring two glasses and she can't think of why she's been resisting it. No doubt, her father will wander in, and catch her at it, or Paz, who is as condescending as ever. The crystal makes a nice loud clink as she pours it in and she's just about to take a sip when she hears the front door slam shut.

"Where's my mother?" she hears Herbie's voice call from the hall, and the ingratiating, sugary reply from that same housemaid who nearly took poor Mrs. Beldenstein's head off two hours earlier.

Herbie appears at the door and makes a show of leaning in the doorframe, casual, like the boy who delivers the ice. "Drinking by yourself, are you?"

"You're late."

"And you, Mother, are very early."

"It's six o'clock."

"Not quite." Herbie wanders over and pours some sherry into Mrs. Beldenstein's glass and knocks it back. "Cheers."

"You could ring for a clean glass, Herbie."

"Maybe I will."

"Not now. We have to be at the Nicholsons' in an hour."

"Oh Lord," says Herbie. He sinks into the chair beside her and discomposes his limbs. "Do we have to go?"

397

"What do you think? It's a courtesy to your father. And you know Nicholson was just appointed head of the Royal Flying Corps. His son is training as a pilot."

"Will he be there?"

"I doubt it. They do have a daughter about your age." Sarita sips her sherry. Herbie looks disheveled and she wonders what he's been up to. "You smell like cigarettes."

"That is because I smoke," says Herbie.

She's shaking her head again, a gesture that is fast wearing out, but she's not sure how else to communicate her resigned disapproval. "Get dressed, quickly. And tell your grandfather we're leaving."

Herbie pulls himself out of the chair. "Can't you let Grandfather know? Every time I see him, he makes me recite 'Hiawatha.'"

"It's not every time." But it is with fair frequency and at this point even Sarita knows the first lines, the shores of Gitche Gumee, the shining big sea water, and that Nokomis. "Just tell him we're late, and if he insists, just say it quickly. And have someone tell Paulson to bring the car around."

"And what will you do?"

"I, Herbie, will sit here and drink my sherry."

Herbie is down the table with Joyce but, as Nicholson is addressing him, it would seem the entire cohort is invited to their conversation. They're already on dessert as Nicholson is one of those people who likes to fly through the courses, as if adding a squandering of time along with the waste of ice and silver polish and food is what would tip the scales.

It has already been established that Charlie has enlisted with the 10th Royal Warwicks, and that all the other enlistable-aged sons have enlisted in equally acceptable regiments. Herbie is the only boy at table, being barely old enough to sit through a dinner, and young enough to not be billeted. He's been entertaining this Joyce all evening, and now has Nicholson's attention.

"How, sir, is it decided who can train as a pilot?" asks Herbie. And this is innocuous enough a question given Nicholson's position and Herbie's age, but something sets her nerves on edge.

"No one knows how to fly a plane, so we ask them if they can ride a horse or operate a boat."

"Really?" says Herbie. "I would think that knowledge of motorcars would be more appropriate."

"This is not a widespread skill."

"Or perhaps a good understanding of maps."

"Herbie was telling me," says Joyce, "that he drove his family three hundred miles through France when the Germans were advancing."

"Sarita," says Nicholson, "is that true?"

"I suppose it is."

"And," adds Joyce, "he did all the navigating on secondary roads. He has an amazing sense of direction. It's uncanny."

"That is also true," says Sarita. "And if he weren't sixteen years old, he'd be a good candidate for a pilot."

"I'll be seventeen in a couple of months," says Herbie.

"Still useless for the war effort," says Sarita.

At this point, Mrs. Nicholson stands, signaling that it's time for the women to leave. She has two tall feathers woven into her hair, which stick up over her head. Along with her glass-blue eyes, narrow nose, and large-shouldered black dress, she looks like a cassowary or an emu or one of those exotic birds. Maybe that's the intention. Sarita rises with her, pulling herself to full height. She stares down at Nicholson, who raises an eyebrow. There is Herbie, reaching for a cigarette. She sees his eyes following Joyce, who is an exceptional creature—one of those lean, golden Dianas that England churns out every now and then, to churn out its ruling class. She gives Herbie her strongest cautioning look. He responds with a face composed in the sweetest confusion, and mouths with brilliant, false innocence, one word: *What?*

*   *   *

When they return to Eaton Square, it is nearly midnight. They were among the last to depart the Nicholsons' South Kensington house, most of the guests having left a half hour earlier. Herbie was "walking around the garden" with Joyce, which left Sarita chatting with Amy Nicholson, who, small kindness, is a straight-talking, intelligent, although terrifying sort of woman. "Good looking, that son of yours," she'd said. But she knew what the source of Sarita's discomfort had been.

In the car on the way home, Herbie had chattered on about how he did like Joyce. Who wouldn't? He'd added something about Charlie's absence working in his favor, how Joyce pretended she'd never even heard of Charlie. And Sarita, patient, had let him unspool the fullness of that blathering until he ran out of nonsense and found himself left with the only thing he really wanted to share with her.

"I want to be a pilot," he'd said.

"Your father is against it," she'd replied, which was true, "and so am I."

Herbie's response? "Glad to know you two agree on something."

Who knows what's going on in his head? There's golden-haired Joyce and his fantasy of soaring miles above the earth—in the clouds with the gods—and there's his mother with a gaping collar and thin hair. She reaches the top of the stairs and hears herself sigh. At the end of the hallway, she can see the light spilling beneath her father's study door. She taps on the door and opens it.

"Father, what are you doing still up?"

"Waiting for you." Her father stands from the desk and she sees that he's accompanied his usual jacket and tie with pajama pants. "What does Nicholson have to say?"

"A lot. You must be referring to something in particular." She sinks down into the wingchair and props her feet on the hassock. Her father pours drinks for them both.

"You actually talked of something other than the war?" She feels like she's his agent. Truth is he has moved large amounts of money—the budget of entire nations—from one account to another based on snippets of information that she picked up at dinner parties. He comes over with the glass. He's a bit stooped now, but still strangely vigorous. Vigor in a man that age can seem psychotic, particularly as his eyes have not lost their youthful glimmer.

"Nicholson wants Herbie."

"Herbie? What on earth for?"

"To be a pilot. To join the RFC."

"Herbie?" A few moments tick by. "Better in the air than in the trenches," he finally says.

"Better at Cambridge," Sarita responds. She takes the glass and restores herself. "So, how was your day, Father?"

"We should invest in jute."

"Jute? What is jute?"

"It's the stuff needed to make the sandbags, which are used to reinforce the trenches."

"We can't profit from the war," says Sarita.

"I'm sure we won't, no matter what we do." Her father looks grim, yet confident. "Do you think Charlie can kill a man?"

Sarita thinks this through. She's seen the boys lined up in the fields, running at the sacks of straw, bayonetting them through, aiming for the heart. Could Charlie do that to man? "I'm sure he could. If other boys do it, he can do it."

"What about Herbie?"

Herbie with his butterfly net. Herbie with his canoe, and his modern poets, and his peppermints and cigarettes. And his oysters. She's stopped breathing.

"Let him be a pilot, Sarita. Otherwise he's a sitting duck."

The house in Weston-Super-Mare is cramped, drafty, and obsessively decorated with trimmings, knickknacks, sea shells, seascapes, cloying figurines of barefoot children brandishing little spades. The windows are hung with lace that further filters winter's gray light. There is little to do but walk the narrow footpaths of the town, stop in at the markets in search of something fresh. The house is staffed with people from the village—an old man to fix the fires, a bent woman who is most often dragging a bucket around with grimy water, a girl to do the cooking who is too simple to have been recruited for one of the factories. Grim company, perhaps, but Sarita has little need for company. In the morning she dresses, writes to Herbert, picks her way through cold meat and cheese at lunch, takes the daily letter from Herbert with the two o'clock post, and reads about the goings-on in his hospital that was once her home.

This house echoes and whines with the wind. The exchanges between old man and bucket woman are carried on the damp air, as if they were whispering at her ear: their language sounds like moaning, composed in pain and strangely absent of consonants. The girl has a high-pitched voice and complains when addressed, her voice ringing like a cat with its tail caught in the door. Sarita should be more generous. Money has made her brittle. No. Not money. This war. If Villiers were here, she would have company, although Villiers is up to her elbows creating vats of bland, gentle food for the damaged men who now inhabit Rolleboise. Madame Villiers—Margarite—reduced to her surname as a way of making her accept that she has English employers.

Sarita's read Herbert's letter twice. Apparently, the majority of his patients—all officers—are suffering from tremors and other odd symptoms. Some of the men can't speak, or see, although the doctor can find no medical reason. At any rate, they're not fit for the Front. Herbie has been indispensable as a driver. Apparently a shipment intended for one of the field hospitals had accidentally been sent to Rolleboise. Some of the items were not essential—a box of glass eyes, for example—but there was also a crate of bottles of hypochlorite for the Dakin's solution and Herbie had been the only one who could take it up. Herbie described the camp as a rage of noise—explosions and shouting. In one of the wards, he'd seen a boy who had been a few years ahead of him at Eton. His legs were gone, which is a common injury. Herbert says it's as if the men have fallen victim to an enormous scythe. The boy had died with Herbie holding his hand.

That you had been here to comfort him and me, but it is quite impossible. And perhaps it is, because there is now a rule that no nonessential women are allowed at Rolleboise, Army Rules, but also impossible because she doubts she has comfort to give.

As it's Saturday night, Charlie is joining her for dinner and he'll spend the night. He's been given the rank of Lieutenant, a natural leader. His steely exterior has no doubt communicated that he has all his emotions under control, but the bravado's been slowly leached away by the growing death toll, and his first act on entering the house is most often to reach for the paper and, with lit cigarette, start scanning the lists for people he knows. He usually finds a few.

Sarita's started praying, although she's not sure who to approach, and wishes she'd made some sort of diplomatic advances towards the creator in a time of peace as now she's obviously in a disadvantaged position. A week earlier, she'd taken her father to Eton to see Roddie, who was marching in some sort of parade. And there the boys were, in their ceremonial top hats and tails, all in step, and—a horror—carrying rifles. Some of these boys, like Roddie, were only twelve years old. She'd looked from face to face in the onlookers to see if anyone recognized the terrible image that this presented, but the women had their faces composed in stoic sacrifice and the men were aping pride. Her father had taken her by the elbow and led her to a tent where tea and biscuits were provided as some sort of civilizing restorative.

Charlie is cheerful. Apparently he's found some willing girl in the village, but he is not yet inclined to supply her name. He's worked his way through recent events, his routines, and she's listened to him go on and on about what they do all day. March—which is essentially walking, which he already knew how to do. Shoot, which he also knew how to do. And order people around, at which he's a natural. To the regular soldiers, however, listening to Charlie must be a novelty: something to learn. Training has been conceived to replace actual thought with reflex. One naturally runs from bullets and this training brainwashes you into running towards them. If somehow you manage to overcome the training, your own officers will shoot you for cowardice. All of this Charlie finds obvious and as it should be as he's already been trained—brainwashed—through his years in the British public school system. He finds her opinions entertaining in their bizarre singularity.

"But that's really it. We've been drilling in the same formation for the last week. We've got it."

"Best that you get it right." She pours herself some wine, shifting in her chair that responds by releasing a ghost mold from the cushion. "You do understand I have no idea what you're talking about."

Charlie smiles. "I can't believe you're letting Herbie go in for flying."

"Since when is anything my decision?"

"The trenches are one thing, but you know the life expectancy of the pilots is really bad. They send them over Germany when they've had half an hour of flying time. That's it. They're playing an odds game with planes."

"An odds game?"

"If ten percent get back, it's worth it."

"What are the chances of them calling him up? Herbie will live out the war in Rolleboise driving your father around. Maybe all this exposure to hospitals will make him want to become a doctor." She can't believe she's comforting Charlie. But they always do this. In another ten minutes, they'll be talking about Herbie again and he'll be bringing her back from the cliff edge.

Charlie sips the wine, and sips again. "What is this?"

"It's one of the bottles that we took when we evacuated. It ended up getting tucked into a bag of my clothing. Perhaps I should have saved it, but what's the point?"

"Definitely one of the good bottles."

The chops are overdone as this local girl cannot cook, but the food—at least for Sarita—is just an excuse for the wine. "Charlie," she starts in, but what exactly does she want to say?

"Chris Landsman is dead. Do you remember him?"

"I remember you talking of him." She chases the peas around the plate with her fork, then gives up. "Charlie, what will you do in Flanders?"

He considers carefully. "I will have men under my command. I will lead them wherever they need to be led."

"A lot of them won't come back."

Charlie tears at the mutton, gets a large piece off, and chews it thoughtfully. He hasn't bothered to tell her not to worry, as he has worn out that phrase. He's also stopped telling her to eat. He swallows and takes the wine again. "I know that."

It's her move. "We need to figure out a way for you not to go. There is money for that."

"Money for what?"

"If you had a condition—"

"Do you mean to buy a doctor's statement? Do you think that anyone would believe that I have a weak heart? Or bad eyesight? Or do you mean to send me to Argentina to hide until it's over?"

"Those are all good ideas."

"I'm actually good at soldiering, Mother." His voice is measured and calm. "I'm a good soldier. I'm a good leader. I'm as fit a man as there is in England and people know that and I need you to know that."

"This is not about being good at something, Charlie. You've won everything you tried your hand at. But it's not about winning, it's about surviving."

"Mother, in times of war—"

"You think I don't know what I'm talking about, because I know nothing of battle. But if anyone would take me, I would fight. And I would shoot a man. If I thought he might shoot at me, I could do it. I might even like it. And you know why?"

Charlie is listening, curious if nothing else.

"Because I am a survivor. I know what it is like to be hungry and barefoot and scared. This life that you've been living—boxing, Oxford, girls— that's a game. But there are times when it isn't a game. This is one of those times and the loser does not get second place." Her voice is cracking and there are tears, but she is still strong.

"There are men fighting with more money than us. There are earls and dukes in the trenches. I need to do this in order to have a life on the other side of it, after the war. Avoidance of this is guaranteed to create failure in my life."

"You're reasoning with me," she says. "You are trying to push me back so that I will not have false hope."

"What else can I do? If there was a way out, I wouldn't take it."

"You wouldn't take it," she repeats, a bitter whisper. How could he put such little value on his golden life? She pushes the chair away from the table, pulls at her face with the back of her hands to clear the tears. He seems surprised to have her approach and what is she doing. She finds herself smoothing his hair almost violently, down on his head. She takes his hand, looking at each perfect finger. "Charlie, I cannot send my child to war." She gets it out, but broken with sobs.

At least she's upset him, disturbed that unearned sense of purpose. He says, "All mothers feel this way."

"No," she says. "No, that is impossible. No one can feel this way."

"I'll be careful," he says, looking up at her, scared to see her so unhinged.

"If you don't come back," she says, "it will kill me."

She sits in the chair beside him. He's smoking and she's not sure how long they stay there, silent. The food grows cold, the fat congealing. He walks to her place for her glass and the bottle of wine. Their silence comforts her with its brutal chill. She reaches for his cigarettes and lights one, inhales.

"Mother?" Charlie says, chiding.

"What?"

"I didn't know you smoked."

She blows out a series of rings, sends the smoke streaming into her nostrils, exhales completely. "And now you do."

VII

Limburg

January 1915

Casement can't understand a word they're saying, but from the frequent glances delivered by the front-seat passenger, a Hauptmann Molden, he knows they're talking about him. Adler says he's paranoid, and he often is, but not right now. He should be steeling himself for the spectacle of Irish prisoners of war, for the reek of the camp, for the sight of malnourished, hopeless men. He should be working out some phrases to get the blood boiling, to inspire them to once more pick up the rifle and fight, but he has thus far not been successful. Five men—that is the extent of his Irish Brigade, and what can five men do?

What can one man do?

His hands are shaking and he can feel cold leather pressing into his seat bones through the wool of his pants as he is worn to nothing and there's no more flesh to cushion. He has a crate of Alice's *The Making of Ireland and Its Undoing* next to him on the seat, although the author no longer supports him. Alice. Clearheaded Alice. She says he is now in league with the Americans, who can fight all they want because they suffer no consequences.

Certainly she would buy weapons from the Germans, but that is not the same as inviting them as conquerors. Does he not see how many Irish have enlisted with the Allies? Does he not see how they've suffered at the hands of the Kaiser? What happens when those men come home? But he is trying to recruit Irishmen, not Germans. And her book might work as a weapon, bought on the sly in Ireland and shipped from the United States.

Does he really want to send these men back into battle?

He has not seen the trenches but several months ago was brought to tour the site of an August victory in Ardennes. This was to impress on him the might of Germany. Victory, apparently, was embodied by a mass grave. His translator, a tall, dark-haired man from Tubingen, a tutor of literature, had related the chatter from the higher-ups, citing figures, casualties in other fronts, the disorganization of the French, but as the man drew up to the edge of the pit, he grew silent. The stench of spilled blood and rot made them cough. Together he and Casement witnessed the incomprehensible tangle of limbs, the gape of mouths and eyes, muddied hands, tufts of hair and torn flesh. The image was untranslatable, impossible as a whole, resistant to being broken down into the men who formed its elements. Someone had desired this carnage and was now pleased. Casement looked to his companion, who was cleaning his glasses with a handkerchief. He placed them back on his face, looping the stems over his ears, and exhaled carefully. A look over to the higher-ups, who were hacking words into the air with practiced vehemence, and he said, "They say it is good for morale. But it is not good for my morale."

Casement, looking into the pit, said, "Are they all French?" And immediately regretted the insensitivity, which was intuited by his companion.

The translator managed, "Who is it who said, 'War condemns all who yearn to peace'?"

"I don't know," Casement replied. "I don't know if I ever knew." But he is so condemned.

In his quiet moments he acknowledges that he has lost his faith in Germany, but not in Irishmen: these Irishmen who will form his Irish Brigade, fighting on the side of Ireland, against the English tyrant. Again, he sees Molden peering at him and realizes that the lip is wobbling again, in and out, like a toothless man masticating his bread.

There is the usual officious rubbish at the entrance to the camp. They all know who he is. The driver of the car is laughing, as is this Molden, and the guard, letting the rifle slip from his shoulders and holding it in both hands, comes over to inspect Casement, who is trapped, like an exotic animal, for anyone to ogle. The sun is breaking through the cloud cover and the men are assembled, standing in the clear air. Guards hover at the perimeters, but these men look beaten to the extent that it seems hard to imagine them attempting to overcome anyone. No one has tried to escape. Casement comes to the front, and instantly the barrage of insults begins.

"How much is the Kaiser paying you?"

That's the favorite, and emanates from all quarters. And then longer phrases, shouted, and impossible to decipher given the cacophony, but he knows what they're saying, that his presence and recruiting for the Irish Brigade make the conditions for the Irish prisoners miserable—shortened rations, beatings, refusal of blankets.

"If you would just let me explain what our goals are," tries Casement. He can see the guards rolling their eyes, chuckling to each other. "England is not our friend. England is what landed you here, in this prison, not the Germans. The Germans did not bring you here, but the English."

It had seemed a good enough argument when he conceived of it in the black of night that had turned to a cold, perverse morning light. But the men are not having it. And something just hit him that might have been a rock. No, just a pebble. He has an odd moment of humor and wonders if he should yell, *Whoever threw that is a good shot and we could certainly use you!* He looks out at the group assembled, maybe a hundred men, although the current count of Irish prisoners that he has spoken to is now close to two thousand. "Will no one talk to me?" There's a knot of conversation in the back, and a young man steps out. He has black hair and light blue eyes and such a worn and patient expression that Casement finally breathes. He sees the man exchange a quick volley of words with one his friends, and then he raises his hand, fingers relaxed, to ask for a moment's understanding.

"Mister Casement," he says. There's a smattering of *Sir Roger* called out, a derision, a cause for humor, from all corners of the assembled men.

"And you are?" asks Casement.

"Sergeant Gordon Kelso."

"I am listening."

"A word in private, sir. Do you think that can be arranged?"

They sit across a plain table on bare wood chairs. A guard posted at the door exercises his boredom by chewing his nails like a schoolgirl, and then examining his work. Kelso is composing his thoughts and he looks over to Casement.

"Do you not remember me, sir? It was a long time ago."

"I'm sorry, Sergeant Kelso. When did we meet?"

"Ten years ago. It was at Mister Biggers's house. You gave me an award for reciting a poem." The man waits to see if Casement can find that boy somewhere in all those years filled with all those faces. "I also captained one of the hurling teams."

"Those were good years," says Casement. He doesn't remember the boy, and so does not know the man. "The Irish Brigade could use a man like you," he says.

Kelso responds by shaking his head. "You come here thinking that we don't understand, but I'm here because I know you and I know that if you understood, you would not be asking us to do this."

"Sergeant Kelso—"

"Listen to me," says Kelso, and his voice is pleading. "I don't want the English in Ireland, but I don't want the Germans either. And after spending time here, I'm sure that you too see that would not be good for Ireland."

Casement searches around the worn arguments for something that is perhaps not too shabby, not rote. He thinks he might remember this boy now, from Biggers's time, because the gentle of timbre of his voice is something that would earn him a prize in the recitation of a poem. "Sergeant Kelso, the whole world order will be altered by this war. We have never had an allegiance to England. We are merely making a wise decision in allying ourselves not only with the victors, but with a party uninterested in governing Ireland."

"German greed leads me to believe otherwise," says Kelso, eyeing the guard, who seems to understand no English. "I believe that we will achieve Home Rule, but that we must do so through peaceful channels. We are not a nation of thugs but of thinkers, and by gaining the respect of powerful nations, we will achieve our goals."

"Our long history," says Casement, "makes such a statement seem naïve."

Kelso covers his face with his hands. "No one is listening to you," he says, his voice reedy. "You have no followers. Look at the numbers, Mister Casement. Redmond is a Nationalist. We enlisted because we are fighting for ourselves, not the English."

"Sergeant Kelso—"

"I was less sure before Flanders. Before that, as a prisoner, I would be standing by your side begging the men to see reason. We all want a free Ireland." He pushes back from the table, searching around the corners of the bare room as if reason lurks there, as if it can be shaken free of the torn curtain or found in the margin of dark shadow by the door. "You have not seen the Front, have you?"

And Casement has not, only its aftermath. His war has been fought in cheap hotel rooms and offices with German officials who cannot disguise their disdain, who speak a tongue of their own and can therefore conceal their intentions.

"The English need us, but we also need the English, because if we cannot stop the German advance now, we will all be overrun."

Casement drops his voice to a whisper. "The situation is not ideal, but as Irishmen, we have few choices."

"True, true." This man speaks gently, in the same voice that men use to calm nervous horses. "I have led men into battle, delivered orders, obeyed orders. I have sent men over the top to be mown down. I was captured, as is obvious. I was close to the German line, in a hole, and I sat there for hours—with a man that I knew from the trenches. He was English, from Dorset, and I held him as he bled out. It took a long time. I don't know how long. The bullets never stopped flying. When the Germans found me, he had died. I was covered in his blood. He was a brave man and he was my brother."

"Your brother?"

"The closest thing I had to one, at the time. We had been through so much together. You might find it strange, given my politics, that he and I grew so close." Kelso takes a moment to escape the memory. "None of these men will bear arms against those who they've suffered with. Some of the soldiers you are trying to recruit owe their lives to Englishmen. And none of them can bear the lofty talk when they lack food and are treated like animals by the very men you are telling them to trust."

Casement nods because he cannot deny what this man has told him. He reaches beneath the desk for one of the copies of Alice's book. The book sits there on the table between them, *The Making of Ireland and Its Undoing*, but from the look on Kelso's face, it would seem that Casement is the subject of the book.

Kelso gestures for Casement to draw closer. At this distance, he can see a louse crawl quickly back into the forest of Kelso's hair. "If you come back," he whispers softly.

"Louder!" says the guard.

So he can speak English.

And in the softest of whispers, "I am begging you, do not—"

The guard jumps up and hits Kelso in the shoulder with the rifle butt, knocking him to the ground. Kelso looks up and raises his hands, not so scared as careful. He gets up and begins to make his way to the door with the guard smacking him in the back, although more to propel than to injure. "Can I get the book?" says Kelso. "The book, to tell the other men."

The guard wearily gestures to the table, watching closely.

Kelso tracks quickly into his memory. And then he's speaking in Irish—school Irish with a stiff accent. And then again, in Irish, that rises to shouting as the guard attacks again. Words flying, and Kelso's Irish is not good, nor his. But he pieces it together as the men shout at him and he makes the shameful walk back to the car. *Please. No. Return. Please. Please. Kill. Kill.*

Or, *please do not come back because if the Germans still have hope in this Irish Brigade, they will kill us all.*

Munich wears its war heavily. Casement has been once before, so he understands that most often the people are a cheerful lot—the sort of Germans who link arms and sing while drinking beer, the sort of Germans who people liked when people liked Germans. Dancing girls in dirndl skirts, laughing boys with clean teeth, a clear sun, a river of beer—these are his memories of Munich, but that was fifteen years ago. Sitting in this tram, the rattle of it, and the dour-faced woman opposite him, who tracks her eyes to the American pin in his lapel and across his features, then down at her shoes, that is the Munich now. She looks into her purse, digging around, and closes it. This is the third time she's done that, as if she's lost something and lives in the expectation that it will magically reappear. If he had any German, he would exchange pleasantries with her, but all he can do is nod as he makes his way out of the tram, onto the street. He thinks he knows where he's headed, but he's only been there once, and that was with Adler, who can find this place in whatever state of being.

It is a shabby tavern and sparsely inhabited, to be expected as the population is already feeling the first grip of poverty. Adler is the youngest man at the bar. He greets Casement with a broad smile, turning on his bar stool. He pats the seat next to him.

Casement obliges. He must not be too strident, or sanctimonious. "Adler, from the tone of your note, I thought you were being dragged off by the police."

"I was worried you would not come."

"Why?"

"Because the last time you said, 'This is absolutely the last time.'" Adler breaks into laughter as he says this. He raises two fingers to the bartender who sets about preparing two drinks.

In a week, Adler will be heading back to Norway to meet with Findlay and his cronies. They need to work out what information to feed him. Any attempts at coordinating this with Germans are met with indifference, which is nerve-wracking. The German Foreign Office claims that the information is changing constantly. They are not privy to the latest naval developments, or what is being shipped where, so how can they advise Adler and Casement? Casement knows that he is being lied to and is not sure what to do. If he and Adler just make things up, it's not going to convince the English that Adler's information is worthy. They will know that Adler is still loyal to Casement. The whole thing is beyond Casement's intelligence acumen. Communicating the amount of arms shipped into Lorenço Marques and creating plans to blow up a railroad in Komatipoort are one thing, but coordinating false information on the presence of U-boats in the North Sea for the British Navy is beyond his purview. And why can't the Germans see the value of this connection? It is because they don't trust Adler. They don't want to give him real information. So he will have to make something up about "pipes" being shipped somewhere for some reason, as if he is a man with no allies.

Whose side is Casement on? Who is he fighting for, or fighting with?

"You look like you need some fresh air," says Adler, patting him on the shoulder.

The bill is, thankfully, less than what Casement had expected.

"Good, no?" says Adler. "It's because they won't let me run a tab anymore."

"Maybe it's time to cut back on your drinking." But he knows that Adler has taken this recent development as a suggestion to find a new watering hole.

"Look," says Adler, stalled on the pavement. "The sun has come out. Let's walk through the English Gardens."

It's a cold day, but with a warming sun a walk will be pleasant, although Casement knows Adler has suggested this because there's a beer garden on the other side. A path runs alongside the river and he and Adler gravitate there naturally. Mothers with prams circuit the walkways, but the winter cold has kept the majority of people indoors. Trees bared of leaves scratch at the humorless blue sky. Afternoon is Adler's best time of day. By evening, the drinking has made him harsh. And after that, he is clumsy, thuggish. Mornings are hard for him. He sits on the edge of the bed, rubbing at his forehead with the heel of his hand, breathing with his mouth open. Every joke has been made a million times. *I thought I was drinking the bottle, but I think it was drinking me. I guess the whiskey won that round.* But Adler in the afternoon, when the drink has warmed his mood and softened the edges, and loosened his tongue so that his simple philosophy finds its way to conversation . . . What can Casement do to resist that? In private moments, Adler will tousle Casement's hair as if they're school chums. He'll respond to Casement's black moods with a cajoling *Sir Roger.* And they will make love, although only at Adler's instigation. Perhaps that adds a level of excitement.

"Nice day," says Adler.

"Certainly," says Casement.

When he was last in Munich, there were young men swimming in the river, splashing and laughing, although this now seems a memory written over for better sunshine, with handsome boys. As they make the top of a rise they can see soldiers drilling on an open, flat expanse that must have once been a football field. These are young soldiers, pink-faced, barely through their teens if that. They are marching in time, many bodies made into one company with the purpose of killing other men.

"You can look," says Adler.

"Whatever do you mean?"

"Perhaps I am getting too old for you."

"You are just fine," says Casement, "although I am getting too old for me." He remembers good humor, and sometimes the words present themselves, like a script. This is what Casement would have said six months ago, and this is what his brain produces. Casement does not like soldiers, does not find the virility of war exciting or tonic. Armed and marching expressionless men are gears—or fuel—of the machine of the present that's grinding everyone, including him, into powder. He has a hard time believing that the past really happened. Was he ever truly in the Amazon among the Indians? Was that really ten years ago? Hard to imagine that, harder still to pursue his life further. There's an image of him on a ship, stiff wind, salt air, and he looks back at England as it vanishes into the promise of Africa. Who was that who sighted into the endless reach of future and did not blink, who sighted back and saw little but a few hard schoolboy years running up to the brick wall that marked his birth? Who was that man?

Now he is so completely aware of his mortality that he has set aside a package to be given to Ward should he die. This is stored, with other things, at his friend Germain's Ebury Street apartment in London. In the package, letters, books, souvenirs from the Congo to go into Ward's Paris studio, photographs of Amazon youths and some purchased while in Sicily—young male nudes in classical poses, as if Bacchus and Apollo had been given life, brought to the present. This last gesture of friendship, waiting in a trunk, oppresses him with its clear-sightedness.

"Looks like you could use a rest," says Adler.

He could use a rest. That is true. He is so very tired.

"How can you be so depressed all the time?"

"One might make a similar inquiry into your persistent vigor."

"People disappoint you," says Adler. "And no one disappoints me. The Germans disappoint you. And now the Irish disappoint you. The English, even when they behave the way you think they should, disappoint you. And I must disappoint you, although you can guess what I will do every day, every minute."

"I can't expect you to understand," says Casement, indulgent.

"But I do. Everything for you is personal. You believe in loyalty, that when you put your trust in people, they will value that."

"Adler," Casement says, stopping on the path, "this is a basic way to be."

"Basic for you, but loyalty is a ridiculous thing. What is loyalty? Loyalty says, 'You know this is bad for you but you must do it because it is good for someone else.' It's a stupid thing, made up by someone, so that people doing stupid things can feel good about themselves."

"You have thought about this."

"And for once, you haven't." Adler gives Casement a patient look, holds it long, with the background music of shouted German commands. "What is good for you, Sir Roger? What would be best for your well-being? Do that, and then you'll cheer up."

But he doesn't know. There is Adler on the path, coaxing him forward. Come on, he gestures with a quick jerk of his head. Casement follows. He does not know what would be best for him, but clings to what is best for Ireland—an Irish Republic that hovers in his mind, an Irish parliament, industry and busy ports, an educated population, a living language, a system of agriculture that feeds the people rather than lines the pockets of the conquerors. It is all so reasonable, so why cast it as a fantasy? People are willing to die to make Ireland free not just because of their bravery and conviction, but because lives so devalued have a hunger for sacrifice.

February finds him in a sanatorium in Grunewald. His old ailments are there to keep him company, but the nerves are what have undone him. He's collapsed again and he knows that people are wondering if he'll ever get out. He is wondering the same thing. Adler has gone to Norway to meet with Findlay, also to expose Findlay's perfidy. Adler, who does not understand why he expects more of anyone. Has Casement not said that the English are not to be trusted? Isn't Findlay's behavior just an example of this? But Adler at least has some sort of intelligence to trade along with express instructions to expose the misconduct of the English legation in Norway. Adler says he'll do this because it seems that, as long as he's representing Casement, the English government will see this attack on them as a good way of covering his tracks. Adler is a natural double agent, although he can't seem to keep the larger goals straight. Casement has been trying to get his letter exposing Findlay in the American papers, but only one will publish it, as it seems that American sentiment is tending towards the support of England. But if the Americans knew the conduct of the English, they would support Germany.

There is a knock on the door, and a nurse enters bearing newspapers. She speaks in rapid-fire German, her distaste for this English-speaking patient poorly disguised. She throws the papers down on his bedside table. There is a question, pointed and stern, to which he cannot respond. She repeats it as if to amp her frustration and then leaves with strident step, shutting the door loudly behind her.

The English papers are a week old and bear the usual news. There are fabrications of German slayings of women who have helped the French. And more atrocities in Belgium, pits full of bodies—babies, children, mothers—dumped by the advancing German armies. He skims the headlines. In Bukovina, Germans supposedly forced Serbians to assist in their own executions. The punishing temperatures in Galicia have not stalled the intense fighting. And in Sydney, Australia, there was a partial eclipse of the sun. Then he sees his name. *Sir Roger Casement.* It is there in bold letters. He scans quickly through the matter, of how he ". . . accuses Mister M. Findlay, British Minister of Norway, of conspiring to kidnap him . . ." and of Findlay's promise to give Adler ". . . Casement's manservant, who is Norwegian, £5,000 in the event that he captured Casement."

This is not his letter as he wrote it, yet there is some satisfaction to see his accusation in print, although buried in a longer piece. At the bottom of the article is some biographical matter and his heart sinks as he discovers, along with England, and therefore Ward, that his pension has been withheld pending further investigation as this known Irish Nationalist is now in Germany negotiating with the Germans for preferential treatment of Ireland.

Of course there is no going back. He has known this, pushed it to the perimeter of his consciousness because it is an inconvenience. And he pushes it away again, but his hands on the paper, his eyes scanning the list of casualties, he realizes again that he is searching for Charlie Ward, and perhaps for Herbie, although he is not yet old enough to enlist.

He has heard through Countess Blucher, an Englishwoman married to a German and now in Munich, that Ward had turned the house in Rolleboise into some sort of hospital. Beyond that, he does not know, as this Countess Blucher does not know the Wards well, although she had been entertained by Sarita and Herbert, brought to the country house by mutual friends motoring out from Paris for the day. And this is all he has to go on: a newspaper that he hopes bears no information and an indication that Ward has leapt into the war effort with his usual energy and will not be sympathetic to Casement's position. This is the same Ward, after all, who went off with Stanley to find Emin Pasha, who throws himself into every endeavor with no thought as to his own well-being, who has great valor, although often for the wrong side. Would not Ward say the same of him?

He finds himself standing, out of the bed, making his way to the window. A weight of snow lies on everything except for one assertive tree, alone by the fence: a lonely tree that casts a pale blue shadow.

VIII
Rolleboise

May 1915

The furniture has been moved back into the drawing room, although there is no carpet as the one that once covered the floor had to be stored in the attic when this room served as an infirmary, and was there chewed through by mice. It was a valuable rug, one that is now in Père Fabrice's cottage, sliced to remove the majority of the damaged bits and roughly seamed against fraying by Père Fabrice's wife. Ward had felt strangely despondent about the rug, and then realized that he'd actually been feeling sorry for it. Sorry for the rug, that it had fallen from its former glory. He has such an excess of empathy of late.

In the past, Ward loved spending time in Vernon. People were happy to see him, offered a flower for his lapel, made urgent, welcoming gestures for him to pull up a chair at the café and take a glass for wine. Now, the town is denuded of men, except for the really old ones, and that's not good for Ward's mood. He doesn't want to think of himself as one of the sidewalk gentlemen with splayed knees and long mustaches, who sit and look and look, just hoping that you'll walk by and interrupt their vision. But as those are the only males around—other than boys in short pants—it's hard to feel a part of things.

If he had only been allowed to keep the hospital going. Everyone was made happy by that. Even Sarita had come around to her exile, noting with some comfort that Herbie was so useful as a driver that he might stop agitating about the flying as he felt essential to the war effort. But it was not to be. One of the officer's wives had shown up unannounced for a visit, and as there was no place to put her up in town, Ward had offered her an upstairs room. Because of that, the Red Cross shut him down. An unauthorized woman, they said, had no business in a hospital. It was improper. Had they seen Mrs. Newcombe? She was so impossible to imagine in any but the most proper way that Ward wondered what had drawn Captain Newcombe to her in the first place. It's concerning that the organization of shipping ammunition to the Front can fall between the cracks, while the comings and goings of Mrs. Newcombe are tracked with such diligence.

Rolleboise is not the place for him. He has begged his way into the Ambulance Corps and is himself shipping to the Front. He'll get there before Charlie. Six months ago, he thought that Charlie might never see combat, but he's given that up. This war needs to be ended as quickly as possible before it destroys anything else.

Casement.

Why would he go to Germany?

Just a week earlier, Neave from the Foreign Office had arranged a meeting with Ward in Paris. He wanted to know, casually, if he and Casement had been in communication.

Ward had not heard anything from Casement. He knew he'd gone to New York to discuss Home Rule with the Americans, but beyond that, he wasn't sure. There had often been times when he and Casement lost track of each other for months here and there, despite Casement's committed letter-writing. He'd wondered. Sarita had seen Casement in London not too long ago and she thought he was involved in some sort of intelligence work in the North Sea, because he'd mentioned Scotland. Ward knew nothing and struggled, in Neave's office, to keep his composure. He could see Neave studying his response to the news and he must have looked bad because Neave, an unemotional type, had his face composed in an almost painful sympathy. Neave had filled in the blanks. The conversation was, as assumed, confidential, but Casement was recruiting Irish prisoners of war. Of course the Germans were just stringing him along, but if the Irish started fighting right at home, it would draw troops away from the crucial conflict.

Casement was exploiting this terrible war to realize his sentimental obsession with Ireland. He must have been planning it for a long time, as he strolled the gardens of Rolleboise and ate their food, as he wrote to Ward asking for money, and for more money. Ward assured Neave that he would let him know if Casement tried to contact him. Ward stood and, as he shook hands, had managed, "What an ending to what promised to be a brilliant career." He could hear the hitch in his voice.

For some odd reason, this betrayal has sent Ward back to thinking about his father, and that time when he signed on to the *Wishart*. He was fifteen, younger than Herbie, when he left for the sea, just a child, and the fact that his father had let him—no, had made him do that . . . also that his mother stood by as her favorite son went into the care of men who, in another time, would have been pirates, is some sort of rent that, even at the age of fifty-two, he has not managed to mend. He is a different man now—well, at least a man—and he survived, obviously. But Ward doesn't like feeling as he did then. The intervening years, washed over with all the bravado of what he managed through physical health and good humor and the friends it brought, that life literally scripted into books, all seems worn to nothing in the early morning hours, or when he walks the perimeters of the property alone. Yes, he's been betrayed. Betrayal. It's a man's word. What he really feels is abandoned.

Ward has only an hour before he needs to be in Vernon on the first of a series of transports that will take him to his position on the Front. Sarita has been making herself scarce. In the hallway, he sees Beatrice shuttling by with a stack of clean linen.

"Beatrice!" he calls.

"Oui," she says.

"Could you please tell Madame that I would like to speak with her and that I am leaving soon?"

Beatrice nods, taking in Ward's uniform as she does so. From her furrowed brow and pursed mouth, it would seem that she shares Sarita's opinion of his actions. He cannot expect Sarita to understand that which he himself doesn't fully comprehend, but she has to support him. Isn't that demanded of one's wife? However, Sarita is an exceptional woman and uses her knowledge of this to except herself from all accepted behavior.

She stands at the door in a simple blue dress, holding the leather-bound book where she records the daily expenses, hesitating before entering the room. "So you are intent on leaving."

"Yes, Sarita, I am."

"Have you looked at yourself in that uniform?" She sinks into a chair and places her hand over her forehead. There's a moment of silence. Beatrice appears in the doorway and, noting Sarita's posture, immediately withdraws.

"Do you have a headache?"

"No," she says, outraged. "I do not have a headache. I'll tell you what I do have. A stupid husband."

"That's not helpful."

"Helpful? Have you thought this through at all? You have a heart condition. You're also deep in middle age. I don't know why they're taking you. Can you even lift a stretcher? Have you lifted anything heavier than a forkful of omelet in the last ten years?"

"I must do what I can for the war effort."

"All right. Well, let's consider it. Charlie will be headed to the Front in two weeks. Herbie will be making his first solo flight sometime in the next few days, and then he'll be headed for Germany. And now we're supposed to send you along too? How about Roddie? Why don't we tell him to pack his bag and you can take him with you?" Sarita stares at him. "This is some variety of suicide. You realize this."

"It's nothing of the sort."

"Listen to yourself. *Nothing of the sort. War effort. Not helpful.*"

"Sarita," he says patiently, "you are not showing your most attractive side."

She calms herself, although, from the catlike stretching of her hands, he knows she's deeply aggravated. "Have you been paying attention?"

"To what?"

"To yourself. One minute you're listening to Northcliffe's advice that the best place for you is in New York getting America in the war, and the next you're dressed like a Boy Scout headed for the Vosges. You've been depressed. I've seen you staring out into space for reaches of time, and that's not like you. It's like me, but not like you. I know we've had some blows." She's referring to Casement and he hopes she won't name him because he doesn't know how he'll react. "You are forgetting that you are a powerful man from a powerful banking family. There is no better place for you than the lecture circuit in America, and Northcliffe has already volunteered to set it up and do the necessary publicity. You are married to an American. You are an internationally renowned artist. You are an explorer and a best-selling author."

"You left out circus performer."

"That supports my argument."

"I'm not ready for the lecture circuit in America," says Ward. He's sure he won't convince her, no matter how hard he tries, so he thinks he can basically say anything. "That is the refuge of an old man."

Sarita leaps from her chair and, taking him by the shoulders, steers him to the mirror. "Take a good look, Herbert. What do you see?"

"I know what you see," he says, ruffling the ever-useful metaphor of his thinning hair, "but I see a man who might be able to save a few lives. You don't know what I'm like under fire. I get frightened, but it doesn't stop me from doing my job. I cheer people up. I give them comfort. And I'm going, so you should make peace with it as soon as possible."

She meets his gaze but glances away. He follows the path of her eyes to the poker in its brass stand but knows she's looking inwardly. "It's as if you have no regard for me."

"You know that's not true." He turns her so that they're facing each other. "One of those boys who I pull off the field could be Charlie. I think of that. Tell me truthfully that if anyone would take you, you wouldn't do the same."

In the garden, larks are singing, intent on performing the music of summer. Sarita's gray eyes rise to his face. "You'll be in the line of fire."

"That, unfortunately, is where stretcher-bearers are needed." He watches her thinking, her twitching brows, but knows better than to ask after her thoughts.

"And what am I supposed to do?"

"Sarita, you do what you've always done."

"And what exactly is that?"

"Keep the planets in rotation."

She shakes her head, an act of defiance that actually shows her resignation. "I suppose you'll write every day."

"I will find the time."

They sit side by side on the stiff, little loveseat and go over the small things that need attention, how to send packages as the food will not be sufficient, a quick rundown of what Sarita's doing with the expenses to see if she's left anything out, when they might meet in Paris when he has leave, whether Roddie can stay in France for the summer, which he's against as the boy just wanders about muttering to himself, enacting his loneliness, as if he's the cripple from the *Pied Piper of Hamlin*.

Ward gets up. "We should head to the train station."

"I'm not going."

"You're not seeing me off?"

"Take Roddie."

"You won't come?"

Sarita shakes her head, and when he goes to embrace her, she won't raise her face to him. He has to wrap his arms around her folded limbs that are holding the accounting book. And right there, he wonders if he's doing the right thing, if he has any right to abandon his wife, who is holding so much together and is now doing it completely alone.

The lease on the house in Weston-Super-Mare is up at the end of the week, because Charlie will be gone, and she will no longer need a place for him. Herbie, too, is gearing up. He will be stationed in France—also Charlie—so there's no reason for Sarita to be in England. Roddie will be back in school, within easy reach of her father, who is a good influence on the boy. Dimples is in London, nursing baby number two—another boy—and Cricket is still in New York, because she's sick of the war and New York is certainly more fun than London.

And Herbert? He is indeed carrying the wounded in the mountains of Alsace. A minor relief is that he is not responsible for the removal of injured from the battlefield. Those stretcher-bearers—as she was informed by Harmsworth—have an average survival rate of two and a half weeks. Herbert's job is to get the injured from the Posts to the areas accessible by ambulance and from the ambulance to the hospital. So he is carrying a stretcher, but not in the line of fire, although he's far from safe. Herbert has witnessed plenty of death: ready corpses, and people about him being blown up, taken away by shrapnel, pouring blood—out of holes that were once legs or arms or abdomens—and sometimes collapsing like wet paper bags as their lungs are crushed by poisonous gas.

Herbie is here for the night to spend time with Charlie. Herbie has to be back at Brooklands tomorrow. She has her two boys under her roof and she is not sharing them with anyone, not with Roddie, who begged to be let off from school but who would have, no doubt, suffered an attack of anxiety upon being returned to Eton. Not with her father, who is preparing for a trip to New York. And not with Herbert, who is waiting at the Front. She remembers Charlie as a boy jumping off a boat landing and Herbert, in the water, catching him. That's probably what Herbert thinks he's doing in the Vosges.

These are magical days, magical hours. It's as if she can hear each second expire as she wills time to still, to not pass. And the boys? They understand the war better than she does. They've lost friends, people they know, but wrapped in the banner of youth, they can't escape joy. Because it is a joy to be that young, to be that beautiful. Now she's old and she's wise, and that is no fun at all. Herbie's voice, plaintive, bounces down the hallway, and there's Charlie, a bark—who would have thought this music would be taken from her?

She should not be false to herself. She always knew that Charlie would leave, and then Herbie. This is what boys do when you do your job well. This is why it is so taxing to be a mother, to get your sons' legs under them with all tenderness and then to bravely walk away. Do not look over your shoulder. Believe that they're capable of handling it all, even when they reach for you. Give them back their hand. Tell them you're not needed anymore, that anything they might require to survive is all there, within them, and if it isn't, that they're capable of creating that strength.

Minute to minute, even when there's no clock for her to look at, she knows that time is passing. The war is hungry and wants to take everything.

Charlie and Herbie are in the hallway, arguing. She tries to think of something cheerful to say, or at least not desperate. She could mention the boiled beef, since it was cooked in such a way that it had neither tenderness nor flavor—miraculous because, in this dish, one is usually sacrificed for the other. Perhaps it wasn't beef at all. Bucket Woman has been very quiet as of late, and she certainly would have provided a tough joint for the table. Humor can be manufactured—must be—as otherwise she is a dark presence, not a support, yet another thing to remind of the death that lurks everywhere, of the death that is celebrating its proximity to all this vigorous youth.

"You're still here?" she asks the boys. "I thought you were going out."

"We are," says Charlie. "Although Herbie is being a complete bore."

"I'm not," he protests. "It's just that Charlie always has to have his way."

"What does Charlie want?" asks Sarita. She sees Herbie roll his eyes. He thinks she favors Charlie, wants to give Charlie anything he desires, and maybe she does, but it's out of habit, not because she prefers him to Herbie.

"I just want Herbie to have a good time," says Charlie, squaring his shoulders at his brother. "If I have to hear another thing about Joyce Nicholson—"

"You wouldn't say that if you'd met her."

"What makes you think I haven't?"

There's a moment. Charlie has that dispassionate look and Herbie's rattled, showing that the last blow landed well.

"I would like to remind you," says Sarita, "that the war is actually with Germany."

"Charlie is relentless," says Herbie. "He just won't give up."

"Charlie is a relentless person who never gives up," says Sarita agreeably. "What is going on?"

"Charlie has set something up with that girl in the village."

"That girl in the village is Jane, and you are actually set up with her lovely sister Bernadette."

"I doubt that Bernadette is lovely."

"You wouldn't say that," Charlie lathers up the sarcasm, "if you'd met her." He smiles and waggles his eyebrows in the exact same way as does his grandfather. "And I've told her wonderful things about you, about your pretty blond hair and how brave you are, being a pilot and all that."

Herbie's knuckles are chapped because it's cold flying up so high, even in the summer, and he's always had a problem with dry skin. He picks at it as he assembles his thoughts, and announces, "I feel like Charlie is prostituting me, Mother."

Charlie probably is, and it's funny, thank God—an easy laugh for her. "You should go, Herbie, have some fun, just don't drink too much. Remember, you're flying tomorrow."

Charlie begins to steer Herbie out the door, his hands on his shoulders. "You'd be surprised just how generous these girls get when they hear you're heading out."

"Charlie, that's enough—" says Sarita.

"And Herbie, you could use some experience."

"I am standing here," says Sarita. "You could wait until you're outside."

"It's just that I told Joyce—" says Herbie, although the protest has worn out.

"Bernadette might be your soul mate," says Charlie.

"Soul mate?" says Sarita. "What are you talking about?"

"Herbie's been brought up on that tale of your romance with Father, how he found you on the upper decks of the *Saale* in the middle of the night looking out to sea and fell instantly in love."

"Is that how he tells it?" says Sarita.

"Do you have a different version?" asks Herbie.

She waves them both off. "Herbie," says Sarita, "Joyce will still be there, in London, tomorrow. Go have fun with your brother."

In the evening, she is knitting with Rose, the girl who—despite her poor cookery—is actually a machine when it comes to turning out socks. Socks are difficult, particularly with this regulation yarn, which is on the thin side. Rose manages three socks for every one of Sarita's and they are all the same size. No one expects Sarita to be knitting socks, but no one expects Sarita to be doing anything.

Rose has a sweetheart fighting up near Cantigny. His name is Derrick and he has a good writing style. Rose finds this surprising and doesn't seem to quite trust Sarita's assessment of his letters. Derrick says things like, "When you get away from the Front, the silence kind of screams at you," and "I'm glad I've got you, because the lads who don't have girls only have their mothers to miss and that's sort of embarrassing." Sarita has started sharing bits of Herbert's letters too, describing caves that serve as operating theatres and steep slopes garlanded with barbed wire. In this manner she and Rose have become friends, although it is a cautious friendship maintained with lowered eyes and constant activity. They haven't actually admitted to being friends and chances are—class difference and all—that they won't. They each roll out their personal narratives as a means of escape for the other woman, eager to be similarly relieved themselves. Here's what Derrick's up to and what he says, and this is what's happening to Herbert and Charlie.

And Herbie, who is struggling with the other officers as he's younger than them all—the youngest pilot in RFC by at least a year. Herbie actually looks his age too, which doesn't help. He's not shaving, unless one calls the removal of the fine line of soft whiskers from his upper lip "shaving," and is the butt of many jokes. Being Charlie's brother has prepared him for this and he weathers it just fine. Apparently, the previous week they had been in training with the gunners and Herbie had been matched with a heavyset Yorkshire man, who took one look at Herbie and refused to get in the plane. He didn't want to be killed, and on English soil, because he was being sent into the air with a twelve-year-old. Herbie understood and was actually hoping that they'd give him someone closer in age and more fun, but apparently the fact that Herbie weighs in at 130 pounds means that he does get matched with heavier gunners. The reason that Herbie shared this story is that his superior had, firstly, pointed out that the man from Yorkshire had to get into the plane even if Herbie was twelve because it was a direct order, and then added that the man was being an idiot because Herbie was actually the best pilot they had. He never got lost, was so mechanically astute that he could probably build a plane from scratch, and—at this point—had the most flying hours of anyone at the school. Also, as he was light, whoever was with him could carry extra ammunition. "They call me Sparrow," Herbie shared, "and I'm supposed to be good luck." So Herbie is not only the best pilot at Brooklands but also the company mascot.

At midnight, the door to the hallway slams open. Sarita doubts that she's been sleeping but doesn't exactly know how she's been passing the time otherwise. Her sock confirms a lack of progress. Rose left for bed hours ago. She thinks Herbie and Charlie are trying to be quiet, but if that's the case, they're failing so extravagantly that it's hard to tell.

She stands up, leaving the knitting on the chair. The door to the parlor leads right on to the front hall so she leans there, in the entrance. Charlie is smoking and Herbie is untying his bootlaces, which she suspects is supposed to facilitate his not waking her up.

"So," says Sarita, "how was the lovely Bernadette?"

Herbie transcribes an arc with his eyes and manages, "She was all right." Charlie smacks him in the shoulder with the hand holding the cigarette, sending Herbie into the coat tree. There's a lot of snickering.

"Don't tell her anything," says Charlie.

"I would prefer that," says Sarita. "I shouldn't have asked." She raises her hands and steps back.

"I wasn't going to," says Herbie. "Charlie thinks I tell you everything, but I don't." He manages to kick his boot off and stares his brother down. "I've been smoking since I was twelve and I never told her that."

"You just did," says Charlie. And it is funny, thank God. "Can you make sure I'm up?"

"What time?" asks Sarita.

"Five."

"What makes you think I'll be up?" But of course she will. She doesn't sleep more than an hour at a stretch, and will just make it a point to check the clock in her waking episodes. She'll lie in bed listening to them. Herbie snores, which might have something to do with the fact that he was a child smoker. And Charlie harrumphs, yells at people, straightens them out at intervals. She wonders how their fellow officers handle this, because Roddie wouldn't share a room with either of them and, on holidays, had to bunk in with the girls. But her room in this little house is right beside theirs, and she's glad they're loud. She'll stay up listening.

IX

Berlin

June 1915

Despite the lungs, Plunkett is tenacious. He's a terrier and his diplomacy consists of sinking one's teeth into another's leg and hanging on until that person gives up. And what is Casement's diplomacy? He proceeds with reason, knowing the facts, knowing what is worth compromise and what is not, but this Boehm, who's been assigned to monitor the Brigade, has been unresponsive. The flickering awareness that he reads in Boehm's face confirms nothing. Boehm is just wondering when Casement is going to land back in the hospital and Casement's awareness of this makes him flustered, confirming Boehm's assessment. To be honest, Plunkett has been the more successful in realizing his ends. Although he can't seem to get his head out of the streets of Dublin and in order for this engagement to sustain, one has to bring England to her knees. That's why they are in Germany.

Plunkett is a good listener but has little patience with Casement's long-range planning. Plunkett doesn't think that sending the Irish Brigade into Turkey is a good idea, although where else will they fight? They can't exactly remain in prison camps if they are, indeed, fighting alongside Germany.

They can't pretend that they're soldiers if they have no weapons, no uniforms, no freedom. And Turkey is more than a convenient exercise.

If the Turks break through the Suez Canal, then the English will lose Egypt. Ireland will act and then certainly India will take the opportunity to assert herself. Without India, there is nothing to fill the English coffers, and England will therefore be undone. But Plunkett seems to think it's enough to push the English past the boundaries of Howth and Bray, and how long will that hold? And yes, one has to do something, but not that. A shoot-up on the streets of Dublin will only anger the locals and extinguish whatever momentum might be in play.

"Are you all right?" asks Plunkett.

"That's the second time you've asked me that, so I'll assume the first response was not satisfactory. I am still fine." Casement likes Plunkett, who looks as fragile as he himself does. The Irish certainly look like they can use all the help they can get. Casement cannot live with the present, with his senses frayed and his mood as shifting and as beyond his control as weather. The future forks into a myriad of possibilities and each channel he explores in turn, and each is a horror. They don't get the guns to Ireland and they stay in subjugation. They do get the guns to Ireland, resulting in pointless loss of life. They don't form an Irish Brigade and are futile. They do form an Irish Brigade and are traitors to their own. Casement escapes to America and he is a failure. Casement is held in Germany and he is a prisoner. They sell to him to the English and he's hanged. He thinks of the word *happen* and the ticking of time it implies, the fatalism of it. *Things happen. What will happen?* Because he's waiting, like a child, like a vassal, for his cues from the Germans and how he got here, how this *happened*, he is not sure. "What did Boehm have to say today?"

Plunkett shifts his head from side to side as he sorts it out. "We're close. We're at least discussing weapons. That rings as a vote of confidence."

"More volunteers?"

"We're up to eighty."

"Is it your charm?"

"It is my bribery." Plunkett pushes his glasses up his nose and settles into his chair. "I can promise the men good pay and good conditions. And my pragmatism has a certain appeal."

"What is the substance of your pragmatism?"

"You're not into contingencies, Roddie, but I've worked some out. If the Germans win, the men get Home Rule, and if not," he makes a face here, as if he's spilled something, "we'll send them all to America with ten pounds and promise of employment."

"So Devoy too is losing faith in Germany?"

"It's not that bad, Roddie," says Plunkett, who is willing to take a good deal of bad to get to a little good, probably a life-lesson taught to him by his pocked lungs. "Also Boehm's agreed that the Brigade will only serve under Irish officers."

"How did you manage that?"

"That," Plunkett winks, "was my charm." If Casement were a different sort of man, it would actually be more funny. Or less funny. "Here's the declaration." Casement takes the sheet of paper and reads it over. It says all it needs to, that the Irish are being armed by the Germans but are fighting for themselves, no more traitors than Wolf Tone for appealing to the French. It ends, *With the help of our countrymen in Ireland and throughout the world, we hope either to win the Independence of our country or to die fighting for the glory of God and the honour of Ireland.* "There's some nice writing here," says Casement. "And it's wonderfully concise."

"I hear you gave them *The Making of Ireland and Its Undoing.*"

Casement laughs, but it's a sad laugh. "Did they not like it?"

"Oh, they did. You know they're short on paper in the camp."

Casement takes the joke. "I seem to have misjudged my audience."

"Don't take it personally. They're just not great readers. And I'm sympathetic to you, as you know." Plunkett, when he's not functioning as senior-level officer for the IRB, is an editor and poet.

"Do you have a book with you?" asks Casement, suddenly hungry for the specific solace of poetry. "Or some poems?"

"What? Of mine?"

Casement nods. "Since I am a great reader."

"No, I don't. I am, eh, incognito. And that's a bit disappointing because I can probably count on one hand the number of people who have asked me for a poem in the last year." Plunkett takes the flyer back from Casement. "I'll scribble one down for you."

Plunkett pauses in his scratching, looks to Casement. "Don't look so concerned, Mister Casement. I may not look like much of a soldier but it's all up here." He taps his head. "I'm a great strategist, trained and everything."

"I have tremendous faith in you, Joe."

Plunkett looks at the paper, shrugs, and hands it on.

I saw the Sun at midnight, rising red,

What a relief that this Plunkett hasn't given him a love poem.

Deep-hued yet glowing, heavy with the stain
Of blood-compassion, and I saw It gain
Swiftly in size and growing till It spread
Over the stars; the heavens bowed their head

The thing reads like a meditation all the way to the end, Christ and metaphysics, tuberculosis and guns. That's what this Plunkett is about.

"Are you a man of faith, Roddie?"

"It has its appeal, but I wouldn't characterize myself that way."

"Well, I don't often ask people that, but you've done so much good for the poor people in the Congo and in the Amazon, I just thought it was worth asking."

Truth is, Joe Plunkett, he did that for them. For the poor people in the Congo. For the Indians, certainly not for or because of God. God was used more as leverage for people with religion as in *support this as it's obviously the right thing to do*. Then, he was always sure of the right thing. And now?

435

Everyone seems to have righteousness on their side and if there is a God, he's gone quiet.

"You are a man of great faith," says Casement.

"And poor health. Did you like the poem?"

"Yes, I did."

"That's the right answer. Here's another question. Do you think you can get us the guns?"

"Joe, I don't think the Germans are inclined to be generous with me. And also I have serious misgivings about the use of the weapons."

"That's not for you to worry about, Roddie. We have our leaders and meetings and all of that, and what you need to do is to help us out in your capacity."

"And what would that be?"

"You are our man in Germany." Plunkett looks suddenly serious, but he is still only in his twenties, and the grave look does not accomplish much. "You have leverage, you know that." Casement shakes his head. "Yes, you do. Boehm has to give you something you want. What if you go back to America and let Devoy and Montieth and all know that the Germans are just jerking us around? We're at a tipping point and the Kaiser needs us happy. It is generally believed that the Americans are about to enter the war. Now, I know—although you seem to be in denial—that America is likely to come in on the side of England."

"What makes you think that?"

"Shipments sneaking into England on passenger ships from New York."

Casement folds himself deeper into his chair. He feels a tremor along his limbs.

"Roddie, there is going to be an uprising in the streets of Dublin. You can't do anything about it, and surely knowing the certainty of such a thing, you will work as hard as you can with whatever you've got to get us weapons."

How many times can a man break down without it being final? Nerves, they say. Malaria. Arthritis. All those doctors with their diagnoses, and how could they miss the truth of the matter, which is that his heart is broken? He is also suffering from the unavoidable reality that he is pathetic, that a man in middle age has no business being in love, that the state of it—nausea, intoxication, obsession—is for the young, certainly not for those with as much responsibility as he. How many people are counting on him, have always counted on him, and he has resolutely buried his own feelings and nature and respected this larger need? He runs the narrative through his head. Roger Casement could have stuck to it and created an independent Ireland. Instead he fell apart when he was rejected by his lover. Of course it's more than that. There are nerves, malaria, arthritis, and also age. But age plays into love, makes one wish to win the hand as it might be the last. For old men, the bounty of the future is decidedly diminished and all in love are young.

As the sand runs out, he panics that even the greater needs of Ireland are being lost while he flails about like a schoolboy trying to recover his bearings.

Adler is always there with him, like a ghost, haunting his peripheral vision, his wrecked voicing of warped philosophies shattering Casement's perspectives. What Casement has left in this cold hospital room, along with the collapsing body and quivering mind, is his untethered conviction. His courage. Something that Adler saw in him, and actually—was this love?—tried to talk him out of.

"Sir Roger," Adler had said, "courage? If you don't have a choice, it's not courage, and if you do, it's no different than stupidity."

Of course it was funny, but hard to find funny because once you peeled back the humor, it was the very stuff of Adler's religion.

Casement had known there was someone else. Why wouldn't there be? And he hadn't let his mind explore the possibility that much because Adler always came back at some point, and maybe it was for money, but as that was the only kindness that Adler understood, it was not insignificant. But a wife? And Adler's explanation?

"It's not that interesting. Men marry women."

"But Adler, you've married two."

And this had made Adler giggle, as if bigamy was a crime on par with having eaten all the biscuits. His wife? Margarette, a German, a woman that Adler can't even have a viable conversation with. Adler is to bring her back to America. Apparently, Devoy has been bankrolling this wife whilst under the impression he was helping to support the other, the "Red Indian," who is probably on the streets now with Adler's child.

Adler is not reliable and Devoy has been angling to pull the plug on him for months, but he is good at certain things. They are plotting to get Montieth into Germany and Adler is the only one who can do it. And they need Montieth, a military man, much decorated, who has spent sixteen years in the English Army. He has been drilling the Irish Volunteers, and will now be in charge of the Irish Brigade. Montieth was exiled from Dublin as a result of his refusing two English commissions and is now in America awaiting some sort of directive that will get him to Germany. And how did he get to America? Emigrated with his entire family as the English thought this was a good way to get rid of him. And how do we get this known rebel back into Europe with all the patrols prowling the Atlantic? The only person who can manage this is Adler. Although Adler won't say how it's to be managed, just collapses into a Cheshire cat smile and says they need to trust him.

Loyalty? Courage? Bravery? Wouldn't Adler add trust to that list of survival-instinct circumvention, also known as stupidity? Casement knows that Adler can't tell them what his plan is because he has yet to figure it out. He'll show up in New York and prowl the docks, make some friends, play some cards. He'll identify a bribable steward and Montieth will find himself jammed into a closet for his journey, shuttled around should the patrols board the ship, and that's if he's lucky. Short on stevedores, men are often hired for this work with spotty background checks. Montieth could find himself shoveling coal the entire breadth of the Atlantic. This particular labor has been one of Adler's educators and what has it taught him? Do anything to never do this again.

Once Montieth is there, he will begin drilling the men. But for what? Will the Germans actually listen to him? His sixteen years in the English Army will at least be seen as valuable knowledge, and the Germans like virile feats, claim to like bravery, but are suspicious of the romantic perfume that the Irish attach to it, as if to the Germans bravery is the means to an end, a few meters into No-Man's-Land, a grenaded English dugout, an excuse to burst into one of their cacophonous, juvenile, hearty songs that spring from a philosophic desire to be happy, destructive, and loud. But surely Montieth's performance at the Battle of Ladysmith—he was lead horse of the gun carriage—will impress.

This hospital room could be anywhere. Wrapped in the cold, white sheet, he could be in Dublin, convalescing, with Alice stopping by. He could be back in England after surgery, waiting for Ward to pick him up. But he has never been so alone, devoid of company, isolated in his opinions. His final urging to the Germans has been to say that arms can be landed in Ireland but should be hidden until the time when German naval power can reinforce whatever is managed on land. And all that smirking, that Deutsche language that he should have learned but somehow didn't, admonishing himself all the while with the memory of his expedient Bakongo—no, they don't think it is in the best interests of the Central Powers to do that right now.

The Germans insist that they will only supply weapons if the Irish use them immediately. Ireland is a beautiful tinderbox. The specter of conscription has already been raised and those who have not signed up in Ireland do not wish to be fighting this war and could well do just about anything—including participating in a different conflict—to avoid it. The Irish will have their rebellion, whether they want it or not. To Casement, it seems that the Germans have handed the Irish a grenade with the express instruction that once they have it they must pull the pin and not let go. And the Irish seem to think that if there's a chance that some English person will be alongside when they do this, it's not a bad deal.

X

The Vosges

November 1915

Ward is trying to get the man ready for the operating table without hurting him, but he's frozen to the stretcher in a mixture of water and his own blood. How old is he? No more than eighteen. As Ward tries to pry him free with gentle rocking, his fingers hooked under the man's torso, he sees the poor soldier's face rigid in pain. All around him Ward can hear shouting. There are things that need to be done, things he could do. And after the rush, the stumbling with the stretcher over the uneven ground, the practiced duck beneath the beam that forms the transom of the surgery, his blinking adjustment to the light that shows the surgeon, up against the back wall, illuminated at his work like a figure from a painting by Joseph Wright of Derby, lit by a lamp held and moved by the nurse, work he himself has done, he thinks himself stalled.

"Easy," he says to the man, but it's an abdominal wound and he doesn't know what damage he might do by moving him. "Is there a nurse who might assist?" Ward asks, hoping that one of this number, dimmed to shadowy figures, might offer some direction.

"Leave him," says a voice. Or maybe he said it himself. They are near enough the heater, so perhaps he will thaw sufficiently to be removed with more ease. Maybe being frozen is holding everything in place. What can Ward do? He hears his driver, Kavanagh, shouting that he needs to find him, to find Ward, and the other stretchers must be empty and now loaded on the ambulance for another trip.

There is no shortage of injured here in the Vosges.

"I'm so sorry," says Ward to the man on the stretcher, and he is, for everything, for the conditions of this hospital, for the freezing weather, for his ineptitude, for this war. He is trained to think of this eighteen-year-old as a man, because if these are all boys, it is impossible to proceed.

There is Kavanagh at the doorway. Ward looks up, helpless, then stands, wiping his hands on his trousers. They are sticky and although the darkness makes it impossible to see, he knows it's blood. "Lieutenant Ward, we have to go. Leave him. They'll know what to do with him."

Ward gets up front with Kavanagh and they begin the drive to the Post. Ward has been feeling sharp pains in his chest and he thinks that, in any other situation, it might be a good idea to mention this to someone, to say that he should possibly sit this one out, but he can't think of how to do it and isn't even sure if he wants to. And sharp chest pains alongside boys with their insides unraveling and frozen to stretchers seems insignificant. But he is uncomfortable and, seeing his expression, Kavanagh, a Tipperary man who thinks that talk is the cure for nerves when singing is not an option, is studying his face.

"Nice weather we're having," he says, almost a shout, over the struggling engine and the tires spinning in the dirt, hitting holes, rolling over rocks.

"It reminds me of home," says Ward. It's not really a joke, but given circumstance, Kavanagh will have to forgive him.

"Where did you say your boys were?"

"My older son Charlie is with the Royal Warwickshire Regiment, tenth Battalion. He's a lieutenant, stationed at Neuve Chapelle."

"An officer." Kavanagh must also be struggling for conversation, dealing with nerves of his own, for this is a poor relative of his usual chatter. And Kavanagh knows all this.

"And the other?"

"Herbie. He's a pilot."

"A pilot? He must be very clever."

"He must be," says Ward, "but growing up he's always been the family clown. And you, Kavanagh?"

"No one in the war. I have a daughter," says Kavanagh, "and the poor thing looks just like me."

Is there any way to make Kavanagh shut up? It is bad enough to be struggling like this without having to maintain a politeness. If he were anyone else, he would just stop the idle talk. Sarita would think of something to say, sharp and funny that would quiet him. There's that sound, a screeching. Ward feels his shoulders pull up, as if that might protect him, and there's an explosion. Rocks fly up and the windscreen cracks. Kavanagh slams on the brakes and the engine dies. He's swearing up a storm now and Ward is not sure what has just happened.

"The road's been blown up. Fuck!" says Kavanagh. He strikes the steering wheel and leaps from the vehicle. Now what? Kavanagh runs to the front of the vehicle and there's another shriek as some explosive tears through the air. There's the boom. They are buried in dust and Ward struggles to see Kavanagh in the thick air at the hood of the vehicle. He reappears, apparently unharmed. "Let's go on foot," he says. "It's not that far."

Kavanagh moves quickly to the back of the ambulance. Ward wonders how far is *not that far*. Ward gets out, giving the sky a cautious look. It's purple, edged in smoke, portentous, as if hatching problems of its own. He and Kavanagh stack four stretchers, one atop the other. Together they move quickly over the busted road and torn trees. Men are running on the ridge above and Ward has the sickening feeling that the Front has moved, that if he wasn't willing to find the Front—his promise to Sarita—the Front has found him. Ward is not sure how Kavanagh knows where he's going.

They could encounter Germans—lost Germans, brave Germans—as it happens all the time.

"Stretchers!" comes that disembodied yell. At least they've been seen. And then it's double time. Ward's chest sends an occasional jolt of discomfort, but his lungs are giving him a few warnings of their own.

It's tough going. They must be up around Lac Blanc. Kavanagh stumbles ahead but recovers. There's a ditch or something. Kavanagh is an absolute goat and Ward does his best to keep up. It occurs to him that he is now a porter, that he is often exceeding his regulation sixty-five pounds, but in his mind—is he ill?—he hears Casement's voice telling him to bear up, to carry this weight, and he thinks of that chopped-up elephant carcass of so long ago and how it dripped blood down the porters' heads and shoulders. He's going to have to tell Kavanagh to slow down, but if he can just make it the next 200 meters to the station, that will at least give him time to breathe as they're loading the stretchers. And then he sets his foot on a rock, and the rock slides, and he's down. There's a searing pain in his knee and he's knocked his head. He's probably bleeding. He struggles to get up, and there's Kavanagh at his side, helping him, but he can't hold his weight. He screams as he tests the leg.

"Wait here," says Kavanagh. And he's gone. Ward hunkers down in the ditch, cowering behind the stretchers. Could he die here? He really doesn't want to. The last kindness drains away from the landscape in a wash of blue watercolor.

Herbert is back at Rolleboise with the war raging inside his head. He has been back for two months. The doctors are still in disagreement as to how to handle the torn ligament in his knee. Surgery? No surgery? But with the heart they are in agreement. General sentiment seems to be that Herbert has shortened his life span with his stint in the Vosges, but to look at him one would think that rather than taking that hit at the end of his life, he is meting out this death sentence over each of his hours, a sort of tax on his vitality. At least she knows where he is—sitting on the terrace watching the Seine that asserts its serenity as a sort of poor-taste joke on the present circumstance.

Charlie is stationed at Neuve Chapelle. The last time he had leave, he said little about the trenches. He's led patrols right up to the German wire but beyond that is tight-lipped about what goes on. Charlie struggles to sound cheerful, but as he's not inherited her sharp wit, he doesn't have the refuge of gallows humor and is most often grim. All he has is an encroaching silence and a parody of manhood. Sarita's begged him not to be a hero, tried to introduce possibilities to get him off the Front, for example, they could set up a farm somewhere and he could do that work. Maybe he could wave his arm at the Germans and get that shot in order to bring the rest home. He tolerates all her madness with a look of such extreme sympathy that she composes herself. And Herbie? Taking pictures, flying a plane, while better-armed Germans try to kill him.

She cannot stand the visitors at Rolleboise, all those lieutenants and majors with their collars strangling their dewlaps, men who have let their own sons fertilize the earth in Flanders and walk around draped in their pomposity as if this infanticide somehow enhances their own commitment to the cause. Oh, she is angry. She can barely rein it in to speak to her own husband. She should be grateful to have him home, but all her tolerance of him has turned to acid and when she looks him in the eye it is with such a ferocious coldness that he cannot hold her gaze. He understands. It's his fault, all of it. His fault, men like him, fathers who resented the youth of their sons and—so accustomed to spending energy keeping them aware of their inferiority when balanced against the strength of their elders—are now smugly resigned to watch them struck to corpses. She forces down the bread with some water. She has to eat. Charlie needs her, and Herbie. She has to keep asserting her forces, whatever they are, to bring them back, to give some strong pull to keep them alive.

Herbert is writing another book, a ridiculous thing with little water-colors of noble soldiers and sketches of stoic farm folk. It is a celebration of the bravery of Mr. Poilu, the term given to the French soldier, who is always cheerful, always brave, and just the thing that the English can see fighting for, and maybe the Americans. At this point, it all hinges on America. The war needs to end now and so she tolerates this book that Harmsworth will publicize. It will be the occasion for Ward's lecture tour in the United States.

This is Harmsworth's war. He makes it whatever he wants it to be, sinks some people, raises others up, brings the trenches into the living rooms of London, although his trenches are characterized by cheery, brave men whose patriotic singing is only halted to let off a round of bullets. Or when shot dead. If Harmsworth could figure out a way to win the war and still have it, he would. No one can live without a newspaper now and the growing roster of the dead is just more saleable ink.

Herbert sits in the sunshine, turning his head to one side and the other, spinning the anecdotes together into a pithy little tale. There are the nuns who pick flowers in the moonlight to present to the injured men. There is Herbert himself cooking a rustic sausage meal in a helmet. Who wouldn't want to join this cloying war? And she would make him eat it, eat the book, and fantasizes about tearing each page and stuffing it into his mouth, choking him, but she too wants America in the war and she has no book. She is a woman and has nothing to give, except her boys. All she has left is her rage.

The phone is ringing. Beatrice will answer, and although Sarita is sitting in the drawing room right by the hallway, Beatrice will walk the extra distance to fetch Herbert as Sarita is better to be avoided. She hears Beatrice's polite *Oui, oui, Monsieur* and then her walking to the end of the hall, the opening of the door, her footsteps muted by distance as she reaches Herbert. There's her high-pitched mumble, followed by his low growl. There's the screech of chair legs as he pulls himself to standing and his new, signature limp as he goes to the telephone. And now her heart is pounding. Is it her heart? It rather feels that her entire torso is being inflated in rapid, short bursts like an expiring fish. She hopes that Herbert will take the call quickly, and then return to his chair and his view and his book. Or if he comes to find her, it will be a matter of setting the table for guests, or maybe even a room for an overnight visitor. She breathes consciously as Herbert's limp comes closer. She looks up to see him at the door, his face pale. Was his face pale before? They look at each other, not saying a word. She feels her lower lip quiver, as if she'll start crying, but she stills it and pulls her spine straight.

"That is not an attractive expression," she says.

"Sarita."

Is this when she says, *Yes, that's my name*? Is he waiting for her to make the news easier for him to deliver? He approaches in a tentative step, but she stops him with a raised hand. "Anything you need to say, you can say from there."

Herbert looks around, lost, again lost. He is desperate and she feels her resolve shattering.

"Out with it."

"Herbie's been shot down."

"That's not possible." She does not know where this statement comes from. It just leaps out as if it's been waiting in the wings these long weeks.

"He could still be alive. No one is sure. One person was seen crawling from the plane."

"Who was that person?"

"It was impossible to tell."

"Was it a big person or a small person?"

"There is no news."

Sarita doesn't know how to process this information. She doesn't. She can't believe it and feels that Herbert has delivered a line handed to him as an actor in a play. "Thank you for letting me know."

"Sarita," he says again.

"What can you possibly have to say to me?" she manages. "Why are you standing there? I heard it."

He makes another step to her.

"Leave me alone." She raises her face to him, finally, and he has tears, but she has none. "I beg of you, Herbert, if you have any ounce of consideration for me, that you leave me alone, just for a while. Please."

She lives like this for weeks, in and out of reality, eating bread, sometimes a little fish or broth. Charlie writes almost daily from the Front, telling her not to lose hope. Pilots are pulled from the aircraft by the Germans and treated well, almost as heroes, as there is a great deal of respect among those who fly. If Herbie were dead, they would all know by now. She can hear that Charlie is appealing to his good public school training and that the regulation hope—a restrained thing that may or may not have a basis in reality, but is, beyond doubt, the correct response to this situation—has been set in motion. She and Charlie bat this thing back and forth in their letters as if they are playing badminton, because that's all they can do. Herbert applies himself with telephone calls, pulling strings. The higher-ups find his bravery and courage appealing. How many of these men lifting phones have carried stretchers? Herbert is a person that powerful people like to help, but there is nothing they can do.

At dinner Herbert eats his pigeon with carefully restrained enthusiasm. He can feel her eyes watching him. Herbert would ask what she thinks he's done, but he would hate to learn, so he is a coward in this respect. He prefers the cold silence. He rests his fork on the side of the plate and, looking across the table, says, "Herbie is my son too. I took him to see that flight at Bagatelle Field. I held his hand. He had a runny nose."

"No anecdotes, Herbert," she says, the gall rising. "I cannot bear it."

Another phone call. She thinks of Charlie, but that would be a telegram, and she calms herself. Herbert tends to the call and she realizes that she has her hands covering her ears, something she has taken to doing each time the phone rings. Each time she thinks of Herbie, she sees him standing in the pear orchard with his butterfly net, his nose peeling from exposure to the sun, his eyes both alert and dreamy, trying to tease some joke out of the current circumstance. He is such an angel that she has taken to worrying that his image is actually a visitation. And there is Herbert at the door.

"Sarita," says Herbert, "Herbie is alive. There is a note. A German pilot dropped it just yesterday. They are sending it to us."

Sarita rises from her chair. She stands beside Herbert, tentatively tapping his shoulder, but warding him away at the same time, and tears come, choking sobs. Herbie is alive.

Paris is gloomy, which suits Ward's mood. A sleeting rain, hunched pedestrians slinking along the sidewalk, a dog raising its leg cheerlessly to the ornamental myrtle. But Cricket is here, will be for the next few days, and that does help to make things tolerable. She's got her coffee and some fashion magazine that must be two years old. The house in Paris accumulates things like that—old magazines, ill-fitting jackets, fancy razors that the children give you for your birthday when you don't really need them. Roddie has spent the holiday with his grandfather in America. They have all been waiting for him to mature out of his nerves, but if anything he seems to be worse. The strain of the war and his mother's anxiety are no doubt compounding this. He wishes Sarita could rally for her youngest son. Although Roddie was actually quite pleased with the trip to America as he has become enamored of American musical theatre. Fine. But Ward doesn't even know what American musical theatre is, nor do any of the family. It could be very good.

Sarita has taken to waking at four in the morning and applying herself to the accounting, although what exactly she's accomplishing, who can know? She has had all the shelves taken out of the downstairs linen closet and moved in a desk. In this tiny, windowless room she retreats for hours at a time. Her explanation? *I need this.* He suspects she's avoiding him. Ward has again appealed to his doctors to see if they won't try surgery on his knee, and they say an operation would be to no purpose. What he needs is a new heart. He receives occasional missives from the center of operations in Lac Blanc asking if he's well, if he's able to return to the Vosges, and that even if he can no longer bear stretchers, there is a lot for a man like him to do. The doctors say no. A man like him—old, weak-hearted—can accomplish nothing but provision yet another of the injured, or worse, a corpse, and does that help anyone?

"Father," says Cricket, "so where is it?"

"Where's what?"

"The Croix du Guerre."

"That? It's in my desk drawer."

"What's it doing in there? Shouldn't it be displayed or something like that?"

"I could do, but it might set your mother off."

"Set her off?" Cricket takes that new expression: determination. It's a recent adult thing for her and he suspects Cricket's determination is very effective. "I'll give her another half hour, and then she's got to get out of the closet." Cricket spins her coffee cup, which clatters in the saucer. "You know, I came here to check up on you, because of your injury, but Sarita's the one who's falling to pieces." That's another development of his daughter's: referring to her mother by her first name.

"I don't know if that's accurate. I think she's holding herself together and it's taking all her strength to do it."

"When does Charlie have leave?"

"Not for another week."

Cricket heaves a sigh. "And Herbie is in a prison camp. I hope he doesn't do anything stupid."

"Like what? Isn't that the situation in prison camps? You can't do anything?"

"Herbie will find something. He doesn't calculate risk the way the rest of us do. He just doesn't care. That's why he can fly a plane, and why he was always in trouble at school."

Ward sees Sarita stirring at the end of the hallway, and he raises a finger to his lips to silence Cricket. His daughter looks at him and shakes her head pointedly.

"Mama, come here. I want to talk about Herbie."

Ward looks at his daughter and again cautions her, but she meets him with clearly enacted disdain.

Sarita comes and sits beside her daughter, folding her hands in her lap. "There's no news, not since the postcard that I showed you, the one where he writes about forgetting his birthday."

"You don't think he's going to do anything stupid, do you?"

Sarita processes this and, to Ward's surprise, relaxes her expression. "Of course he's going to do something stupid," says Sarita. "He's Herbie. Let's just hope the Germans have a sense of humor."

Cricket is staying through Ward's birthday, which is tomorrow, and leaving on the twelfth. And he's not exactly sure what she's doing with her mother, but Sarita is responding. She ate a little more at dinner where the conversation was all about Charlie's most recent letter, so heavily censored that the effect was, "Dear Mother and Father, XXX, yesterday, XXX, tomorrow, XXX, Love, Charlie. Cricket's tack is, rather than avoiding the topic of Charlie and Herbie, to talk about them nonstop. Ward wonders if some of this is her desire not to speak about her marriage as she's left the husband and children—the baby is not even a year old—in London and is in no hurry to get back. It's true that she is needed here in Paris, but Ward wonders what her husband has to say about it. Cricket seems content to lie on her old bed in her old room as if she's still a girl of twelve. She's very disparaging of Dimples and her happy marriage and her children, Mervyn and Allan, whom Dimples is devoted to. "God, it's Mervyn and Allan everything. Mervyn and Allan had a poor night of sleep. Mervyn and Allan prefer Scottish rolled oats to the English. Mervyn and Allan sneeze around horses. Mervyn and Allan. Mervyn and Allan," she'd said. "They sound like a magician duo, or some carbolic compound for cleaning ovens."

And now Cricket is up in her room, writing a letter, although he doubts it is to Colville Barclay and this concerns him. Her legion of suitors has probably not given up, despite her marriage, and he wonders with whom she's corresponding. But he doesn't want to know, and he's worried that if he asks, she might actually tell him.

He and Sarita are sitting at the fire. She has a book in her hands and the page turns, but much more slowly than in the past. He is still working on his manuscript and has the same problem with the narrative as he always did: There is an attractive gathering of little stories, but he's not sure if they add up to anything, and in this episodic, erratic way, don't really create the emotional payoff that he wants. He was never much of one for reading novels and suspects that this has compromised his ability to create a narrative arc out of so much disparate, anecdotal material. He is editing the piece about the chicken who nested in No-Man's-Land, amid the barbed wire, and how protective of this bird they all were, how the soldiers themselves saw this chicken sitting on her eggs between the lines as somehow an expression of the resilience of the French. Which sort of makes sense, but why is a chicken that has chosen to nest in the most idiotic of locales a symbol of *élan*? Why? And yes, he can see why people would care about a chicken when their comrades are dying all around—people do this all the time—but how can he make this a thing to admire?

There's the bell.

Ward checks his watch. It's almost midnight. He hesitates. The servants are all asleep so he'll have to get the door himself.

There's the bell again.

Sarita closes her book and looks at him. Ward rises from the table. Sarita rests the book beside her on the couch and gets up. "Sarita, stay here." She shakes her head and follows him into the hall. He makes his way to the door. He opens the door. Standing on the step is the uniformed boy. He is looking out at the street but turns to look at Ward, his face composed.

"Monsieur," he says. He hands him a telegram. Ward thanks him, somehow, and shuts the door against him. He looks at the envelope. He would like to put it down and return to his editing, but that is not the correct thing to do. He tears the envelope open. Sarita's hand rests lightly on his elbow. He hears footsteps down the hall and there is Cricket in her bare feet and nightgown.

"What is it?" she says.

Herbert's eyes scan over the telegram. His eyes read it again. "It's Charlie." Cricket's hands fly up to her mouth and he begins to read out loud. "It is my painful duty to inform you that a report this day has been received from the War Office notifying the death of Lieutenant Charles Sanford Ward, Royal Warwickshire Regiment, which occurred while on patrol on the tenth of January, 1915 and I am to express to you the sympathy and regret of the Army Council at your loss. The cause of death was killed in action. Any application you may wish to make regarding the late soldier's effects should be addressed to The Secretary, War Office—"

He stops reading.

"Oh my God," says Cricket, and runs to her mother, who has collapsed to her knees in an uncompromising silence.

XI

Banna Strand

April 1916

It is a burial at sea. However, Casement has always thought burial would offer peace, and this is an odd coffin packed with activity and actors. He would turn to face the wall, but the bunk does not accommodate this. His head is shoved up against a circuit box, the heels of his shoes rest against a steel plate covering a nest of wires. His knees project into the space before him and are routinely struck by the sailors passing through the cabin, although it's not a cabin, really, just a few yards marked off and two bunks, this one—longer than the other and at times occupied by the Quartermaster—and that across from him. Montieth is sitting there and would be looking into space, but there is no space, so he's focused on a patch of wall just above Casement's head. The walls are slick with condensation and drops of water spatter onto his face with fair frequency. The air is thick and unwholesome, heavy with heat.

Montieth takes a vial from his pocket and shakes it. You can hear the tablets rattle. He laughs, and then composes his face into grim resignation. He and Montieth have pills and a tube of curare, poison, with express instructions to use it in the event that they're captured, although right now survival seems of more importance than orchestrating death.

"You're awake?" says Montieth, nodding at Casement.

"I'm afraid I haven't been much company."

"Ah, there's been plenty of that." The sound of a man vomiting can be heard from beyond the curtain. Casement too would be vomiting, but he's done with that, emptied himself completely an hour or two ago. The scent lingers with that of urine and a reeking medley of sweat-soaked wool.

"So I asked the captain how he could manage to be in this tin can for so long, with all the smells and closeness, and I'm expecting some sort of condescending German speech about superior races and all that. So I say, 'Captain Weisbach, how do you do it?' And do you know what he says to me?"

"No," says Casement.

"Opium. They're all on opium." Montieth shakes his head, looks at the vial again.

"That's not opium, Bob."

"Ah, don't worry about me. I'm not one for that sort of thing, and we know fuck all anyway. I'm not sure what secrets they're worried about us giving up." Montieth may not be inclined to take his own life, but it's a suicide mission they're on, poison or not. At least they've managed to keep the Irish Brigade out of this, because to send them to Ireland now would surely be the equivalent of lining up all those men against the wall to be shot. Instead they are accompanied by Beverly, or whoever he is, because that's not his real name, who has been sent over from Ireland and is now speeding back to no good purpose.

Casement's not sure when he signed his own death warrant. The music of rattling pills accompanies this knowledge, but even if he dodges that, he's destined for the noose. He knows it. The night before, he had brought his personal papers to Countess Blucher and had broken down into a fit of weeping. He's just out of the hospital, so it was predictable, although perhaps somewhat of a surprise to her ladyship. The Countess can't really be trusted but there is no one else, and the fact that she knows Ward—or has at least met him—provided connection to some kinder time. It is its own particular torture not to be able to comfort Ward for the death of his son, not to be able to grieve this child in a public way. He carries the loss of Charlie in silence. He harbors hope that there's been some mistake made in the *Telegraph*, which is where he'd read the news, looking for it as he lay in his hospital bed, finding it, and then trying not to believe. He tries to articulate the stuff of Sarita's grief, of Ward's grief, and of his own. He keeps from thinking over what he knows must be the case—that his friendship with Ward has bled out on the fields of Flanders along with all things good and youthful and true.

He has held his grief in silence, buried it under papers and planning, shot-up ideals, and doctor's reports. He has struggled into meetings and as he shouted, his voice cracked, he knew that he was speaking as a man on the edge of destruction, clinging to a dream to stop from slipping over. Negotiations on what was finally going to be shipped to Ireland, and how, had been fraught. And what was the point of fighting when it was clear the Germans wouldn't budge? What was the point in arguing over mode of transportation, number of weapons, quality, ammunition? The vast majority of the 100,000 men that Devoy wished to arm would go without rifles. That was clear. Everything else is mired in a fog of poor planning. In Ireland, people are waiting for the arms, prepared to rise up on Easter Monday. There is to be a rendezvous with a ship in Tralee Bay, but they only have 20,000 rifles and these are of a vintage that does not inspire confidence. Devoy had said something about rifles like this being good enough for Napoleon, but that was when the enemy wasn't wielding something far better. Such statements are easily made from one's armchair in New York.

The ship, the *Aud*, has a four-day window to meet with the escort off of Banna Strand. The U-boat will be reaching the coast of Ireland in the next couple of hours and then, Casement hopes, he can contact the leaders of the uprising—although who these men are, other than Plunkett, is not known to him—and convince them that they are better off waiting for naval support from Germany. Although, as he articulates the thought, he knows it represents a false hope. There is to be no German naval support. This is it for now and waiting—which is what he'd wanted before he fully understood—will just take the current situation and transport it neatly into the summer.

The Volunteers too are angling for a conflict. Whatever distractions the Germans are giving the English works well for their cause. But even should the arms land, and the men occupy Saint Stephen's Green and what else—Four Courts? Dublin Castle?—how long can they possibly hold before England crushes them? The civilian casualties will be high because occupying places like Saint Stephen's Green means ridding it of dog walkers and students and shopgirls with sandwiches and nodding drunks, not English soldiers.

He did have a glimmer of what was at stake when Plunkett was still around. Plunkett had his little document for the Irish Brigade and that was effective. And Pearse's address at the burial of O'Donovan Rossa—Casement had the souvenir booklet mailed by Nina—was a brilliant piece of writing. There, by the old Fenian's graveside, the identity of Ireland had suddenly made sense. You could see it emerge from the primordial gel and stand, fully formed, in your mind. One would have to be insensible not to join this God-ordained war against oppression. Apparently, what Ireland needed was some pretty words on a bit of paper and a body for gravity, and suddenly she was an intelligible nation. Suddenly, your blood was heated and you'd pick up a gun and head for the streets, feeling that anything less was cowardice and worse, a negation of self.

Casement has a curdling feeling in his gut that right now that one of these language teachers or poets or editors or painters or whomever else seems to be fueling the passion of this doomed uprising is coming up with some bit of paper, and, given time, will find the bodies to sign it in blood.

"You've gone all quiet again," says Montieth.

"Did you think you'd lost me?"

"I did just check you out of the hospital."

Casement nods. "I'm thinking of the Pearse speech." The last line has anchored itself in his memory. "'Enough to know that the valiant soldier of Ireland is dead; that the unconquered spirit is free.'"

"Ah yes, the noble dead." Montieth groans. "We all know that the Irish are willing to die for Ireland, but what's needed is some men who can manage to stay alive long enough to shoot a few of the English."

They are silent for some time. Montieth takes the pills out a few times and puts them back. He has a wife and daughters in America. He must be thinking about them because there's something regretful in his features, almost sentimental. "Are you a lucky man, Roddie?" asks Montieth.

It is a good question. Looking back on the matter of his life, it would seem that he has dodged a few disasters, although found himself mired in others. He has had friends and experience and fame, but also loneliness and despair. Here, on this U-boat, barreling towards the coast of Ireland, wasted and weak after those long, frustrating months in Germany, it's hard to feel lucky. Adler is lost to him, lost to everyone, vanished and leaving no trail. Who knows what will happen? There it is again, *happen*, as if the very presence of that word implies the existence of a creator, a *happener*, someone who may or may not be feeling kindly towards Casement. And if there is a God and he is the familiar one, he is not known for treating his loved ones gently. "Lucky?" says Casement. "Ask me that tomorrow."

Casement is not really asleep but not exactly conscious when he is roughly roused. It is close to two o'clock in the morning.

"What are we doing?" asks Casement.

"Weisbach wants us out of here. He's getting worried about running into a patrol."

Casement swings his legs around and sits up.

Beverly sticks his head around the curtain. "Got everything?"

What is there to get? Casement pats himself down in a perfunctory manner. He has a German code, although he's sure it isn't an important one. He has his poison, the pills, the tube of curare. He has a gun that he doesn't know how to operate.

"Let's go," says Montieth.

The U-boat has surfaced to a surging sea. A rowboat bucks in the waves. One of the nameless sailors holds the rope. The water roars and breaks around the submarine, sucking at the sides. Casement holds fast to the railing, feeling hollowed and weak. He will not be able to row, that he is sure of, and is even wondering if he will make it to shore in consciousness. The moon, skirted in cloud, watches on coldly. Montieth is the first to reach the boat, stumbling in like a drunk. He recovers quickly, gestures for people to hurry.

"You next," says Beverly to Casement. He's to be handed in like a child. Holding the railing, Casement takes cautious steps. The observation deck is slippery and narrow. The Germans watch, eager to finally be rid of him, as eager as he is to be back on Irish soil. He swings his leg over the edge, sees Montieth's burly hand extended, and he grabs for it, managing two quick steps before a sudden surge up-tilts the boat and knocks him from his feet. He folds himself into the bow of the boat.

"There's a blanket for you," says Montieth. Beverly is next, hopping in from the side. They start rowing for Tralee Bay, guided by the reach and dip of the Little Fenit light. The U-boat stays afloat just long enough to get its men back into its belly, and then it sinks beneath, as if Casement's imagination is what had called it to the surface.

Casement takes the blanket and pulls it around his shoulders. The boat rocks up and falls away. He'll have to hold fast not to fall out. Montieth is a skillful rower and throws himself into the troughs, angling across the waves. A wave breaks over the bow, soaking Casement, bringing him into a more articulate consciousness. There's a lot of water accumulating in the boat, and a shouting match—or desperate conversation—has sprung up between Beverly and Montieth. The great shattering of waves upon the Strand means they are drawing close. Montieth is dealing with the shore break, trying to keep the boat at the correct angle, but his hand is wrapped—when did he injure it?—and he's weak with the left oar. They swing around, no longer across the waves, and there's one last roll that takes the boat and holds it and flips it over. Into the drink he goes. There is Casement, sinking beneath the water. He reaches the ocean floor, its shifting surface of powdered stone, and hears the clash and clash of rocks raked along the margin as the waves beat and mold the shore of Ireland. And here he'll die, a fitting end, a drowning on the eve of the futile uprising, and his lungs are filling with water, and it is a rough falling off, not as gentle as sleep, but a persuasive, brutal love. And then there's a tug at his neck and he's pulled from the water, dragged with his face just in the air and the sea still smacking his cheeks.

"I've got him," says a voice, Montieth's.

"Is he alive?"

"Don't know. Jesus Fucking Christ."

He is rolled on his back on the rocky beach and Montieth begins to chaff his arms and legs. "Roddie, are you there?"

Casement begins to cough in streams of water. His nose is running. He is more liquid than solid.

"Well done, well done."

"We have to get going," says Beverly. "I'm sure they've seen us."

"Three men," says Montieth. "Smallest invasion on record."

"We have to move," says Beverly.

"What do you suggest we do with Sir Roger?"

"We'll hide him somewhere and get a car."

"And come back for him?" Montieth's pause seems to suggest that he's not in favor of the idea but can't think of a better one.

Then Beverly is on his left side and Montieth is on the right and they're dragging him along and the toes of his shoes are scuffing up the beach. He's seen legless drunks carried like this, and men after being beaten senseless. He's not sure which of these groups he belongs to, and also not sure that he justifies the creation of a third.

"I think it's a ring fort," says Beverly, in response to something. "It will keep him out of sight."

He's lying in the long grass. At a distance he can see an outline of beer bottles, maybe some empty cigarette packets. This must be a place where young people come for fun, out of sight of their elders. And this is where they will leave him, sheltered from the wind, cushioned by the grass.

"Roddie, don't go anywhere."

"He's not going anywhere," says Beverly.

"We'll back as soon as we can. Don't make any noise."

"He's not going to make any noise," says Beverly.

"Shut your gob, Beverly. What is wrong with you? It's Roger Casement, for fuck's sake."

And that's the last he hears before he drops into sleep. He has made it home. He has made it to Ireland. And if he never wakes he will be all right, for his head is cradled gently and the grass, stirred by the night air, is caressing his cheek, and there is the harsh whispering of waves on the Strand and the raking of rock against rock at the brink of a cold sea and the rattle of some night bird's wings. He is all right. He is better than that. He is home.

XII

Paris

April 1916

After Charlie's death, Sarita had stayed in bed for two weeks and then one morning, arbitrarily, had appeared at breakfast. She wasn't wearing black. Ward had watched her butter the toast. She gave it a look, as if it wasn't friendly, before taking a bite.

"I couldn't stay in bed any longer," she said in response, although he hadn't asked her anything.

In his mind he heard *stiff upper lip* and *best to soldier on*, but had nothing of his own to give. Sarita looked at him with mild disappointment, as if understanding the corners of his silence.

"You know I thought if Charlie died, it would kill me. And here I am, breathing, eating."

"That's good, Sarita."

"It is the most depressing thing I've ever learned. No matter what this life does to me, I will keep going. Just like that. I'll survive anything."

"I count on your strength."

Sarita had shrugged, indifferent to Ward's needs. "Herbie's still out there." She'd been suddenly disdainful of the toast. "We can't just sit here in Paris."

"You have something in mind?"

"I'm going with you to America." Ward had been unaware that he himself was undertaking the trip. "I'm not worrying about Charlie anymore and I have to think of Herbie."

So they had gone to America. There, Sarita had brought out the black and had spoken so passionately about the man who had been Charlie, about his accomplishments and personality, of how he had not died in vain and that America, as a moral nation in support of all that was good, had to join the war. She would bring tears to Ward's eyes and at these times he would forget that Charlie was his son, that he wasn't just tapping into the gentle feeling of an alien grief that struck through eloquence.

He had done his thing, had spoken of the plucky French who whistled in the cold mountains, sniped at, starved, low on ammunition and high on spirit. He talked of his own injuries, of how he had returned to his ambulance service in the Vosges, but thought he could do more good in America, here with the support of friends. He had lectured about the chicken and her nest in No-Man's-Land. In London, he'd attended benefits arranged by Harmsworth, and felt the full flush of activity. But any hopes he'd held of life returning to normal have died. Even now, sitting in his Paris drawing room with the newspaper, he knows that he's performing his role in a darker world and the food has lost its flavor, the wine its capacity to bring levity. He is all motion and motion without substance. He reads through the headlines, the battles, the lists of dead.

Uprising in Ireland. Yes. There it is. The traitors to England and there it is. He reads about Casement's arrest and they are just words, more print, more despairing fact. Captured in Kerry trying to land arms for the Germans, transported to the Tower of London, trial scheduled, execution probable. He folds the paper roughly, crumples it.

"Herbert?" asks Sarita.

"Well, they've got him. And he'll be hanged."

Sarita blinks a few times but keeps her true thoughts to herself, searching for some words that will not betray her feelings. "Will they not shoot him, like Pearse and Plunkett and the others?"

"Traitors are hanged." Ward doesn't know what this feeling is. It is an out-of-body sensation. "There will be a trial. He has his supporters."

"He could be pardoned."

"They should hang him."

Sarita has her hand covering her mouth.

Ward says, "We'll have to change Roddie's name."

She watches Ward, her face sympathetic and tentative.

Ward says, "He can be Rodney Sanford Ward."

Sarita nods and gets up quickly, bumping the small table, upsetting her teacup. She walks quickly to the window and presents him with her back. He thinks she's crying but is incapable of getting up to see, or even asking. "Casement's death will solve nothing, Herbert."

"Sarita, there is such a thing—"

"It's just another body."

A week passes in a distraction of conflicting emotion, but what must be done is at least clear. Ward will have to list the change of Roddie's name in the papers. That much he can do, although it's impossible to distance himself from the evidence of his long friendship with Casement. The letters from Casement's friends have already started to arrive, letters assuming that Ward will come to his aid. Alice Green is raising money for Casement's defense and has asked how much Ward would like to contribute. He hides this correspondence from Sarita, ushering it quickly from his desktop to the fire.

The telephone is ringing in the hallway. There is Beatrice at the door. "Captain Nelson would like to speak with you," she says in her country French.

Who is this Captain Nelson? "Tell him it is not a good time and that I will ring him back."

"He says it is urgent."

Sarita is suddenly alert. "I'll take it." She follows Beatrice into the hallway. He hears her voice, a bright, "Oh my God. Yes, yes of course. We will be there as soon as we can. Yes. Allow me to get my husband, who I'm sure will wish to speak to you, given the circumstances."

Sarita presents herself in the doorway. She looks stunned.

"Sarita," he says. "What is it?"

"It's Herbie." She shakes her head in disbelief and there is something wild in her demeanor. "He's here."

"Here?"

"He's in Paris."

The chauffeur takes the major roads, the familiar roads. Captain Nelson had not offered much information. Herbie and one other have walked out of Germany, sneaking across the Swiss border. The boy is in good health, although extremely fatigued. His appearance might startle, as he's very thin.

Ward holds Sarita's cold hand. They are both silent, as if reacting to some good news might inadvertently scare it off. Captain Nelson had said that Herbie has been in questioning since his delivery to Paris. Ward can sense the disbelief of the authorities that such a slight soldier could make it all the way across enemy lines, especially as he is the first to do it. They are concerned that Herbie is a spy, which is ridiculous, but the escape is unbelievable.

The war office has high ceilings, marble floors, a sense of permanence, although just months ago it was a bank. Sarita is looking at the desks, the office doors, spinning around as if making the wrong choice will cause Herbie to vanish. The officer running the reception makes a quick call and rings off. "Sergeant Peal will take you up," he says.

Ward follows Sarita following Sergeant Peal up the stairs. She's looking around his broad shoulders, as if he's moving too slowly. They stop at an office and Sergeant Peal raps three strong times. A voice calls out, *Enter*. And Peal opens the door.

There is Captain Nelson standing behind his desk. There, standing by the window in an ill-fitting jacket and rough trousers, his hair in disarray, looking like he's twelve years old, is Herbie.

There's a moment where no one moves. Herbie says, "Hello."

Sarita shouts something that is neither a name nor a word and then she's on the boy, holding him tightly, her arms wrapped around his shoulders, pinning his arms to his sides. There's a ferocious weeping coming out of her and Captain Nelson seems shocked at the violence of her emotion. She has her face buried into Herbie's chest. Her words are sorting themselves and she seems to be saying *You're back, You're back*, over and over, but it's muffled through Herbie's shirt and the crying. Herbie looks over at Ward with a clumsy smile and says, "Hello, Father."

Ward wakes into the moment. He salutes Captain Nelson, who salutes back. "Lieutenant Ward," says Nelson.

And Ward says something, but who can know? He wants to go home.

". . . and I'm sure that you understand that we still haven't received a satisfactory explanation as to how Lieutenant Ward managed to circumvent a series of enemy patrols—"

"Captain Nelson, I am not going home without my son. I don't have a choice. Perhaps you can think of a way of extricating him from his mother, but I can't. And despite his proven skills at escape, neither can Lieutenant Ward."

"We've lost Charlie," says Herbie, an attempt at a whisper, but Sarita's making so much noise it's audible to all, "Charlie is dead."

Sarita manages some calm. She raises her eyes to meet Herbie's. "I know," she says. "I know."

Sarita insists on running the bath herself. She checks the temperature, and it's really hot, hotter than most people would tolerate but just how Herbie likes it. She can hear Herbie chatting with his father, his laughter in the hallway, and it sets her off crying again. She hears Herbie say, *Will you tuck me in tonight, Father?* They must be making fun of her.

He enters the bathroom with a lit cigarette and takes a powerful drag, burning it down to his knuckles.

"The water's hot," says Sarita.

"Fantastic," says Herbie

"Is there something in particular you want for dinner? And don't ask for oysters."

Herbie begins to undress. "Villiers must have already started dinner." He undoes the first button but can pull the shirt over his head after that and tosses it on the chair. "I'm actually missing vegetables." His ribs stand out. His spine is knobbed up the center of his back.

"She's making stew, mutton, with the white wine. I can have her put in extra carrots."

"Sounds unbelievably good."

"All right." Sarita heads for the door.

"Don't go. Why don't you stay?" He's now naked and he slides into the tub. "You can light me a cigarette. And I know you know how because Charlie told me you smoke."

"In that case," says Sarita, "I'll have one with you." She pushes Herbie's clothes onto the floor and takes the seat. She reaches to the cabinet across the sink where there are some matches and a packet of cigarettes—Philip Morris's Bond Street—that she keeps there because, on occasion, she will have one while lying in the tub. She knocks the soap into the sink as the soap dish will serve as an ashtray. Herbie responds to her casual arranging with an approving laugh of disbelief.

"You have to tell me," she says, handing him a lit cigarette, "how you made it out of Germany alive."

"I'm going to have the same problem with you that I did with Nelson, because I'm really not sure how I did. It makes it hard to explain."

"Just tell me what happened." She lights her own cigarette and takes a contemplative puff.

"They were transferring all the Russian and English officers. We had managed to get some civilian clothes from the French orderlies. There was a yellow stripe down the back of the jacket and we just removed it. And there was some sort of map, more of a sketch made from memory, which showed the area. The train was headed from Vohrsbach to Heidelberg, bringing us close to the Swiss border. They loaded us into three carriages with guards on either end."

"What was the plan?"

"Well, there wasn't one. There were four of us with civilian clothes that we were wearing under our great coats, and we'd agreed to go in pairs. We decided to wait for a good moment and then escape. The train pulled in to some small town and the Russians struck up a conversation with the guards. They spoke some German, which was good. And while the guards were distracted, the four of us went to the middle car and climbed out. The window got stuck halfway, so it was a bit of a squeeze. I was with Champion and we watched the two other men go first. I don't know what happened to them. But Champion and I went out the window and sort of began walking off in the other direction. Since I broke my leg in the crash, I have a limp, so that explained why I was out of uniform. Champion tried to look bow-legged."

"That worked?"

"It must have. Champion is South African, so he was mumbling at me in Afrikaans, and I was *javohling* back at him and trying to look German. We wanted to run but knew we couldn't. I kept thinking I was going to get shot. But neither of us was. And we somehow walked into Switzerland."

"How long did it take you?"

"Days. We didn't have much food. We spent a night in a German guard-house, which was a risk, but it was cold. And then a Swiss border guard outside of Bergen saw us and brought us in. We were about to wander back into Germany."

They hold a benevolent, sweet silence. Sarita says, "Joyce Nicholson is very happy to know that you've escaped."

"Is she?"

Herbie sits still in the tub. He reaches over to Sarita and puts out his cigarette in the soap dish that she has rested on her knee. "I miss Charlie," he says.

466

"I do too."

"You know they're not going to send me back. They say I'm ruined by proximity to the Germans, that POWs make bad killers because they know the enemy."

"Really?"

"They're right. I don't want to shoot any Germans. I'm to be sent to Northolt as a flight instructor. And I picked up some Russian in the camp, so I'll be teaching Russians how to fly."

Herbie had asked after Casement at dinner. What followed was an awkward silence. No doubt Sarita will fill him in on what has happened during his time in a German camp. And the two will likely indulge in maudlin sympathies.

Ward will not grieve for Casement. He will not share with him that decent feeling that he has assigned to his eldest son. Because of this, he has no line of thought, but just the knowledge that his friend is no longer his friend, that this man who was once all things noble and admirable to him is in a cell somewhere awaiting judgment. Ward knows what to say, he has his lines. Hang him. He is a traitor. He is a disgrace. He rolls these out without feeling, envying Sarita her surreptitious perusal of the newspapers, her sadness. But he is stuck, like a car spinning its wheels in a rut. People will ask him his opinion. What happened to the great man, the great friend, who was not only a brother to Ward but also an embodiment of the joyful, youthful past?

He will probably come up with something about Casement's obvious mental illness, not to solicit forgiveness, because Ward knows Casement too well to think that he would not rise above his frailty to follow a noble idea—that he thought that terrorizing the English was what he had to do, what he believed in, even as Ward's sons were in the line of fire. It is as if Casement had stood on the field in Flanders and held that rifle, aimed it at Charlie's head, and pulled the trigger. Casement had made that assessment. He had made that choice. And there is the old conversation in his mind, that fragile psychic bond that Ward has always felt with Casement, as if he can hear him on some remote wavelength sending him messages, his thoughts lifting from the prison cell and crossing the Channel, reaching Ward, saying *forgive me, forgive me*, over and over, but Ward cannot. Casement is a traitor, and if not to England, than to his brother, this brother, who loved him more than anyone.

Ward can hear Sarita chatting in the hallway with Villiers. Of course the likelihood of oysters is remote, but if they are available, take all and hope they're fresh, spare no expense. And Cricket will be arriving in the afternoon, on the first boat to France after learning of Herbie's arrival. The sheets on her bed are clean but should be changed regardless because they might be dusty. Herbie will be back in England soon enough, so Sarita has managed to put off Sanford and Roddie for the moment.

Despite Herbie's upbeat demeanor, he's still in fragile health. He's smoking over a pack a day, but maybe it's too early to suggest he cut back. Dimples says she's put a pound cake in the mail, which will make Herbie happy, as butter and flour are hard to come by. So all are accounted for, except for Charlie. Charlie, who is buried in Flanders, along with others, in an unmarked grave. Charlie, whose spirit should not be at rest, but who has ceased to exist so completely that even the memories are beginning to seem stiff, as if Charlie is a mere paper cutout of who the boy was. Better the screaming spirit begging for his bones to be brought home, beating at the window, than this impossible stillness: the doorbell that does not ring, the clothes still in the closet, the boxing gloves quiet on the peg, this one-sided conversation with his boy Charlie that will continue to the end of Ward's days.

Herbie is still asleep at noon. Ward goes in to wake him, but Herbie isn't in his bed. He's chosen to sleep in Charlie's and for a moment, Ward's heart leaps because he thinks his elder son too has found his way home.

XIII
London

June 1916

This is what he knows. He knows that the *Aud* failed to rendezvous with the Volunteers and, scuttled, is now in a long sleep on the ocean floor along with her cargo. He knows that he was picked up by the constabulary as he dreamed in the long grass of McKenna's Fort and was taken quickly to London. That the uprising went on without weapons, without him, and all the major players were starved out or hunted down. That these people, for the most part, are dead. Plunkett, executed by the English rather than his lungs, married in Kilmainham just hours before facing the firing squad. Pearse, shot dead against the prison wall, although the Proclamation still lives. James Connolly, Seán MacDermott, John MacBride, all dead—executed without trial. Should he go on?

Casement has been questioned and then placed back in his cell, then questioned again. How could he have learned anything since his last interview, when his only company has been mice, his only communication with a guard who kept him up-to-date on the fate of the uprising in harsh, uninflected whispers? Was this out of sympathy or in order to twist the knife?

469

Casement does not know. When asked if he supported the uprising, he had responded honestly. No. He did not support it. Then how does he explain his presence in Ireland? He doesn't. He can see all the individual events, but when he puts them together, they make an unviable whole. He doesn't know how he got into this cell. He knows he will never be free.

Casement has tried to control his destiny. While held at the Tower, the poison still in his pocket as they had not seen fit to give him a change of clothes, he had managed to cut his thumb and rub in the curare, which ought to have ended his life. But he was caught at it and saved to this greater purpose. In poor health for years, how is it that now life persists?

Duffy, who is his lead council, shuffles through the papers.

"Have you been completely honest with me?"

"What are we talking about?"

"All right," says Duffy. He writes something at the top of a sheet of paper, then leans back in his chair, swinging one leg over the other. He bites his lower lip and the way he does it lets Casement know that he's hitting unpleasant material. "Adler Christensen. Can we talk about him?"

"He was my manservant in Germany."

"Casement, I'm your council. You need to tell me everything."

Casement would tell him, but he's still figuring it out. Will he tell him that Adler Christensen broke his heart? "What would you like to know?"

"All right. I have testimonies here from hotel staff in Christiania: 'The entire time Christensen was checked in at the hotel, his bed was never slept in. He always spent the night in Mister Landy's room.'" Duffy switches the papers around, squinting at the print. "'I opened the door to Mister Landy's room and found the two men half-naked on the bed in a suggestive position.'"

Casement feels a cold wash of panic. He's dizzy and is sure he looks ill. "Doesn't say which half was naked."

"Casement, is that a joke?" Duffy stacks his papers and lets out an almost passionate sigh. "Look, I am your solicitor. I represent you and I will do that to the best of my ability. I worry about you because you're in fragile health, but I have to tell you that this Christensen has made numerous presentations to the authorities that your relationship was not of a whole-some nature. And the first of these dates back to October of 1914. It's in a statement to a Mister Findlay"—he searches around his notes—"who was with the Foreign Office, that's the English Foreign Office, in Christiania."

"Findlay cannot be trusted," says Casement.

"That may well be the case," says Duffy, "but neither can your friend Christensen."

Casement takes a moment to think things through, meditating on the painted tabletop where some other poor soul, in an equally unenviable position, has scratched *FUK* into its surface.

"Casement, the police are going through some boxes of yours that were stored at the apartment on Ebury Street. I want you to think carefully. Are they going find anything in there?"

The pictures for Ward.

The diaries.

Casement states with grave reserve, "I have kept a diary."

"Lots of people keep diaries. What's the nature of the information con-tained therein?"

"Mostly accounting."

"Look, I'll say it because you don't want to and we don't have time. I'm under the impression that you are a homosexual and the only reason you're mentioning the diaries is that you must have recorded some of your actions in there. I don't care who you choose for sexual relations. As long as it's not me, I'm fine with it. All right? But if I am going to do my job as your solicitor, I need you to be more direct in stating your past actions, if only to get to a place where I know who my client is and what we're facing."

"It would seem you understand the nature of some of what is contained in the diaries." Casement sits up straight. The world is suddenly strange. "Will this come up at trial?"

"To be honest, I'm not sure." Duffy pushes the papers around the table-top. He's perspiring, sweat beading at his temples, although Casement feels cold. "The current sentiment seems to suggest that you are to be made an example of as a traitor. The charge is likely to be High Treason. Certain people of influence, Arthur Conan Doyle, for example, are hoping for an insanity plea. You were hospitalized several times in Germany for mental instability and homosexuality will help in this characterization. It would seem that at the moment, the authorities are committed to presenting you as an organizer, a man of reason, a man in full control of his actions. But there is already outrage at the executions of the other organizers, Pearse and Plunkett, who easily fill the role of martyrs to the cause of Irish Independence. Evidence that attests to your degeneracy becomes useful in that, should you find yourself cast as a martyr, this will serve to discredit you."

Should he find himself cast as a martyr. He is as good as dead.

"There is a packet of things in the Ebury Street rooms that I have requested be sent to Herbert Ward on my death. Contained in that packet is a series of photographs that I purchased in Italy that I thought he would find inspiring, as he is an artist. I need the pictures to be destroyed. I would not want him to misunderstand the gift."

Duffy is frustrated by this request. That much is clear. "Is this the Herbert Ward that has refused all contact with you?"

"He is my oldest friend."

"That may be, but he has declared himself hostile and I don't see the importance of a gift of pictures—"

"There is nothing more important. And as a man of few options, I would appreciate you following through in this matter, which might not be vital to my defense but is of unimaginable importance to me."

"Casement, can we just—"

"I beg you to do this. Consider it one of my final requests."

The trial proceeds.

Casement is charged with High Treason, as he has acted on behalf of Germany during a time of war.

A knight of the realm has not suffered such an accusation in several hundred years. And what is his defense? That he was not acting on behalf of Germany but of Ireland and—ostensibly—England is not at war with Ireland. There are several other pertinent points. He was against the uprising, tried to call it off, is on record for this, so to accuse him of being an instigator in this act is incorrect. But the prosecutor's closing statement makes the opinion of the King—and therefore the hangman—clear. Any action undertaken that strengthens an enemy in a time of war qualifies the perpetrator as having committed an act of High Treason. Whether or not the uprising was successful and that Casement saw it as doomed is irrelevant. And there is the matter of the Irish Brigade. Evidence is presented stating that rations had been withheld from captured Irish troops to entice them into serving the Kaiser and that Casement had been paid to see it through. His life is the subject of legal banter—some abstract thing, a palimpsest—as if Casement the man is not bound to it. He has responded to the accusations with an articulate statement written with clarity and passion.

There's his bit of paper.

He is dead and, as a true Irishman, has the document to bind to the body. He is not going to fail his people in the one moment when the world can be made aware of what it is to be Irish. He has asked to be tried before an Irish court, which is rhetoric, just a taste of a thought that ought to be a practice. Why is it noble to lay down one's life for England, with its history of harm and oppression, yet not noble to lay down one's life for Ireland, who never harmed anyone?

Perhaps it will be noble to sacrifice himself but he will not see the fruit of it.

He has grown used to the parade of people in this plain room, the seat that presents a roster of possibility in a place where none exists. Alice Green, who, absurdly, tells him to take care of himself. Canon Ring and Father Carey, whose advising timbre instructs that caring for one's self is, at best, a sentimental occupation.

Gee takes the seat in her gray dress, her hair lopsided and eyes reddened, hopeful and despairing, swinging between each with mounting hysteria. There is a bare bulb on a wire. There is the whitewash of the wall flaking. There is a cough down the hall, the tread of official shoes, a cough again. A warm August sun paints the window yellow.

This is his last visit.

Petitions have been circulated. Powerful people, fashionable people, have written on his behalf. Powerful people, fashionable people, have derided him. His lawyer had listed off a few writers and artists who supported him, Lytton Strachey, Duncan Grant, others of that circle, and made the wry observation that they were freaks and weirdos, but at least they were on his side. Perhaps this was an attempt at humor, but with Duffy's dry delivery, who could know? Writers and artists have influence on influential people, but Casement is already feeling the itch of the noose and finds these discussions of a decidedly academic nature. If Ottoline Morrell were to circulate a petition on behalf of a knight accused of treason, for example, Sir Roger Casement, and if it were signed by a healthy contingent of the powerful and interesting, would it suffice to warrant an appeal?

Apparently the answer is no.

He feels ill as he watches Gee's frenetic gesturing, listens to the patter of names—Joseph Conrad, who has deserted him; Edward Morel, who cannot sign his name to this cause lest it damage his defense of the enslaved—his heart vibrating oddly like the hull of ship struck with a hammer. He cannot find an appropriate response.

"What of Herbert Ward?" he says.

She is stunned by the question. "What of him?"

He accepts the Catholic faith as he has accepted many things, being a man inclined to faith—the concept of faith, in strong belief that defies reason.

He believed in God once and as the contours of his life slowly took form, he felt God's disapproval. Still, there was comfort in it, a comfort in being but a small player in the greater plan. And then he lost that faith, that belief, out of an accumulation of reason. He began to think that he was valid, not perfect, but just a man in a world of individuals and as such not remarkable. How could one believe in that and God? He chose himself.

474

That old faith seems but a dream, like a wine that you know was delicious without being able to recall the flavor. He can summon up the grief—the horror of solitude—that overcame him once his faith was gone. He is conscious that at one time he had felt the beauty of a clear path—the box-ticking approach to salvation—but as he disassembled his fears about his actions, that process had started an unraveling not only of the conventional but of convention itself. And what was religion if not convention?

But as each hour wastes itself, a small response to his loneliness stirs—a voice in answer to an inarticulate question.

His acceptance of Catholicism has forced him to abandon the earlier, impossible idea that Ireland could be a nation undivided. The use of religion by the leaders of the new Ireland will no doubt put the people under another yoke. But, as he has already begun his steps to the scaffold, he must create a martyr, and Catholics like martyrs and also like other Catholics, which must be acknowledged. And America likes religion, or at least the fear of God, so this is not a bad statement to make, not bad, for those who will live with its results. Confess. Confess. Confess. After a life in secret, confession is oddly exhilarating, and there is the Canon making his four-cornered gesture over Casement's bowed head and his spirit is soaring somewhere. Or will be soon.

He should be afraid, but he is not.

His hands are bound and he's glad for he would not know what to do with them otherwise. It is but a short distance to the scaffold. No tears come. No thoughts flood his mind. His is a strange perspective. He looks out at the small crowd of factory workers who have gathered to watch him die. From this vantage point, they seem small and he above them, as if he might deliver a speech or a benediction and perhaps this act is a variety of one of these. But no friends are with him now. No sympathizers are at his side. Who does he wish were watching? Who should be the custodian of these final moments? Nina is in America. He has made his peace with Gee. Mbatchi, whom he raised, has disappeared into his untranslatable existence. And Ward? Could love be so extinguished?

A warder pinions his legs. The hangman fits the hood over his head. He is aware of his breathing—a simple operation of the living body—and he hears a prayer end, a pressure on his shoulders, followed by a practiced manipulation of the rope.

God surprises, whispering in his ear. Not a word, but a breath. Has he always been there?

The prison bells are surely tolling now. Ward has some paper on the desk and a sheet, half-covered in his schoolboy scrawl, ready. The script is from an early and rejected draft, but he has not been able to produce any text in the last hour. He is pretending to write a speech that will be presented from New York to San Francisco. America is nearly in the war and just needs a little nudging.

Casement is dead.

Ward hears Sarita's footsteps to his door. She pauses there. He has asked to be alone so that he can finish his speech, but she's looking for him. He holds his breath and her footsteps pick up, continuing down the hall.

He doubts Casement intentionally deceived him. They never spoke in any deep way about Casement's persistent bachelorhood. Had Casement confided his problems, Ward would have had to repudiate him, but this *thing* was always there, so how does knowing its particulars change who Casement was? Still, he feels betrayed, and, like a once-deceived wife who now sights down the length of her marriage and questions all of it, he wonders what he and Casement had actually shared.

Ward has thought a lot about the Congo in the past few days. He has gone through his things and dug up the old photograph taken in '88 or '89 with the other Company men. In the picture are him and Glave and Parminter and Casement. They had all been in Boma on leave and a photographer was in town. On the spur of the moment, they decided to sit. The photographer was not a regular fixture and made his money this way, traveling here and there. Ward remembers Casement suggesting that he contact a missionary friend, who was raising American money to help the natives and might want slides.

There was no studio and the men had grouped together against a sheet hung over a wall in the company manager's front office. They could not take the picture standing because of the height of the camera, so chairs were arranged, although only three could be found. Finally, a stool, normally occupied by a small boy who fanned the manager as he did his correspondence, was located. As Ward was the shortest of the group, it was decided that he would occupy it. Originally, Ward had been positioned between Glave and Parminter, but as they were not much taller than he, Ward found himself on a completely different visual plane. He looked like their father, or as if he were haunting them, or—Casement's observation—as if he wasn't invited to join and had insisted at the last second. Ward said he could bend his knees and that would bring him to the right height, but the photographer was not convinced that Ward could manage this and stay absolutely still, despite his having been an acrobat. He'd argued with the photographer—a remarkably small Belgian man with an epic beard—who had argued back, pointing out that acrobats were best known for leaping about. As the group had already had a few drinks, probably why they'd decided to get photographed in the first place, significant merriment followed. As they settled, it was decided that Ward would sit by Casement, as he was the tallest by several inches, although Ward would still have to sit behind the group as the camera didn't accommodate all four men sitting side by side unless they squeezed together. And when arranged this way, Ward's anomalous height was more obvious. So he positioned himself behind Casement and Parminter, several inches taller than them both, the three forming a sort of pyramid, with Glave off to the right. And they collected themselves.

And they were blinded by the flash.

In the photograph, Parminter looks almost morose. Ward's recollection is that Parminter was laughing hardest and, in his effort to control this, had achieved a look of constipation. Glave has tamped his smile into a look of pleased acceptance. Ward is a bit hunched over the others and had been just about to compose an appealing look when the flash went off. Casement, with his full beard, looks at the camera at an angle, a smile playing at the corners of his eyes. Casement. Probably the most handsome man Ward has ever known.

Years ago, Casement had been visiting in Berkshire in that crazy old house with the ghost that they'd rented before moving to France. Ward had gone into Casement's room to find him and, discovering the room empty, had absentmindedly picked up a book—some French novel—that Casement was reading. A photograph that was being used as a bookmark had fallen out. It was the Boma photo. Casement had folded it down the middle so that Glave and Parminter were on the one side, and he and Casement on the other. With just Casement and Ward in the photograph, the dynamic was significantly altered. It appeared that they had been photographed as a couple. Ward's lack of composure, in this composition, seemed dynamic and Casement, his shoulder touching Ward's jacket, his face angled with the ghost of a smile, looked pleased. Almost tender.

There are Sarita's footsteps in the hall. He has asked to be alone, but he knows that she will not be able to stay away. She knocks and without waiting for an answer opens the door.

Grief has hardened her features and her look is accusatory. "Do you know what time it is?"

"No," he says. "And I'm not at a good stopping point." He watches her eyes arc over to the desk, at the page half-filled with scribble.

"I am beginning to despise you," she says.

"Despise me?" He takes his pen and nervously scrawls *The*. "What an odd thing to say."

"You couldn't even send him a note? You sent that woman away empty-handed, weeping."

"What was I supposed to do?"

"You were supposed to write to him and tell him that you loved him, that he was your brother."

"Given recent developments, I don't think that would have been appropriate."

"It would have been appropriate because it was true." Sarita has started to cry. She presses her fingers hard against her lips to compose herself. "And what are these recent developments?"

"The diaries," he says and he's nervous, although he's not sure why.

"The diaries? Are you saying you didn't know?"

Ward can feel himself blinking. "Are you saying you did?"

Sarita's eyes fly into an unreal gaping and she swings her head around like a birch in a storm. "How could you not?"

"And you let him into our house."

"I welcomed him, even when he made me uncomfortable, because no one made you happier. No one. Not me. Not the children. And that gentle man who got nothing out of life and just gave and gave and gave was happy enough with that, pleased enough to see that he made you smile."

There's a moment of panic. As he feels that he is unhinging, he sees Sarita summoning her strength. He says, "After the death of your son, I find it difficult to understand how you can take such a position."

"If my Charlie were still alive he would have written the letter himself and sent it on your behalf. And I wanted to, but I didn't. And I'll never forgive myself." She presses her hand to her forehead. "He was alone. They put a hood over his head and a rope around his neck—" She can't go on. "I'll never forgive myself and I'll never forgive you." Because she won't. She keeps seeing Casement on the sidewalk in London. It was the last time they were together and he already had an unnamed tragedy weighing on him. "Germans killed my son but the English killed my friend. And I stood by silently, as if it didn't matter."

Ward feels the battered word groups rising to the surface *In times of war* or *We must not allow personal sentiment to cloud* or *He knew what he was getting into*. He dare not speak such useless phrases to his wife. He says, "I could not write."

Her eyes flicker over the shelves of books and a watercolor painted in the Vosges and back to him. She delivers an almost imperceptible nod. "Then you are a coward."

Ward's not sure when she leaves or how long he sits suspended in time, but when he returns to the moment he finds the room cold.

XIV
Paris

August 1919

She accepts her role in her husband's death. She looks at it and sees its measure for she is no coward. In response to the moaning of his friends who wonder what Herbert had hoped to prove, she would like to say that he was trying to regain the admiration of his wife. But perhaps she is overstating her importance in his choices. His life was a catalog of risk: He put himself in canoes to be shot at by savages, carried stretchers in battle zones, exhausted himself despite the subpar heart, did all those things that spun the wheel of fate. But he had known this last venture to the Near East would kill him. Dr. Bathurst, the "old croaker," had told him as much. Sarita told Herbert not to go. He was no coward. How many times had she taken those words back? She had, in an uncharacteristically generous moment, apologized and blamed grief and the general hysteria that electrified her nerves throughout the war for that indelible accusation. To be truthful, he was most often not a coward. He was a brave man, undeniably so. Her injury had been in convincing Herbert otherwise.

He had needed to prove his valor to himself and so when the opportunity arose to be part of a commission to investigate the economic situation in Bucharest and Belgrade, he had insisted on joining. The war may have been over, but its aftershock was still being felt and Herbert was committed to see it through, despite the fact that the "old croaker" had determined his heart so weakened that the winter had to be spent in some southern clime. Herbert needed a place with lots of rest, steady sun, and a situation where all activities could be performed in a robe and slippers.

His current situation could be performed in a robe and slippers.

Herbert had gone off in his uniform and with his cough. She hadn't heard from him for two weeks and when the letters finally arrived, they were addressed from Rome. She read the most recent letter first. He had been recovering in hospital and would be sent to Paris as soon as he was fit. The situation was very grave. She had accepted the news with calm resignation as she had been waiting for it, then gamely decided to read the rest of the letters in chronological order. The first dated from the eleventh of March and had been written en route to Bucharest. To start, the letters were cheerful. Herbert was getting plenty of rest, eating well, and felt that he was doing much good. There were the usual charming anecdotes of unsinkable lads, the usual descriptions of costumed girls. He asked how Roddie had done in his boxing tournament, which was insensitive. She hated that Roddie had gone in for boxing as it was Charlie's sport and Roddie was no good and had been pushed to it by his father and her father as a way of making him more manly. Of course, being battered by other boys accomplished no such thing.

Herbert's letter from the end of March describes bitter cold and everyone in fur coats, although Herbert had left his in Paris, where the weather was mild. He is on his way to Belgrade. In Craiova, he admits that the doctor is worried about the condition of his heart. Suddenly he needs to get back as quickly as can be managed. He travels with the party on to Trieste, writing of tremendous tiredness, incapable of levity. He is eager to be back in Paris, however once in Trieste is determined too weak to make the journey, and sent to Rome.

The packet of letters had reached Sarita in England, where she was visiting Herbie and Joyce as Joyce had just given birth. The baby was a girl and Sarita's first granddaughter. With the end of the war, Herbie had become adrift. His marriage to Joyce had done nothing to anchor him. He did have a significant Sanford income, but needed a profession and had turned to sculpture. He was very good, which surprised her, and no one else. But she was worried about Herbie, whose natural distractedness had been pressurized by the war into something unfathomable. She had watched Herbie struggle with trying to figure out how to smoke and hold the baby until Sarita had pointed out that these two actions should not be performed simultaneously. He gave the baby odd looks, as if he wasn't sure where she had come from or what she was. He had a similar look for Joyce but hid it from her, managing cheer whenever she might notice.

Sarita rushed back to Paris. Herbert had beaten her by a day and was already set up in the house. Villiers too was there, having traveled from Rolleboise to run the kitchen, and when she intercepted Sarita in the vestibule, tilting her head in grave sympathy, Sarita knew to steel herself for Herbert's appearance.

He had lost weight and seemed crumpled into his chair. There was a blanket across his lap, which he tossed onto the floor when she came into the room. His eyes were tired or unfocused; she did not know which. His breath sawed through his body and his attempt to make it mild resulted in a dramatic coughing fit. He immediately spoke of his recovery, but even he didn't believe in it. He wanted to return to Rolleboise as soon as could be managed. Sarita arranged for travel that very evening.

Herbert hung on through the start of summer, although he slept most of the time. Speaking set off his coughing. He liked to watch the light play on the river while holding her hand. The weight of his love for her was almost more than she could bear. He would look at her as she sat consciously arranging her limbs into a relaxed posture. He kept returning his waning eyes to her, kept squeezing her hand. "Of course I love you," she said. Why the *of course*? The war had made her hard. Or perhaps she had always been hard and when the war had killed off some, and altered others, she had survived, with all her strength, which made her appear callous.

When she looked at her husband it was not love she felt, but an immense pity. And sadness, because she could not remember what it was to love at all. She clung to thoughts of their first meetings. She remembered him tying her shoelace in New York, long ago, before they were married, the tremors rising in her from the simple pressure of his hand through the leather of her boot. How she had adored him. Life without Herbert would go on, just as life without Charlie had continued. She would spend more time with her daughters and all her grandchildren would know her. And then his eyes would rise to hers again. "Herbert," she said. "Let's just enjoy the view." He may have wanted her weeping in his lap but, at this juncture, was probably better served with her quiet.

Herbert had been buried in Père Lachaise with a civilized, gentle drizzle as benediction. She had known there would be a good turnout, was not surprised to see so many faces she did not know because Herbert had been most successful when she was not around. His war-related efforts accounted for many of the people, although there were quite a few artists present, all old. She had produced a few weary tears, but only as she made her way up the steps of the Paris house did she truthfully understand her loss. She would never be with Herbert again and, maddening as he had been, she had never had and never would have a better friend. She had outlived Charlie and Casement and Herbert. She had survived the men undone by war, and was now left alone in its rubble.

Cricket was still in Paris, having volunteered to stay after the funeral, although Dimples too had wanted to look after her. Dimples's personality was a little less taxing than Cricket's, but with Dimples you got Phipps, and any time Dimples paid attention to anyone who wasn't Phipps, he began to get agitated. It was, one had to admit, a happy marriage, even though Phipps had begun to look like an overfed housecat.

Herbie had kept quiet. He took his father's death very hard and confided to her, secretly, that he and Joyce were having problems. She was seeing an analyst. And then he added, with a giggle, that he thought she was sleeping with her analyst. Sarita should have been appalled, but for some reason she too found it funny and, standing hidden behind a hedge, smoking one of Herbie's cigarettes, she felt almost normal, almost herself. He was going on a journey to South Africa, something that Joyce, and her analyst, wholeheartedly supported.

Roddie seemed fine. He'd been spending a lot of money, according to Sarita's father, and had little to show for it. Sarita had a hard time mustering appropriate concern for she felt that the boy was best left alone. He seemed happiest that way. And her father? Cricket, with her usual sensitivity, had whispered in Sarita's ear while all were still arranged around the grave, "Why is Grandfather still alive? He's going to outlive us all." Which seemed a possibility.

Sarita has been flipping through the dressmaker catalogues. She had not ordered any mourning clothes while Herbert was still alive as she knew it would have upset him and she didn't want to hide it from him. But now she lacks the necessary outfits and has been in the same dress, which reminds her of Charlie in the worst way, for days. Sarita has made some decisions— mourning is nothing to get excited about—and is just about to ring for Beatrice to set up an appointment with the seamstress when Cricket crashes into the room. She flops onto the couch opposite where Sarita is sitting, looking intensely grieved.

Cricket says, "It's just so horribly sad. All of it."

Sarita is trying to think of some mild thing to say about mourning, but Cricket is not yet finished.

"Do you remember what it is to fall in love?"

Sarita looks for the words. "Your father was buried the day before yesterday."

"And I'm still alive, but I wish I were dead."

"How you can possibly say anything so stupid?"

Cricket thrusts out that defiant jaw. She will not be outdone by the noble dead and there is something glorious in that. "You just don't remember. I want to die."

Cricket is in love. Who could she possibly be in love with? Sarita hopes he's not married, although at Cricket's age, just about everyone is. Including Cricket.

"You never had to deal with it. You and Father and your perfect relationship."

"We had our troubles. You've heard about his scandal, the one that broke right after we were married."

"Oh. Wasn't he rumored to have a cannibal concubine, or something like that? But that's ridiculous. Father would never have done anything like that."

"When I asked him about it, he would never outright deny it." Sarita has Cricket's attention. "We had our troubles, even recently."

"I know you fell out when Uncle Roddie was executed. But what was Father supposed to do?"

"Your father should have stuck by Casement, especially after the diaries were exposed. He should have said they were forged, but when he was called to verify them, he said it was Casement's writing, both hand and style."

"He couldn't exactly lie to the police."

"I would have. So many people were supporting Casement. So many people were on the fence. The petition did have a chance and if we, with our American influence, had cast our lot with your uncle Roddie, it might have made a difference. Remember, this was August of 1916. America hadn't entered the war."

"But Uncle Roddie really was a homosexual?"

"Absolutely. Not only that, but for many years I suspect he was in love with your father."

Cricket finds this hard to believe and she makes the same face that she does when the fruit is not as ripe as it ought to be. "Didn't that bother you?"

"Not as much as it bothered your uncle Roddie."

Cricket gives her mother an appraising look. "You're such a radical, Sarita." Cricket adjusts herself on the couch, but she still has her knees spread out as if she's about to give birth. "But your story with Father is still the most romantic one out there."

"Not the story of our meeting on the *Saale*?" Sarita sighs heavily.

"Handsome Englishman. Beautiful American."

Sarita supplies, *penniless Englishman, rich American.*

"Your shipboard romance. Him finding you on deck, your hair flying."

"My hair was most certainly not flying. We used a kilo of hairpins in those days. And he wasn't looking for me. I wasn't supposed to be up there at night ever, and certainly not without a chaperone. I had some bad prospects that I'd been managing with sherry and needed some fresh air. Your father was actually looking for Paz."

Cricket finally looks scandalized. "For Paz?"

"Remember, she was my lady's maid. She often trawled the upper decks late at night, cutting a romantic figure, hoping to snare a gentleman. But she wasn't that night, as your father had hoped."

"How do you know this?"

"I know. He put his hand on my shoulder and when I turned, he was beyond surprised. I had obviously been crying and he was drunk—we both were—so he kissed me. He didn't know what else to do."

"He thought you were Paz?"

"Until I turned around."

"And you let him tell that story all these years? His realizing he loved you and tearing up to the first-class deck and seeing you—"

"Windswept."

"Windswept. Why?"

"He wouldn't have made it up if he didn't love me. And you know your father. After he told it a couple of times, he believed it. And it's much better than," she drops her voice, "*I was up on deck tom-catting after your mother's maid.* So I let your father tell it however he wanted."

"Well," says Cricket, "that was very valiant of you."

Sarita considers. Valiant? It seemed like an insignificant and obvious choice of word, but perhaps valor was composed of that, these small moves in a minor key that made up the narrative of life. "It didn't seem so at the time," she says, "but I suppose it was."

Acknowledgments

As I write this, I have recently delivered a talk at Kellogg College, University of Oxford, on the "Pleasures and Pains of Writing Historical Fiction," which could have easily been called, "Historical Fiction: Why Do It?" Why, when there are so many texts that better explain the matter that filled the days of Roger Casement and Herbert Ward and his wife Sarita, write a fictional account? There is a fantastic biography of Roger Casement by Seamas O'Siochain that I consulted throughout the process of writing this book, *Roger Casement: Imperialist, Rebel, Revolutionary*. And a very interesting book by Jeffrey Dudgeon, *Roger Casement: The Black Diaries: with a Study of His Background, Sexuality and Irish Political Life*, provided a lot of detail. Herbert Ward wrote several books, all of which I read. As for Sarita, who provides the other voice for the novel, she wrote her own book about her husband: *A Valiant Gentleman*. She was particularly provocative in what she chose not to include, and her book, because of this, sent me in a number of interesting directions.

The reason I decided to write a novel that took on these particular historical figures is because I became fascinated with what it was like to be these people unaware of what the future held. What was it like to be

Roger Casement and ignorant of the outcome of the Uprising? What was it like to be Herbert Ward, a realist sculptor in a time of great artistic change? What was it like to be Sarita Ward, a mother, as the First World War threatened to break? History is essential in the writing of a book like *Valiant Gentlemen*, but I wrote this book to understand what it was like to not know the outcome, to look at history that had not yet become history. So, in my mind, this historical fiction is fiction set in the past that refuses to recognize its historicity. The prime narrator—actual event—does not exist and we must turn the pages blindly.

A more complete list of books consulted can be found on my website, sabinamurray.com.

Many people were helpful in the execution of this book. James Kelly of the University of Massachusetts Library System provided assistance early on with genealogies and various other hard-to-track-down material. Vyvyan Harmsworth supplied information on Lord Northcliffe and the activities surrounding exploration ventures of the *Windward*. Alexander Chee furnished photographs of the famous urinals of the Old Town Bar in Union Square, New York. Okey Ndibe texted me the correct 1894 Niger Protectorate term of address for Casement, while on holiday with his family in Utah. Roseanne Guille took me fishing on Sark, and Richard Axton let me into the archives. Neil Guerra, nature guide, showed me a wild rubber tree somewhere up the Amazon in Peru. Anston Bosman put me up in Cape Town. Keti Mbogile took me around villages in Maun, Botswana, which altered the landscape of my mind. Danny and Deborah Devenny gave me an insiders' view of the murals, pubs, improvisational museums, and other sites of Belfast, my favorite being their living room. Cloddagh, last name unknown, translated what the men up at the bar on Inishmaan were saying. Margaret O'Brien read an unwieldy early draft to make sure that I would not (ironically) be strung up by the Irish. My husband John Hennessy—in addition to listening about this book for close to a decade—prevented the children from starving and going feral. The children, Nick and Gabe, neither starved nor went feral, and provided much needed levity throughout.

I was supported in other ways. I received grants from the Guggenheim Foundation, the National Endowment for the Arts, and various travel and research grants from University of Massachusetts at Amherst. I was also resident at the Tyrone Guthrie House in Annaghmakerrig, County Tyrone, Ireland, which is an official gig, and a resident at Sunetra Gupta's and Adrian Hill's house in Oxford, England, which isn't.

There are also a number of people who maintained an astounding level of faith in this book through the years. First of all, my agent, Esmond Harmsworth, who makes everything seem possible. Elisabeth Schmitz, my long time editor who is always supportive, and Katie Raissian, my editor on this book, who said she loved it and then made me change a bunch of stuff, which I—wisely—did.

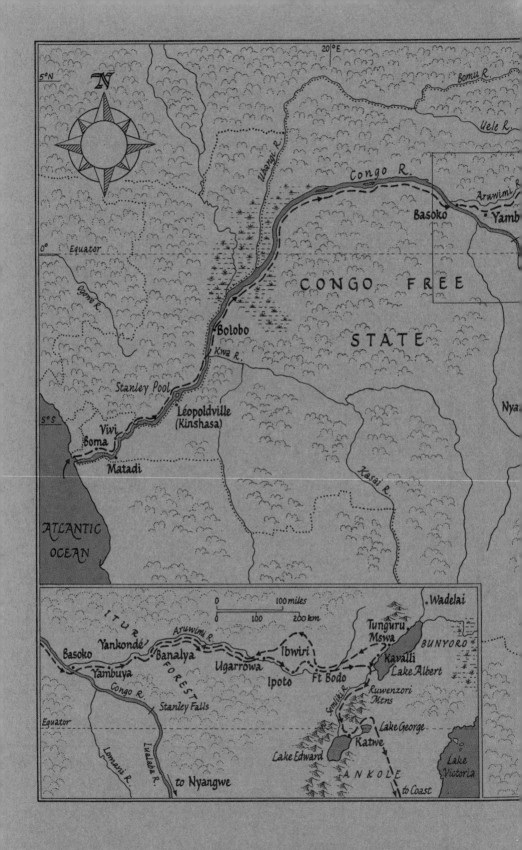